A
GHOST
AND HIS
GOLD

ROBERTA EATON
CHEADLE

TSL Publications

Published 2021 By TSL Publications, Rickmansworth

Copyright © 2021 Roberta Eaton Cheadle

ISBN / 978-1-913294-94-6

Cover image: Tim Barber, Dissect Designs

This book is dedicated to
my mother, Elsie Hancy Eaton.
She reads every word I write and
provides me with valuable and truthful feedback.

MAIN HISTORICAL CHARACTERS

Main British officers

Major General Barton – commander of the 6th (Fusiliers) Brigade under Sir Redvers Buller. After the relief of both Ladysmith and Mafeking, Major General Barton was sent to the Western Transvaal, where he commanded in the Krugersdorp and Pretoria districts until the end of the war.

Colonel Baden-Powell ("B.P.") – garrison commander during the siege of Mafeking, which lasted 217 days.

Sir Redvers Buller – commander of the British forces in South Africa from early September 1899 to January 1900 when he was replaced by Lord Frederick S. Roberts. He subsequently commanded the army in Natal until his return to England in November 1900.

Lord Edward Cecil – Chief Staff Officer to Colonel Baden-Powell during the siege of Mafeking.

Major General Clements – commanded the Colesberg front in early 1900. Led the disastrous Battle of Nooitgedacht in December 1900 and the subsequent retreat of his forces to Pretoria.

Captain Cowen – captain of a squadron of the Bechuanaland Rifles during the siege of Mafeking.

Captain Fitzclarence – captain of a squadron of the Protectorate Regiment during the siege of Mafeking.

Lieutenant-General French – commander of the Cavalry Division during the march to relieve the siege of Kimberley. Prior to this, he won the Battle of Elandslaagte near Ladysmith, escaping under fire on the last train as the siege began. After the relief of Kimberley, he conducted counter-insurgency operations in the Cape Colony.

Lieutenant Colonel Charles Hore – second-in-command of the garrison in Mafeking and, later, commander of the garrison at Elands River.

Lord Kitchener – Chief of Staff to Lord Roberts from December 1899 to November 1900. He succeeded Lord Roberts as commander of the British forces in South Africa from December 1900 until 30 May 1902.

Major General Hector MacDonald – commander of the Highland Brigade under Lord Roberts. He prepared the way for Lord Roberts' march to the relief of Kimberley by seizing Koedoesberg in February 1900. He also took part in later operations in Bloemfontein and Pretoria.

Lord Methuen – general officer commanding the 1st Infantry Division of the British Army during the Second Anglo Boer War.

Lord Milner – High Commissioner for South Africa and Governor of the Cape Colony from 1987. After the discovery of gold in the Witwatersrand area of the Transvaal in June 1886, Milner wanted the whole of South Africa quickly brought under British control.

Colonel Plumer – commander of the mounted infantry force which came to the relief of Mafeking on 16 and 17 May 1900.

Lord Frederick S. Roberts ("Bobs") – succeeded Sir Redvers Buller as the commander of the British forces in South Africa from January 1900 until 12 December 1900.

Lieutenant-Colonel Henry Roberts – commander of the Lincolnshire Regiment company which arrived at Silkaatsnek pass in the Magaliesberg mountains late on the afternoon of 10 July 1900 to relieve the Royal Scots Greys cavalry.

Lieutenant General Sir George White – commander of the British forces in Natal at the beginning of the war. He commanded the garrison during the siege of Ladysmith.

Lieutenant-Colonel Gordon Chesney Wilson – aide-de-camp to Colonel Robert Baden-Powell and husband of Lady Sarah Wilson.

Other British characters

General Frederick Carrington – commander of 1,000 Australians from the New South Wales Imperial Bushmen along with some South African irregulars, who failed to relieve Elands River during the siege.

Dr Kaufman – Viennese doctor who attended to sick inmates of the Mafeking Concentration Camp. He spoke little English and no Afrikaans.

Mr L. McCowat – superintendent of the Mafeking Concentration Camp.

Cecil John Rhodes – British businessman, statesman, imperialist, mining magnate, and politician in southern Africa who served as Prime Minister of the Cape Colony from 1890 to 1896, when he was forced to resign due to his support of the failed Jameson Raid. Rhodes and his partner, C.D. Rudd, launched De Beers Consolidated Mines in March 1888. Rhodes was in Kimberley during the siege which lasted for 124 days from October 1899 to 15 February 1900.

Lady Sarah Wilson – born Lady Sarah Isabella Augusta Spencer-Churchill, aunt to Winston Churchill and one of the first women war correspondents in 1899, when she covered the siege of Mafeking for the *Daily Mail*.

Boer officers

General Piet Cronjé – general of the South African Republic's military forces during the First and Second Anglo Boer Wars.

General Koos de la Rey – one of Piet Cronjé's field generals when the Second Anglo Boer War broke out. He was commander of the Western

Transvaal Boers during the years of guerrilla warfare from June 1900 to May 1902.

General Christiaan de Wet – second-in-command to General Cronjé until General Cronje's surrender at Paardeberg on 27 February 1900, when General de Wet assumed the generalship of the Free State forces. He was regarded as the most formidable leader of the Boers in their guerrilla warfare.

Combat-General Petrus Liebenberg – one of General de la Rey's senior commanders who was charged with organising and leading guerrilla resistance in the Potchefstroom District.

General Snyman – General of the Rustenburg and Marico Burghers[1] who served at Mafeking under General Cronjé. He took command of the Boer forces around Mafeking when General Cronjé left the area on 18 November 1899.

Commandant-General Piet Joubert ("Slim Piet") – Commandant-General of the South African Republic from 1880 to 1900. He led the siege of Ladysmith in Natal from 2 November 1899 to 28 February 1900.

---

[1] "Citizen-soldiers" who, between the ages of 16 and 60, were obliged to serve without pay in the two Boer republics commandos. Most of them were Burghers.

TIMELINE OF

MAJOR HISTORICAL EVENTS

1895

Dec 29 – Jameson Raid – a botched raid against the South African Republic carried out by British colonial statesman, Leander Starr Jameson, and his "company" troops, who were in the employ of Alfred Beit's and Cecil John Rhodes' British South African Company, together with the Bechuanaland policemen.

1899

May 24 – Petition of Uitlanders[1] to Queen Victoria with regards to their grievances against the government of the South African Republic.

May 30 – Conference at Bloemfontein between Lord Milner and President Kruger to discuss the Uitlander issue. These were terminated without an outcome.

September and October – British troops were dispatched to Natal in South Africa.

9 October – Boer ultimatum, making war between Britain and the South African Republic inevitable. The Orange Free State joined the South African Republic.

11 October – Expiry of the Boer ultimatum. War between Great Britain and the two Boer Republics breaks out.

12 October – Capture of the British armoured train by the Boers at Kraaipan near Mafeking.

12 October – Colonel Baden-Powell prepares for a siege of Mafeking in the Cape Colony (near Bechuanaland), by taking up a strong defensive position.

13 October – Commencement of the siege of Mafeking by the Boers, led by General Piet Cronjé.

14 October – Commencement of the siege of Kimberley in the Cape Colony by the Boers.

16 October – Commencement of shelling of Mafeking by the Boers.

1 November – Invasion of the Cape Colony by the Boers.

2 November – Commencement of the siege of Ladysmith in the Cape Colony by the Boers.

---

[1] A British immigrant living in the Transvaal who was denied citizenship by the Boers for cultural and economic reasons.

17–22 November – Transports deliver 22,000 British troops to Cape Town.

19 November – 4,000 Boers under General Piet Cronjé are redeployed to the Modder River area near Kimberley. 1,500 Boers remain to continue the siege under General Snyman and *Kommandant*[1] Botha.

10 December – Defeat of the British troops, under Sir William Gatacre, by the Boers at the Battle of Stormberg.

11 December – Defeat of the British troops, under Lord Methuen, at Magersfontein, during his attempt to relieve Kimberley.

15 December – Defeat of the British troops, under Sir Redvers Buller, at Colenso, during his attempt to relieve Ladysmith.

17 December – Lord Roberts appointed as Commander-in-Chief in South Africa with Lord Kitchener as his Chief of Staff.

1900

15 February – Siege of Kimberley ends when a British cavalry division, under Lieutenant-General John French, came to the town's relief.

18–27 February – Battle of Paardeberg between Boer General Piet Cronjé and British troops under Lord Kitchener. General Piet Cronjé surrendered with 5,000 Burghers on 27 February which was also Majuba Day.

28 February – Siege of Ladysmith ends after Sir Redvers Buller finally broke through the Boer positions on 27 February.

13 March – Lord Robert's occupies Bloemfontein, capital of the Orange Free State.

12 May – *Veldkornet*[2] S. Eloff, led a force of 240 Boers in an assault on Mafeking, which ends in defeat by the Boers.

17 May – Siege of Mafeking ends when a flying column of 2,000 British troops, including volunteers from Kimberley, relieved the town after fighting their way in.

28 May – British annexation of the Orange Free State.

31 May – Lord Roberts occupies Johannesburg in the South African Republic.

5 June – Lord Roberts occupies Pretoria, the capital city of the South African Republic.

12 June – Lord Roberts defeats the Boers, under General Botha, at Diamond Hill near Pretoria.

---

[1] Afrikaans word for commandant, the title given to the officer in charge of a commando.

[2] The *veldkornet* was responsible for calling up the Burghers and also for policing his ward, collecting taxes, issuing firearms and other materials in times of war. He reported to the *kommandant* in charge of the commando.

14 June – War council meeting of Transvaal officers at Balmoral where new guerrilla warfare tactics are accepted.

2 August – Skirmish at Silkaatsnek between defending British troops and the Boers under General de Wet with a successful outcome for the Boers.

4 August – Commencement of the siege of Elands River by the Boers.

16 August – Relief of the siege of Elands River by Lord Kitchener.

14 September – Lord Roberts issues a proclamation calling on the Burghers to surrender.

25 September – British annexation of the South African Republic.

20–25 October – Battle of Frederikstad which ends in defeat for the Boers under General Liebenburg.

1902

15–31 May – Series of meetings at Vereeniging to negotiate for peace with Great Britain.

31 May – Signing of the Peace at Melrose House in Pretoria, the treaty that ended the Second Anglo Boer War.

MICHELLE

HELLO, WHO'S THERE?

March 2019

"These sausage rolls are amazing." Carl stuffs another one into his large mouth.

"Thank you, Carl," Michelle smiles brightly.

The evening is going well, and Carl's appreciation of her cooking skills pleases her.

A strange sense of foreboding about this house-warming party has bothered her all week.

There is something strange about this house, she thinks. *I've seen such weird things since we moved in; shadows of people who aren't there, flickering movements with no apparent cause, and that hair. Yuck!*

A shiver ripples up her spine, causing her hands to tremble slightly.

Nothing untoward has happened so just relax.

Tom bounds over. His shoulders, usually slightly hunched with stress, are relaxed and his grin is boyish and charming.

"She's a great cook, Carl." He grabs a few of the delicious home-made pastries from her tray.

Michelle returns his contagious grin. She's absurdly pleased that her distinguished husband has praised her catering, especially in front of his best friend and long-term colleague. Carl and Tom are both partners at the prestigious auditing and advisory firm, Kellerman, James & Thompson.

"I love what you've done to this place." Sue takes a large sip of her wine and makes an expansive gesture to incorporate the room. "You are very creative, Michelle."

"Thank you," Michelle laughs. "It's my night for compliments."

Glancing around, she also thinks the room is attractive. Against the right-hand wall is an antique sideboard. Michelle recalls her delight when she found it in a local antique shop soon after their move. She'd questioned the owner about its origins.

"It is believed to have belonged to Pieter van Zyl, one of the original Boers in this area," the shop owner told her. "It comprises of two pieces.

11

A large kist, originally used to store clothing and linen makes up the bottom piece, and a glass fronted display cabinet makes up the top piece."

She pointed at the legs of the kist which ended in the large paws of a lion. "Just look at the beautifully carved legs of the kist, such wonderful detail."

The fact that the two pieces came apart interested Michelle, and she asked about it.

Delighted at her interest, the shop owner shared a bit more about the history of the Boers. "A lot of Boer furniture was designed so that it could be easily disassembled and packed into an ox wagon when they trekked from one area to another."

The shop owner spoke with a strong Afrikaans[1] accent and wore her thin, grey hair drawn back into a tight bun. Her dress, while made from a pretty floral material, was old fashioned in its design, and her shoes were sensible lace-ups. Michelle suspected she'd lived here in Irene, and been a part of its community, all her life.

Casting her mind back, Michelle remembered her school history lessons about the mass migration of the Afrikaner farmers, called *trekboers*, into the interior of South Africa to escape British rule.

Imagine packing all your worldly possessions into an ox wagon and heading off into unknown territory. A brave thing to do.

The dining room also holds an eight-seater Rhodesian teak dining room table and matching chairs, as well as a vintage book cabinet made from stinkwood. Michelle's taste runs to the old and unusual and stinkwood furniture is now rare. Owning a piece of furniture made from this endangered wood, native to South Africa, appealed to her and she'd paid the high asking price unhesitatingly.

Behind the glass inlayed doors of the cabinet, her prized books, including a vintage copy of *The Collected Works of Herman Charles Bosman*, a well-known collection of short stories about the Transvaal at the turn of nineteenth century, stand in a neat row.

Michelle smiles when she remembers Tom gifting her this heavy book for Christmas.

It is wonderful when your husband knows exactly how to please you.

Tonight, the dining room table is covered by an antique tablecloth,

---

[1] A southern African language derived from the form of Dutch brought to the Cape by Protestant settlers, including French Huguenots, in the 17th century. It is an official language of South Africa, spoken by around six million people as their first language.

gifted to Michelle by her grandmother. Candles in a pretty silver candle-stick holder, a wedding present from her mother, illuminate the room. The highly polished wood of the table and cabinet gleams softly in the mellow light which also picks up the embroidered detail on the cream silk curtains and the rich patterning of the floral tablecloth.

The curtains, made to her specifications by her father, are deeply satisfying.

The walls are so plain and bland, they ruin the decor. I must go shopping for some suitable paintings. There is no rush. Tom's given me a generous budget for furniture, and I'll find what I want eventually.

Bottles of brandy, whiskey, vodka, and rum stand on a folding table, sparkling in the soft light. Tucked neatly beneath the table is a cooler box full of soda mixers, cans of beer and water. Although Tom and Michelle rarely drink heavily, the installation of a proper bar is high on Tom's list of home improvements.

"It's all about appearances. I can't have clients and friends coming here and being offered drinks from behind a folding table."

Well, some of us aren't heavy drinkers.

Tom's friend and colleague, Trevor, stands at the table refilling his glass. His hands shake slightly.

Drink in hand he ambles over to her.

"Well done on a great party," he mumbles.

His red eyes and whiskey laden breath horrify Michelle.

Why has he done this to himself. It's not surprising he's divorced. What woman would put up with his binges, even if he does somehow manage to hold it together at work and earn a good living? I wonder how he and Tom came to be friends? I must ask Tom sometime.

"What should we do for the rest of the evening? I'd like to do something different and fun."

Michelle's best friend from school, Alice, is single and a bit wild. A talented make-up artist, she's always in demand for the biggest theatre productions that take place in South Africa and she's used to being continuously entertained.

The Ouija board.

A surprising find among Tom's things when she'd packed up their old apartment, Michelle had kept it. It had resurfaced when she unpacked and, after looking on the Internet to see how you played the game, she had put it away in the cabinet in the television room.

In her slightly inebriated state, her desire to entertain her best friend overwhelms her common sense and she makes an unusual suggestion.

"How about trying out our Ouija board."

"You have a Ouija board?" Sue's eyebrows rise. "I didn't know you were interested in that sort of thing."

"I'm not, although I've been known to consult Tarot cards. I found it when I was packing and I thought it looked interesting, so I kept it."

"I think it's a great idea. Who wants to play?" Alice giggles.

"What do you think, Sue? Do you want to play?"

Everything about Sue, from her carefully straightened professional greying bob to her plain jeans and tee-shirt, shout sensible and no-nonsense; she's always the hand break in the group.

Sue shrugs indifferently. "If the rest of you are keen, I'll play along."

"I'll play," Carl supports Sue, as always.

"I think Ouija boards are a waste of time," Tom sniffs disdainfully. "Why don't we rather play poker?"

"Don't be such an old fart, Tom," Alice's eyes sparkle with mischief, "Let's play the game. It's not dangerous, unless," she goads him mercilessly, "you think the spirits are unfriendly tonight."

Tom sighs heavily, "Okay, Alice, if you want to play that badly, I'm in."

Going into the lounge, Michelle takes the flat board and the panchette from the cabinet.

It is marked with the letters of the alphabet, the numbers 0 to 9, then the words "yes", "no" and "goodbye" along with some other symbols and pictures. She sets it up on the dining room table.

"We need some paper."

Sighing heavily in exaggerated disgust, Tom gets up and goes into her office, returning, a few minutes later, with a sheaf of paper out of the printer in his hand.

All six occupants of the room sit down at the table, enthusiastic to join in this unusual and unexpected form of entertainment.

"We three women will go first," says Michelle. Sitting down at the table, Alice, Sue and Michelle each place their fingertips on a different side of the triangular shaped wooden gadget standing on three short legs with the pencil pointing down.

"Ask it a question, Alice." Michelle grins at her friend.

"Are there any ghosts in this house?" Alice giggles again, shaking back her unruly auburn curls and taking a sip of her pink gin cocktail.

For a moment nothing happens. Disappointment lurches in Michelle's stomach and then the planchette starts to move, slowly and shakily. Shivering, she watches, suddenly feeling inexplicably cold. It moves, stops, moves, stops, moves, stops. It spells out the word P-I-E-T-E-R.

"Pieter?" Michelle raises her eyebrows slightly. "I don't know a Pieter. Does anyone else know him?"

The group around the table shake their heads, their eyes glued to the paper. Tom's expression is a curious mixture of amusement and ... could it be anxiety?

Weird.

Michelle studies Tom carefully.

He doesn't believe in the occult or ghosts. He's such a typical chartered accountant, seeing everything in his life as black or white with no shades of grey. That's why I haven't mentioned my recent experiences to him. I know he'll scoff and make me feel like an idiot.

Alice shivers violently, as if in response to a cool draft of air. She catches Michelle's eye.

Is Alice the one driving the planchette? It's not me, so it must be either her or Sue.

"You ask it something now, Michelle?"

"Where are you from Pieter?"

The planchette moves again, slowly spelling out: I—A-M—F-R-O-M– –H-E-R-E.

Alice, always irreverent, bursts into more uncontrolled giggles. "You'd better watch out, Tom. Pieter's from here."

She turns, grabs her light cardigan, which is draped over the back of the chair, and puts it on, before replacing her fingers on the planchette. Michelle suddenly notices how long and elegant her fingers are, like those of a pianist.

"It's writing some more." Sue's fingers on the planchette look like plump white sausages.

I—A-M—G-U-A-R-D-I-N-G—M-Y—G-O-L-D, the planchette writes laboriously.

Despite the stifling heat of the summer evening, Michelle's arms break out in gooseflesh. "I'm from here. I'm guarding my gold."

Michelle inhales sharply.

What does it mean?

The planchette jerks sharply under their fingers, causing Alice's loosely held pink gin to slop onto the table. A gasp whistles through her suddenly white lips.

"Did you feel that?" Michelle jerks hard, trying to pull her fingers away, but they seem glued to the planchette. Sue's shoulders move backwards, as if she's pulling strenuously. Her fingers don't detach from the planchette. The air is oppressive and humid. It settles like thick sludge as Michelle draws it sharply into her lungs. Alice's eyes are huge and frightened.

The planchette spurts forward. H-E-L-P—M-E, it writes in hard, slashing letters and then stops, flipping onto its side.

Yanking her hands away quickly, Sue's eyes are large and shocked inside dark holes. Her make-up stands out harshly on her pale and waxen skin. Touching each of her fingers lightly, as if to check nothing has adhered to them, she lets out a slow, shaky breath.

Alice is gazing at the Ouija board, as if hypnotised.

BANG! BANG! BANG! BANG!

The terrible loud explosions shatter the quiet. The bottles of alcohol on the folding table, and cans of beer in the cooler box beneath it, burst apart in an eruption of glass shards, twisted metal and liquid. Water boils out of the open cooler box as the plastic soda and water bottles rupture and twist into lumpy shapes. The candles flicker and blow out in the wake of a sudden, icy breeze that whips through the room, leaving the group in darkness. A heavy thud shakes the table and then there's silence.

A shriek destroys the quiet. Michelle heaves back her chair. It falls to the floor with a thump. Moving towards the doorway, she gropes, finds the light switch on the wall, and flicks it on. The harsh electric light illuminates the scene of destruction.

Sue, who is standing, and Tom, who is sitting at the head of the table with his back to the bar, have received the brunt of the unexpected shower of booze and water. It drips from their hair and clothes. Tiny splinters of glass have speared their exposed faces and arms, causing lacerations which ooze beads of blood.

Fortunately, the explosion knocked over the folding table, shielding them from the worst of the spray of metal and plastic fragments erupting from the cooler box.

"Sue," Michelle shouts, "Are you okay? Tom?"

Tom nods his head; he is okay.

Sue croaks, "Okay," and then bursts into braying sobs which seem to wrench themselves out of her throat like vomit.

She's in shock!

Michelle rushes away to get some towels, while Carl placates his distraught wife.

Re-entering the dining room, Michelle hears Sue's whispered question. The same one on all their minds.

"Wh... wh... what happened, Carl? How could the bottles explode like that?"

Her eyes are bulging from their sockets in a most unflattering way and continue to stream tears as she struggles to make sense of this assault on her orderly and structured life.

Michelle hands Sue and Tom a towel. She gives a third to Alice, who has been splattered.

Carl's at a loss for words.

"Maybe the heat?" Tom ventures. "I've never heard of bottles exploding like this, but it is unusually hot."

"The heat," Sue repeats.

Her hunched up shoulders visibly relax at being offered this reasonable and ordinary lifeline. She clutches at it.

"The heat, yes, that makes sense."

Having dried herself off, she walks unsteadily into the adjoining lounge to retrieve her handbag.

"It's getting late, Michelle. I think Carl and I should get going."

"Yes, of course," Michelle moves towards the sideboard where her keys lie, looking modern and out of place on its dark wooden surface. "I'm so sorry about how tonight has ended. I'll let you out."

"Can I help you tidy up, Michelle?" Alice asks. Her eyes are glassy and shocked.

Michelle shakes her head. "No, but thank you for offering, Alice. I'll sweep up the mess in here and mop the floor. There isn't much else to do except pack the dishwasher. I deliberately served finger foods to avoid a huge pile of dishes and a lot of work." She offers her friend a watery smile.

I can always rely on Alice for help. She's such a good friend. Of course, I'm going to have to polish all the furniture, wash down the walls and dry clean the curtains, but I'll sort that out tomorrow.

"In that case, I'll be off now too. I have an early start tomorrow." The two friends embrace.

"Goodbye, Michelle," Trevor's breath is rank. Agitated eyes peer out of a pale face, topped by greying hair, "That was really weird."

"Are you okay to drive?" Tom claps Trevor on the back.

"I've called an Uber. It'll be here any minute."

The house is quiet when Tom and Michelle come back inside, locking the front door behind them.

"That was ... bizarre," Michelle hugs Tom, seeking comfort in his strong arms.

"Yes, it was. I can't imagine what could've caused the bottles to explode like that."

Tom's face is set in lines of perplexity and worry. Michelle can almost see the wheels turning in her husband's mind as he tries to make sense of the irrational and puzzling events of the late evening.

"It doesn't make sense. What the hell happened with that Ouija board?" He looks at her expectantly, as if she can provide the answer.

A slight grimace twists her face as she thinks about what transpired with the Ouija board.

It didn't feel as if one of us was exerting undue pressure and guiding the planchette. It felt like an outside force, but Tom will ridicule that notion. What can I tell him?

She is aware of his eyes on her, waiting for her response.

"I expect Alice guided the planchette so that it appeared to move. You know how mischievous she is. Teasing us with those messages would be right up her street."

Tom considers her words. They satisfy him and he nods assent.

"Where did you get it anyway?" Michelle asks. "Messing around with the occult is not like you."

"I saw it in a novelty party shop years ago and it looked like fun, so I bought it," Tom looks away shiftily as he speaks.

She doesn't press him although she knows he's lying. "Could heat really make the cans and bottles explode like that?"

"Heat can cause extreme pressure to build up inside a bottle or can and make them explode," Tom is matter of fact and decided. "I'm going to put the Ouija board in your office for the time being. I think we should throw it out on Friday when the rubbish truck comes. Right now, I'm exhausted. I'll clear up the mess in the dining room while you pack the dishwasher. Then we can go to bed. I'm too tired to think clearly about all of this tonight."

Michelle understands that Tom does not want to continue their discussion.

But the cans and bottles of soda and beers were in an ice filled cooler box. How could heat have made them explode?

An hour later, Michelle gratefully slips between the cool sheets of her bed. Despite her physical fatigue, her mind is whirling, refusing her the absolution of sleep. The events of the past few weeks, following the move into their new home, drift through her thoughts like flotsam.

"Those boxes go in the kitchen." Michelle pointed to a door a couple of metres away from where she stood. The removal men shuffled in that direction, straining under the weight of their loads which contained crockery and cooking utensils.

Michelle had risen before dawn, packing the last bits and pieces of their belongings and sealing the boxes, ready for when the removal van arrived.

Fine strands of long blonde hair clung to her sweaty face and fatigue nipped at the heels of her sensible, flat shoes.

It's so hot. Why, oh why, did we have to move in February?

Excitement had kept her going over the past whirlwind six weeks since Tom had come home and announced that he had found them the perfect townhouse to buy.

"It can be ready for occupation by the middle of February if we want it," he said.

Michelle did want it. They'd both agreed that this new and modern townhouse in Irene near Pretoria was ideal for them. Due to Tom's forward thinking, they had a pre-approved bond and, following their offer to purchase, the purchase process had gone smoothly.

The packing had been time consuming and tiring. The amount of junk they had managed to accumulate since their marriage, just over two years before, was unbelievable. It had taken them several weeks to sort through the cupboards and garage and decide what to keep and what to dispose of.

Tom had brought a few boxes of miscellaneous items with him when they moved into their rented apartment after their wedding. They contained old photographs, medals, books and other bits and pieces that his mother had packed up for him years ago, when he moved out of her home and into his own apartment. He'd never unpacked the boxes and Michelle had decided to sort through them and throw out those items that weren't worth keeping.

She'd kept the photographs and medals as well as an Ouija board she'd found carelessly shoved into the top of one of the boxes. The gaudy box sported a large picture of adults gathered around a table, drinking and enjoying themselves with their fingers on the planchette, implying it was a party game. The box was undamaged and a quick peep inside divulged a heart shaped wooden planchette still covered in plastic, confirming its newness.

Michelle's knowledge of the occult was limited to tarot cards and she didn't know much about Ouija boards, but she wanted to ask Tom how he came to have such an item. It was out of character.

Who knew, it might be fun to experiment with the board some time.

Our mutual friends might be interested in playing the game one evening, she thought.

* * *

Having deposited Michelle's and Tom's furniture and boxes in the correct rooms, at least Michelle hoped that was the case, the movers prepared to leave at 5.30 p.m. The house was in complete chaos with dismantled beds, rubbish bags full of bed linen, and piles of curtains filling the upstairs bedrooms.

I must hang the curtains tonight. I'll also have to find the towels, soap and other toiletries if we want to shower.

"Let's get the bed assembled, Mich," Tom had taken her hot hand and led her upstairs. Fortunately, it didn't take long to push the two three-quarter bed bases together and hoist the cumbersome king-size mattress over them.

God, I hate this damn mattress. It would be so much easier to have two three-quarter mattresses.

Tom had now done his bit towards getting the bed ready for the night. "I'm starving. Shall I go and get us some takeaway food. What would you like?"

"Okay, that's a good idea. I'll have a vegetarian pizza."

Tom's thumping footsteps descended the stairs and the front door slammed. Michelle set about wrestling the king-size duvet into its cover, a task she loathed. She pulled the enormous fitted sheet over the mattress and then shoved the pillows into their cases.

Too late she realised that she'd forgotten to fit the bed frill over the two bases before placing the mattress on top of them.

I just can't try to get the frill on tonight, especially with Tom gone. I'll fix it tomorrow.

Pulling the stool of her dressing table over to the window, she climbed up and hung the curtains on the rail. Knowing she would need to hang them immediately in the new house, she hadn't bothered to remove the hooks when she took them down in their old apartment. The curtains didn't reach the floor and hung limply, looking old and ill fitting.

We'll have to get new curtains; these ones look tatty.

The sun was going down and its bright rays caused Michelle to look out of the window, into the garden. A massive jacaranda tree dominated their small space. Its trunk was twisted and gnarled, and it gave an impression of great age and mystery.

What's that?

Michelle leaned closer to the window. Next to the huge shadow of the tree another shadow had appeared. It was faint and wavering, but definitely a man in a large hat.

Panic shot through her.

Who could be lurking in our garden? Did Tom lock the door when he left.

Shifting her gaze to the tree, she tried to spot the intruder; stories of criminal attacks on people when they moved in or out of houses flooding her mind.

There was no one there. A moment later, the shadow disappeared.

Michelle let out her breath, which she realised she'd been holding. *Strange, I wonder what threw that shadow. Probably nothing. I must try to calm down and not get carried away by my imagination. Time for a quick shower, that'll help sooth my nerves.*

Entering the bathroom, Michelle turned on the shower tap. Pulling off her tee-shirt, damp with sweat, and stepping out of her jeans and underpants, she reached into the shower and felt the temperature of the water. Warm. A sigh of pleasure escaped her as she stepped into the fast flow, closing her eyes and enjoying the freshness of the water on her hot, sticky body.

A few minutes later, her feet were covered by water which was pooling in the bottom of the shower.

The drain must be blocked. Bugger!

Peering into the drain, water beating down on her exposed back, she saw the obstruction.

Oh my God! It's clumps of hair!

Hurriedly turning the tap off to prevent the water from overflowing the pan, she stepped out and wrapped herself in a thick towel. The water level had not dropped.

It must be well and truly blocked to stop the outflow so completely. I'll have to go and find something to poke down the drain and try to unblock it.

After slipping on her light summer pyjama top and shorts, she headed downstairs with a plan to find the wooden skewers she used to test if cakes are baked. They are sturdy and long enough to push a little way down the drainage pipe.

Luckily, the package of skewers was near the top of the box containing

21

her baking and cake decorating equipment and Michelle was soon on her way back upstairs, with the packet clutched in her hand.

She poked a skewer into the drainpipe. From this close she could see it was human hair blocking it. Grimacing in disgust she wriggled the skewer around and dragged out a clump of long, dark blonde hair. It was packed so tightly into the drain; Michelle thought the previous occupants of the house could not possibly have ever used drain cleaner or pulled the hair out by hand.

After repeating the process, several times, the drain seemed to be cleared of hair and the water started to empty out of the shower. The clumps of hair were quite revolting, mouldy and rotten, as if they had been there for years and years and not just a few months since the townhouse had been inhabited. The house had only been occupied for six months when the previous owner decided to sell.

Annoyed with herself for not thinking to bring a plastic shopping bag upstairs with her when she went down to fetch the skewers, Michelle hurried back downstairs. On her way back upstairs, she decided to ask Tom to take the bag outside when he returned home and put it into the outside dustbin. The hair revolted her, and she didn't want to leave it in her kitchen overnight.

In front of the shower stall she gasped, shocked. The horrible clumps were gone. The drain was clean, shining brightly in the artificial light from the ceiling downlights. Leaning over the drainpipe she peered into the dark hole. *It looks like a toothless mouth.*

A burst of cold water from overhead made her jump and she leapt out of the shower stall at its sudden wet assault. Shock turned to annoyance as she realised it was only the shower that had come on. *How on earth did that happen? I'll have to ask Tom to have a look at it.*

The sound of Tom's key opening the front door, spurred her into action. In the bedroom she changed into a dry pair of baby-doll pyjamas and headed downstairs to join her husband for their meal. She didn't mention her strange experience with the hair, thinking that maybe she had imagined it. She was tired and had been pushing herself for days with her work and all the packing. She didn't want him laughing at her, or worse, think she was going nuts.

* * *

The following morning, Michelle unpacked her study. She needed to get her office up and running quickly. February was not only a bad month for her to arrange a move because of the heat, it was also tax year-end which increased her workload significantly.

Trained as a chartered accountant, she had soon discovered that she didn't enjoy the routine and unyielding pressure of life in an auditing firm and had elected to run her own small business providing tax and financial services to a selection of clients.

Needing a creative outlet for her artistic side, she had started writing short stories a few years previously, attempting to learn the craft of creative writing. To date, several of her short stories had been published in various anthologies. Writing always made her happy and the publication of some of her stories vindicated her efforts.

Running her own business gave her more flexibility to indulge her writing hobby and she was grateful for her life and Tom's understanding of her objectives.

Of course, I don't need to work for financial reasons and none of Tom's colleagues' wives work. That may have contributed to his enthusiasm for me to leave the firm.

Michelle pushed this uncharitable thought away, a bit shocked that it had voiced itself so clearly in her mind.

The Ouija board was near the top of the box, just under one of her "in progress" client files. Michelle pulled it out in surprise.

How did this get here? I left it in the box with the rest of Tom's bits and pieces that I kept.

She inspected the board and, after removing the plastic covering, the planchette. There were no instructions on how it should be used. "I must look up how it works," she murmured to herself.

A shadow shifted on the far wall of her office and an unexpected cold draft made her shiver. Glimpsing a subtle movement out of the corner of her eye, she swung around quickly, but saw nothing at all. There was no shadow on the wall.

Michelle picked up the Ouija board and planchette and placed them next to her laptop.

As soon as I finish my work, I'll do some research on these and how they work.

PIETER

THE KHAKIS ARE COMING

June 1900

The muffled rapping penetrates Pieter's thin early morning sleep. He stirs and rolls over. The insistent rapping continues, forcing his reluctant consciousness upwards, towards full awareness.

Sitting up quickly, he awakes fully, sudden fear acting like a bucket of cold water. The blankets drop away from his body and the frigid iciness of the early June morning chases away any remaining vestiges of sleep.

Over the past months, fear has eaten into his mind's core like a malevolent caterpillar. Fear of the future. Fear of the soldiers. Fear of losing his farm. It's been there, rotting his brain matter, ever since the declaration of war in October the previous year. The injury he sustained early this year exacerbated its effect until his mind is a worm-infested apple, brown and soft inside. He takes some deep breaths, determined to prevent the poison from spreading and affecting his reactions. Poor reactions could result in his death and that of his family.

He stares into the total blackness, trying desperately to see, while his body reacts to the biting cold, with gooseflesh breaking out on his torso and arms.

Who can be knocking on my door at this time of morning? It can only be bad news.

Next to him, his wife, Marta, starts to stir as she too responds to the intrusion.

"Pieter, are you awake?" The piercing voice competes with the wind that rattles the slats of the wooden blinds, and whistles under the ill-fitting front door.

Something's wrong.

Clambering out of bed, he stumbles across the uneven floor of the bedroom and down the passageway. By the time he reaches the front door, his eyes have adjusted fully to the darkness, and he can make out the shapes of the furniture in the *voorkamer*, a large room at the front of the farmhouse where Marta receives visitors.

Grabbing his loaded Mauser rifle from its hooks on the wall near the

24

door, he hesitates for a moment to admire its smooth and shiny wooden length. The feel of the gun in his hands gives him confidence; he is an excellent marksman.

This gun brought me a lot of respect.

His ability with a gun had been his saving grace when, as a young man, his peers had been mystified by his interest in books and writing and had liked to share their derogatory thoughts in that regard.

The chilly wind strikes him as he opens the door in his nightclothes and bare feet, the gun raised cautiously, ready to fire. The wind blows straight through his clothing, leaving him feeling vulnerable and naked, despite his trusty weapon. The cold front that arrived during the night has dropped the temperatures below freezing.

I'm tired of winter and it's only June. We still have the whole of July and August to get through.

He shivers as he peers into the heavy dark, searching for the owner of the voice. "Who's there?"

"It's François Naude," comes the hoarse whisper.

On the far side of the enclosed outdoor area, referred to as the *stoep*, a dark shape manoeuvres itself around the two wooden chairs that stand side-by-side under the overhanging roof. Its movements are quick and impatient.

Pieter does not recognise the dust-roughened voice of the whisperer and strains to identify the shape as it moves closer, his rifle at the ready.

Is it really François? I must be careful. It could be a bywoner *looking to cause trouble.*

The profile of his old friend comes into view and Pieter's breath, which he has been unconsciously holding, escapes with a whoosh. Despite François' dusty and dishevelled appearance, this is no migrant labourer with no farm or land of his own. This is a well-known face and form.

"François, what are you doing here?"

Pieter lowers his gun despite the dread that tightens his stomach as he takes in the heavy-set man's exhausted appearance.

"The Khakis[1] captured Johannesburg yesterday and are now marching to Pretoria. Your farm is directly in their path. You need to pack up as much as you can and leave with your family or you will be made a prisoner of war."

---

[1] Khaki refers to the British forces because of their change in uniform from bright red in the First Anglo-Boer War to khaki in this one, having learnt the value of camouflage in the African bush.

The harrowing words seemed to hang in the air like the puffy white clouds of vapour that escape from François' mouth. They smash into Pieter's heart like arrows.

This farm is my life and now the British soldiers are coming.

He swallows hard, "How long do we have?" His voice sounds strained and gravelly to his own ears.

"A few days at best. You should go as soon as possible."

"Thanks, I'll get Marta and the girls moving as quickly as possible. Can I get you some coffee before you leave?"

"Thanks, but no. I need to warn the other Boers. At least those who plan to resist and continue to fight." François' lips briefly form into a rueful smile. "Many of the Boers are so demoralised they had laid down their arms."

Pieter grips his cold hand and gives it a firm shake. "Thank you, my friend. I'll be rejoining my commando[1] and continuing the fight."

Praise God for our tight knit farming community where everyone helps each other.

The sky has brightened to a pale grey as Pieter watches François galloping away in the direction of the Nel farm. The clouds of dust kicked up by his horse's hooves hang heavily in the dry air, drifting down slowly as if reluctant to return to the earth.

Pieter shivers violently. He pushes the door shut, cutting off the vicious wind. Bangs and muffled thumps attract him to the kitchen.

The inevitable has happened and the Khakis are coming.

In a way it is a relief to finally have his fears confirmed and to be able to take definite action.

Marta, a strong and resourceful woman who can handle a rifle as well as him, is already up and dressed in her floor length dress of dark cotton. She obviously overheard the conversation and knows they need to leave as soon as possible. Pieter stands for a moment, watching her pack food and cooking utensils into grain sacks. Her back is as rigid as the unforgiving bun into which she has twisted her long, dark hair. Sensing his presence, she turns and attempts a smile, but it does not reach her pale, blue eyes.

"I've started the fire and the coffee is almost ready."

He nods. Just what he needs, a cup of very strong, very black and very hot coffee.

---

[1] Volunteer military units of armed combatant soldiers, organized by the Boer people of South Africa.

Pieter has not hidden the facts of this disastrous war from Marta. She is aware that the British Empire formally annexed the neighbouring independent Boer country, the Orange Free State, on 28 May. The following day the Boer government of their independent home state, the South African Republic,[1] had abandoned the capital city, Pretoria. The occupation of the nearby city of Johannesburg on 1 June by the British soldiers, known locally as Khakis, was not a surprise and, over the past few days, he has observed the subtle signs of Marta's acceptance that they would need to flee their farm quickly when the inevitable Khakis march on Pretoria commenced.

The alternative was for him to surrender and hand in his weapons and that would never be acceptable to Marta. Her loathing of Burghers, called hands-uppers, who laid down their arms and took an oath of allegiance to Britain was palpable.

His three daughters, Estelle, Renette and Suné, have been helping wash clothing, blankets and linen and packing them into sacks, ready for transport. The pantry has also been emptied of candles, soap and other necessities.

Marta pours the coffee and they sit for a few minutes at the rough wooden table, drinking the strong brew and reading the Bible. The words fortify them both.

Pieter drains his mug. "I need to see to some business and then we must get ready to trek. We'll go to my brother's farm. Although it's close to the western border with the Cape Colony, it is remote and isolated, and you and the girls will be safer there. It's a long trip, about one hundred and fifty miles, but my injuries have healed well so I can manage it. When we get there, I can find out what's happened to Willem and what our officers are planning next for this war."

"That is a good idea. The girls will enjoy spending time with their cousins and Sannie and I will be company for each other while you and Willem are away fighting. I'm sure our military officers are already planning a new strategy to continue the struggle. We can't surrender, we have too much to lose."

The words are impassive and controlled and her eyes, as she gazes at her husband, are calm and accepting. Pieter could be forgiven for thinking she has no regrets about leaving the home they have built together, but he knows better. This is as devastating for her as it is for him.

"I've heard no recent news of Willem. I'm sure he'll have returned to

<hr />

[1] Also known as the Transvaal.

his farm after the relief of Mafeking by the Khakis last month. He's probably waiting for further instructions from our leaders."

Standing, he heads for the door. "I'll be back for breakfast. Straight afterwards, Estelle must round up the chickens and get them into their cages ready to go under the wagon."

Marta nods. Her face shines pale and white in the soft light of the lantern and the corners of her mouth sag downwards even though her lips form the words of a silent prayer:

Our Father, who art in heaven, hallowed be thy name; thy kingdom come; thy will be done on earth as it is in heaven.

* * *

By the time Pieter enters the main bedroom the sun has crept over the horizon and bright chinks of light are squeezing through cracks in the shutters making dappled patterns on the floor. The wind has dropped, and Pieter opens them, letting light into the cave-like room.

He takes a moment to reflect on how yellow the sun looks in the clear blue sky. It looks warm and inviting, but the layer of frost on the worn-down grass outside the window refutes the lie of a summer's day.

Picking up his woollen shirt, trousers and jacket from the top of the kist at the bottom of the bed, he quickly dresses. His feet are two unmalleable lumps of ice as he jams them into his sturdy *veldskoen* and ties the laces. Initially stiff and unyielding, the leather soon warms. His toes begin to tingle, and he wriggles them to get the blood flowing.

Opening the kist, he removes a small metal file and walks over to the bed.

The old iron bedstead slides along the floor easily. Inserting the metal file under a loose floorboard, he pries it up. Grunting, he lifts a few heavy sacks from their dusty hiding place beneath the sprung wooden floor.

His fingers work the leather thong holding one of the bags closed. It loosens and he plunges his hand into the bag and pulls out a handful of coins. Setting the coins aside on the floor, he re-ties the bag with dextrous fingers and drags the ungainly sacks over to the window.

Peering out he sees that no one is about, but smoke is rising from the direction of the farm workers' huts, which are set out in the traditional circular formation referred to as a kraal. He needs to move fast.

Manhandling the sacks out of the window, he hears them hit the ground outside with heavy thuds.

Smoky clouds from his warm breath plume in the frigid air as he carries the sacks, one in each hand, to the nearby thicket. Despite the cold, sweat beads his forehead and dampens his armpits as he pushes his way for a couple of hundred feet through the dense bushes until he reaches a wide clearing.

Pain, from the broken ribs he'd sustained in February while opposing the march on the besieged town of Kimberley by the British relief forces, hampers his movements. He fights against it.

Sighing heavily, the memory of the British defeat of the Boers at Kimberley still weighing on his morale, he offers up a silent prayer of thanks that he was injured, but not fatally so, during the British advance on the town, and was not part of the subsequent disastrous battle at Paardeberg Drift on the banks of the nearby Modder River.

I hoped for the best and prepared for the worst, but I didn't know at that time what my personal worst would be. I've since learned that surrendering and becoming a prisoner of war is the worst outcome imaginable, and I thank the Lord I escaped that fate.

His part in the fighting had started with his commando's first triumphant engagement with the British troops at Kraaipan in October 1899, just over six months previously.

Kraaipan was located south of the town of Mafeking where the British had chosen to store their supplies in anticipation of war with the two Boer republics. Despite Mafeking's isolated location at the northern tip of the British controlled Cape Colony, and its closeness to the Boer controlled areas, its choice by the British was strategic due to the town's proximity to British controlled Rhodesia and the Bechuanaland Protectorate.[1]

Despite this win, Pieter harboured a secret certainty that the British were going to rally. The British Empire was a formidable opponent and its imperialistic and capitalistic Queen Victoria was determined to have the gold that had been discovered in the Boer Republics.

Thoughts of his commando's win at Kraaipan come unbidden into his mind.

September 1899

By September 1899 the Boers knew that war was coming, and Boer commandos were being called up from all districts in the South African Republic. Grave discussions were taking place in many households as Boer women attempted to goad their reluctant fathers, husbands, brothers and sons into taking up arms and fighting for the independence of their home state.

---

[1] Current day Zimbabwe and Botswana respectively.

All Burghers, or fully entrenched citizens of the South African Republic who had the right to vote and own land, aged between sixteen and sixty, were obliged to serve in a commando during times of need.

Each commando was attached to a town, after which it was named, and each town was responsible for a district which was divided into wards. Each commando was overseen by a *kommandant*. A *veldkornet*, who reported to the *kommandant*, was responsible for each ward. Each *kommandant* reported to a general who oversaw four commandos.

Pieter originated from the Lichtenburg district, close to the western border with the Cape Colony, and his brother and cousins still lived there. They would join the Lichtenburg commando under Assistant *kommandant* General De la Rey, and Pieter had decided to return to his family home and serve with them.

He believed he would be safer among family and friends, having quickly learned that being obligated to fight for your country did not necessarily translate into an eagerness to do so. The reluctance of some of the Burghers to take up arms surprised him, and he chuckled at some of the conversations he'd overheard.

"I don't want to go to war now," said François Naude, "it's spring and I need to be here to oversee the planting."

Pieter, who was waiting to collect his grocery order from the proprietor of the Irene General Store, hid a smile at this amusing comment.

What does he think our government should do? Ask the British if they mind waiting for a more convenient time before we commence hostilities.

"You have no option but to fight if our government declares war. You're a *Burgher* and it is your obligation to fight for our independence if you're called upon to do so." The proprietor, Stefan Wolmarans, added the few extra items Pieter handed him into the grain sack containing the rest of his order and wiped his sweaty hands on the front of his apron.

"That's true, and for no pay too. Maintaining our independence from Britain is important but why do we have to start a war now? Can't it wait until the beginning of winter when all the crops have been harvested and the fodder for the cattle stored? Then I'll have time to fight in a war."

This time Pieter couldn't control his grin. Stefan noticed and winked at him conspiratorially.

"I don't think our government thinks this can wait that long, François, and there'll be no out for you, my friend. Your wife is one of the biggest supporters of this war. I've rarely met a more blood thirsty shrew. She'll be taking your horse and Mauser rifle and fighting on your behalf if you don't join your commando quickly. Her women's group are just as bad, don't you agree, Pieter?"

Pieter glared at the overweight storekeeper, his lips a thin line of irritation at these insulting words. He wasn't going to disrespect François by supporting Stefan's derogatory comment.

"I think you're being a bit hard on Mrs Naude and her friends, Stefan. The women know that any conflict will result in much bloodshed and the deaths of their loved ones. The independence of our nation is being threatened and they consider it their duty to put their own selfish considerations and emotions aside and to serve our country regardless of the personal cost."

Stefan Wolmarans' eyes in their puffy pockets of flesh twinkled with wry amusement. "I should have known you would try to explain the women's perspective, Pieter. Some things never change, and you were always thoughtful."

A red flush crept across Pieter's cheeks and down his neck at this reminder of his liberal views.

"You're right, Stefan," François slapped the portly man on the back with a meaty thud. "I'll get ready my thirty rounds of ammunition and enough rations for two weeks. After that, central government must resupply me, as promised."

Pieter finished his business at the store and set off for home to continue his own preparations for war.

Marta had spent several weeks making him serviceable corduroy clothing, knapsacks, and bread bags in readiness for his leaving to join a commando. Now that war was imminent, Pieter was grateful for her efforts which facilitated his swift departure and appreciated that it was a gesture of her love for him and their family.

Pieter planned to leave for Willem's farm the following week in accordance with the two men's arranged plan for when war came. From there, the two men would travel to the nearby town of Polfontein, a gathering place for the Western Frontier commandos.

In anticipation of Pieter's journey, Marta and the girls had baked large quantities of *harde beskuit* or rusks. Marta made the bread dough and the two girls rolled it into round balls and packed them into the bread tins. These were baked in the same way as bread.

After the initial baking, Marta used her knife to slice the bread into pieces which the girls laid out on a baking tray. These were baked again until the pieces were quite dry. The doubled-baked bread would last a long time and sustain Pieter while he was away fighting.

He packed these up, together with mielie meal, a course flour made from maize; biltong, a spicy dried meat cut into strips; and his personal Bible, and set off early one morning, accompanied by his farm worker, Mhlopi.

Mhlopi came up to him the day before he left. "My *Baas*," he said, "I know you are going to join a commando. Let me come with you and help look after you."

Pieter was pleased that Mhlopi had volunteered to go with him and join his commando as an auxiliary or *agterryer*. Not only was he trustworthy, he would be useful to collect firewood, light the fires, cook, and look after the horses.

Tall and strong looking, with flawless skin, a wide smile and a cheerful disposition, Mhlopi had been in dire need when he'd knocked on Pieter's door five years ago, looking for work. His previous employer had spoiled his pass, a metal badge carried by all natives working in the South African Republic, by scratching across it. This spiteful but effective action had marked him as undesirable, rendering his chances of long-term employment in the Republic virtually non-existent.

When Pieter had opened his door to him, he had been moved by the sad acceptance in his dark eyes. The man who stood before him expected nothing and didn't dare to hope.

Pieter had given him a chance, employing him to help prepare the fields for planting. In return, Mhlopi had given him his loyalty and devotion.

Pieter had never learned why his previous employer had punished him so harshly, but he thought it had something to do with that most destructive of human emotions, jealousy.

His other farm manager, Mosiko, also volunteered to accompany them.

"No, Mosiko," Pieter said firmly. "I need you to stay here and look after the Missus and the girls. You need to see to the farm while I'm away and oversee the spring planting."

Mosiko nodded agreement, "Yes *Baas*."

I'm fortunate to have an employee like Mosiko. I know I can trust him explicitly after all his years of service. He knows it is his responsibility to look after my family during my absence. He'll also see to the needs and safety of the other farm workers and their families, as well as his own.

Mosiko was only ten-years-old when Pieter's father, Hendrick, had discovered him hiding in the veld.[1] Mosiko's parents were both dead and he had been unhappily living with uncaring and abusive relatives. He had recently run away and was attempting to make his own way in the world.

---

[1] Open, uncultivated country or grassland in southern Africa.

Willem and Pieter, young teenagers themselves, had been with their father at the time and Pieter had given a share of his lunch to the thin and hungry looking boy.

From that moment, Mosiko had attached himself to Pieter, looking out for him and seeing to his every need. He had followed them back to their farm and asked to stay and work for Hendrick. Hendrick, a kindly man, had agreed, and Mosiko had been working for the van Zyl family ever since, choosing to accompany Pieter when he married and left to establish his own life and farm.

When the time came for Pieter to start his journey to meet Willem, Marta told their three daughters to kiss him goodbye.

"You must be good girls," he said. "Help your mother and learn your Psalms every day."

"We will, Papa," they chorused.

Sadness clouded Pieter's expression as he watched tears slipping from Renette's and Suné's eyes. He knew that their soft hearts were already grieving for the loss of their father, even though the loss was only expected to be temporary.

Estelle managed to give him a weak smile. She didn't cry but the redness of her eyes and their anxious look betrayed her overwhelming sadness and the poor night's sleep she had suffered.

"Goodbye Papa," she whispered.

"Remember to say your prayers every night and read from your Bible every day, Pieter," Marta said. Her expression was inscrutable, but her eyes resembled those of a wounded animal.

Pieter and Mhlopi, mounted their horses and trotted away down the dusty track.

When Pieter glanced back, a few minutes later, Marta and the girls had gone inside. The house was quiet and peaceful.

The idea of going to war seemed surreal except for the pack horse Mhlopi was leading, loaded with spare ammunition and other supplies. Sighing deeply, he turned his back on his home and family and rode towards his future.

It was a couple of days' hard riding before they reached Willem's farm. As they travelled, Pieter studied the terrain around them. Its wild beauty filled his heart with wonder. The long grass was green at the bottom of its shafts and wildflowers broke the endless continuity of the veld with their bright splashes of colour. His sharp ears could hear the bees as they went about their daily task of gathering pollen.

It's a wonderful thing to be far away from the shackles of authority and free.

Resolve to fight for his freedom steeled him for the period of fighting to come. *I do not want to live under the yoke of Britain.*

Eventually, the two men arrived at Willem's farm in the early evening, exhausted and dirty. Mhlopi happily joined Willem's workers in their *kraal* for the night. Pieter and Willem sat in the *voorkamer* and discussed their travel plans.

Through the doorway, Pieter caught glimpses of Willem's wife, Sannie, and their two daughters preparing the evening meal. Lena, who was seventeen, and Hannekie, who was fifteen, were lively and talkative girls and Pieter was aware of the steady hum of conversation while the three of them worked together. He thought how nice it was for Sannie to have their company and support while Willem was gone.

His own girls were much younger with the oldest, Estelle, turning thirteen in December. She was a hard-working girl and helped her mother extensively with the housework and cooking, but she was a loner and liked to spend her spare time by herself, dreaming her strange and lonely dreams. He knew that Marta found their oldest daughter difficult to understand and the pair did not always get along well.

He sighed deeply as he half-listened to Willem, who was now complaining about the unreasonable behaviour of the British towards their government and pushed his concerns about the relationship between Marta and their oldest daughter aside.

Sannie was famous for her *potjiekos*, a rich stew comprising beef, potatoes, and plenty of vegetables which she cooked slowly, in a three-legged cast-iron pot, over hot coals until the meat was tender and the vegetables soft.

Pieter's meals for the past few days had comprised rusks, dried bread and *biltong* with water from their water-skins, and his mouth watered as the rich fumes from the stew wafted through the house.

When the meal was ready, Pieter and Willem tucked into the food with gusto, knowing that they were unlikely to enjoy such a good meal again for a while. The main course was followed by Sannie's home-made *melktert*, a traditional dessert consisting of a sweet pastry crust containing a custard filling made from milk, flour, sugar and eggs, and sprinkled with cinnamon.

After the meal, Willem produced his fiddle. Eyes shining with joy, he played into the night, his foot tapping in time to the music. The evening was happy with Willem looking strong and fit as the smooth wood of the fiddle gleamed in the soft lamplight.

Sitting back in his chair, Pieter listened while Willem played his eldest daughter's favourite song, *Jan Pierewiet*. He sang with the fiddle, his voice rich and mellow.

>Jan Pierewiet, Jan Pierewiet
>Jan Pierewiet stand still.
>Jan Pierewiet, Jan Pierewiet
>Jan Pierewiet stand still.
>Good morning my wife,
>Here's a kiss for your life.
>Good morning my man,
>There is coffee in the can.

Pieter forgot his worries temporarily while the rollicking tune filled the night.

The following day, the men set off early, travelling in a westerly direction towards Polfontein.

Polfontein was a strategic choice for the gathering of the Boer commandos as, in addition to being close to the border between the South African Republic and Cape Colony, it was also close to Mafeking.

The Boers were determined to occupy Mafeking, partly due to its role as the British administrative centre of the region and the headquarters of the peace-keeping Bechuanaland Border Police, and partly because the town had been used as the base for the Jameson Raid in December 1895.

The raid was purportedly not supported by the British government but comprised a party of volunteer armed forces backed by mining magnet Cecil John Rhodes, and other British and Jewish businessmen who wanted to overthrow the government of the South Africa Republic and turn the Transvaal into a British colony.

The Boers remained bitter about this unsuccessful raid and it was one of the contributing factors to the current hostilities between the Boers and the British government.

Willem was accompanied by his *agterryer*, Sipho. Before they left, Sannie replenished Pieter's supplies of *harde-biskuit*, dried bread and biltong as well as providing Willem with substantial amounts of these foods.

Willem was in high spirits. "This war will soon be over, Pieter. It'll be the same as the last one. We'll defend our borders against the invaders, and it will be over in three months. We'll be home by harvest time."

Willem shared the sense of excitement and euphoria that many of his fellow countrymen were experiencing, but Pieter did not.

War brings bloodshed, grief and tears. This time the British will probably send many more soldiers. I think this war is going to be a much harder win.

He had not shared his own thoughts with Willem. There was no point and he had learned many years ago to keep his unpopular opinions to himself.

Just after dark one evening later that week, the foursome rode into the Boer laager[1] at Polfontein. The huge number of fires burning in a vast circle was a welcome and encouraging sight and they could also see a significant number of wagons in the soft yellow light from the fires.

They reported to the *veldkornet*, who showed them a place where they could camp and assigned them to the division led by Assistant *Kommandant* General de la Rey. The other two divisions were led by *Kommandant* Snyman and General Cronjé.

As the *veldkornet* walked away, Willem said to Pieter, "I'm sorry we have not been assigned to Cronjé's division. I'm sure we could learn a lot from such a distinguished general. His successes in the last war will inspire his men to greater bravery and military achievement. He was also in charge of the force that rounded up Jameson at the conclusion of the Jameson Raid." Willem's shoulders sloped downwards with disappointment. "Instead we'll ride with one of his field generals."

I don't agree with Willem, de le Rey is a brave man and a good leader too. I'm happy I'll serve with him. I've read about General Cronjé's involvement in the controversy surrounding the surrender of the besieged British garrison at Potchefstroom during the First Anglo Boer War. The British accused him of treachery because he did not inform the garrison that an armistice had been concluded before they surrendered. While I wouldn't personally call his behaviour treachery, I do think it was dishonourable and I don't trust him to act with integrity.

Willem's comments about his success with the defeat and arrest of British colonial statesman, Leander Starr Jameson, and his troops after their botched Jamison Raid, are true. I hope Cronjé will lead his men to a similar success in this war.

Mhlopi and Sipho set about starting a fire and making coffee while Pieter and Willem joined a group of men standing around a fire in front of one of the wagons.

"Tomorrow afternoon at 5 p.m., our government's ultimatum to the British government will lapse," said one of the men who had introduced himself as Hendrik van Staden.

"The British government is unlawfully interfering in our affairs," declared Willem. "Our government is right to give them an ultimatum."

---

[1] An encampment formed by a circle of wagons.

"Agreed," said van Staden, "the British government must remove all their troops from the borders of our country. They must also send their reinforcement troops back to England."

"And they must agree to Oom[1] Paul's proposal for the Uitlanders," Willem spat the word "Uitlanders" out, as if it was a piece of rotten food.

The men who had gathered at Polfontein were all aware of the reason for the ultimatum. The president of the South African Republic, Paul Kruger, affectionately known as *Oom* Paul, had refused to give in to British High Commissioner Lord Milner's demand that the Uitlanders receive full voting rights after five years residence in the South African Republic.

The problem of the Uitlanders outraged them. Immigrants, mainly from Britain and given the name of Uitlanders or Outsiders by the Boers, had flooded into the South African Republic during the Witwatersrand[2] gold rush in 1886.

The expectation by the Boer government that the Uitlanders pay taxes despite lacking any civil representation until they had been resident for fourteen years increased tensions between the Republic and Britain.

The Boers believed that granting the Uitlanders full voting rights would eventually jeopardise the independence of the Republic due to their continuously increasing numbers in comparison to the number of Burghers.

The Boers, including Pieter and Willem, believed in the principles of the war and were happy to play their part in the on-going fight.

There were few women living in the laager and there was a shared awareness by all the men that their womenfolk expected them to act as the Lord's vessels in extracting revenge on the British Empire for its breach of trust towards the Afrikaner nation.

Their women carried themselves bravely, firmly believing that their collective suffering was for people and fatherland and would be justified by their independence.

"*Oom* Paul was most reasonable in his offer to Lord Milner. He was prepared to offer the Uitlanders naturalisation after two years' residence and full franchise after a further five years," Willem ranted.

"Yes," said a large man with a bushy, dark beard and sharp eyes, who

---

[1] Uncle in Afrikaans – used as a respectful and affectionate form of address to an older man.

[2] Witwatersrand, also called The Rand, ridge of gold-bearing rock mostly in Gauteng province, South Africa.

Pieter recognised as a farmer from Zeerust, a farming district which neighboured Lichtenburg, called Stoffel de Bruyn. "He was also prepared to give them increased representation in government and a new oath."

"Milner just wants control of the Witwatersrand gold-mining complex in our country," Willem agreed.

Why, oh why, did gold have to be discovered on the Witwatersrand? thought Pieter.

In his usual reticent and quiet manner, he had not verbally joined in the heated debate, although he listened intently. As a young man living in a rural farming community, Pieter had quickly learned that most of his poorly educated peers could not understand his complex viewpoints and if he tried to explain them, they said he spoke in riddles and ridiculed him mercilessly.

The words of Piet Joubert, *Kommandant* General of the South African Republic, repeated in Pieter's mind: "*This gold is going to soak our country in blood.*"

The topic of the ultimatum, the expected war and its justification was eventually exhausted. The men roasted pieces of a buck someone had shot over the coals of the fire and the conversation turned to everyday topics. The men discussed whether the mielie crops would be good this year, the problems encountered with the cattle-smuggling business, and the rinderpest, also known as cattle plague.

The next morning, in anticipation of the lapse of the Republican ultimatum that evening, General de la Rey called together the men forming his commando and spoke to them. "We are going to mobilise as soon as war is declared, be ready."

Pieter and Willem spent most of the afternoon resting in the shade of a group of acacia trees. It was a refreshingly green spot among the waving yellowy brown veld grass, rocks, and clumps of khaki-*bos* that comprised most of the landscape.

By 2 p.m., most of the men had settled on their backs under the wide-spreading branches of the acacia trees with their hats tipped over their eyes, whiling away the hottest hours of the African spring day in this pleasant manner.

It's practical as we are going to be awake all night, Pieter thought dreamily as his eyes closed.

Late in the afternoon a lone rider rode into the camp. Bright and excited eyes stared out of a youthful face; the messenger could not have been much older than sixteen.

"The ultimatum has lapsed. We are officially at war with Britain," he shouted. His pleasure at this development was evident on his dirty and travel-worn face.

The date was 11 October 1899. The announcement sent the encampment into a frenzy of final preparations. Just before midnight that same evening, eight hundred Boers, including Willem, Pieter and the young messenger, set off southwards under General de la Rey's command.

Mhlopi and Sipho were left behind to look after their additional supplies and equipment.

Pieter watched the young messenger, whose name was Adrian Opperman, part from his mother, who was one of the women brave enough to have accompanied her husband and son to the laager.

"Goodbye my son. Let your ways be in the fear of the Lord. If I do not see you again on earth, I pray to find you again in heaven."

His heart constricted at this touching parting and he wondered if they would see each other again. He thought of the wording of the vow taken by his pioneer ancestors, the Voortrekkers,[1] before the Battle of Blood River on the 16th of December 1838 when four hundred and seventy Voortrekkers, led by Andries Pretorius, fought against ten thousand Zulu warriors on the bank of the Ncome River.

> We stand here before the Holy God of heaven and earth, to make a vow to Him that, if He will protect us and give our enemy into our hand we shall keep this day and date every year as a day of thanksgiving like a Sabbath, and that we shall build a house to His honour wherever it should please Him, and that we will also tell our children that they should share in that with us in memory for future generations. For the honour of His name will be glorified by giving Him the fame and honour for the victory.

The words of this vow gave Pieter comfort.

He wondered how Marta was managing on the farm. *She's a tough woman, she'll be fine.*

The October evening was warm, and the men were confident that their objective to drive off a small British force of about one thousand men at the nearby railway station and to destroy the railway line would be easily

---

[1] Boers who took part in the Great Trek, an eastward migration of Dutch-speaking settlers who travelled by ox-wagon trains from the Cape Colony into the interior of modern South Africa from 1836 onwards, in an attempt to become independent and live beyond the Cape Colony's British colonial administration.

achieved. They rode through the darkness of the early morning hours, only stopping to refresh themselves when the first streaks of pink coloured the horizon. Pieter's coffee and *mielie pap*[1] tasted good as he rested during the short stop after dawn. It was good to be alive, enjoying the rich smell of the dew dampened veld and the brisk morning breeze.

All day they rode, through the relentless heat of late spring until, at 3 p.m. that afternoon, they reached their destination. Kraaipan Station stood lonely and deserted under the blazing sun. As they approached, Pieter saw the distant form of a domestic dog skulking across the platform; nothing else moved. Seizing the opportunity presented by the lack of opposition, the men set about cutting the telegraph wire and damaging the railway line on both sides of the station. Sweat streamed down Pieter's face and soaked the back of his shirt as he ripped up the rails.

Within a short time, they had finished and were riding away, their confidence bolstered by the ease and quickness with which their task had been achieved.

Maybe Willem is right, and this war really will be over quickly, Pieter thought, relaxing into his saddle. *The British are significantly outnumbered by our men and their old-fashioned ideas of advancing in shoulder to shoulder formations and firing volley after volley in ridged lines will not serve them well in the veld.*

Tired out by their early start and the excitement of fulfilling their mission so easily, the men set up their rough camp in the late afternoon. While their supper of meat, from a buck shot while they were travelling, cooked over an open fire, most of the Boers took advantage of the nearby river to replenish their drinking water and wash their weary and sweat drenched bodies and clothes. The cool water was refreshing and invigorating after their long and dusty ride.

It is fortunate that it is only October and the stifling heat of summer has not yet arrived. Mind you, I'm better off in my loose shirt and trousers than the British in their heavy helmets, high necked and long-sleeved khaki shirts and knee-length boots, thought Pieter as he hung his dripping clothes on a bush to dry.

After eating his share of the simple fare, Pieter spread out his handmade sleeping bag beneath a convenient tree and dropped off into welcome sleep.

Hours later, he was awoken by one of the sentries.

---

[1] Maize meal flour that has been stirred with water until it is stiff and crumbly (called *phutu* in Zulu) and eaten as a starch with savoury meals and with a thick tomato and onion braised sauce.

"There is a train coming." The man's whisper was grimly urgent.

In the cool darkness of the night Pieter could hear it approaching. Moments later, metal wheels screeched, and voices cried out in shock.

"The train's derailed," the English words pierced the darkness.

Leaping to his feet, Pieter moved in the direction of the noise. There was a bright moon, but also some thick dark clouds which drifted across its face. For a minute, Pieter's world was completely black and then the cloud passed, and he could see the armoured train, its engine leaning drunkenly to one side where it had left the tracks.

De la Rey gave his orders and Pieter, together with a group of his peers, moved to the south to break up the railway line behind the armoured train.

It won't be able to retreat now, Pieter thought triumphantly.

Banging floated through the blackness.

What's happening? Pieter stood still, listening carefully.

His eyes picked up movement in the darkness. Shadows were working frantically, trying to repair the damaged line.

Bang! Bang! Shots aimed at the Boers shattered the air, the thick darkness seeming to amplify the sound.

The Boers opened fire in return. Within minutes, the exposed British soldiers had bolted back inside the train to escape the Boers' barrage of gunfire.

Invigorated by this further victory, the Boers settled down to wait for the dawn.

Bang! Bang! Bang! Three shots were fired by the Boers when the new day broke. After the third shot, the crew of the train, followed by the soldiers, surrendered.

Entering the train, the Boers crowed with jubilation when they saw its useful cargo comprising three 7-pounder field guns, many shells, thirty rifles and ammunition for them as well as a few cases of dynamite.

"We'll put all of this to good use," Willem shouted in delight.

"The first encounter of the war has ended in total victory for us," de la Rey announced to his cheering commando.

The following day, Pieter and Willem were among a group of men who set off on the more leisurely return journey to the Polfontein laager.

Their triumphant arrival corresponded with the start of the shelling of Mafeking on the 16th of October, three days after the siege of the town began.

Pieter and Willem quickly learned that, two days previously, General Cronjé had issued a note to the British Commander in Mafeking, Colonel

Baden-Powell, demanding that he surrender the town to the Boers. This demand had been rejected and General Cronjé had ordered the Boers to besiege the town.

The gatherings around the campfires on that first evening of the shelling were exuberant due to the Boers' expectations of a quick victory.

Pieter, doubtful of a quick resolution to this conflict despite the initial victories enjoyed by the Boers, watched solemnly as those men who had a musical talent pulled out their violins, playing for the assembly while the sound of laughter and excited talk filled the star-studded night. His apprehensions about this war prevented him from embracing the celebrations with the same enthusiasm as his peers.

Willem had not brought his fiddle, but he joined in the singing when Jannie Snyman, a middle-aged Boer with a light brown beard, started playing a popular new song.

> My Sarie Marais is so far from my heart
> but I hope to see her again
> She lived in the area of Mooi-river
> before the war began.
>
> Chorus:
> *Oh bring me back to the old Transvaal*
> *where my Sarie lives*
> *There by the maize*
> *by the green thorn tree*
> *there my Sarie lives.*
>
> I was so scared that the Khakis would catch me
> and send me far across the sea
> So I fled to Upington
> there next to the Grootriver
>
> *Chorus*
>
> The Khakis are just like crocodiles
> they always drag you to the water
> They throw you on a ship for a long, long trip;
> who knows where they're taking you.
>
> *Chorus*
>
> Relief came and it was possible that we could go home
> back to the old Transvaal
> My love will probably also be there
> to reward me with a kiss.

"When the Long Tom arrives from Pretoria and starts bombarding the town, the British will soon surrender," a burly Boer called Pete Grobler declared after the music and dancing had died down.

Another Boer caught up the refrain: "Our general is experienced in this type of warfare. He forced the British garrison at Potchefstroom to surrender during the last war, and he'll do the same thing this time."

Pieter listened quietly while the men extolled the virtues of the French siege gun called the Long Tom. The government of the South African Republic had bought four of these great guns with their 4.2-metre-long barrels in 1897 for deployment at the four forts they had built around Pretoria. Now that war had been declared, it had been decided that the guns would be deployed as field and siege guns around the country.

A small smile turned up the corners of Pieter's mouth as he went to sleep that night. He dreamed of the successes of the day and the eminent capture of Mafeking by the Boers after the arrival of the Long Tom.

June 1900

Pieter's mind returns to the present day and he reflects on the recent news that the Boers have finally been beaten back at Mafeking after a siege that continued for two hundred and seventeen days.

A deep sigh escapes his lips. The Mafeking debacle was not a success for his people. In his secret heart he knows that this war can only end in defeat for the Boers now. His mouth will never utter his thoughts, they lie deeply hidden in his inner most mind. Marta would berate him for having such thoughts, for even considering the prospect of defeat for the Boers. He knows this and he keeps silent, but the thoughts remain, tormenting him during sleep and causing him to thrash and turn in his bed.

Focusing his attention on the task at hand, Pieter makes his way over to a freshly dug hole in the centre of the clearing and shoves the sacks into it. He manoeuvres a young tree that is standing nearby, mud clinging thickly to its root system, into the hole and proceeds to cover up the roots and the sacks with the rich, dark soil.

As he continues working, he thinks about the recent meeting he had with *Oom* Paul at his house in Pretoria.

May 1900

Oom Paul's deep-set eyes were underscored by pouches of dark, bruised-looking flesh and new deep lines had etched themselves into the skin of his face.

"Pieter, I'm confiding in you as one of my most loyal and trusted citizens. The government has decided not to defend Pretoria against the Khakis. I'm preparing to leave the city shortly with several my advisors. We'll establish a provisional capital in Machadodorp."

"Why has this decision been made, *Oom* Paul? We have our four forts that were specifically built to defend the city. Why are they not going to be used?"

Oom Paul's shoulders slumped, and his large frame seemed to crumple momentarily. Then he pulled himself upright and straightened his shoulders. "The government fears that the British will destroy all our beautiful buildings in a bombardment if we attempt to defend the city. For this reason, we have decided to abandon the city, as was done with Bloemfontein. Johannesburg will not be defended for the same reason and is expected to fall imminently."

Pieter thought it was a strange decision, but he smiled at the elderly president. "I understand, what do you need of me?"

"I want you to take this, Pieter," *Oom* Paul said, pointing to the two heavy sacks on the floor. "The Boers in your area will need it to rehabilitate themselves after the war, whatever the outcome."

Whatever the outcome. Those are not the words of a man confident of victory.

"Thank you, *Oom* Paul."

Two days later, on the 29th of May, *Oom* Paul had left Pretoria, travelling by train to Machadodorp, which was on the line to Delagoa Bay in neighbouring Mozambique. When it became known a day later that the government had left the city, rumours started to spread among the Pretorians and to the Boers living on the surrounding farms.

One rumour was that the President had made a secret deal with Lord Roberts to hand the city over to him in exchange for a huge financial reward. Pieter had scoffed at that one. The second rumour did not seem to be as groundless.

It was said that the President had taken all the gold from the National Bank with him when he left. This rumour led Pieter to reflect on the sacks that *Oom* Paul had given to him and to wonder if the Kruger coins they contained had come from the National Bank. He thought that they did. *What's happened to the rest of the gold? Oom Paul must have given some to other Burghers and not just too me. It's worth a fortune.*

June 1900

Pieter stands up and stretches gently, trying not to escalate the ache in his ribs to an unbearable pain. The 30,000 gold Kruger coins he'd been given should be safe until he could get back for them.

With a sigh of relief, Pieter makes his way to the barn which houses his wagon. Mosiko and Mhlopi arrive to assist him. First, they stretch the white canvas cover over the wooden arches attached to the wagon to create an enclosed area, and then they assist with inspanning the oxen in preparation for the trek to his brother's farm which is quite a distance away from their current location. It's quite a process to attach yokes to the sixteen oxen.

The other farm workers are sent to round up his cattle and goats, a tedious task which will take two to three hours.

Pieter checks the yokes, skeis and strops for each pair of oxen. He does not want his animals to be damaged in any way during the journey. Next he checks the trek chain, wooden wheels and spokes and the iron tyres covering the rims of the wheels. He fills the water barrel and hangs it under the wagon next to the cages filled with chickens. He is pleased that Estelle has managed to catch them all and get them into the cages on her own.

When he is satisfied that the covered wagon is ready for the journey, Pieter speaks to his farm workers. "The British soldiers are coming. Mosiko and Mhlopi will come with me and lead the oxen. Feile and Kleinbooi will help me to drive the cattle. Their families will come with us, but the rest of you must take your women and children and go back to your villages until the danger has passed."

Pieter can sense their anxiety and sadness.

I wonder what the fall of Pretoria will mean for them. Will they join the Khakis in the fight against us Boers or will they remain loyal to us?

He is aware that his farm workers hold him in high regard. Despite his quiet nature, Pieter's actions towards his workers and their families demonstrate his kindness and consideration. He knows all their names and the names of their wives and children. He allows them to keep their own cattle which graze on his land alongside his own livestock.

As he dismisses his farm workers and tells them to travel safely, bitterness burns in his heart like acid.

My farm is lost to me now. It is time for me to assess the future for me and my family.

The gold coins he took from the sacks feel heavy in his tobacco pouch and he finds their weight reassuring.

The wagon is loaded with farm equipment, seeds, kitchen utensils, bedding and clothing. Marta and their two younger daughters, wearing their button-up boots and carrying their rag dolls, climb into the back of the wagon, under the canvas covering.

Estelle climbs up and takes her place as the driver. From his position on his horse next to the wagon, Pieter sees Marta's annoyed glare. He knows Marta does not approve of Estelle sitting in the open on the wooden chest, driving the wagon.

Marta's just being narrow minded. We have no sons and Estelle is capable and willing. She is good at driving too and has expressed her preference for sitting outside in the air rather than sweltering under the covering at the back. Marta will just have to learn to accept my decision.

"Put your bonnet on, Estelle," he calls, hoping to pacify his wife.

Estelle drags on the thick white ties attached to her bonnet, pulling it up over her bright hair and plunging her beautiful face into shadow. Pieter smiles at her and moves away, walking his horse slowly down the line of oxen.

The young son of one of the farm labourers assumes the position of *voorloper*,[1] taking his place at the head of the oxen to lead them. Mhlopi, the driver, will walk next to the oxen while Mosiko and the other farm labourers will drive the livestock. Mhlopi cracks his *shambok* and the heavily loaded wagon lurches down the rutted track that leads away into the bushveld.

Pieter drops back and looks behind Estelle and into the wagon. He smiles reassuringly at Marta. "Sannie will be glad to see us and she should be able to give me information about Willem. Leaving our farm for the time being is the right thing to do. I do not want to be forced to surrender and hand in my guns. Once Pretoria falls, the Khakis will declare martial law in the city and surrounds. It'll become difficult to leave as people will have to apply for permits in order to travel."

Marta returns his smile, despite her sadness at leaving their home. Pieter knows it is her enormous patriotism and determination that the South Africa Republic should not surrender to the merciless invaders that is sustaining her through this difficult time in their lives.

---

[1] The person (usually a young boy) who walks with the foremost pair of a team of draught oxen in order to guide them.

MICHELLE

HOW MANY ARE THERE?

March 2019

The dull throbbing of her over-full bladder forces Michelle from sleep.

Bugger! I don't want to get up.

Rolling over, she ignores the persistent niggle and attempts to go back to sleep.

Five minutes later she accepts defeat and hauls herself out of bed. Eyes barely open, like those of a new-born kitten, she makes her way to the bathroom. The electric light shines through the gap between the door and the doorframe, painting a bright stripe across the floor and illuminating her way. Tom accommodates her night light, provided the door is only open a crack. It helps control her nyctophobia and darkness induced anxiety.

A few minutes later, and only slightly more awake, she walks back towards the bedroom.

The bright green digits on the alarm clock next to the bed flash 4 a.m. The curtains billow with an unexpectedly cold early morning breeze, drawing her eyes in that direction. Gooseflesh breaks out on her bare arms and legs as the coolness wraps itself around her like a blanket. A dark shadow stains the light curtains. It's indistinct in the dim light but has a distinctly human shape.

It's a burglar! The man I saw in the garden, he's returned and broken in.

Adrenaline floods her body and each nerve seems to vibrate. Her fingertips tingle unpleasantly.

What should I do? If I scream, he might shoot me.

She stands, staring fixedly at the shadow, waiting for it to move. The temperature in the room plunges and she shivers uncontrollably.

The shadow takes a step towards her and her heart gallops, pounding against her ribs.

It is a man. From beneath a battered cloth hat, bright eyes peer at her from a face partially obscured by a thick, greying beard. He wears a white shirt and a bandage soaked in dark, sticky blood is wrapped around his chest.

Behind the shadow, the curtains continue to dance and sway.

Her stomach is a tight knot of horror. The tingling in her fingers spreads and her skin begins to smart unpleasantly.

The phantom tips his hat at her.

Crash! The en suite bathroom door slams shut.

Michelle jumps and whips her head in the direction of the noise. She makes out a second shape dimly outlined against the door's stark white paint. The figure's khaki uniform, knee-high boots and helmet are clearly visible, as well as the rifle he holds in place over his left shoulder. The front of his tunic is stained an inky black.

It's a soldier. A dead one. Holy crap!

Her scalp prickles as the hair on her head tries to stand up and fails due to its length and weight.

A movement from the bed briefly attracts her attention. Tom moves restlessly, but, strangely, the slamming of the door has not woken him. She opens her mouth to call out, but no sound issues from her strained throat.

Her eyes dart back to the first shadow. The man in the hat has closed the gap between them; his back is rigid and his posture aggressive. Unlike the soldier, he appears to be unarmed. He stands in front of the dressing table, and she can see her own reflection right through him. It's distorted, like looking through the bottom of a coke bottle. He has no reflection.

She closes her eyes and takes a deep and steadying breath.

I'm dreaming. The weird events of last night disturbed me and have manifested as a nightmare. What's happening is not real. There is no such thing as ghosts.

Opening her eyes, she glances quickly towards the bed. Tom sleeps on, his breathing soft and restful.

There's no help coming from him. Irritation at his complacent slumber briefly displaces her fear, crowding it out like the incoming tide.

A soft rustling gives the soldier's movements away. He has stepped forward and is standing at the edge of the king-sized bed. His weapon is raised and its wooden stock shimmers in the faint light. Michelle can see his face now, its handsomeness marred by lines of bitterness and anger.

A shudder wrenches its way through her body, as her eyes skitter from one apparition to the next, trying to see which one will move next. A strong wind rushes past her as the soldier streaks across the room and collides with his adversary. On impact, both shapes disappear.

Michelle backs up a step or two, scouring the room for the two figures. They are gone. She stands frozen for a few minutes, breathing deeply and trying to regain control of her chaotic thoughts.

Should I wake Tom? No, he'll laugh at me and say I'm imagining things.

Wrapping herself in her dressing gown, she goes downstairs stealthily and sits, drinking a strong cup of coffee, in the kitchen, while she reflects on what she has witnessed.

Did I really see the figures of two men? Did the Ouija board summon them? Could one of them be the mysterious spirit that seemed to take control of the planchette last night? If so, what help did he need?

"The first man was unarmed. Maybe he needs help to escape the evil intensions of the soldier?" she murmurs to herself.

She hears a sound behind her. Turning around quickly, an embarrassed flush on her face, she expects to see Tom standing there. She can almost hear his cocky comment that talking to yourself is the first sign of madness. There is no one there.

I'm tired after the move and the party yesterday. We got to bed late. There is nothing there and I didn't see anything upstairs either. I'm just tired!

Michelle spends the next two hours cleaning. Unhooking the curtains, she puts them in the washing machine together with the soiled table-cloths. Turning on the radio, she listens to the news while she scrubs down the walls and polishes the table and each of the heavy wooden chairs.

The host is talking about the Reserve Bank's impending decision to either cut or maintain interest rates. People are dialling in and sharing their views and thoughts. Michelle's own anxieties fade as the normalcy of everyday life encircles her.

By the time Tom finally opens his eyes, ninety long minutes later, Michelle is convinced she imagined the two phantoms.

My overactive imagination scared the shit out of me, but it's over now and I don't need to tell Tom about it. He'll only laugh and make me feel ridiculous.

After a light breakfast, Tom leaves to meet his mates at the gym and work off his mild hangover. Michelle indulges herself in a warm and soothing bath. The scented bubbles relax her, making her visions of the early morning even more surreal.

I definitely imagined it. Thank God I didn't tell Tom. How he would have laughed.

Climbing out of the bath, she dresses for the day, and goes downstairs to her home office. The idea of doing some research on how a planchette works attracts her.

Once I understand how the planchette moves, it'll dispel any concerns I have about what happened last night. There must be a scientific explanation for what happened; there always is.

She starts her laptop and types "What makes a planchette move?" into the computer's search engine. A few moments later she is reading the response.

> According to some psychologists, a planchette is moved as a result of tiny movements by the finger muscles of a party or parties holding the instrument. These minute movements reveal the player or players' unconscious thoughts as they move the planchette in the desired direction without consciously recognising that they are doing so.

How fascinating. One or all of us made the planchette move last night and write that peculiar message. I'll bet it was Alice acting the billy goat and giving us a good scare. There is nothing to be afraid of, nothing at all.

Still reflecting on this information, Michelle goes into the kitchen and makes herself a cup of coffee. The idea of writing a book about the Second Anglo Boer War has been niggling at her.

I wonder if the historical ownership of the original Irene farm, on which this housing estate was built, is a good place for me to start my research. The estate agent mentioned that our town house was built on the site of the original old farmhouse which dated back to before the Second Anglo Boer War. He also said that our jacaranda tree is protected and was planted by the first owner of the farm. Did I mention the history of the property to Alice? She is such a prankster; she could easily have initiated that peculiar Ouija board experience as a joke on her friends.

She searches, but little detailed information about the original farmhouse is available on the Internet.

Maybe I should visit the Irene Library sometime this week when I get a work gap. I've heard that it's well stocked with books and information about this area. Maybe I can find out something more or find a librarian or someone else who can point me in the right direction.

Michelle is so absorbed that she fails to hear the front door slam announcing Tom's arrival home. Skulking up behind her, he runs his finger lightly down her spine. Michelle jumps and lets out a short scream. Swinging around to glare at him, she catches his wink.

"I think that Ouija board scared someone," he laughs.

* * *

Michelle works non-stop the whole of Monday morning. Usually she takes a break from her work, going out for a thirty-minute walk and then making herself a cup of coffee to drink in their small garden, but not today.

By 3.30 p.m., Michelle is on top of the bulk of her work. Suddenly ravenous, having not eaten since her 7 a.m. bowl of cereal and cup of tea, she makes herself a tuna sandwich. While she eats, she thinks about the events of Saturday night, pulling out each memory and examining it carefully.

Are they real memories or did we have a group hallucination? Could Alice have moved the planchette? I certainly didn't see her do it, but it is possible. Perhaps I should ask her.

Her phone starts to ring as she walks back to her office. "Hello."

"Hi, Shells, how are you?"

"Hi Alice, I'm fine. A little confused about the events of Saturday night and wondering on and off if I'm going a bit crazy, but otherwise I'm fine."

"Why do you think you're going crazy? We all witnessed the drinks bottles and cans exploding."

"Tom is convinced the heat caused the bottles and cans to explode."

"Really? I suppose it is a possibility, but it seems highly unlikely. I've never heard of bottles and cans exploding due to hot weather. Even if that could happen, weren't they in a cooler box full of iced water at the time of the explosion?"

"Yes, they were. I agree that Tom's explanation isn't very feasible, but he won't discuss it further. That isn't why I said I think I'm going crazy. It's what happened with the planchette that is disturbing me."

"Do you mean the strange messages?"

"No, I'm talking about the fact that I couldn't pull my fingers away from the planchette when it started to write its final message. My fingers were glued to it. It was the scariest experience I've ever had."

"I couldn't pull my fingers away either, Michelle. It didn't only affect you. Think about how Sue reacted when the pencil broke. She jerked away as if the planchette had burned her. I'm sure she also couldn't pull her fingers away while the planchette was writing."

"Did you move the planchette, Alice? I know you like to kid around, but this is serious for me. I'm scared that we have unleashed evil spirits in my house."

"I didn't move the planchette," Alice promises.

"I know I didn't move it. I didn't know how a Ouija board worked when we played on Saturday. That only leaves Sue, and she's an unlikely candidate."

"I agree that Sue is unlikely to have moved the planchette or tried to trick us. Her shock and fear at the Ouija board's peculiar behaviour were genuine. Why do you think you have spirits in your house? Have you seen one?"

Michelle tells Alice about her peculiar experiences with the hair in the shower and the two apparitions she'd seen in the early hours of Sunday morning.

Every now and then, during their conversation, Michelle glances at the Ouija board which is still sitting on her desk. I must remind Tom to throw it away.

There is something strange about that Ouija board. I think it has opened some sort of portal to another dimension. After this call, I'm going to do some more research about Ouija boards. Maybe I'll also read up about séances. If there are malevolent ghosts in this house, we may need to investigate ways of getting rid of them.

Ten minutes later, Michelle says good-bye and hangs up. She's agreed to let Alice know if she has any new ghostly encounters.

Okay, it's time to get this research show on the road. Tap, tap, tap. "Risks of using a Ouija board," appears in her Internet search tab.

An article pops up, "Six reasons not to play with Ouija boards."

> You could become possessed while using a Ouija board and, even if you don't, it doesn't mean that you won't let loose some sort of bad spirit or phantom into your home. Spirit boards are believed to be portholes to other dimensions, and you don't know who or what you'll end up contacting. After playing with a Ouija board, you may start to hear strange noises, items may start to move around in your home without anyone touching them, and electronic items may even start working on their own.

"You may let loose some sort of bad spirit or phantom into your home," Michelle repeats dumbly. She stares at the scene with a sort of incredulous avidity and her fingers twitch slightly.

The mouse jerks free of her hand. The curser moves to the top of a fresh page and stops, waiting … blinking brightly on the blank screen.

Oh my God. What's happening? The words scream in her head.

"Hello Bitch."

Michelle stares in shock at the words that have appeared on her screen.

"You betrayed your sex by marrying a man like Tom. I'm going to get that lying, cheating husband of yours and then I'm going to get you. I'm going to teach you both a lesson you won't ever forget."

"Nooooo," the moan rasped from her dry throat. "I don't believe this."

"You'd better believe it, Bitch."

The face of a girl of about thirteen years old appears on the screen. She has long blonde hair tied neatly into two plaits which peep out from beneath a bonnet that covers her head and makes her face shadowy. Michelle can see her eyes; dark and hate-filled they glare at her from beneath its wide brim. Only the top of her old-fashioned dress shows; it has buttons running down the front and a lace collar.

The girl's mouth moves, and Michelle can hear her voice through the speakers. "Don't think that Pieter van Zyl or that pompous Englishman, Robert, can save you. I'm in charge here. I moved the Ouija board to ensure you found it and opened the gateway. Unfortunately, those two stupid men can also use it, but, be warned, if they interfere with me, I'll take care of them too."

Michelle hangs her head and clasps her forehead in both of her hands. Her temples have exploded into a migraine. She sits, holding her head for what seems like hours, but it's only twenty minutes, before the pain recedes sufficiently for her to look up.

The late afternoon sun is streaming through the window and the bright light obscures her computer's screen. Pulling it roughly across the desk, she sees that the screen has reverted to her screen saver. She reaches out and moves the mouse. The screen is perfectly normal, her Internet home page is still open at the article about the risks of using a Ouija board. She shuts her computer down and gets to her feet.

Picking up the Ouija board, she heads for the kitchen. She glances at the inside dustbin but makes a quick decision to dispose of the board in the large black garbage bins in the yard outside. *I want this out of my house.*

The box looks bright and almost obscene lying on top of the black garbage bags in the bin. Michelle slams the lid down and goes back inside.

* * *

"I had a great day." Tom bounds over to her and wraps his arms around her. "I love living closer to the office. It gives me more time with you," he nuzzles her neck.

After dinner, they sit outside on the patio drinking wine while Tom tells her about his day.

"My team started a new project today. It is a complex transaction, but I enjoy a challenge and I'm looking forward to finding some innovative solutions for them."

Michelle listens attentively to Tom's numerous ideas and plans. Her headache has receded to a mild throb and it's not hard for her to give him her undivided attention. Tom's work in corporate finance is interesting and sometimes he shares information she finds useful for her own work. On the odd occasion, his comments have even inspired an idea for a story.

In bed later, Michelle lies awake listening to Tom's deep breathing beside her. As her mind floats freely, seeking the respite of sleep, the words that appeared on her screen earlier that day, replay in her thoughts.

You are a traitor to your sex marrying a man like Tom ... a man like Tom. What does it mean? What is wrong with Tom?

A series of memories marches through her weary mind: Sitting next to Tom at a client event, during the final year of her training contract to qualify as a chartered accountant. Recognising him as an equity partner at Kellerman, James & Thompson, the firm where she also worked as an articled clerk, awkwardness had coloured her conversation, making it stilted and uninteresting.

Relaxed and confident, he'd made light and amusing conversation until she overcame her discomfort and the evening had evolved from her personal nightmare into an entertaining and enjoyable one. The following day, she'd been disappointed when several people warned her that he had a reputation for drinking and womanizing. Avoiding him seemed the best plan.

Being allocated, a few months later, to one of Tom's corporate finance engagements. His division had been exceptionally busy and had borrowed some junior staff, herself included, from the audit practice to help them. Impressed by her competency and excellent work, Tom had invited her to join his division when she completed her training contract at the end of that year. She'd agreed, intrigued by the solutions-based nature of his work and flattered by his praise of her report writing skills. Working exclusively for him in her new role, they had gradually become friends and then, eight months later, lovers.

Watching for signs of the "playboy" side of him she'd heard so much about, but which never presented themselves.

Going out for dinners at expensive restaurants of his choice and to see the odd movie had become her new normal. The perfect boyfriend, he'd deferred to her selection of movies and sat through her favourite musicals and romantic comedies without compliant.

Moving in together, eighteen months after their initial meeting.

Getting married a year later.

So far, their marriage had been a good one, despite their age gap. On

54

their wedding day, she had been twenty-six and he, forty-two. Tom was ambitious and had worked his way up over the past two years, becoming the partner in charge of the corporate finance division.

Michelle had continued to work at Kellerman, James & Thompson for another two years after their wedding, and then she had left to run her own small accounting services business. This move enabled her to work mornings only and pursue her writing career in the afternoons.

The emotional support and encouragement Tom had given her as she set out on this new path filled her heart with gladness and love for him.

They never talked about having children. Comfortable and happy with her current life, Michelle is in no rush to embark on motherhood. The driving urge to procreate some of her friends had experienced had not reared its head, forcing them into this discussion.

... a man like Tom. What does it mean?

Michelle slips into sleep and the thoughts cease.

In the early hours of the morning, she awakes again.

Tom is breathing in long, heavy gasps and he is curled up in a foetal position in the bed. As she watches him, he becomes more uneasy and disturbed in his sleep, moaning and thrashing wildly. He is in the grip of some sort of nightmare.

She shakes him roughly to wake him up. He opens his eyes and stares at her in surprise, his greying hair is sticking to his sweaty scalp and face.

"You were having a nightmare."

"Strange," he mumbles, rolling over and sinking back to sleep.

Her mouth feels dry and her tongue thick as if she has been sleeping with it open. It's unpleasant and she hopes she isn't getting a cold. Knowing she won't go back to sleep without moistening her mouth, she gets up and walks to the kitchen to get a glass of water. She also takes an immune boosting tablet to ward off any attacking germs.

Turning off the kitchen light, she walks towards the bedroom and passes through a patch of frigid air. It's icy touch on her warm skin shocks her. "Eeek!" Squealing, she leaps backwards and a shadow slips past her towards the kitchen door. A glimpse of a khaki uniform and helmet catch her eye. The shadow is not malevolent or threatening, but it disturbs her.

Back in her bedroom, she sees that Tom is fast asleep and breathing softly. She climbs back into bed and lies awake until morning.

* * *

When Michelle walks into her office, the first thing that greets her tired eyes is the Ouija board. It is back on her desk, exactly where Tom had put it after the party.

The adults on the cover grin at her mockingly, dancing and swirling as a wave of dizziness washes over her. Taking ten deep and calming breaths, she decides not to touch it.

I'll think about it later.

Sitting down in her chair, she focuses intently on her work, channelling her fear-induced energy into her outputs.

Her email is busy, and she is fully absorbed by her work until after 12.30 p.m., only glancing at the Ouija board occasionally.

Her unusual night-time experience and the reappearance of the awful Ouija board have firmed her resolve to go to the library and see if she can dig up a bit more information about the original farm that her house is built on and Pieter van Zyl.

The name Pieter has come up three times in the past several weeks, once in connection with the display cabinet she'd bought from the antique shop in Irene, once while she was using the Ouija board, and once when her computer had gone haywire the day before. It couldn't be a coincidence. Pieter van Zyl must be connected to her current strange experiences in some way.

He's the only lead I've got, and I have to start somewhere.

After lunch, she drives to the beautiful, old library in the town centre. Maybe she'll find a link to either Pieter van Zyl or the ghost wearing the khaki uniform that she has seen twice during the early hours of the mornings. Following the incident with her laptop, she is convinced that the visions are not imagined, but are a real phenomenon of some sort.

Parking her car on the street outside the library, she hurries over to the building and pulls open the door. The slight smell of parchment and old paper wafts out. The shelves are packed with books of all shapes and sizes.

A lady with grey hair twisted into a neat bun, and wearing an old-fashioned blouse, sits in front of a computer behind the counter. Looking up, she smiles, "*Goeie dag.*"

"*Goeie day. Praat jy Engels?*" [Good day, can you speak English?] Speaking Afrikaans is not one of her strengths. The woman smiles understandingly and switches to English.

"Good day, how can I help you?" she says in perfect English.

Flushing slightly with embarrassment at her incompetency in speaking Afrikaans, Michelle responds in English. "Hello, I wonder if you can. I'm looking for information about the land my townhouse development is

56

built on. I understand the property was originally a farm. Do you have any suggestions about where I could start looking?"

The woman smiles again. "Where is your townhouse located?"

Michelle provides the address and stand number.

"That land originally belonged to a Boer called Pieter van Zyl. Let me see what information I have about him and the property."

She taps on her computer and scrolls down the screen. After a few minutes, she looks up.

"The van Zyl family fled their farm in June 1900 when the British soldiers marched on Pretoria. Pieter van Zyl was married to Marta van Zyl and they had three daughters, Estelle, Renette and Suné. He never returned to reclaim his farm after the war and is assumed to have been killed in action."

"How sad," Michelle glances at the woman's computer. "How did you find that information so quickly?"

"My name is Corné Bardenhorst. I'm a historian and the two Anglo Boer Wars are my main focal areas. I've lived in Irene all my life and I know the history of many of the original local families in this area and its surrounds. I know exactly where to look for information like this."

Corné looks thoughtful. "There is a bit of a legend about Pieter van Zyl. The story goes that when he became aware that the Khakis were approaching and he needed to leave his farm, he buried a fortune in gold Kruger coins somewhere on the farm. The gold is alleged to be part of the missing Kruger millions and was given to him for safekeeping by Paul Kruger before he departed for Machadodorp during the war."

"Why would he bury it? Why not take it with him?"

"The gold would have been heavy to transport, and the risk of the family being stopped by Khakis, the wagon searched, and the gold discovered, would be high. I'm sure Pieter believed that even if he was killed in action, his wife and family would return to the farm eventually and could use the gold to rebuild their community."

"That does make sense. Do you think the legend is true?"

"I don't know, but it is a long-standing story. Many people have searched, but the gold has never been found."

"I don't know much about that period of history or the concentration camps," Michelle confesses, "but I've been planning to do some research about the Second Anglo Boer War. I'd like to learn more about it."

She doesn't mention the possibility of her writing a book about it in case the librarian doesn't like the idea of an English woman writing about this war.

There is long standing bad feeling between English and Afrikaans speaking South Africans because of the two Anglo Boer Wars.

"Would you like me to find you some books on these topics to read?" the librarian asks.

"Yes, that would be lovely. Thank you."

Heading towards some large shelves, holding large and heavy looking books, at the back of the library, the librarian glances over them and pulls out a couple on the Second Anglo Boer War and the concentration camps.

"These books will provide you with all the facts and details of the war. Once you are familiar with the history, you might like to read some personal diaries and fictional accounts of life during the war. You can let me know if you are interested and I'll find those books for you."

"Thank you, I appreciate your help."

Sitting down at a table in the corner, Michelle turns the pages of one of the heavy non-fiction books. The history is unexpectedly fascinating to her and she settles down to read in earnest.

Michelle reads about the scorched earth policy that was implemented by Lord Kitchener during the Second Anglo Boer War. The photographs of the burning farmhouses and dead animals are shocking. She has vague memories of learning about this policy at school but doesn't remember any details.

She reads through the section on the concentration camps. It provides a factual account of the various camps by location.

I don't remember being told that there were separate camps for white and black people. Actually, I don't remember ever learning anything about the fate of black people during this war.

The information on the concentration camps is useful and interesting, but it doesn't provide any insight into the daily life of the inmates.

I can't believe one hundred and fifteen thousand people were imprisoned in over one hundred camps across South Africa. The death statistics presented here are horrific, over twenty-eight thousand white people and twenty thousand black people died in these camps. I don't remember being told those figures at school, but maybe I just didn't appreciate what I was learning. Twenty-eight thousand bodies, lined up next to each other, would be an incredibly long line. When I think of it that way it is overwhelming.

The poignant photographs are more emotionally impactful than the stark and bare facts, despite the shocking death and disease statistics presented in the many graphs. She studies old black and white photographs of lines and lines of small white tents in huge barren fields with no trees or foliage of any kind. There are also slightly fuzzy sepia photographs of large groups of children, their unsmiling faces and sad eyes turned towards the camera. The faces of the supervisory women in the background are obscured by their wide-brimmed sun bonnets.

The girl on my computer was wearing a bonnet just like these. Could she have lived during this war? Did she die in one of these camps? Why is she so malevolent towards Tom and me?

A rueful smile pulls at the corners of her mouth as she realises what she is thinking. She has accepted that she is seeing some sort of ghostly phenomena in her home.

If I tell Tom that I've been seeing ghosts in our home, he'll think I've gone mad. He's so rational and scientific in his thinking. His mind could never stretch to acceptance of the supernatural.

Scanning through the stack of books, she susses out their contents. The psychology and sociology of the various groups of people who were involved in this war particularly interest her. All aspects interest her, from the motivations and thoughts of the British troops, to the attitudes and emotions of the Boer women and children left alone on the farms and who were later interned in the concentration camps, to their men on commando, fighting for their country's freedom, and finally to the black people who either fought alongside the Boers or defected to fight on behalf of the British Empire.

Learning more about the plight and circumstances of the thousands of black people interned in the sixty-four African concentration camps is also one of her objectives, although she suspects that the research will be more difficult.

She reaches for another volume. This book is written from the perspective of the British soldiers fighting in South Africa and includes a chapter in the front about why the war initially resulted in such heavy defeats for the British forces.

The introductory paragraphs give an overview of Leo Amery's withering criticism of the performance of the British army, under the generalship of Sir Redvers Buller VC,[1] during the first few months of the war. Leo Amery, a correspondent for British daily national newspaper, *The Times*, during the Second Anglo Boer War, wrote that the pre-war army was "largely a sham", and the home army was "nothing more or less than a gigantic Dotheboys Hall."[2] Amery's writings contributed significantly

---

[1] Recipient of the Victoria Cross, the highest award for gallantry in the face of the enemy that can be awarded to British and Commonwealth forces.

[2] Dotheboys Hall is the brutal Yorkshire school, of which the evil Mr

to Buller's sacking and replacement by Lord Frederick S. Roberts VC, as well as the perception by the British public that the British army initially failed to measure up, particularly during the Natal campaign.

Her eyes fly over the pages as she becomes immersed in an intriguing analysis about how the British military leadership and troops gradually came to realise that their Boer opponents were not mere farmers, unskilled in warfare, and that they had underestimated them.

The British troops had arrived in South Africa following spectacular military successes at Dargai Heights in India and Omdurman in Sudan during 1897 and 1898, respectively. They were filled with self-confidence and held themselves in high esteem.

The book describes how the British troops quickly came to realise that more was required from them than just checking "raids" by a few thousand farmers, and that they were significantly outnumbered. Gasping involuntarily, she reads about the losses suffered by the British forces during the period from the 10th to the 17th of December 1899, which came to be known as Black Week.

> On the 10th of December 1899, twenty-six British troops were killed during the battle at Stormberg in the Cape Colony, with an additional sixty-eight being wounded and six hundred and ninety-six being captured by the Boers. The following day, two hundred and twenty British soldiers were killed during the battle of Magersfontein near Kimberley, with the wounded amounting to six hundred and seventy-five men and sixty-three being captured. The battle of Colenso in Natal that commenced on the 15th of December 1899, resulted in the deaths of one hundred and forty-three men, with seven hundred and fifty-six being wounded and two hundred and twenty being captured.

No wonder the British soldiers came to hate the Boers. The pride of the officers would have been seriously undermined and the loss of friends and colleagues by the ordinary soldiers must have been shocking and tragic. It would have made them fearful and knocked their confidence in their military leaders.

She reads a comment reported to have been made by Major-General Neville Lyttelton:

> Few people have seen two battles in succession in such startling contrast as Omdurman and Colenso. In the first,

---

Squeers is the headmaster, depicted in Charles Dickens' *Nicholas Nickleby*.

fifty thousand fanatics streamed across the open, regardless of cover, to certain death, while at Colenso I never saw a Boer all day till the battle was over, and it was our men who were the victims.

Michelle is intrigued to read how the attitudes of the British forces towards their Boer enemies hardened after these defeats. It makes perfect sense to her that revenge had crept into the hearts of these soldiers who'd watched their comrades fall in battle.

Michelle is fascinated by a statement that is attributed to a Devonian officer service in Natal:

> What a lot they are teaching us, these farmers! When we have settled them, we shall be the most magnificent army in the world ... Fighting begins at 3 000 yards. You never see your enemy, even at 900 or 500; and the Boer is a busy fellow if he feels so inclined. He will stay and fire 300 shots at you before you can clap your hands. If he wants to go to a better place he will go, but you can't see him move. Taking one consideration with another, the Dutchman[1] is a fine enemy, and if he did not misuse the white flag, he would be universally respected.

There are some black and white photographs of the three battles and Michelle recognises the helmets and khaki uniforms worn by the British soldiers as being the same as the one worn by the strange apparition she has seen twice in her home.

The phantom girl called him Robert. I wonder who he is. Why is he appearing to me? He attacked the ghost I assume is Pieter van Zyl? Why? Why? Why?

At 4.30 p.m. Michelle stands up and prepares to leave. She decides to check out a non-fiction volume about conditions in the South African concentration camps. It contains details of the reports and accounts written by Emily Hobhouse, a British welfare campaigner who aimed to bring the plight of the Boer women and children incarcerated in the concentration camps to the attention of the public, thereby forcing change.

Later that evening, Michelle settles down again with the library book. The terrible conditions in the concentration camps and the numerous deaths due to illness among the prisoners has completely captivated her. A new idea to tell the story of the Second Anglo Boer War through the

---

[1] In this context, the term *Dutchman/Dutchmen* is derogatory, insinuating stupidity and being uneducated.

life and experiences of Pieter van Zyl and his family has come into her head. She could take the bare bones facts that were available about him and write a fictionalised account of his role in the war using other available historical facts and her imagination.

This book idea grips Michelle so she stays up until after 12 a.m. reading and plotting the outline of her book.

Later that evening she goes up to bed alone. Tom had retired earlier saying he had a headache. In her excitement over her reading and research, she hadn't paid much attention to his complaints, but now, as she climbs the silent stairs, she feels slight remorse at not having been more sympathetic.

She stops, puzzled, outside their bedroom door. It's closed. She has never known Tom to close the bedroom door before.

He must be feeling bad if he closed the door to prevent me disturbing him. Poor man.

Reaching out, she turns the door handle, but the door doesn't open.

It can't be locked, there's no key.

She jerks down the handle and pushes on the door with all her strength. It gives suddenly, and bursts open. Falling headlong into the room, she lands heavily on her hands and knees. Pain shoots through her kneecaps and her elbows.

Looking up, she is appalled by the sight that greets her. Tom is lying on the bed, his faced flushed in the dim light from the partially open curtains. In the throes of a terrible nightmare, he thrashes about, legs kicking out at an unknown enemy. Standing over him, her hands circled around the shaft of a kitchen knife, is the phantom from the computer.

Turning to face Michelle, her eyes glowing red with anger and malicious passion, the poltergeist takes a step towards the door.

"Die whore of the rapist," she hisses, her face distorted with fury and her teeth gnashing with rage.

She lunges towards Michelle, her flashing blade held high.

Michelle recoils from the advancing spirit, a harsh whining sound erupting from her throat. She can hear it but can't control it.

She can feel the girl's nearness. A warmth, like hot breath, envelops her face. The knife draws downward in a shining arc. A strong gust of wind whips past her and the British soldier slams into the girl in an explosion of bright blue flames. They burn with a ghostly brightness but do not illuminate the room in the way a physical fire would have done. Within moments, the blue flames dissipate, and both ghosts are gone.

Michelle looks at the bed. Tom has quietened and sunk into a deep stupor-like sleep. She wants to wake him and draw comfort from his embrace, but her mind is in turmoil.

Why is this phantom intent on harming us? I don't understand what she meant when she called me the whore of a rapist.

She sits on the edge of the bed, her body leaning over so that her elbows rest on her thighs and her hands cup her face. She shudders uncontrollably, making the bed beneath her shake. Tom does not stir. The horror finally overcomes her, and she slumps down unconscious into the bed.

ROBERT

THE BEST DAY I EVER SAW

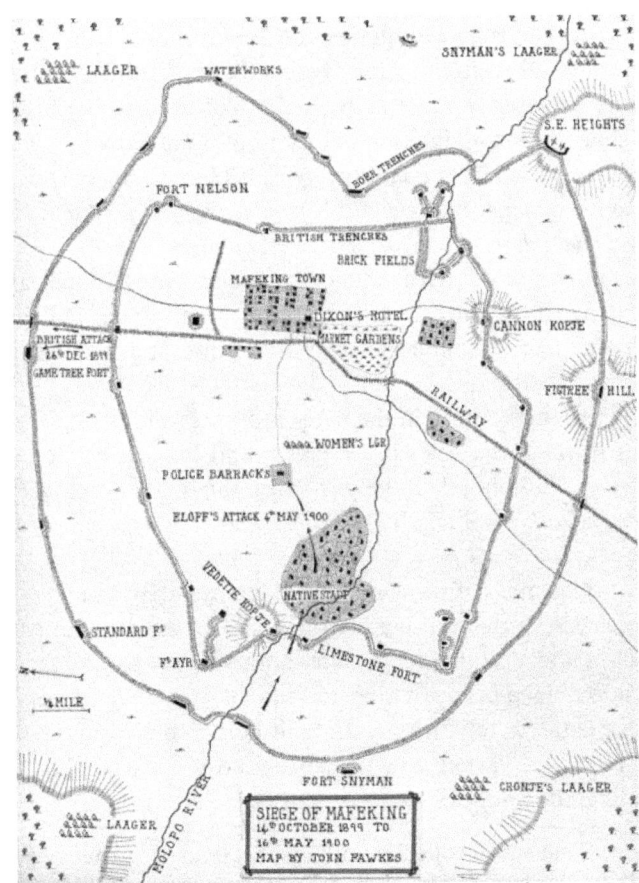

Map of the Siege of Mafeking 14th October 1899 to 16th May 1900 in the Great Boer War: map by John Fawkes (BritishBattles.com)

Boom! Boom! Boom!

Robert wakes instantly and lies in the dark, listening intently to the sounds of heavy gun fire to the east of the town.

Glancing at the clock on the bare wall of the barracks, he sees it's 4 a.m.

Around him, men are stirring. A soft cacophony of grumbles and complaints about the early hour swirl around the room like a gentle zephyr, as the men, cranky and irritated at being awakened at this early hour, hurriedly dress.

Robert drags himself from the comfort of deep sleep and joins his colleagues in preparing for the day of fighting ahead.

This is it. The Dutchmen's last stand. They know this is their last opportunity to capture Mafeking before the British relief forces arrive.

Minutes later, he is at headquarters. After arming himself, he joins the throng outside, all waiting to receive instructions from Colonel Baden-Powell, affectionately known as B.P. He is pleased to see his favourite cadet, Richard Johnson, looking out for him in the crowd.

That boy's mental strength is unbelievable. He's been through so much over the past few months, but he's still here, smiling and lending support to us soldiers. No self-pity and no dwelling on the past. He's a real trooper.

"The assault on our eastern defences is a feint," the Colonel studies the assembled men, assessing their mood, "the real attack will be on the Native Stadt.[1] Get your horses ready for action and we'll wait for the Boers to make their move."

Standing around waiting in the early morning cold is unpleasant. The cold seeps through the soles of his boots and his feet become stiff and unresponsive. Stamping them helps to keep the blood flowing.

It's bloody cold this morning. I'm acclimatised to the warmer temperatures in Bulawayo.

Richard Johnson is overflowing with excitement, his young face shines with enthusiasm in the dim light. Robert's heart swells with pride as he contemplates the useful role in defending the town that these young English cadets, aged between nine and fifteen years old, are playing. The troops have come to rely heavily on their help in delivering messages by bicycle between the various town defences and acting as lookouts to warn them of impending attacks.

---

[1] The Native Stadt was a collection of huts that housed the native population of Mafeking. It lay to the west of the railway line and extended to both sides of the Molopo River.

"Coffee's ready."

Trooper Watson's call is welcome and Robert and Richard head over to get their cups of coffee. Robert wraps his hands around his cup, its blissful warmth in his cold hands almost outweighing the pleasure of the drink itself.

"When are they going to begin?" Richard asks eagerly.

Robert opens his mouth to reply when the sudden red glow in the west catches his eye.

"I think it just started. Let's go and see what's happening."

He leads the way over to a nearby single-storey house and they climb up onto the corrugated iron roof. They watch the fire fan out like a destructive burning spider-web. The flames from the Baralong[1] huts that have been deliberately fired by the Dutchmen, jump in fiery tendrils from one to the next. Within minutes the Stadt is a conflagration.

Behind them the sun starts to rise, throwing its cheering rays across the horizon. The sunlight gradually creeps across the sky until it embraces the glowing red haze of the fire and merges into one.

Unease at the burning washes over Robert, but he is the only one. In the quad below, his fellow troopers are hurrying in the direction of the fire.

"We're going to have a good fight," the shout rises above the medley of excited voices and sounds.

The eighty-one men of the Bechuanaland Rifle Volunteers, under the direction of Captain Cowan, follow hot on their heels in the direction of the gunfire.

Robert and Richard descend from the rooftop and separate; Robert joins the swift moving river of men flowing towards the fire and Richard runs towards the bicycle shed.

Robert sees the British South African Police, or BSAP, fort, which lies on the outskirts of the town and is occupied by Colonel Hore and a squadron of the Protectorate Regiment, looming up ahead. Warning shouts that it has fallen into enemy hands grab his attention.

Squinting at the men running across the front of the fort, Robert can hardly believe they are the enemy until he realises that shots are being fired in his general direction. The two sides meld together in a turbulent mix, making differentiation between the opposing sides virtually impossible.

---

[1] Baralong [British] or Barolong Boo Ratshidi [South African], a section of the Tswana society who settled in Mafeking.

On his left side, a man falls, his chest exploding in a spray of blood and shattered flesh and cloth. In the melee, it takes a few moments for Robert to realise it was Joe Thompson, a personal friend of his from back home. The shock barely registers as he continues running towards the fort.

"Re-group men," the order penetrates his confused mind, "Re-group."

He stops running and veers towards a group of men he recognises. They are formulating a plan of counterattack.

When he re-enters the fray a short while later, order and confidence are in the process of being restored among the British forces as word-of-mouth swiftly shares the plan through the chaotic ranks.

The men of the Artillery, the Bechuanaland Rifles and those members of the Protectorate Regiment, commanded by Lord Charles Bentinck, who escaped the fort before it was taken, start returning the Boers' fire in a calculated and methodical way.

Up until this point, the British forces had been the recipients of a heavy fusillade of gun fire but had not returned it. Smiles appear on the faces of the men as they begin to really fight.

Now we've got the beggars, he thinks as they concentrate their collective efforts on preventing the Boers from achieving their goal of reaching the town.

The Boers are trapped in the fort.

"That cheeky bugger, *Veldkornet* Sarel Eloff, used the telephone in the BSAP fort to tell B.P. that his Boers have taken Colonel Hore and some of his forces prisoners." The story travels like wildfire through the ranks of the British soldiers.

This boastful claim by the leader of the Boers, infuriates the troops who fight with increased determination. Robert watches as McLeod, the man in charge of the telephone wires, sets off towards headquarters with his staff of black assistants.

"The telephone operator who received that call had to disconnect it and then reconnected it to Major Godley at his fort. A direct telephone connection between all the forts and headquarters will help provide accurate and timely information to our leaders," he loudly informs his officer and everyone else in hearing distance.

Men from the town appear to join the fight. They are armed with guns of every sort; anything they could get their hands on.

We all just want this siege to be over. A fight to the finish is an appealing prospect after all this time barricaded in this town.

The tide of the fight is turning. The Boer casualties are rising as they get picked off by British fire whenever they show themselves.

Robert and a few other troops go down to the jail which is the commanding point of the fort and surrounding barracks. The jail prisoners have all been released, but there are no signs of an imminent attack by the Boers. It's gone quiet.

During this lull, breakfast is served, and the men partake of the food in groups. Having kept going for hours on coffee, served earlier by a townswoman who braved the front lines to support the men, Robert devours his portion with gusto.

Excited talk of imminent victory, together with the food and drink, inspires the troops, who are like giants ready to crush the enemy.

"We've had a seven-month long wait," one man declares, "and now, at last, we are having our decisive fight."

After breakfast the next phase of the fighting commences. Additional British forces arrive, having come through the town, and Major Godley devises a plan to round up the Boers. A significant group of about three hundred Boers still occupies the BSAP fort and they must be dealt with before nightfall.

"There are also two smaller groups of Boers who are continuing to fight from defensive positions in the town. One is holed up inside a stone kraal in the Stadt and the other is attempting to safeguard their position on top of the kopje,"[1] says Captain Godley. "Captain Fitzclarence's and Captain Marsh's squadrons will go and round these men up, assisted by Silas Moleno and Lekoko."

I'm glad I'm not in those Dutchmen's shoes. Silas and Lekoko and their Baralong have a real axe to grind with them because they burned their Stadt.

The fighting for possession of the BSAP fort continues. Robert notes with satisfaction that the firing by all the British troops, including himself, has become more deadly and accurate.

We all want this matter settled by nightfall. Fighting through the night is not an option.

A group of about a hundred Boers breaks away from the larger group inside the fort and attempts to escape. Robert takes careful aim and fires.

A puff of red billows from the back of one man's head and he falls to the ground. Others fall with clouds of red blood blooming from their backs and buttocks. A few of the Baralong take off after those who manage to get away.

They'll try to kill them and take their rifles. The Baralong are always begging for rifles which we can't supply. Now's their chance.

---

[1] A small hill in a generally flat area.

A short while later the remaining Boers surrender to Colonel Hore. Robert joins a group of his fellow soldiers and they follow in silence as the Boers are marched into town. The streets are lined with soldiers who salute the prisoners as they pass. The Boers are brave men who tried and failed, and the British troops respect them. The Baralong, however, fill the air with hoots of triumphant joy.

In the distance, the notes of God Save the Queen and Rule Britannia reverberate through the air as all along the lengthily lines of the British defences, men raise their voices in song to celebrate this victory.

Each Boer marches up to the cadets, who have been under fire with the troops all day, and hands them his weapon. Robert spots Richard and sighs with relief that he has survived to stand in the town, collecting weapons from their attackers.

He remembers meeting Richard and his father just after he arrived in Mafeking in early October the previous year. He and the young cadet had become good friends during those first few weeks of the war.

October 1899

Slinging his heavy bag over one shoulder, Robert stepped off the train and onto the platform.

The early afternoon heat hit him like a physical force, leaching the moisture from his body and the air from his lungs. Even though he knew from previous experience in this part of the world that the average temperature in Mafeking during October was approximately 84 degrees Fahrenheit and could reach highs of 100 degrees Fahrenheit, the overwhelming heat still came as a shock.

It doesn't take long to forget how searing this heat is. I feel like I've stepped into an oven.

Standing with the few other British troops who had travelled with him from Cape Town, he inhaled a deep breath and immediately choked on the dust which clogged the air with its fine particles. He noticed how it had settled on the platform and the roof of the railway station, coating them with a thin layer.

Peering around, he took in the nearby town, which comprised mainly of single-storey houses built of soft bricks and roofed with corrugated iron. There were only two exceptions, the station and one other two-storey building. The town was well positioned for defence, with flat open country all around it. The only section of higher ground lay across the Molopo River to the south-east of the town.

To the north-east, approximately one mile away, he saw the town's waterworks.

That is liable to be cut off when the Dutchmen attack. Knowing B.P., I'm sure he's made a backup plan.

A man and a boy came out of the station.

"Hello, I'm Mr Johnson, I work at the Standard Bank in the town," the man greeted the new arrivals. "My son, Richard, will show you to your barracks."

The boy was about fourteen years old. His blond hair was cut so short it stuck up like a bottle brush and he sported the biggest grin Robert had ever seen. He was dressed in a khakis uniform and held a wide-brimmed hat in his hand.

"Good afternoon, Sirs," he said, "please follow me."

They set off at a fast walk through the dusty streets of the town towards the place that Robert would call home for the next seven months.

* * *

Early the following morning, Robert gathered with the rest of the troops in the quad outside Dixon's Hotel, which was being used as a temporary headquarters for the garrison.

His night's sleep had been severely interrupted, obliterating any vestiges of relaxation remaining after his military leave. During the night the alarm bells had rung frequently and the inhabitants of the town, who seemed to have taken to sleeping in their clothes, had rushed to their various stations in preparation for an attack by the Boers.

During the brief walk between the barracks and Dixon's Hotel, Robert had seen the town guard, which included the able-bodied shopkeepers, businessmen and residents of the town, being drilled by some men from his regiment. The high spirits of the men were palpable, and he noticed Mr Johnson marching with the rest.

The boys of the Mafeking Cadet Corp were lined up in neat rows in the quad and standing to attention. Robert caught the eye of young Richard Johnson and give him a nod of recognition. The boy's face lit up in a delighted smile.

B.P. gave the men an inspirational talk and updated them on the status of the impending hostilities with the Boers.

"War is imminent," he said, "President Kruger issued an ultimatum to our government yesterday, giving us forty-eight hours to withdraw our troops from the borders of their two republics. Several Boer commandoes have already massed several miles away from here, along the western border of the South African Republic. The guns and reinforcements I requested from Cape Town have not yet arrived, so we must rely largely on our existing garrison and weapons to defend the town.

"The good news is that we did have a few men arrive yesterday to join the Protectorate Regiment. The boys from our Mafeking Cadet Corp are here to show our new joiners the defences we have put in place."

An enthusiastic cheer went up from the boys under the leadership of their thirteen-year-old sergeant-major, Warner Goodyear.

"Our forces comprise five hundred men from the Protectorate Regiment, three hundred from the Bechuanaland Rifles and the Cape Police, about three hundred men from the town and the fifteen new arrivals. Three hundred of the Baralong have also been armed with rifles. I have intelligence that the Boers currently number seven and a half thousand men."

"What artillery do we have, Sir?" Robert asked.

"We don't have anything modern. We have four old muzzle-loading 7-pounder guns with a short range, a 1-pound Hotchkiss, one Nordenfeldt and seven .303 Maxims."

Our artillery is even feebler than I thought it would be. It's just as well B.P. is so knowledgeable about the veld and is such a resourceful man or we wouldn't stand a chance of staving off an attack by the Dutchmen.

B.P. asked the new arrivals to stay behind for a tour of the town's defences and dismissed the rest of the men. Warner Goodyear stepped forward and introduced his cadets to the waiting men before they set off to inspect the town and surrounding countryside.

To the west of the town ran the railroad, which crossed the Molopo River using an iron bridge. It ran due north and south and its embankments would furnish good cover for the defending forces.

Additional rails had been hastily flung down around the circumference of the town to accommodate the armoured train which had arrived from the south on the 3rd of October. The armoured train, together with the natural protection offered by the railway line, was to protect the north-west front of the town.

To the west of the railway, was the Stadt, which lay on both sides of the river. The ground in front of the Stadt's northern end rose up and then gradually sank away, a natural feature which would afford good cover to an attacking force on that side.

The Stadt lay directly between Cannon Kopje, an old circular stone fort, and the town on the southern bank of the river.

The brickworks lay on the northern bank of the river about twelve hundred yards in an eastward direction from the town, with MacMullan's farm occupying a ridge about three and a half miles from the town.

The two-storey building that Robert had seen in the north-eastern corner of the town turned out to be a convent.

Major Godley, whose fort was to the south-west of the town and at the north of the Stadt, commanded the western outposts, including the BSAP barracks and fort, the women's laager, the refugee camp, and the Stadt.

The bluffing tactics, which had been improvised on the spot by B.P. and his officers and which had utilized every bit of available material, were impressive.

Warner Goodyear pointed out areas on the outskirts of the town which were marked with warnings for the townspeople and cattle herders to stay clear of them.

"The Colonel discovered that the Boers have a great fear of land-mines," he said. "He incorporated this knowledge into his design for the defence of the town. He ordered the preparation of a whole lot of metal boxes filled with sand which the people of the town were asked to carry to these sites. Our officers visibly issued them with dire warnings not to drop or bump them. The boxes were buried, and the affected areas marked as dangerous. The new mines were even tested, and the towns-people were warned to stay inside while the tests were undertaken."

Richard Johnson was standing next to Robert while Warner narrated this story. Emboldened by Robert's clear amused interest, he shared the details of the fake testing.

"Major Panzera and a colleague went out into the minefield and stuck a stick of dynamite into an ant-bear hole. They lit the fuse and ran for cover. My father and I were watching from the railway station when the dynamite exploded. It made a tremendous roar and threw up a huge cloud of dust. We heard later that a man on a bicycle was cycling past just at that moment. It's generally believed that he'll have carried the story of the dangerous mines surrounding the town over the border of the South African Republic to the gathering Boer forces."

Robert laughed at Richard's story and the boy blushed red with delight.

I have an admirer, Robert thought.

The idea pleased him. Robert came from a big family of eight children and Richard reminded him of his younger brother at home.

* * *

The following morning, Robert had breakfast in the mess with the troops. He was joined at his table by Cadet Johnson and they fell into casual conversation.

Richard's mother had volunteered to assist at the Victoria Hospital if the need arose. She had been training to become a nurse when she met his father. After their marriage, she had discontinued her training, and moved with him to Mafeking. Together with Miss Hill, the young matron, and the three trained nurses, the volunteers would need to minister to the needs of the whole garrison when the anticipated attack finally took place.

"One of the tasks of the cadets is to help in the hospital when the time comes," Richard told Robert. "We'll also be assigned to an officer to carry out their orders and do small jobs for them like deliver messages between the town defences. We've been training to do that and to act as lookouts."

The boy's pride in his job was evident and warmed Robert's heart.

Under the leadership of the veld crafty and resourceful B.P. and with the experience of some of the officers who fought in the Matabeleland Wars and in the Jameson Raid, we have a fighting chance despite our small numbers.

"I have two younger sisters," Richard confided. "Eliza and Emily. Eliza is twelve and Emily is turning ten in December. They are both scared that the Boers will capture the town. They don't know what will happen to them if they do. Mother is doing her best to keep them occupied so that they do not dwell on their worries."

"Your mother sounds like an admirable woman, Richard. How is she keeping them busy?"

"They learn their lessons every morning. Mother teaches them spelling and writing and they read to her from the Bible and some other books she ordered from England. They also each have a pony which they have been riding every morning and evening. I sometimes ride with them. I love looking at the flatness of the countryside around the town. I find the isolation invigorating, but they find it scary," he finished, glancing up at Robert.

After breakfast the troops gathered in the quad for an update on the latest position.

"I received news late last night that eight thousand Boers have amassed on the border. When President Kruger's ultimatum lapses at 5 p.m. tonight, we expect war to be declared. We anticipate that tomorrow morning the Boer force will attack the town and we'll have to fight our way out."

Afterwards, Robert overheard Major Hamilton Gould Adams, Resident Commissioner of the Bechuanaland Protectorate, who commanded the town guard, say to B.P., "What about Lady Sarah? She must be protected at all costs."

"She left Mafeking at dawn this morning for Setlagoli store and hotel in Bechuanaland. From there I've advised her to continue on to the Native Stadt of Mosita, a further twenty-five miles from the border."

Robert had been surprised to learn that Lady Sarah Wilson was in Mafeking when he arrived. The daughter of John Spencer-Churchill, 7th Duke of Marlborough, and the wife of Lieutenant-Colonel Gordon Chesney Wilson, aide-de-camp to B.P., she was a lady of some importance.

I would have expected B.P. to repatriate her to Cape Town when it first became obvious that war was inevitable.

He enquired about her presence in the town and was told she had stopped in Mafeking on route to Cape Town from Bulawayo.

She left leaving too late. B.P. obviously realises that the Dutchmen will not allow another train to pass south and if one tries, they are likely to wreck it by tearing up the rails.

The day passed slowly, with everyone anxiously waiting for the ultimatum to expire at 5 p.m. The town guard spent the day drilling while the troops continued to progress the town's defences.

Wagons were drawn across the roads leading into the market square and a few breastworks, aimed at providing protection to defenders who could fire over them, were thrown up. A few strands of barbed wire were run between these higher points.

Later that evening, the men again assembled in the quad to receive the news that they were at war with the South Africa Republic.

"At least," said B.P., "this intolerable waiting is over."

* * *

The waiting was not over. The following day passed quietly. Robert's regiment under Colonel Hore took up a defensive position on the Heights which overlooked the town, but the Boers did not come.

Around midday, the news of an initial success by the Boers at Kraaipan reached the town. An armoured train carrying two 7-pounder guns, rifles, ammunition and supplies for the Mafeking defenders had been derailed and captured by the Boers.

B.P. shared further news during the evening line-up in the quad.

"Captain Nesbit and his twenty men were all taken prisoner by the

Boers after continuous shelling of their damaged train for five hours."

This news cast a pall over the evening.

"Not only is the much-needed artillery and supplies not going to arrive," Robert grumbled to Richard, "they've fallen into the hands of our enemy."

* * *

Another long day of waiting commenced at dawn. Robert and his colleagues took up positions on the Heights. Robert had suggested that Richard accompany them. The Boers had fired on both the north and south of the town that morning and his services might be required to deliver a message to the town.

From their advantageous position above the town, Robert watched an engine run two trucks full of dynamite that had been standing in the railway station, up to a northern siding.

Wise to get those clear of the town.

As he watched, the Boers engaged the engine and trucks about eight miles from the town, firing on them with field guns. From a distance, he could see the engine moving back towards the town.

The Boers continued to bombard the trucks, obviously thinking they were full of soldiers. The dull booming reports of their guns floated on the still air.

The trucks exploded with a tremendous whirr-rump sound. The enormous noise rolled across the barren countryside like thunder. The two balls of flame that had been the trucks, burned with a brightness that Robert couldn't look at. Dark, oily fumes rose in the air, fanning out into a huge mushroom cloud that hovered above the veld like a malevolent genie in a children's storybook.

The tiny figures of the Boers scattered, all running in different directions.

Out of the corner of his eye, Robert caught Richard gazing in astonished horror at this unexpected inferno. He put a comforting arm around his shoulders.

"Go down to the town and tell them what has happened." The look of relief and gratitude in Richard's eyes caused Robert's own eyes to mist up slightly.

It is a terrible thing that these young boys must witness such vicious scenes of death and destruction.

Later that afternoon, Robert was among the men who went out in the armoured train to inspect the damage. A large hole in the ground, surrounded by displaced earth and twisted chunks of metal, denoted the site, but, as the tracks had been pulled up, the train had to stop some distance away.

A group of Boers mounted on horses, were gathered around the hole. Robert and his peers proceeded to fire on the gathering with a Maxim from the cover of the train. Two fell from their horses in a shower of red and the remainder hurriedly galloped away towards their laager to the north-east of the town.

* * *

Saturday morning commenced with the Boers firing heavily on the small units of British troops making up the outward defence of the town.

Robert was at breakfast when the sound of firing came from the direction of the cemetery to the north of the town. His breakfast having lost its appeal, he gathered in the market square with the other troops to wait for orders.

The bark of the Maxim, boom of heavy guns and continuous rattle of musketry permeated the air. No one knew what was happening and when the order came through for Robert's squadron to go out in support of the armoured train, he and his fellow troops set off with no idea of what they were heading into.

His squadron mounted their horses and followed the sounds of gunfire, arriving just as the armoured train moved out in support of the early morning patrol, under Lord Charles Bentinck, which had encountered the Boers about four miles out of town.

The Boers had pursued the patrol and tried to cut them off, but Lord Bentinck and his right flank patrol had managed to gallop to the armoured train and direct it to move out in support of the rest of the troops.

Robert and his peers engaged the Boers, who were withdrawing towards their own laager, firing on the train all the time. Unfortunately, they quickly lost the support of the train as the railway ran due north and south of the town and they were heading north-north-east.

Adrenalin pumped through Robert's veins as his squadron galloped madly after the darkly clad Boers, pelting them with their well-directed fire. He felt invincible, as if he was on some sort of exciting adventure despite the British troops numbering only seventy to the Boers five or six hundred.

Flying bullets whizzed past him and he saw two of his compatriots,

Walshe and Parland, fall; shot through the head by a Boer who had ensconced himself in a tree. Robert picked him off like the vulture he was, and he fell to the ground, dead.

The squadron realised that several other Boers had climbed up the nearby trees and they set about shooting them down. The Boers did not like this treatment so they changed tactic and made their usual move to try and work around their aggressors, cutting them off from their base.

Robert knew this was a serious situation for his squadron, their flank was nearly turned, and the Boers had managed to interpose themselves between them and Mafeking. Just at the point when all seemed lost, Lord Charles and two more troops with 7-pounder guns, arrived within striking distance. Two rounds of shrapnel sent the Boers scampering away. Through the dust and smoke, Robert watched their fleeing forms with satisfaction.

Once the withdrawal of the Boers was assured, the troops placed their wounded onto the armoured train and returned to Mafeking where they received a hero's welcome.

"Well done, Robert," said Richard, clapping him on the back.

His exuberance was a stark contrast to Robert's own fatigue, which had struck as soon as he re-entered the town and safety.

Squadron D reported to head office where they were again congratulated on their success. The British loss was two men dead and twelve wounded, two of whom died later. In addition, four of their horses were killed and a further twelve were wounded. The Boer losses were estimated at eighty killed and more than double that number wounded.

Robert later learned that B.P. and the other head office staff had experienced great anxiety during this four-hour altercation, knowing that if the engagement proved to be disastrous, it risked their entire defence as they didn't have anyone to send to their support.

* * *

The peace and quiet of Sunday morning was strange and out of place after the intense fighting of the previous day.

Due to their religious practices, the Boers did not engage in warfare on Sundays.

Robert attended the morning service at the church and later met up with Richard and his family at a sort of impromptu gymkhana that was set up to entertain and distract the people of the besieged town.

B.P. was in great form following the success of the previous day, chatting to everyone and dispensing tea from a travelling wagon.

"Can I ask you something, Robert?" Richard said.

"Yes, of course, ask away."

"Why did the Boers not respect the Red Cross flag? Isn't that dishonourable?"

"Well, yes, it is dishonourable," Robert replied.

The boy was referring to the firing on a relief party including Major Baillie, Father Ogle and Mr Peart, the Wesleyan minister, who had gone out to recover the bodies and, if necessary, attend to any wounded Boers who had been left during the retreat.

The train had stopped near the scene of the fight and the party, armed only with stretchers and preceded by a large Red Cross flag, had moved towards the spot.

The Boers had fired on them about half a mile before they reached their destination and they'd been forced to withdraw. The Boers had tried to work round to the line to cut them off from the train.

"Dr Pirow, General Cronje's doctor, came for lunch earlier today, under cover of the Red Cross flag. He claimed that the firing on the Red Cross flag was a mistake and the Boers thought it was the armoured train returning. Dr Pirow left with whiskey and beer for his general and the ambulance was sent out to collect the dead."

"Okay, I understand," said Richard.

The innocence of youth. Some of those Dutchmen are awful hounds and I'm not sure I believe their story.

That evening, Father Ogle presided over a ceremony to bury the dead. The makeshift coffins were closed, due to the fact, Father Ogle said, that bodies went rotten quickly in the heat and attracted flies.

Richard attended the moonlight service, together with his father, and Robert saw a few tears slip down his cheeks.

Robert was unable to shed tears. He knew why the coffins were closed. He had seen the headless bodies of Corporals Walshe and Parland. His attitude toward the Boers had hardened almost overnight as he thought of his mates whose high spirits and joy in life had been squelched so ruthlessly. The circumstances of their deaths, and the deplorable way the Boers had hidden in trees and taken pot shots at his squadron from above, as well as their later suspected abuse of the flag of the Red Cross, enraged him. He wanted revenge for their deaths and was keen to "have another smack at Johnny Boer".

* * *

The events of the following day compounded Robert's growing disgust for the dishonourable behaviour of the Boers and their complete disrespect for the flag of the Red Cross.

The Boers brought two 12-pounder guns to a long-range position north-east of the town and proceed to bombard it relentlessly. The small body of British troops at the head of the waterworks had to evacuate their positions and the Boers occupied the trench. They then proceeded to fire mainly upon the town and station, doing significant damage to the near-by convent, which was flying the Red Cross flag and was fitted out as a hospital.

Robert later learned that a shell had gone through one of the wards, but, by some miracle, no patients had been injured. A woman from the laager, recovering from a wound caused by a Mauser bullet during a previous bombardment, had died of fright.

The following day, when Richard asked Robert why the Boers had shelled the hospital despite its flying the Red Cross flag he had replied. "I'm sure it was by accident."

He saw no point in disillusioning the boy by telling him about the cowardly nature of some of the attacks.

Several shells that missed the station, landed around the BSAP fort, which was occupied by another squadron of the Protectorate Regiment under Colonel Hore. To Robert's immense relief no one was injured despite the shelling continuing for the entire day.

The Boers, having occupied the waterworks, cut off the water supply to the town, just as Robert had suspected they would on the day he arrived in Mafeking.

B.P. and the other head office staff had provided for this possibility and all the wells had been cleaned out and reopened, ready for use by the townspeople. As a result, there was no shortage of water.

* * *

Nine days later, the Boers introduced the besieged town to Creaky, an enormous breech loading canon, by discharging forty shells on the town.

The inhabitants quickly learned to fear the loud whump as Creaky's shrapnel shells exploded above the town, expelling its deadly cargo of spherical individual bullets and fragments of shell casing. This was followed by a whizzing sound as they tore through the air, inflicting grotesque injuries on any poor soul they struck.

Through a telescope installed on the Heights, Robert had watched this formidable weapon, which discharged 96-pound shells, being mounted on a specially constructed platform on a height called Jackal Tree, about 3,500 yards south of the town.

He gazed mesmerised at the long barrel, shining wickedly in the bright sunlight, and ending in a large black hole like a mouth.

The intense shelling continued incessantly for the next two days, with 7-pounder guns, 12-pounder guns and recoil operated machine guns called Maxims, supporting Creaky's efforts. It was during this time that the residents of the besieged town came to really understand and appreciate the extraordinary versatility of B.P., who the Baralong took to calling *Impeesa,* or the wily wolf who never sleeps.

On the evening of the first day of earnest shelling, the men discussed the Boer's latest tactics and B.P.'s countermeasures over dinner in the mess hall.

"Over the past few weeks, the Boers have shelled the convent repeatedly in an attempt to destroy the nearby station. It's been reduced to rubble," said Joe Thompson.

"They've also pulled up the railway line all around the town, rendering the armoured train useless. It's been withdrawn to the railway station, out of harm's way," he continued.

"Well, they won't easy outmanoeuvre B.P. Under his direction, a small earthwork has been erected at the corner where the convent stood. It's garrisoned by the Cape Police who've been provided with a Maxim gun," said Robert.

"B.P.'s clever and that's a fact. The series of defensive forts he's built have significantly improved the defences of the perimeter of the town," said Joe.

"He's had telephones installed in the bomb proof headquarters of each of the forts, connecting them with headquarters to ensure instant communication. I'm really grateful as it's greatly reduced the need for the orderlies or cadets to deliver communications personally and risk being sniped," said Robert.

"Cannon Kopje is now defended by two Maxim guns and a 7-pounder.

"I also understand that B.P.'s 'placebo' land mines continue to be a deterrent for the Boers who are frightened of them." Robert grinned at the thought.

"I've also heard that. Thanks to the larger earthworks surrounded by barbed-wire fencing B.P. ordered thrown up around the town, and the massive barricades of wagons and sandbags we put in place across the principal streets, our defences are as good as possible in the circumstances.

"I'm impressed by B.P.'s boldness and adventurousness in extending the town's defences over a wide five to six-mile area, despite our small garrison and the overwhelming number of Boers," said Joe.

"I agree," Robert nodded. "If the town's defences had been limited to the market-square, as the garrison originally suggested, any concentrated shelling effort by the Boer artillery would have quickly overwhelmed us. Instead, the Boers have been required to spread their shelling out over a much wider target."

Robert, together with six of his men, spent eighteen hours of the second day of shelling in a rifle pit. They couldn't leave throughout this period as their Boer aggressors were only six hundred yards away. Any attempt at movement drew a hail of bullets in their direction.

It was hot and uncomfortable in the pit with its crumpling earth walls and strong earthy smell. It was like being buried alive.

From his position within the earth, Robert could not see anything, but the sharp ring of bullets from the Boers' Mausers on the corrugated iron roofs of the houses pierced the still air. *It sounds like the hard, bullet-like hail we sometimes get in this part of the world.*

Southern African thunderstorms were savage and wild, with bright streaks of lightening and rolling thunder accompanying the rain which fell in sheets, as if being poured from the dark clouds.

It's nothing like the soft and continuous rain that usually falls back home.

He pushed the thoughts of home away as a stab of homesickness seared his heart.

When the enemy's Maxims came into play, he could hear a loud hammering, quickly repeated, and almost simultaneously a whirring as the shells flew. If they exploded, there would be four tremendous bangs.

The bangs didn't always come, as not all of the shells burst. Expected bangs that didn't happen frazzled Robert's nerves and made him frustrated and irritable.

This combination of sounds, intermittently embellished by shells fired by Creaky, disconcerted Robert. His disdain for these seemingly cowardly Dutchmen grew as he and his men treated them to an on-going deluge of bullets.

Braver men would come out of their trenches and rush us. We would soon be dislodged if they did because of their greater numbers. Of course, many of them would get shot during the advance across the open space between the trenches, but it would be the right military strategy to follow.

When he and his men were finally able to emerge, they learned that the casualties from Creaky were few, but its impact on the moral of the townsfolk was great.

One man had been blown to pieces with his legs being found later on the roof of a building, while another had his right leg torn off.

Robert did not know either man so this news did not have as great an emotional effect on him as it could have, but their horrible deaths still caused his stomach to knot and twist with horror.

The town had many civilians who needed to be protected.

Robert's thought of Richard's family. Richard had two younger sisters and a mother who was currently overworked helping to look after patients at the hospital. He made a mental note to check on the Johnson family as soon as the opportunity presented itself.

* * *

As Robert knocked on the Johnson's front door, the sound of the warning bell rang out, shrill and clear in the hot stillness of the late afternoon. There had been a lull in the shelling during the sultry noonday hours and Robert had seized the opportunity to check on Richard and his family.

Richard jerked the door open. "Good afternoon, Sir. Please follow me to our shelter."

Robert followed Richard as he herded his sisters as quickly as possible across the garden and down the twelve wooden steps leading to the shelter. They passed rows of sandbags piled up outside the entrance to guard against shrapnel from the shells and stray bullets.

Once they were all inside, Richard slammed shut the door and sealed off the small room from the outside world. The shelter was standard in its construction, about eighteen by fifteen feet and eight feet high. It was dimly lit by three horizontal apertures which could be closed with wooden flaps.

The roof of the shelter was composed of two layers of steel rails, placed one above the other, covered by sheets of corrugated iron and then a huge tarpaulin to keep out the rain. These four layers were covered by nine feet of soil, making the shelter safe and secure from the shelling above. Three stout wooden posts inside the room helped to hold up the heavy roof.

"I'm taking care of my sisters while Mother works at the hospital," Richard said.

Robert nodded. He knew Mrs Johnson must be run-off her feet. There were limited trained staff available to see to the needs of the patients, some of whom had horrific injuries and wounds.

The hospital's close proximity to the convent continued to make it an easy target for the Boers. The constant shelling added to the anxiety of the over-worked hospital staff.

"Where's your father?"

"He's helping man one of the forts," said Richard.

Robert told the scared girls a funny anecdote.

"The monkey at the post office, who usually spends his day on the top of the pole he is chained to, has taken to seeking shelter when he hears the alarm-bell. When it rings, he scurries down his pole and pops under a large empty biscuit-tin."

The youngsters, including Richard, all laughed, and Robert was relieved at the easing of tension in the room.

As he took his leave, Robert gave Richard a friendly slap on the back.

"You are doing well, Richard, keeping your sisters safe. Keep them distracted so they are not scared."

Glancing back, before turning the corner of the house, he saw the door was tightly closed. Richard and the girls would continue their mole-like wait in the shelter until the "all clear" sounded.

* * *

That evening, Robert's squadron, under Captain Fitzclarence, and two parties of the Cape Police, made a night attack on the Boer trenches.

B.P. had decided to give the Boers a taste of cold steel. Excitement abounded at this opportunity to exact revenge on their opponents using only their 12-inch sword bayonets.

Rolling clouds obscured the moon and the night was dark as Robert's squadron crept stealthily towards some Boer trenches on the British side of the racecourse and to the north of the Malmani Road. The two parties of the Cape Police had moved towards the brick fields in order to support the squadron with gunfire directed from a flanking position along the length of the selected trenches.

The moon sailed out from behind the cloud, as the men lay waiting for the order to charge. Their lethally sharp bayonets glimmered in a bright moonbeam.

The order came and the men surged forward, inundating the trenches.

The Boers lying under tarpaulins in the trenches did not hear their advance until they were almost upon them.

A tremendous din commenced as the bayonets flashed downwards, hurtling towards their targets. The Boers awoke, shocked, and immediately started struggling to free themselves from their confining coverings.

Screams of pains melded with loud, wild yells of horror.

The sides of the trenches collapsed, throwing up clouds of thick dust, causing all the men to cough and splutter.

Gunfire exploded from the flanking parties as they fired on the rear trench, adding to the cacophony of deafening sounds that swirled around the opposing parties.

The Boers pulled themselves together and commenced a heavy and wild return fire in all directions.

Robert's bayonet plunged downwards and came up dripping blood. The scream of his victim quickly died away into a wet, gurgling sound. He moved along the trench, plunging his bayonet into living flesh with deadly precision.

He no longer heard the screams and shouts of his victims or the continuous gunfire that ran along the line of fighting men in both directions, like ripples of water. His body had taken on a life of its own; his striking arm rising and falling like a machine, coolly enthusiastic about its task.

He brought his bayonet down again just as his unseen victim emerged from beneath the tarpaulin. It missed the man and pierced his right hand. The Boer, a large fellow with a thick brown beard, yanked himself free of the tarpaulin, clutched his injured hand in the other, and shouted at Robert in English.

"Stop!"

The clouds parted again and, in the momentary bright moonlight, Robert gazed into a pair of bright blue eyes. They were rimmed with a dark outline of deep blue and interspersed with flashes of lighter and darker blue like a snowflake. The eyes shone with a keen intelligence and Robert realised with a shock how wrong he was to have assumed that all their opponents were ignorant farmers.

"You speak English?" said Robert.

"Yes," answered the man, "I read in English too." His English was heavily accented, but perfectly understandable.

"Good luck to you," replied Robert and moved away further down the trench. He could not bring himself to kill this unknown Boer. As he moved away, he heard another Boer call out in Afrikaans to the man he'd spared. He couldn't understand what was said but he heard the name Pieter.

Robert killed and wounded three more Boers before the sharp sound of a whistle pierced the discordant symphony of bullets, shells, shouts, and shrieks. His mental detachment from the chaos had disappeared during his encounter with the man called Pieter.

He was now conscious of his bayonet's destructive journey, felt the momentary hesitation as its smooth downward motion was interrupted by heavy clothing, and then the jerk as it pushed through and sliced into yielding flesh.

The clatter of musketry, hoarse cries as orders were given, and the high-pitched shrieks of the wounded and dying swirled around him, like the hum of swarming bees.

Robert pulled himself out of the trench and, as he did, he heard one poor fellow, badly wounded, call out "Ma". Again his heart was touched, although the dying man was his enemy.

The British troops retired in the same orderly manner as they had advanced, retreating though the dust and smoke and vanishing into the dark of the night.

The Boers continued with their furious firing, confused further by the return volleys fired by the Cape Police. The rattle of gunfire continued for a long time into the night, even after the wounded British, including Captain Fitzclarence, had been tended to and admitted into hospital.

That night, Robert dreamed of the man called Pieter. They were walking through the veld and Pieter was showing him his cattle. In the distance stood a house of the typical Dutch style. Smoke rose from the chimney and drifted lazily on the gentle breeze.

"It is our freedom we want," the bearded man said, "we want to live our lives free from the yoke of British oppression, nothing more."

MICHELLE

A VISIT TO THE DOCTOR

April 2019

Alice sits on the floor behind the glass-topped coffee table. The cute baby doll pyjamas she wears, combined with the thick layer of rejuvenating cream smeared over her face, are reminiscent of the girls' only slumber parties she and Alice had attended during their teens.

"You look like a sixteen-year-old." Michelle hands Alice a frosty glass of kahlúa and milk and drops gracefully to her knees on the other side of the table. "I can't believe you still drink that stuff. It's like drinking milkshake."

"That's why I like it. It tastes delicious and satisfies my sweet tooth." Alice eyes Michelle's drink, "Strawberry daiquiris aren't exactly the height of sophistication either."

The smart wooden box containing Alice's tarot cards lies open in the centre of the smooth glass surface. Fragrant smoke, from the burning incense sticks Alice has shoved into a drinking glass and stood on the table, curls upwards in a thin spiral. It is Friday night and they are both relaxed with the weekend stretching ahead of them.

"Do you remember our high school slumber parties?" giggles Michelle. "You look just like you did then."

"So, do you, Mrs Pot. You should see yourself in your Hello Kitty short pyjamas and pigtails."

"Well, that's a good thing, isn't it? Letting our hair down and having some fun is good for us."

Tom is away on a business trip and the house is quiet and serene. No ghostly presences have manifested themselves since Tom's departure two days ago. It's as if he took them with him.

Confiding her paranormal experiences and resultant fears to Alice during a long telephone discussion the previous day has left Michelle cleansed and refreshed. Alice hadn't laughed or made light of her anxieties. Instead, she had suggested an evening of meditation and a tarot card reading. Michelle had jumped at this idea.

Maybe the cards will reveal something to help me understand what is going on and why.

Alice sips her drink and then settles herself into a cross-legged position. Her back is straight, and her arms relaxed with her hands lying on her knees, palms upwards. Michelle does her best to copy her.

"You need to find your third eye chakra," intones Alice. "It's in the front of your brain, in between your eyes and just above the bridge of your nose. You need to focus on this chakra, Michelle, as it's what you want to open. Your third eye will help you see the world with more clarity."

Focusing on her meditation object, a rose, Michelle concentrates deeply on opening her third eye. Her mind finds solace in rest, as she sits there, repeating her mantra "peace" to herself.

Within her mind, the light of a spiritual eye starts to appear. Gradually it takes the shape of a white star with five points in a dark blue sphere, surrounded by a golden circle. A light pressure builds in the area between her eyebrows and she knows her third eye has opened.

Seeing herself, through the lens of her mind, is disconcerting. The hallway or waiting room in which she finds herself is dark and gloomy.

The ceiling and walls are faraway and have no clear definition. The room is full of faceless people, all standing or sitting as if waiting for something. She can hear them whispering and moaning.

"This is not what I planned for or what I wanted." A single loud voice ricochets through the room like a bullet, bouncing off the distant walls and ceiling. "I never wanted to be trapped here in this place of lost souls," it moans, "you need to help meeeeee."

The words echo around the cavernous room which is getting bigger and bigger.

Michelle opens her mouth to answer, to ask the voice how she can help, but no sound comes out. It is not fear that has made her mute, it is an inability to grasp the words with her mind and force them from her mouth. The voice has an underlying tone of sadness and distress.

After a further period of timeless silence, another presence makes itself known. A shadowy red form. It exudes anger like flashes of lightening, making the fine hairs on Michelle's arms stand to attention. The shadow elongates like a piece of chewing gum and tears down the middle. The rent widens and stretches to form a mouth.

"I hate you," the voice that issues from the rent booms.

The voice frightens her, and she turns and starts pushing her way through the countless milling people, their faceless countenances disfigured by gaping holes from which a collective and continuous doomed moan issues.

She can hear another voice now. It is far away but has a confident and comforting ring to it.

"Michelle," it calls, "are you ready for your reading?"

Michelle follows the voice towards a doorway at the far end of the room. She pulls open the door and follows the voice through a maze of dark passageways towards her own lounge. Looking back fleetingly she sees that the dark windowless room has disappeared. She bursts from the end of the last passage and opens her eyes.

Alice, who is still sitting in her cross-legged meditation position, stares at her with frank fascination. Unease creeps over Michelle.

"What's wrong? Michelle asks.

How much could Alice sense about where I was and what I saw?

"Nothing," she replies, "you were really focused; that's all. I had to call you a few times before you responded."

"Yes, well, I was trying to follow your instructions and open my third eye."

"And did you?" Alice asks, "open your third eye, I mean?"

86

"Yes, I think I did open it."

I'm not going to tell her about that weird dark room and the voices. Not just yet. We'll do the tarot card reading and I'll decide afterwards whether I should tell her or not.

Michelle grabs her drink and gulps a large swig. Delicious sweetness fills her mouth. "Shall we do this reading, then?" Her wide smile feels fake on her lips.

Alice reaches over and opens the lid of the wooden box containing the tarot cards. She lifts the pile out and holds them in her one hand. She starts to shuffle them by taking a small stack and shifting them behind the rest. She carries on until one card seems to pop out of the pack. She grabs it and places it, face down, on the table. The shuffling continues until there are three cards lying face down in a row on the shining glass.

"You said that you wanted some insight into the past, present and future of your relationship," Alice's expression is solemn. "You must remember that you'll not get a definitive answer from this reading. Rather, the cards will guide you about how to make good decisions to support your life goals. Are you comfortable with that, Michelle?"

"Yes, I understand that."

Alice turns over the card on the left. It's the Moon. Paling slightly, she draws in a deep breath.

"The Moon in the past position, as it relates to romance, could mean that you have an inaccurate perception of your partner. It is possible that your partner has not been completely honest with you and has hidden secrets."

Michelle grimaces, "That is rather concerning, especially considering the poltergeist, or whatever she is, said he was a lying cheat and that I was a traitor to my sex for marrying him. What can it all mean?"

"I'm not sure, Michelle, but it may not mean what you think it does. Let's consider the next card and what it tells us about your relationship?"

Alice flips over the middle card and reveals the Ten of Swords.

Starting visibly, Michelle sucks in air through gritted teeth. "That's not a good card in the context of a relationship," she hisses.

"No," Alice agrees, "it means that your current situation is going to come to an end, but this could apply to your life more generally and it may be something else that is important to you that is concluding and not your relationship."

"Remember what I said when we started," Alice continues. "This is just guidance and should not be interpreted too literally. Out of every ending there comes a new beginning and it could refer to your decision to finally write a book. Maybe your day job will come to an end to enable you to do that."

Michelle smiles at Alice, "You are such a great friend. Who else could turn the Ten of Swords into something positive?"

"I'll drink to that." The two women raise their glasses, clink them together, and take large gulps.

"Let's see what the last card is," Michelle manufactures a cheerful smile. "Hopefully it will be an improvement on the last one."

Alice turns it over slowly. "The Chariot."

"That's good, isn't it?"

"Yes, it is related to having confidence and overcoming obstacles in your life. Read together with the Ten of Swords, it means that whatever major life event you are going through now, will be overcome in the future."

"And with regards to relationships?" Michelle asks in a trembling voice.

"It can be interpreted that your relationship is about to go through a rough patch, but the Chariot is telling you that it'll pass and that you'll come out stronger and better because of it."

Michelle nods, the cards have unsettled her and added to her questions rather than giving her any clarity.

"I think we should call it a night," Alice yawns hugely. "It's late and I'm tired."

Michelle nods again and rises to her feet. "I'll rinse out the glasses and put them in the dishwasher. You pack away your cards."

Thirty minutes later, Alice is installed in the spare room and Michelle is lying in her own bed gazing at the ceiling. The interpretation of the first card, the Moon, repeats itself over and over in her mind.

Your partner hasn't been honest with you. Honest … Honest … Honest …

The words follow Michelle into sleep.

* * *

The following morning, Michelle and Alice talk about the reading over their breakfasts of muesli and yoghurt.

"Try not to worry about the cards, Michelle. Tom is a good man and he loves you. He is older than you and everyone has a past. Maybe he had a previous engagement that went sour, or even a divorce. He may not want to tell you about it and revisit a whole lot of negative memories and emotions."

"You are right, Alice. What you've said makes perfect sense. Thank you."

"I've given some thought to the poltergeist you spoke about. There are a few things you can do to ward off evil spirits that don't require much effort."

"We can't do anything that Tom will notice, Alice. Although he seems to be the primary target of this spirit's vengeance, he doesn't know about it and would never acknowledge the existence of a poltergeist."

"I know, but he's unlikely to notice any of the changes I'm thinking of. Firstly, we should smudge each room in the house with dried white sage. Burning sage has been used in cleansing rituals for thousands of years. After the smudging, we'll sprinkle a little salt in the corners of each room in the house and on the doorsteps. This will help prevent the return of negative spirits. Lastly, we'll buy a potted St John's Wart plant. You can put it in the kitchen. St John's Wart wards off evils spirits."

Michelle leans over and hugs Alice: "You are a life saver, let's get busy."

An outing to an esoteric shop in Pretoria provides the two women with the plant and the dried white sage they need.

On their return home, they prepare for the smudging. Alice opens all the windows and doors. She lights the end of the sage bundle with a match. Michelle watches as the tips of the leaves start to smoulder slowly, releasing thick smoke. Holding the bundle in one hand, Alice directs the smoke around her body and space, she then hands the bundle to Michelle and motions for her to do the same.

Taking the sage back, Alice walks around the house in a clockwise direction, directing the sage over all the surfaces and spaces in each room. Thirty minutes later, the pair arrive back where they started. Alice pokes the lit end of the smudge stick into a specially prepared small bowl of sand, successfully extinguishing it.

"It's done," she smiles at Michelle. "Let's hope it chases away your poltergeist and provides for an inflow of positive energy."

***

That evening, Tom arrives home, looking fit and well. Michelle has made his favourite chilli prawn and tomato spaghetti and a walnut and apple salad. They eat their meal at a small table outside on the patio, while enjoying a rare glass of red wine and watching the sun sink below the horizon.

It's one of the last balmy evenings of mid-autumn and the setting and food bring back strong and lovely memories for Michelle. They had not gone on their honeymoon immediately following their wedding, preferring to wait until the European summer holiday period and go to Italy on a tour for couples.

During the first idyllic weeks in their new home, she had cooked every day and they had relaxed every night with a glass of wine and a good meal. May became June and the peaceful evenings they'd been enjoying petered out as the demands of their jobs increased.

During his busy periods at work, Tom often stayed at the office until 10 p.m., eating takeaway meals with his team of staff while they continued to work.

Michelle has continued to make the most of the quieter work periods in Tom's life and keep the romance in their relationship alive by cooking tasty meals for them to enjoy together in a romantic setting whenever Tom's schedule has allowed for it.

His high spirits evident, Tom keeps up a steady banter all evening. He tells her all about the conference. Michelle smiles and laughs at his funny stories about his colleagues, one of whom got so drunk he passed out in the passageway outside his room. It was just like old times before they moved into this house with its creepy and shadowy inhabitants.

She would have been completely happy except for the strangely furtive way his eyes dart around from time to time, as if he is keeping an eye out for something or someone. It worries her a little; she can't help it.

Later that evening, she lies awake, listening to the slow, heavy sound of her husband's breathing and wondering whether there is any truth in the poltergeist's odd words. The message imparted by the Moon tarot card is also distracting. Until lately, her belief in her perfect husband and wonderful life had been unwavering, but now she is beginning to question its authenticity.

Alice's words of advice comfort her. "Keep quiet about your paranormal experiences and see what happens over the next few days. Things may be different now that we have taken steps to rid your house of negative energy."

Michelle's not said anything to Tom about her ghostly visions and the tarot reading. Her restraint is more to do with a lack of courage, and a certainty that Tom will laugh at her and say she is foolish to think such silly thoughts, than because of Alice's sage advice.

The situation in the house has not improved over the past two nights since the smudging ceremony. Every morning Michelle searches for her smart phone and her car keys which have been moved. She finds them in odd places like in the fridge or a flowerpot. Her morning showers are unpleasant endurance sessions with the water temperature constantly changing from freezing cold to boiling hot. Her nights are disturbed too.

Our actions certainly didn't suppress the poltergeist. I think they angered her and made her stronger.

Her mind probes and worries at the problem until she sits up, shivering, and straightens the twisted and damp bedclothes. Sometime much later, she drifts into a troubled sleep. Tom sleeps undisturbed, his body hidden beneath the blankets with only a few tufts of his hair poking out.

A dull throb signals the opening of her third eye. She is lying asleep in bed but can see the bedroom with a bird's eye view.

A young woman stands in the light from the bathroom. Michelle recognises her as the girl who appeared on her computer screen and threatened both Tom and her with a knife.

Moving into the bedroom, the woman looks down at the sleeping Michelle. Reaching out, the phantom's white hands float towards her sleeping figure on the bed.

Adrenaline floods Michelle, but she can't move. Her frozen limbs lie heavily on the bed.

Roll over, her mind screams at her unresponsive body.

The disembodied hands move closer and closer to her exposed neck which begins to tingle in horrified anticipation.

She's going to throttle me! I'm going to watch myself die of strangulation.

The hands stop abruptly as they hit an invisible barrier. Pieter's dark shadow leaps forward and, with a fierce sweep of his arm, he flings the girl aside. Her insubstantial form drifts through the air and flutters to the ground like a silk scarf.

"No, Estelle, don't do this. Don't seal your fate by killing her. She's the only one who can help us escape our diabolical fate," Pieter shouts.

The discarded shadow slowly elongates itself into an upright position like a curl of smoke from a fire. Opening her gaping maw, a terrible screeching laugh rebounds from wall to wall.

"You can have her, but I'll have him. She's easier to contact because she has the sight, but his inability to see or hear me doesn't mean I can't find a way of destroying him."

The two spirits vanish, and Michelle slips back into unconsciousness. When the sound of the alarm jerks her from sleep the following morning, she notices that Tom's face looks clammy and red. The flesh beneath his eyes is bruised and puffy looking and his breathing is again laboured and heavy.

I'm going to have to do something about this situation. Maybe I should do some research on Tom and see if I find out anything about his past.

* * *

Michelle enters Thomas Cleveland into the Google search bar and hits enter. Her face is white and anxious, and her upper teeth bite down into her lower lip. She is expecting her search to return an unwanted finding.

All the usual items come up on the screen: Thomas Cleveland – Director – Kellerman, James & Thompson and Tom Cleveland / Face-book; Tom does not have a lot of social media. These links are followed by a list of links to on-line newspaper articles that Tom has written about the equity and debt markets in Africa and other emerging markets.

She flips to page 2 and a newspaper article comes up entitled "Woman takes her own life months after qualifying as a chartered accountant." She clicks on the link:

> Tracey Atkinson (24) was found dead at her apartment in Morningside, Johannesburg, only two months after qualify-ing as a chartered accountant. Her parents, who had not been able to contact her for over two days, called her friend and neighbour, Sarah Wilson, who discovered the body when she accessed Tracey's apartment.
>
> Thomas Cleveland, a partner at the auditing firm in Pretoria where Tracey worked, expressed shock at her death. "She was a hardworking and dedicated woman and she will be greatly missed at Kellerman, James & Thomp-son."

The article was dated February 2011. Michelle joined the firm in January 2012 and any gossip surrounding this woman's death had peated out by then. She'd never heard the name Tracey Atkinson before, not from Tom or any of her other work colleagues.

Sitting back in her chair, Michelle considers what she has read.

Is it unusual that Tom has never mentioned the suicide of this girl to me? Would I discuss a suicide from the previous year with my new girlfriend? I do remember hearing something about an unfortunate death when I first joined the firm, but I don't recall any details. I don't suppose suicide is something people want to talk about or remember. I wonder why she did it. Could this be the unmentioned event in his past? The newspaper article did mention his name and quote him, so he must have known her.

June 2019

Michelle reverses her car out of the garage and stops. Getting out of the car, she walks around to the passenger door and opens it for Tom, who gets in. The change in him over the past six weeks is unbelievable. His hair has greyed, his eyes are hollow and burn in his chalky white face, and he looks like he is in a great deal of pain.

Out of the corner of her eye, Michelle sees him put one hand up to his head.

"Are you all right?"

"Headache," he sighs and leans back in his seat, closing his eyes.

"Would you like a pill? I have some?"

"No, thanks. Let's wait and see what the doctor says."

Michelle pulls out of their complex and heads towards a private clinic in Centurion. She is taking Tom to see a neurologist for an evaluation. She'd made the appointment at Alice's suggestion, when they'd met for lunch the previous week.

Tom scared, that's the only explanation for his agreeing to see this doctor. Normally, he wouldn't hear of seeing a "head" doctor.

May 2019

Running late as always, Michelle rushed through the mall and dashed into the restaurant where she had agreed to meet Alice for lunch. *I wonder if she's running later than me, I don't see her anywhere.*

"Have you seated a young lady with red, curly hair?"

The waiter smiled and nodded, "Yes, she's sitting outside in the court-yard. I'll take you to her."

Michelle followed the man.

Of course, he remembers her, Alice always makes an impression.

The courtyard was bathed in midday sunshine. Seated at a table, her chair pulled out from under the protective umbrella, she saw Alice reclining with her eyes closed. Her turbulent red curls were wreathed with a sun induced halo just like an angel from a children's Bible.

"Hi, Alice," she announced her presence, not wanting to give Alice a fright by just pulling her chair out from under the table and scraping it across the flagstone floor.

"Hi there, girlfriend," Alice peered at her through a crack in her eyelids. Pictures of giant lizards sunning themselves on rocks and peering around at the world through heavily lidded eyes popped unexpectedly into Michelle's head, and she giggled.

It feels so good to giggle. I don't think I've laughed for days.

Lazily, Alice pulled herself to her feet and came around the table to give Michelle a hug.

"It's great to see you." She stood back and stared at Michelle. "You are looking very washed out, my mother would say you look peaky. I take it things haven't improved at home?"

"No, things are much worse now," Michelle burst into tears.

Alice gave her another bracing hug.

"Let's sit down and order some drinks and a snack. You can tell me all about what's been happening, and we can decide what to do to improve the situation."

Nodding, Michelle pulled out her chair and sat down. Alice did the same and they both studied the menu.

"I can't read it, I'm too upset. You order for us both, Alice."

"No problem. Let's have strawberry daiquiris, your favourite, and chicken and sesame salads. I'll go and find our waiter and place the order." Alice grinned wickedly, "The poor bugger ran a mile when he saw you weeping all over the place."

She's the same old Alice. Always able to make me smile with her outrageous comments.

Michelle pulled a packet of tissues from her handbag, wiped her face and then blew her nose. Alice disappeared inside to place their order.

Her spirits improved by the company, the food and the drink; Michelle told her friend how things had been at home since their last meeting a few weeks ago.

"Tom's not slept restfully once since he returned home from his conference. Every night he thrashes about in bed and in the morning his sheets are soaked with sweat. He's also talking in his sleep and sometimes even shouting out. He's complaining of bad headaches and taking pain killers every day.

"But that's not the biggest problem. His behaviour has changed completely since he came home. He's started having a few whiskeys at home nearly every evening. If he doesn't drink at home, he drinks at work. With his friend, Trevor. Do you remember him from the party?"

"Yes, I remember him. He is a big drinker, isn't he?" Alice's nose wrinkled slightly as the memory of Trevor.

Nodding, Michelle carried on with her story. "His personality has changed; it feels as if it's happened overnight. If I say anything about his heavy drinking, he shouts at me. He's bad tempered and impatient all the time. I know he's sleep deprived and is suffering from these awful headaches, but he's aggressive towards me. I'm scared of him right now."

"Have you tried to talk to him about his drinking?" Alice smiled in acknowledgment of the waiter as he set their drinks down on the table.

"Of course, but when I say anything to him about it, he gets all sulky and sullen. I don't know what to do.

"Tom's never drunk much since I've known him. Occasionally, when we've entertained larger parties of his work colleagues and our friends, he's had a whiskey or two, but never more than that. I've only really known him to drink the odd glass of wine when we have supper together, either at a restaurant or at home. Of course, our home life has always been dictated by his work schedule and he's always had his meals at work with his team during busy periods. I've never considered that he might be drinking at work before."

"Do you mean other than in the bar with Trevor? Is he drinking at other times during the working day?"

"Yes. The firm's Human Resources manager called me last week. She wanted to know if there was a problem at home. She said that his work ethic and behaviour had changed recently. His staff have complained that he is drinking at lunch time and that he is missing conference calls and not showing up for client meetings. His recent behaviour is such unchartered waters for me. I don't know what is bothering him or how to try and help him." Michelle took a sip of her daiquiri. The sweet alcoholic liquid gave her an instant burst of energy.

"That doesn't sound good, Shelles. If he's drinking during the working day then he needs help. Has he seen a doctor about his sleeping problem? Maybe a short-term course of sleeping pills would help until we can find out what's causing his nightmares." Alice's gaze was searching. "He hasn't told you what's causing the nightmares, has he? He hasn't mentioned any visions or paranormal encounters like the ones you've experienced?"

"No, but he doesn't believe in ghosts and the paranormal. I don't think he would ever admit to me he'd seen something that couldn't be rationalised by science and facts.

"He's seen a general practitioner. In fact, he's seen two over the past six weeks. A local GP and his mother's GP, Dr Botha, who has known him all his life. I accompanied him to both appointments. Both doctors examined him, and Dr Botha took samples of blood to test for a variety of ailments. All the blood tests have come back negative." Michelle takes a large gulp of her drink.

"He didn't mention his excessive drinking to either doctor. Dr Botha prescribed some strong sleeping pills, which he might not have done if he'd known about Tom's drinking. Tom's been taking them, I know because I've checked the blister packet, but they haven't helped him to sleep better at night. They've just caused him to be apathetic and fatigued during the day, which makes him even more grouchy and difficult to live with."

Michelle threw back her blonde hair and straightened her shoulders as she prepared for her next revelation. "I've never mentioned it to you before, Alice, but before Tom and I started dating, I heard rumours that he drank heavily and was verging on alcoholism. I never told you, or any of my other friends about these stories, because they no longer seemed relevant. I've known Tom for nearly six years, he's never shown any signs of being a heavy drinker during all that time. The stories about his wild and heavy drinking and status as the firm's biggest playboy were more than a year old when I first heard them. I thought that period of his life was over and would never return."

"Alcoholism can return during periods of stress and it looks like it may have in Tom's case. It could be that there is some other medical issue that is causing his headaches and inability to sleep. I think he should see a neurologist and ensure there is no physical reason, like a brain tumour, for his symptoms and behavioural changes." Alice took a delicate sip of her drink.

"That is a good idea, Alice. Thank you for suggesting it. Can you recommend anyone I could make an appointment with?"

"Dr Stephenson at the private hospital in Centurion has a good reputation. You could try him."

"Thanks, Alice, I'll do that."

"And how are you, Shelles? Have you had any further visitations since we did the smudging?"

"No, I haven't seen any ghosts since then … I've seen nothing at all." The speculative look in Alice's eyes told Michelle that she hadn't convinced her friend that nothing was wrong. Her voice had sounded shrill, almost screechy, to her own ears.

Alice didn't push it. Michelle changed the topic of conversation and they chatted about lighter subjects. Alice took the opportunity to tell Michelle she'd be away in Cape Town for a few weeks with the cast of her latest show.

The rest of the afternoon passed quickly and by 4 p.m., when Michelle climbed into her car to drive home, she was optimistic that everything would turn out okay.

Heavy dark clouds were massing in the sky and by the time she reached home a cold wind had sprung up. Pulling her thick overcoat closer around her, Michelle rushed from the garage to the front door. Her front door keys dropped from her frigid figures and she stooped to pick them up again.

A dark and solid shape, like a large owl, swooshed past her, making her jump. The creature made a terrible wailing sound as it disappeared into the brooding jacaranda tree that dominated her garden.

With shaking hands, she jerked the door open, slipped in, and shut it firmly behind her.

Later that evening, just before they went to bed, Michelle noticed Tom sitting in his chair in the lounge with his head cocked, as if he could hear something. She strained, listening intently, but heard nothing.

"Can you hear something, Tom?" She'd reached out to comfort him.

"I'm not crazy," he shouted at her, his face red with anger. "I can't hear anything except you asking me daft questions."

Shaking off her outstretched hands, he pushed her away and stormed out of the room, shutting himself in the bedroom.

The following day, in desperation, Michelle made him this appointment with Dr Stephenson.

I don't know what else to do. He's rejected all my attempts to discuss his nightmares and unravel their meaning or cause. He'll not listen to the slightest suggestion that our house might be haunted nor let me tell him about my visions and disturbed nights.

Although she hadn't mentioned anything amiss with her own life to Alice, disturbances and visions have intruded on her nightly rest. Ever since she'd opened her third eye on the evening of the tarot reading, she'd been experiencing her own night-time torments.

For the past week, these have overflowed into her days and she feared for her own sanity.

Numerous times, over the past weeks, she'd heard voices whispering together. The whispering had not ceased after the smudging exercise, it had just become more indistinct and obscure, like leaves rustling in a strong wind. This intrusive noise was particularly noticeable when she was working in her home office. When the noise first started, she would swing around in her swivel chair, hoping to glimpse what was causing the disturbance.

Occasionally, she glimpsed a shadow on the wall in the shape of the British soldier, Robert, or the man in the wide-brimmed hat called Pieter. Hysterical laughter intermittently ripped apart the silence. Headphones have proved to be the only viable solution to blocking out these distractions.

She prayed that the ghosts would not infiltrate her computer and channel the whispers and shrieking laughter through her audio system. That might just push her over the edge and into madness.

Every couple of nights she felt the throbbing between her eyes from her third eye chakra and found herself back in the waiting room among the tightly packed mob of faceless men and women, as they milled slowly and helplessly around and around in circles. The dreadful noise of their on-going sobbing and moaning assailed her ears, as she forced her way through them, trying to find her way through the labyrinth to the passageway that led out of that terrible place.

The memory of her last visit still left her cold and shivering with wretchedness. As she ran along a previously unexplored passageway, she stumbled into a room that had materialised in the wall. The room was a bedroom in what looked like a hotel. It contained a large king-sized bed made up with the classic white linen of many hotels. A large television stood on a television cabinet made of some pale and expensive looking wood.

The couple in the bedroom were kissing and she couldn't see their faces. The man roughly pushed the woman towards the bed, forcing her down on the crisp white sheets. She started to struggle, "No," she cried, the word loud and clear in the silent room.

"Come on, Tracey, you know you want to," the man's voice sounded slurred.

An overpowering smell of liquor hung in the air.

He's drunk, thought Michelle.

She wanted to back away, but her feet wouldn't move.

Reluctantly, she was forced to watch as the woman's mouth opened to scream and his hand descended, covering it and stifling the sound.

"Cock tease," he muttered.

He threw himself down on top of her, forcing the air out of her lungs with a long whoosh. Rolling over slightly, he unbuckled his belt and yanked down his zipper. Within moments his pants were around his knees and he had shoved up the skirt of her evening dress. He forced her legs apart as, beneath him, the woman continued to struggle, her hands beating ineffectually on his back.

Michelle's feet released and she turned and ran from the room, sprinting down the passageway towards the dim light of her own bedroom.

"Hi, I'm Dr Warren Stephenson," the tall, beefy man with thick grey hair leans across the desk and shakes Tom's hand and then Michelle's. He is not at all what Michelle expected, looking more like a farmer that a doctor.

"Your wife said on the phone that you are suffering from insomnia and chronic headaches, Mr Cleveland. Can you please give me an overview of your symptoms?"

"Please call me Tom. For the past six to eight weeks I've been experiencing on-going nightmares and sleep disturbances. During the day I've been suffering from escalating fatigue, which I assume is due to my interrupted nights. I'm also experiencing recurring headaches. This combination has started to impact on my ability to perform my job and that is why my wife made this appointment."

"I see. Has anything happened in your life recently, Tom, that could be causing the nightmares? Are you having any martial issues?"

The doctor's eyes move between them, looking for any indications of discomfort with this line of questioning.

"No, we're getting along fine," Tom answers shortly.

The doctor studies him momentarily and then writes a few notes on his notepad.

"What about medications or lifestyle? Any recent changes?"

"No, I don't take any on-going prescription medications. I've been taking pain killers for the headaches, but they haven't helped much. My lifestyle hasn't changed recently, and I've had two complete medicals and a series of blood tests over the past month."

The scratching of the doctor's pen on his notepad makes Michelle's fingernails tingle. It reminds her of fingernails scrapping on a blackboard.

"Which doctors performed the medicals?"

"Dr Anderson at the Irene Medical Centre did the first medical about four weeks ago. He didn't see anything that suggested a medical problem of any sort. I saw a second general practitioner, Dr Botha, two weeks ago. He did a battery of tests for diabetes, thyroid problems and various infections including meningitis. They all came back negative."

Dr Stephenson nods and writes a few more notes.

"Is there anything else you think I should know?"

Tom looks at Michelle out of the corner of his eye and she nods.

He sighs deeply, "I've been drinking a bit more than usual lately, but the nightmares and headaches started before the drinking."

"Okay, that's good to know. Did you follow the instructions I gave your wife with regards to washing your hair and eating and drinking this morning?"

"Yes."

"Perfect, I want to perform an EEG on you, Tom. The procedure involves attaching several small electrodes and wires to your head and connecting them to my EEG machine. The machine measures the electrical signals that form patterns in your brain. This test is used to diagnose conditions such as seizures, epilepsy, head injuries, dizziness, headaches, brain tumours and sleeping problems. Are you comfortable to go ahead with this procedure, Tom?"

"Yes, please go ahead."

"Follow me please, the procedure will take place in the room next door." The doctor stands, gesturing for them to follow.

An hour later, Dr Stephenson switches off the machine.

"We're finished, Tom. My assistant will take the electrodes off you and then we can have a chat in my office."

When Michelle and Tom enter the doctor's office a short while later, he's looking at the brain traces on his computer screen.

As they sit down, he turns to them and smiles.

"I've looked at your EEG and your brain patterns are normal, Tom. No signs of head trauma, tumours or seizures. I'm ordering an MRI for you to completely rule out a brain tumour, but I think it is likely that your insomnia and headaches are being caused by tension and stress."

"That's great news, doctor," Michelle's relief is palpable.

"If the MRI comes back clear, then I suggest you consider physiotherapy and acupuncture to help with the headaches. If you reduce your tension, you may find that your sleeping patterns improve too. You can also continue with the sleeping pills your general practitioner prescribed for you. Make sure you only take them on nights when you are sure you can achieve a minimum of seven to eight straight hours sleep to avoid daytime sleepiness."

* * *

Two days later the results of Tom's MRI came back negative for any tumours. There is nothing physically wrong with him; nothing at all.

ESTELLE

ON THE MOVE

June 1900

When Marta comes into the girls' bedroom, Estelle is not asleep. Eyes wide open in the darkness, she watches the patterns of light on the walls and floor quiver and jump as the lantern moves in her mother's shaking hand.

Mama's scared. She's so scared she's shaking.

"We're preparing to leave, Estelle," Marta throws open the wooden shutters, flooding the room with light.

"I'll help the children get dressed," Estelle throws back the bed covers and swings her legs over the side of the bed. The shock of the cold floor beneath her warm feet, causes her to rise onto her toes.

Estelle has long suspected that they'll have to leave the home she has known for the past nine years. She's a quiet but keenly observant girl, listening carefully to the various conversations going on around her and drawing conclusions. Melting into the background with her unobtrusive manner and slight stature, she frequently overhears discussions that are not meant for her ears. It infuriates her mother, who constantly berates her for being a devious little eavesdropper.

"Stand properly, Estelle. You know I can't stand it when you walk on your toes like that."

"Yes, Mama. Do you know why?"

"Why what?"

"Why we must leave so suddenly."

"The Khakis are coming." An expression of irritation flits across her mother's face. "Stop asking meddlesome questions and get yourself dressed."

Bending over the mattress on the floor that holds the sleeping forms of her two younger daughters, Marta gently shakes Suné.

"Wake up, girls, you need to get dressed and come and have your breakfast."

Her tone is kind and loving, unlike the sharp and clipped speech she used to address Estelle.

"Where are we going, Mama?" Four-year-old Suné trills like an excited bird.

"We're going to your *Oom* Willem and *Tannie*[1] Sannie's farm. You'll find out more soon enough. Now obey me and get dressed as quickly as you can."

"Estelle, strip the beds and fold the linen and blankets ready to pack into the wagon."

Her mother turns abruptly and walks out of the room, but not before Estelle sees her eyes, exhausted and filled with pain.

"Yes, Mama."

Turning back, Marta says, "When you're finished, Papa wants you to get the chickens into their hutch, ready to be packed up for transport."

"Yes, Mama."

Why does she despise me? I always obey her without question and submit to her will on everything, so why?

* * *

Estelle slips out of the front door and sets off towards the chicken run. The icy wind combines with her warm breath to create a foggy cloud that trails behind her as she walks. She is acutely aware of the crackle and snap of the frost on the short grass as her boots trample it.

Her clenched right fist clutches a handful of dried mielie kernels, which she intends to use to encourage the rooster and any hens which have strayed out of the hen house and into the long chicken run, back inside. Once inside, she'll close the door and they'll be trapped until she's ready to catch them.

I'm glad Mama didn't ask me to bring Renette along to help. It's so much easier for me to do this on my own.

When Mosiko arrives for work shortly, she'll ask him to help her carry the cages from the barn, and assist her in setting them up, one at a time, in front of the hen house door. A bit of food sprinkled on the ground would be enough to attract the stupid birds out of their hen house and into the cage when she released them from captivity by opening the door. Once safely inside, Mosiko would then help her carry the cages back to the barn, ready to be hung under the wagon before the family trekked later that morning.

Estelle looks at her thin arms with irritation. Her small stature and

---

[1] A woman who is older than the speaker (often used as a respectful and affectionate title or form of address). The Afrikaans word for aunt.

slender body deprive her of the physical strength she longs for.

Her mother is a tall and raw-boned woman, perfectly adapted to the life of a Boer woman on a remote farm. Marta's waist has thickened as a result of her pregnancies, making her look shapeless in her heavy clothing, and her hands are large and reddened from the endless cleaning, cooking and farm work her life demanded.

At their young ages, Renette and Suné already bear the same physical characteristics as their mother, with thick dark hair and stocky bodies.

They are so lucky to look like Mama. They fit in perfectly with all the other woman in our community. Why am I so different? What man will ever want to marry someone as small and skinny as me?

Estelle sprinkles the kernels on the rough ground and the chickens follow her eagerly. Within minutes her task is complete. She stands for a moment, wondering whether she should return to the house or go over to the barn and see if she can shift the cages on her own. With her lifestyle under threat, her mother is particularly difficult to be around and best avoided for the time being.

Estelle jumps at the sound of heavy footsteps. She shrinks back into the dark shadow of the chicken house. Within moments, Papa comes into view. He is carrying two sacks, one in each hand. From the downward slope of his shoulders, she knows they are heavy.

What is Papa doing?

She sneaks after him, keeping a good distance so he won't see her and send her away. He'll not shout at her, Estelle knows that she is his favourite child.

From behind a screen of trees, she watches her father manipulate the heavy sacks into a hole in the ground and place the young sapling into the hole.

As he works to fill in the hole, his grunts of pain carry on the still, thin air. This is hard for him after his recent injury. Sweat beads his brow and the spade in his hands slides up and down within his slippery palms as he struggles to lift spadefuls of the soil into the deep hole.

He stops and pulls a handkerchief from his pocket, mopping his brow to stop the sweat from blinding him.

Crouching down behind a tree, Estelle watches.

There must be something important in those sacks. I wonder what it is.

As Papa's task approaches completeness, she gets up on silent feet and slips back to the house. She doesn't want him to see her. Her heart is heavy within her breast, knowing that he'll soon return to his commando. Her mother's cold indifference towards her, interspersed with moments of active dislike, confuses and saddens her.

Papa is the one who enjoys sitting and talking to her in the evenings when he relaxes on the *stoep* after a long day's work on the farm.

When she was a little girl, he would speak to her in English and read to her from his few precious books. Sometimes, he would read to her from the English newspaper and discuss the article with her. Papa had strong opinions on a wide range of political and other topics. Estelle quickly realised that if she sat quietly and listened attentively, he would often explain his point of view to her. As she grew older, he had taught her to read in English, patiently helping her sound out the words until she could do it on her own.

"You are just like my Grandmother Anne," Papa told the nine-year-old Estelle one day.

Estelle had been working on a tray cloth she was decorating with tiny and exacting cross stitch. Never having heard of Papa's Grandmother Anne before, Estelle laid down her needlework and stared at him.

"She died when I was sixteen and I was devastated. She was a wonderful and kind woman. Well educated too. She taught me to read in English and Dutch when I was a lad of your age."

"Was your grandmother English, Papa?"

"Yes, her family were among the first English colonists who arrived at Algoa Bay[1] in 1820. Her needlework was excellent, and she embroidered some lovely tablecloths, handkerchiefs and even Christening gowns and dresses. Would you like to see some of her work?"

"Oh yes, Papa, I would love that."

Papa grinned widely and gestured her to follow him into the bedroom he shared with Marta.

The top shelf of the beautifully carved wooden cupboard that dominated their bedroom held a small suitcase. Papa lifted it down and placed it carefully on the bed.

Mama won't like it that he put the suitcase on the bed. She won't comment or complain to Papa, but she's sure to let me know she disapproves.

A small sigh slipped from Estelle's mouth. She soon forgot her anxieties as Papa drew a collection of amazing objects from the suitcase.

"When she died, she left her books to me," Papa placed a large leather-bound *King James Bible* and an old copy of a book called *Aesop's Fables*, wrapped in plain brown paper, on the bed.

---

[1] Algoa Bay is now called Port Elizabeth and is in the Eastern Cape province of South Africa.

These astonishing items were followed by a few letters, written in spidery handwriting on yellowed paper, and some of her clothes and other personal belongings.

"This is the gown my brother and I were christened in," Papa held up the beautiful garment.

The gown was made from a delicate white fabric which had yellowed with age. The sleeves were puffed and a bib of the same material, with white satin ribbons to tie it, lay over the bodice. The entire gown was decorated with clusters of tiny white beads and the most detailed and exquisite embroidery Estelle had ever seen.

Other delights, a gauzy handkerchief decorated with cream lace and a beautifully embroidered tablecloth, were taken from the suitcase and held up in front of her astonished eyes.

"One day, you'll own this suitcase, Estelle. I hope you'll treasure it as I have."

"Oh, yes Papa. I'll treasure it forever. Thank you, Papa."

"I don't open the suitcase often, Estelle, as it holds the smell of my grandmother. It'll eventually evaporate if I keep opening the suitcase. The letters will also become even more faded and the cloth more fragile and yellowed, so I keep it closed most of the time and only open it on special occasions."

"I can smell roses, Papa. Was that Grandmother Anne's scent?"

"Yes, she sometimes used a rose scented toilet water and its fragrance has permeated the items in her suitcase."

Papa packed Grandmother Anne's special things back into the suitcase and returned it to the cupboard.

After that day, every so often Papa would get the suitcase down from the cupboard and they would re-examine the treasured items together. At these times, Papa would read to her from *Aesop's Fables* and once, he'd even allowed Estelle to read some of the stories to him. He'd held the book on his lap while she read and turned the old and delicate pages for her. Estelle longed to touch those pages and feel the smooth fragility of the paper beneath her fingers.

Marta never takes any interest in the suitcase or its contents. She does not enjoy listening to Papa talk about his Grandmother Anne, who was a gentlewoman and of English descent.

Estelle knows her mother is resentful towards her because she speaks in English to Papa. Her literacy in both English and Dutch also displease her mother, whose own reading is limited to her Bible and is stilted and laborious.

Estelle can read Great-grandmother Anne's English Bible and her father's Dutch *Statenbijbel*. Papa told her that he'd ordered the *Statenbijbel* from Cape Town when he converted to the Dutch Reform Church so that he could marry Marta.

* * *

A few hours later, the heavily loaded wagon moves slowly along the track through the veld. Estelle is in her customary position as driver, a thick shawl draped around her shoulders and the long reigns held loosely in her hands, which are gloveless, exposing their mangled nails. Her mother hates her driving, believing that this is the job of a man or boy.

Papa appreciates my help. Why can't Mama understand that and accept my driving?

From beneath the confining flaps of her bonnet, she watches the passing veld, rippling and bending in the cold wind that blows right through her shawl and dress, causing her to shiver.

In the typical manner of a winter's day on the Highveld,[1] the frosty chilliness of the night and early morning succumb to the warmth of day before the wagon has travelled a mile from the farm. The wind drops as if it never existed and Estelle's shivering abates.

The heat increases gradually as the sun creeps slowly along its designated path towards its zenith. It burns down on the long, yellow and brown grass, interspersed with clumps of bushes and thorn-trees.

By mid-day, the temperature has reached its high and Estelle is unbearably sticky and itching in her long-sleeved cotton dress, petticoat and long bloomers. Her shawl lies discarded next to her on the wagon seat. If she hadn't known it would incite unnegotiable wrath from her mother, Estelle would have removed her shoes and stockings too.

From past travelling experience, she knows it is worse inside the wagon. She is sitting directly in the hot midday sun, but it is airless and stifling inside the canvas enclosed wagon with the only fresh air entering through the opening behind the driver's seat.

Her legs ache from sitting and her eyes feel dry and itchy from the thick dust that hangs in the hot air and the brightness of the light. Despite these discomforts, she delights in the beauty and wildness surrounding her and wallows in the freedom of being outside on the wagon seat, away from

[1] The Highveld is the portion of the South African inland plateau which has an altitude above roughly 1,500 metres, but below 2,100 metres and constitutes most of the Free State and Gauteng provinces of South Africa.

the condemning eyes of her mother.

The wagon stops briefly for the travellers to enjoy an unappetising meal of rusks, softened in cups of water, and biltong. Marta doesn't even make coffee as Papa wants to get further away from Irene before they make camp and build a fire.

For a few hours after this short interlude, Papa spares his horse's strength by walking him alongside the wagon. The rest of the time, he rides through the cloud of dust kicked up by the oxen, his large, protective hat drawn down low over his face, as the scorching sun beats down on everything and everyone. Every now and then he scouts ahead, keeping a sharp eye out for signs of Khakis.

Estelle is comforted by his vigilance. From time-to-time she turns her head, squinting into the glare for a few moments in order to watch Feile, Kleinbooi and his teenage son, Klein Frantz, herding the livestock. She cannot see the farm workers' families, but knows they are following on foot behind the wagon.

After so many hours, the wagon's jolting over stones and through ruts in the hard ground is more jarring and uncomfortable than earlier in the day. Its laboured forward motion is even slower. Her sisters could easily have walked alongside the wagon for part of the afternoon, relieving some of their boredom and discomfort.

Estelle could also have relinquished the task of driving to Klein Frantz for a short while and stretched her legs by walking a few miles, but she doesn't suggest it or ask her mother's permission to do so. Marta will not allow it, being afraid of poisonous snakes and ticks in the long veld grass.

It would also go against her deeply ingrained attitudes about how to raise her daughters in a proper and moral way. Estelle knows better than to try and challenge her mother's Puritan and almost childlike outlook on life and the role of Boer women in society.

In the late afternoon, Estelle watches with fascination as fluffy, white clouds gather in the sky. Her vivid imagination assigns human faces to some of them.

How marvellous nature is. God has created such a beautiful world for us to live in and enjoy.

She twists around in her seat, planning to point the cloud faces out to her sisters.

Marta is still sitting straight and quiet in the wagon, her hands folded neatly on her lap and her lips moving in prayer. Her expressionless eyes are untouched by the passing countryside.

Estelle's enthusiasm for the cloud pictures dies and she turns away, her words of delight remaining unspoken.

"... help our leaders rally and formulate a new plan of action to resist the Khakis," Marta's murmurings reach Estelle's sharp ears.

"Give Pieter and Willem the strength and the will to continue the fight ..."

She doesn't care about Papa. She is willing to sacrifice him and Oom *Willem rather than see them submit to British rule.*

Irritation at Marta's unwavering and stoic belief that God's plans for His chosen people will prevail, regardless of the decisions and choices made by men, cause Estelle's hands to tighten painfully around the leather reins.

Mama's attitude is ridiculous. A lot of the Boer women share this belief and it's going to cause a lot more death. People must take responsibility for their lives and not expect God to magically resolve their problems when they make wrong decisions. In Aesop's fable about the lion, the ass and the fox, the lion rejects the ass's proposed solution to his question by killing him. The fox learns from the death of the ass and amends his own proposal accordingly. People need to be like the fox in this story. I know that Papa believes that men must be accountable for their own decisions. He's told me so.

Marta is proud of her husband and his role in fighting the war. Before they left the farm, Estelle had overheard her speaking to Renette and Suné about their father.

"Your papa is no coward. He's recovered from his injury and is returning to the fight. I'm glad that we are going to Lichtenberg and will be able to help the commandos in the area with food and other necessities.

"Koos Steyn and Johannes Badenhorst took their wives and children with them to the front when the war first started. When your papa left to join his commando last year, he told me to stay behind and look after our farm. I gave him a Bible to read every day and did as he asked me. You must always submit to the requests of your husband. It is God's will."

These overheard words caused conflict within Estelle's young heart. Marta's complete submission to the will of her husband confuses Estelle who does not share her mother's firm belief in the authority of men as the rulers of the household and the state.

What if your husband is wrong and his choices are not good for you or your family? There will be no divine intervention when common sense fails.

Marta's outwardly calm appearance hides her anxiety and pain at leaving her home. Estelle knows this in some undefined way that is no more than an elusive understanding within her heart. Like all Boer women, Marta is strongly attached to their land, the South African

Republic and her family and, as with most of her compatriots, she vigorously resists British imperialism.

Estelle recalls hearing her mother sobbing late at night after the news of General Cronje's defeat at the battle of Paardeberg[1] became known.

The newspaper delivering this devastating news had been brought to their farm by François Naude's young son, Tertius. Estelle had read a section of the three-day old article, dated the 2nd of March 1900 and headed "Boer laager at Paardeberg surrenders" to Marta.

> Cronjé and his Burghers were, we are informed, involved in a fierce rifle battle with the British on the southwestern side of the laager early on Tuesday morning (the 27th, Majuba Day)[2]. After about 15 minutes, reportedly, some Burghers raised the white flag. Soon this became a general practice and at six o'clock Cronjé sent messengers to Lord Roberts to inform him that they would surrender. Soon afterwards the general, dressed in an old green coat, was taken to Roberts' headquarters with his sjambok[3] in his hand.
>
> Approximately 4 000 Burghers thus fell into British hands as prisoners of war. The Burghers outside the laager, from De Wet downwards, were devastated by this news, which became known yesterday. Some were angry that Cronjé had surrendered specifically on Majuba Day and had not held out one day longer; others regarded it as a miracle that he had held out that long at all. More important is the fact that many Burghers, wondering if there is any sense in proceeding with the war, are returning to their farms without leave.

Marta's tears were private, shed only in the darkness of the night, and Estelle never mentioned them or openly recognised her mother's distress. She understood in her sensitive way that her mother would think she had

---

[1] The Battle of Paardeberg was fought near Paardeberg Drift on the banks of the Modder River in the Orange Free State near Kimberley.

[2] Majuba Day was a major annual celebration on 27 February in the South Africa Republic in the period between the First and the Second Anglo Boer Wars. The Battle of Majuba Hill on 27 February 1881 was the final and decisive battle of the First Anglo Boer War and it was a resounding victory for the Boers against the British.

[3] Also shambok, a heavy leather whip used by the *Voortrekkers* to drive their oxen when trekking. It was also used by herdsmen to drive the cattle.

disgraced her husband and children if her weakness were ever acknowledged.

Estelle reflects on those long days on the farm, alone with her mother, siblings and the native labourers.

September 1899

After Papa left to go and fight in the war, Estelle tried not to invoke her mother's anger. Pre-empting household tasks before Marta could demand assistance became her way of avoiding conflict.

Estelle bore the brunt of Marta's vexation and discontent at being left to manage the farm on her own, as well as raise her three daughters and look after their home. Despite this, she tried to forgive her mother's relentless complaining and nagging.

Mama's lonely and worried. The responsibility of the farm and us, with no Papa and only the native employees to help and protect us, is a big burden for her to carry. I know she misses Papa so I must try not to let her meanness upset me.

No matter how hard she tried, Estelle could not get close to Marta or offer her any solace. Loudly disparaging Estelle's lack of obedience and humility, her mother berated her.

"Your Papa has filled your head with his liberal ideas about women having a political voice and his unorthodox views about God and religion. You would do better to listen to me and emulate what I do, rather than risk being ostracised by our community. Do you want to end up a spinster with no husband and children? Men don't like opinionated women who think too much."

Try as she might, Estelle could not mould her character into the model daughter her mother desired. Papa was respected in the farming community because he always had the correct answer for any problem that arose. Despite this, he was not popular. The other men in the district thought he was odd with his penchant for reading books and his unusual ideas about politics and religion, as well as his liberal labour practices. Estelle had established this from overheard bits of conversation when she went with Papa to the closest general store.

As the days and weeks passed, she suppressed her tumultuous emotions and continued with her daily jobs of feeding the chickens and helping her mother with the cooking, washing and cleaning. She never voiced her anxiety about her father's fate and neither did Marta. Estelle assumed Marta did worry about her husband's safety but saw no outward signs of concern.

Only Estelle guessed that with her father away and no other adult companionship or emotional support, Marta was crushingly and incurably lonely and tired. She kept herself perpetually busy, expanding her well-worn daily path between the stove, the laundry in the kitchen, the vegetable patch, and the clothesline in the back garden to include the barn. Fortunately, all her stops stood within an area of land Papa had cleared.

Beyond the chicken coop lay a dense thicket of trees which was a cool and shady refuge during the hot summer months and beyond the thicket, stretched the grasslands which teamed with life. Estelle frequently saw a slender mongoose or shy duiker during her afternoon walks, as well as hundreds of scrub hares.

The bird life was rich and varied and included hundreds of different species: small waxbills with their violet cheeks, red bills and blue foreheads and rumps, red-faced and speckled mousebirds, sparrows, crested and black-collared barbets, cape robins, and yellow and black bokmakieries with their distinctive cry of bok-bok-mak-kik. There were also the birds of prey: the black sparrowhawks, buzzards, black-shouldered kites, branded harrier hawks, and the lanner falcons, all of which fed mainly on the smaller birds.

Various species of skinks, yellow-throated or plated lizards and rock monitors lurked among the rocky outcrops and hundreds of butterflies and bees lived in the tall, waving grass. The spiders were dreadful, especially the rain spiders with their large, bulbous and hairy bodies and legs that were more than double the length of her thumb.

Estelle remembered stepping on a rain spider with her bare feet in the dark one night. It went crunch under her foot and something sticky came out of its mangled body. The thought still made her shudder. The rain spiders were harmless, unlike the small light yellow or creamy coloured sac spiders which had a vicious and poisonous bite.

During the months when her father was away, Mosiko proved himself to be exceptionally devoted and Estelle was relieved that her mother had someone competent who she could rely on to help her. Mosiko had worked for her father his whole life and knew exactly what needed to be done. Stepping into the role of overseer, he supervised the work of his fellow labourers and ensured it was done properly.

Even at her young age, Estelle knew that the relationships between the farm workers and their Boer employers had always been tempestuous.

There was often friendship and loyalty, as in the case of Mosiko, who had come to work for Grandfather van Zyl as a young orphan boy. He had become attached to the whole family, but her father had been his favourite. When her father left his parents' home to start his own farm, Mosiko had gone with him. He had proved himself to be a devoted servant and never told lies or stole from her father.

His wife, Ardrina and daughter, Dorthea, lived with him in the workers' kraal. He had accumulated a small herd of his own cattle and was considered by the other farm workers to be a wealthy man.

Papa had told Estelle that many of the farm workers stole from their employers, especially clothing, alcohol, and food. Each Boer dealt with such instances in his own way, and the punishments varied in severity.

Estelle knew that her father was disdainful of some of his peers who treated their workers with unnecessary harshness.

"Sometimes the thefts are understandable and justifiable, Estelle," Papa said. "Some farmers blame their workers for mishaps outside their control and withhold their wages in lieu of costs. There are also instances when a Boer's wife will give a worker a poor reference or spoil their passport[1] in circumstances that are unfair or spiteful."

Every afternoon, before the work of the evening commenced, Estelle went for a walk. Her mother did not like her venturing into the thicket and surrounding veld, but Estelle fought hard for this privilege, which her father had encouraged. While she walked she gathered wood for the kitchen fire, in an effort to make it into a useful occupation that was better tolerated by her mother.

I just couldn't bear to be tied to this house and its immediate environment all day, every day. Papa understood why I need to go walking, so why can't Mama?

Although Papa's absence was hard to bear and it added significantly to her mother's and her own workloads, it did provide for some stimulation in the way of added variety which Estelle welcomed.

November 1899

Isolated on the farm, news of the on-going war rarely reached the family and the small pieces that came their way were out of context and merely fed their anxiety.

One morning in late-November, a horse drawn cart drove up to the front door.

---

[1] Internal passports for blacks were first introduced in South Africa on the 27th of June 1797 by Earl McCartney, in an attempt to prevent non-working blacks from entering the Cape Colony. This idea was copied by the South African Republic which also required all blacks Africans working in the Republic to carry a metal badge.

"Hello everyone," called the heavily bearded man in the driving seat.

"It's Jannie," Marta's face broke into a delighted and welcoming smile.

Oom Jannie and Papa had both grown up in the Lichtenberg area. They had become best friends at a young age and their friendship had remained intact throughout their lives.

Seated next to him on the wagon seat, a wide smile on her round and pleasant face, was his wife, *Tannie* Susannah. Their two young sons, Wynand and Alwyn, sat on a pile of straw in the back of the wagon, each holding the handle of a carefully packed basket.

"We've come for a visit and to share all the recent news," *Tannie* Susannah said as *Oom* Jannie helped her down from the wagon seat.

"That's wonderful, but what about the shop?" asked Marta.

Oom Jannie owned a butchery in Pretoria and purchased his meat from the farmers in Irene.

"Jannie left *Oupa*[1] in charge. *Oupa* helps me when Jannie is away, so our customers all know and trust him. We'll stay overnight and travel home tomorrow."

Stepping up to the wagon box, *Tannie* Susannah lifted down the two baskets her sons handed to her and then each boy in turn.

"We've brought some freshly baked milk bread and an apple pie from the bakery as well as some biltong from the shop. I'm hoping you can supply the cream," Susannah smiled and picked up the baskets, one in each hand.

Estelle went to outspan *Oom* Jannie's horses, which were left to roam, noting bitterly that her mother hadn't commented on how unsuitable this activity was for a woman.

Mama has nothing to say when it suits her that I'm hands on with the horses and other animals.

It was midday when they arrived and Estelle had been in the kitchen with her mother, preparing the midday meal.

Oom Jannie and his family joined them for their repast of mutton *sosaties,* which Marta had marinated in her special homemade sauce for two days before cooking.

"This is delicious," *Oom* Jannie moped up the sauce with chunks of milk bread. "My compliments to the cook."

Marta beamed with pleasure and pride.

Oom Jannie tells them the latest news of the war in Mafeking.

"I was sent home to convalesce after being wounded during a planned

---

[1] Grandfather in Afrikaans.

attack on the Native Stadt. Luckily for me, my wound wasn't serious and has healed well. I'll be returning to Mafeking within the next few weeks."

"Pieter and Willem were both alive and well when I saw them just before I left. I was relieved to see the wound Pieter sustained during a cowardly night-time attack on our trenches by the Khakis had healed. He's most fortunate it didn't fester.

"Don't worry, Marta," seeing her frightened look, *Oom* Jannie reassured her. "After that unexpected attack, we built higher fortifications around our laagers. Our men even planted a telegraph pole next to our fort and hoisted the *Vierkleur*[1] on it."

Marta smiled weakly in response to his attempted humour.

After the meal, Renette and Suné showed Wynand and Alwyn around the farm while Estelle and the two women cleared the table and did the washing up. *Oom* Jannie rested in Papa's favourite chair on the *stoep* and smoked his pipe.

The pungent and rich smell of his tobacco wafted down the passage and into the kitchen, evoking vivid memories of the many warm evenings Estelle had spent on the *stoep* reading with Papa while he smoked. Her eyes pricked with tears and her throat smarted.

Dear Lord, please protect Papa and bring him back to me unharmed.

As they worked, *Tannie* Susannah shared with Marta her anxiety at the increasing number of stories about sexual molestation and rape of women and children left alone on the farms while their men were away on commando.

"I'm worried about you and the girls all alone here on the farm," *Tannie* Susannah said.

Estelle did not understand the word "rape", but she could tell from the horror in her mother's eyes and the way she pressed her lips together into a thin line that it was a bad thing. A terrible thing.

"Who are the perpetrators of these crimes?"

Marta scrubbed the gridiron bars she'd used to cook the *sosaties* over an open fire as if they had committed the crimes she was being told about.

"There is not just one group of perpetrators. As always, men have turned to this most ancient of weapons for demonstrating their power over women,"

Tannie Susannah stacked a dried plate onto the pile and walked across the kitchen to put them away in the cupboard.

---

[1] The *Vierkleur* (meaning four colours) was the flag of the South African Republic.

Estelle stopped her sweeping and glanced at her mother to gauge her reaction to these strange words, but her expression had not changed.

"Have you heard that many of the native labourers on the farms have turned against their Boer employers and are now supporting the British? They are freely roaming the veld and there are stories of groups of them bursting into farmhouses during the night and demanded money from the occupants who are generally women and children." Susannah picked up a coffee mug and started drying it.

Estelle's mother nodded her head, her face had drained of all its colour and her blue eyes stood out against its whiteness.

"Most of us are defenceless," she said, "as our men folk have taken all the weapons in the house with them to the front. The labourers would know this."

"Jannie said that many of the victims of these attacks, together with their children, have resorted to wandering around the veld, too scared to return to their farms. I understand that some of these attacked women were also raped by their assailants."

Tannie Susannah then proceeded to tell Marta about the problems with the *bywoners,* or poor white sub farmers, many of whom had become deserters, called *hensoppers.*

"Some of the *bywoners* have resorted to looting and destroying Boer property after having become *hensoppers* and being ostracised by our men. This is not unexpected, as with no property of their own to fight for, they have no loyalty towards our Republics and don't care about our independence. There have been several claims of inappropriate behaviour by these cowards towards Boer women on the farms.

"Of course, it is not only *bywoners* who are molesting Boer women on the farms, there has also been the odd story of Burghers behaving disgracefully and defiling women."

"What preventative measures are women being advised to take?" asked Marta. "It's expected that we host, feed and care for Burghers who needed food and assistance. What must we do?"

"You must act in the best interest of your children and yourself," said Susannah. "Do not allow false loyalty or misguided pity to cloud your judgement and put your family in a vulnerable position. Regardless of the circumstances of any visitor, you must only open your door to Burghers who are known to you."

"You are right. Mosiko is loyal to Pieter and our family. He'll warn me if he spots horsemen or wagons approaching. I can then lock the girls and myself into the farmhouse and push the heavy wooden table against the door. We'll shutter the windows and wait for any unknown parties to leave."

"You are most fortunate to have an employee like Mosiko."

"I'm grateful for his support of my family, Susannah, as well as for his help with the running of the farm."

Marta suddenly realised that Estelle was there, listening to this uncomfortable and worrying conversation.

"Please go outside, Estelle, and check on the children."

Estelle left the room quietly. She overhead Marta remarking to *Tannie* Susannah as she closed the door quietly behind her.

"That girl has such quiet and unassuming ways about her. She hardly ever speaks, and it is easy to forget she's there. She hears far too much that is not intended for young ears."

Later that afternoon, Estelle brought coffee for her mother and their company as they sat in the *voorkamer*.

The conversation had moved to a lighter topic and *Tannie* Susannah was telling her mother that she had joined one of the women's organisations that had been established to alleviate the suffering of people who had lost their incomes when the big industries and stores in Pretoria had closed due to the war.

"It is a disgrace that so many of the poorer foreigners in the city were left behind to starve when the great exodus of the Uitlanders took place at the start of the war. The women's organisations are helping all innocent victims of the war, regardless of their nationality. They are even assisting the Khaki prisoners of war who are confined in the racecourse in Pretoria by sending them wagon loads of fruit, luxuries and reading materials.

"It is a pity you live here on the farm, Marta. You would have enjoyed working for one of the organisations and it is lovely to have such good company."

After breakfast the following morning, the Oosthuizens left for the three-hour drive back to Pretoria.

The effect of *Oom* Jannie's comforting words during this visit gradually diminished, as the war, which had been expected to be short, dragged on and Christmas approached.

No word or letter came from Papa and Estelle was aware that Marta was becoming more and more fearful about her father's fate and concerned about the eventual outcome of this war.

Was he dead or wounded or had he been imprisoned and exiled? They had no way of knowing and Estelle knew that the uncertainty lurked at the edges of Marta's conscious mind and manifested as nightmares when she slept. She often heard her mother tossing and turning at night and sometimes heard her calling out in her sleep.

Marta continued to find solace in her Bible which she read several times a day to give her strength and peace of mind in God's will for His People.

Sometimes she read quietly to herself, but often she read aloud to the children. Now and then, when she was in a good mood, she would ask Estelle to read passages. These were usually the less popular texts that Marta did not know off by heart which resulted in her stumbling over the words.

PIETER

INJURED

March 1900

Two days after his family learned about General Cronjé's surrender at Paardeberg, Pieter and Mholpi arrived home. Pieter had fractured two ribs when he fell from his horse during an altercation with the British mounted forces who were marching to relieve the besieged town of Kimberley.

Marta removed the dressing that a Red Cross nurse at the hospital in Bloemfontein had applied. The bruises covering Pieter's chest had faded to a light yellowish brown, interspersed with white scars where the thick and crusty scabs had fallen off. The nurse, and then Mholpi, had applied a strong brine solution to his wounds with clean rags to prevent infection.

While Marta went about the task of re-wrapping his chest with her usual stoic lack of emotion, he gave thanks to the Lord for his recovery by reciting Psalm 28:7 about giving thanks. "The Lord is my strength and my shield; my heart trusts in him, and he helps me. My heart leaps for joy, and with my song I praise him."

"Amen," Marta said quietly. "Thank you, Lord, for sparing Pieter's life."

Estelle came to see him later that afternoon. She confessed that she was annoyed with God.

"Why did He let you get injured so badly, Papa, and if the Boers are His chosen people, why has He turned His back on us? Why did He allow General Cronjé to be defeated at Paardeburg?"

"I believe that God helps those who help themselves, Estelle. I think General Cronjé made some bad military decisions and that is why he ended up having to surrender with his men. I'll tell you all about it tomorrow, but I need to rest today."

Estelle hugged him gently.

"I'm glad you are home, Papa. Being stuck here on the farm with hardly any news or information has been awful. We didn't even know you had left Mafeking and were fighting near Kimberley."

The following day, Pieter tells his family about his time on the western front and how, after he'd been injured, the loyal Mhlopi had assisted him home to Irene.

"How did you come to be near Kimberley, Papa? We thought you were still in Mafeking. *Oom* Jannie told us he'd seen you there."

"Willem and I were part of the Boer force that left Mafeking on the 18th of November under the leadership of General Cronjé. We marched southwards to Kimberley. Our generals considered Kimberley to be key to the war on the western front."

"Why is Kimberley more important that Mafeking, Papa?" Estelle looked at him with interest.

"Kimberley's the second biggest city in the Cape Colony and the centre of the diamond mining operations of the De Beer's Mining Company. De Beer's supplies ninety percent of the world's diamonds, and I'm sure this fuelled our leadership's desire to occupy this town."

"Don't forget, Pieter, that Cecil John Rhodes controls De Beer's and the mining activities in Kimberley. I'm sure his being in the town was one of the reasons our generals wanted to occupy it," Marta gently admonished him.

"Yes, you are right, Marta, Cecil John Rhodes' presence in the town was controversial for us."

"Who is Cecil John Rhodes, Papa? Why don't our generals like him?" Renette's smooth brow wrinkled as she tried to understand the conversation.

"He was the Cape premier a few years ago and sponsored a raid by the British to try and overthrow *Oom* Paul and take over the South African Republic. The raid was led by a man called Dr Jameson and it is called the Jameson Raid. Luckily for us, it was unsuccessful, and Dr Jameson was sent to jail," said Marta.

"Your mother is right. There were several reasons why General Cronjé felt it was important for us to join in the fight against the Khakis in the area surrounding the Modder River and Kimberley, and one of them was the presence of Cecil John Rhodes. Whatever the reasons, Willem and I ended up defending the area around the Modder River."

Shifting in the bed, Pieter tried to relieve the pressure on his aching ribs.

"I was injured by falling off my horse during a fight with the Khakis' mounted forces who were riding to relieve Kimberley. When I fell, I feared the worst and thought I would be left behind and captured. Luckily, Willem came to my aide. He managed to help me back onto my horse and we fled the scene and returned to our camp."

"Why did you fall off your horse?" Renette asked. "You are a good rider."

"Yes, I'm an excellent rider," said Papa. "*Oom* Willem and I were scouting with a group of other Burghers when we saw a thick cloud of dust approaching. To be honest, the march on Kimberley under Lord Roberts took us by surprise. The Boers at Magersfontein were engaged in fighting the Khakis under Lord Methuen so they were not able to come to come to our aide. Do you remember that name, Marta? He was the British general who was defeated at Magersfontein on 11 December last year?

"Yes, I remember," Marta leaned forward in her chair. "He was attempting to relieve Kimberley. We heard about our splendid victories at the church service on Christmas Day."

"That's right. It was a black day for us when Lord Roberts replaced Sir Buller as the Commander in Chief of the Khakis in January. Together with his chief of staff, Lord Kitchener, they have implemented massive changes to the scale, organisation and tactics of the British Army. Lord Roberts has brought all the resources of the British Empire to bear against us and numerous reinforcements have increased the Khakis' ranks significantly.

"Anyhow, while the Magersfontein Boers were fighting Lord Methuen, a few other commandos were fighting another division of Khakis, under Major General Hector MacDonald, as he marched westward to Koedoesberg. We were unprepared for a large-scale march on Kimberley, as Lord Roberts had been successful at keeping his plans secret, and our numbers were few between the Modder River and the town. The army we faced comprised five divisions and a whole division of cavalry under Lieutenant-General John French. That equals about forty thousand men, Marta."

Pieter stops talking and gazes into space. Memories assail his mind in a kaleidoscope of sounds, smells and visions.

"At about midday, we saw a large cloud of dust coming our way. Having no idea how many horsemen there were, ten other Burghers,

Willem and I quickly set up an ambush. As they drew closer, we could make out a mass of at least seven thousand horses and men. It was a hopeless situation and we prepared to withdraw, but the Khakis saw us and started shelling our position. My horse took fright at an exploding shell and bolted. I fell and broke two ribs, but luckily my horse is well trained, and he came back to me. *Oom* Willem hoisted me back onto my horse, and we were able to escape."

Marta's pale face and the tension around her mouth and eyes suddenly register with Pieter.

Is she upset because of my injury or because the Burghers ran away?

"It was cowardly of you men to flee, you should have stayed and fought," said Marta, her lip curled with contempt.

How does she think I could have carried on fighting with broken ribs? She's being ridiculous; if we'd carried on fighting, we would've all been killed. A handful of men couldn't hold back such a significant force.

Smiling wryly, he took a sip of water. "Maybe you are right, Marta, but I was in too much pain to influence that decision."

Renette's little face was pinched and anxious.

"Don't worry, little one. I had treatment for my injury at the hospital in Bloemfontein before travelling by train to Pretoria and then home. One of the nurses showed Mhlopi how to apply the healing solution to my wounds. There were also nurses on the hospital train that transported us to Pretoria. I was even gifted a bottle of milk by a woman at one of the stations. Don't worry, Renette, I received good treatment and care.

"Now I think you little girls should go outside and pick some fresh vegetables for dinner. Vegetables will help me get better more quickly."

Renette and Suné left quickly, pleased to have been given this important task to help their papa get better. Estelle stayed behind.

Papa smiled at her.

"Bring me a cup of coffee, Estelle?"

Estelle nodded briefly and left the bedroom.

Some things are best not said in front of young girls, especially Estelle who knows far too much already.

Studying Marta carefully, he shared the bad news.

"I was lucky to receive the care I did in Bloemfontein and that I was able to travel to Pretoria by train. Now that Kimberley has been relieved by the British, Bloemfontein is sure to fall. That is why I decided to travel home before the nurse said I was ready."

He sighed deeply.

"How did General Cronjé end up having to surrender?" asked Marta.

"General Cronjé and his Boers evacuated their camp at Jacobsdal on the 15th of February. That was a good decision as their position at Magersfontein was no longer relevant. Mounted rear guards managed to hold off the Khakis the following day and prevent them from passing the convoy of ox-wagons, but it came under attack when they tried to cross the Modder River at Paardeberg Drift. For some reason, General Cronjé decided to form a laager and dig in on the banks of the Modder River."

"It doesn't sound as if you agree with General Cronjé's decision," Marta's voice was high and strident.

"No, I don't think it was the right strategic decision. He put his men in a position where they would have to withstand a siege by fifteen thousand well-armed Khakis."

"What would you have done?"

"The Khakis had insufficient cavalry. They treat their horses badly and don't care for them properly. Those poor animals arrive at the Cape weak after their long sea voyage and they aren't given any time to rest and adjust to their new environment. Anyhow, it was inadvisable for General Cronjé to form a laager and give the British an opportunity to gather more attacking forces. Given the limited British cavalry, I would have pushed on and joined up with General De Wet's men who were only thirty miles away to the south-east, or Chief *Kommandant* Ferreira's men who were a similar distance away to the north."

Marta's mouth formed into a thin line of disapproval at Pieter's words. Marta continued to hold General Cronjé in high esteem, despite his shocking surrender.

"On the Sunday, Lord Kitchener ordered a frontal attack on the Boer trenches on Paardeberg Hill. This was disastrous for his troops who had to charge down a slope for eight hundred and seventy yards or more to reach the Boer trenches. General Cronjé's men waited until their attackers were only one hundred and ten yards away and then they opened fire. The shelling went on all day and I heard that the Khakis suffered one thousand one hundred casualties with two hundred dead.

"It was a terrible thing, Marta, sending men to be slaughtered like that. The Khakis were brave to have fought all day under those circumstances."

"The only good Khaki is a dead one," Marta's voice was cold. "I've no room in my heart for sadness or pity towards Khakis who fight on a Sunday. The Lord intervened on behalf of our people."

Pieter paused, wondering whether to continue his story or not. *She's become so bitter. The Khakis are people and surely deserve some pity.*

"Go on," Marta waived her hand impatiently.

121

"On that same day, General De Wet attacked and took the British held Kitchener's Kopje, which the Khakis had left practically undefended. This was an important win for the Boers as it changed the strategic picture, allowing General De Wet to shell the Khakis' position on the south-east bank of the river at will. You must remember though, that all our men's wagons, horses and oxen were exposed to the continuous shelling."

Again, Pieter changed the position of his upper body on the plump pillows supporting it.

"General De Wet's men withdrew on the 21st of February. They were faced with an overwhelming number of Khaki forces to their small numbers and feared reinforcements could arrive at any time. General De Wet could not rely on support from General Ferreira's men as they were leaderless after he was accidentally shot dead by one of his own sentries. General Cronjé refused to abandon his laager, so General De Wet was forced to leave without him."

"He shouldn't have left," Marta moaned.

"Well, he did. He was concerned for the safety of his own men. After that, the situation deteriorated rapidly for General Cronjé. Almost every one of his Boers' oxen, mules and horses had been killed. Ammunition had exploded and stores had been ruined. His position was impossible, Marta. Can you imagine the stink and flies with all those decomposing animals?"

Pieter shuddered at the thought, causing his broken ribs to grate painfully against each other. A wave of dizziness forced him to close his eyes and draw in as big a breath as his ribs would allow. By the fourth big breath, the faintness had passed, and he could continue.

"Following a night attack on his trenches on the 27th of February, General Cronjé surrendered with over four thousand men and fifty women. His ill-advised decision to form a laager at Paardeberg Drift caused us to lose about ten percent of our whole army."

Pieter's eyes flashed with anger, but he held his body stiffly immobile, not wanting to bring on another spell of giddiness.

"I heard about his surrender when I arrived in Pretoria, and I was horrified but not really surprised.

"The Khakis also suffered. I heard that hundreds of their men became ill and died from drinking water polluted by our dead cattle and horses."

"Good," said Marta, "I hope they all die."

"But they won't, Marta. The British Empire is throwing men and resources at this war and are using their power at sea to prevent any foreign intervention on our behalf."

Glancing up, Pieter caught sight of Estelle, who was standing outside the bedroom door. She shuddered violently and the coffee cup in her hand fell to the floor, smashing to pieces on the hard wood.

HELLO AND GOODBYE

June 1900

All day the wagon rolls forward across the vast and seemingly never-ending veld. Now the swiftly lengthening shadows warn Pieter that the afternoon is far advanced, and night is coming. The heat of the day is gone, replaced by the raw cold of the Highveld winter nights.

Slowing his horse to a gentle meander, Pieter allows the wagon to catch up to him.

"I'm going to ride ahead and look for water and a suitable resting place for the night."

Estelle raises one blue-tinged hand in acknowledgement. She draws her shawl protectively around her thin shoulders as the biting wind tugs viciously at her tightly braided hair and whips loose pieces around her face.

Over the next rise, a clump of trees, silhouetted against the dark blue sky, comes into view. Pieter rides over to it and dismounts. The scrubby trees encircle a shallow pool of water which has formed in a rocky indentation in the ground.

The sight of the clear water is a relief. Sometimes it takes days to find water when they travel, and their supply drops uncomfortably low.

Pieter scouts about to ensure there are no unwelcome surprises lurking anywhere. Finding nothing, he remounts his horse and heads back to the wagon.

We'll be able to refill the water barrel and give the livestock a satisfying drink too.

By the time the wagon stops at the small thicket of trees, the dark orange sun is slipping into the veld. Estelle climbs down from the wagon seat and lifts her sisters down from the wagon box. They rush around like wild things, eager to stretch their stiff arms and legs.

Pieter and the native women hurry to fill the water barrel and a couple of metal pails with fresh water from the pool.

Marta hands Estelle and Renette a basket each and instructs them to collect kindling for a fire. Suné trails after them, adding bits of dried grass and small sticks to the piles in the baskets.

Mosiko and Mhlopi outspan the oxen and then herd them, together with the other livestock, to the pool to drink their fill.

By the time the children return to the camp, Pieter has cleared an area of ground for the fire.

"We need some rocks for the fire, girls."

Estelle and Renette collect a pile of rocks and place them in a circle around the cleared patch of earth.

Pieter is aware of Estelle's keen attention as he uses the kindling collected by the children and his fire steel and flint to build a roaring fire inside the rocky barrier.

Pieter then sets about digging a deep hole in the ground next to the fire so that Marta can bake *potbrood*.[1]

His tasks complete, Pieter relaxes while Marta mixes the dough and Estelle kneads it. It takes over ten minutes of kneading before the mixture leaves the sides of the bowl clean. Pieter observes Estelle's sigh of relief as she sets the dough near the fire to rise. He makes a mental note to speak to Marta about it. Estelle is a skinny little thing for her age and kneading dough is hard work.

Marta should take a turn during the kneading and give her a short rest.

When the dough has doubled in size, Marta knocks it back and shapes it into a ball. She then places the dough into a greased cast-iron pot and flattens it with her hands until it fills about one third of the pot. Once again, the dough is left near the fire to double in bulk. Once the dough has risen for the second time, Marta brushes it with fat and covers the pot with the lid. Pieter shovels some coals into the hole and Marta places the filled pot on top of these. After placing some more coals on top of the lid, she leaves it to bake until it is crisp and brown.

While the *potbrood* is baking, Estelle helps Marta cook the meat over the open flames of the fire. When the food is ready, Marta serves the *potbrood*, steaming hot and spread with butter, accompanied by chunks of roasted meat.

The family sit on a spread out bucksail[2] laid near to the fire and tuck into their meals with gusto. Marta hands Pieter a strong cup of coffee and pours water into tin mugs for the girls.

---

[1] Bread baked in a heavy cast-iron three-legged pot or a heavy flat-bottomed pot with straight sides, over hot coals in a hole in the ground.

[2] Tarpaulin or canvas covering, often used to cover a buckboard wagon.

After dinner, Pieter sings hymns with Renette and Suné while Marta and Estelle wash the dishes and prepare the beds for the night.

A short distance away, the labourers have set up their own camp.

Klein Frantz has done a great job of building a fire and Ardrina and Dorthea cook their own simple meal of crushed mielies, boiled in a pot over the flames, and roasted meat.

From his seat on the bucksail, Pieter can hear them speaking softly to each other in their own language.

"Papa," Estelle suddenly asks, "why are Mosiko and Mhlopi drinking water. Don't they like coffee?"

Before Pieter can decide how to answer, Marta responds curtly, "I don't have coffee to spare for servants, Estelle."

* * *

"Look, Papa, look," Estelle whispers, pointing towards a patch of veld grass near their camp.

Two green lights shine in the dark, close to the ground. The hairs on his arms stand on end. *It must be an animal of some sort.*

Grabbing his Mauser, Pieter aims it at the eyes, ready to fire. The eyes stop moving forward. They stay still in the dark, looking at them.

Is it a hyena?

Nothing moves in the vast stillness of the African night. The animals are nonchalant and continue to graze peacefully.

Pieter picks up a stone and throws it in the direction of the eyes. The eyes do not move. No wild cackling of a hyena feeling distressed, or snarls of a lioness felling threatened, fill the air.

"It can't be a wild animal," he says quietly.

The tension in Estelle's shoulders relaxes slightly.

Mosiko stands up and moves towards the eyes which slowly draw towards him and, into the firelight, comes the blocky head and well-developed body of a *Boerboel*[1] dog.

The dog is clearly used to people and seems pleased to see them. Pieter sees the wide smiles of his daughters. They love dogs and have missed having one around the house. Even Marta looks pleased as the dog stands there with his tongue hanging out. He looks like he is grinning.

Pieter gives the dog some of the leftover meat and he wolfs it down hungrily. He then lies down near to the fire and sighs a long sigh.

---

[1] The *Boerboel*, is a large, mastiff-type dog breed from South Africa and is bred for the purpose of guarding the homestead and working the farm.

"He reminds me of Hansie, he has the same trusting eyes. I miss that dog," Pieter sighs deeply. "Shooting that dog was one of the hardest things I've ever had to do, but what other option did I have? He'd gone blind from the snake venom and a blind dog cannot survive in the veld."

Estelle visibly shudders. Since Hansie was hit in the eyes by the venom of a Mozambique spitting cobra, she has developed a horror of snakes and won't go anywhere near them.

Pieter had desperately tried to save the dog's eyesight by washing his eyes out using water and milk, but he had gone blind anyway. Marta has mentioned several times that she missed knowing Hansie was there to protect them while Pieter was away. His loud and frantic barking acted as an excellent warning system if any humans or wild animals approached the farm.

"We could use a good dog. He must have come from one of the farms around here. If he's still here in the morning, he can come with us. Now it's time for bed, girls."

Pieter swings Suné into his arms and carries her towards the wagon and her bed.

The dog is still there the following day and takes his place under the wagon when it moves off on its way towards *Oom* Willem's farm. Everyone is pleased that the dog, who they name Karel, has stayed with them.

* * *

Willem's and Sannie's pleasure at the arrival of Pieter's family is obvious.

Sannie hugs everyone. "You're lucky, *Oom* Willem is currently at home. He took a two-week furlough from his commando to come home and check on me and the girls. We hadn't seen him since he left to join his commando with your Papa in September last year."

Lena and Hannekie make a fuss of Renette and little Suné, rushing to hug and kiss them. They greet Estelle with more restraint as her quiet and controlled demeanour does not invite excessive demonstrations of affection, but they are kind towards her.

They soon sweep Renette and Suné away into the house to show them Hannekie's bedroom which they will be sharing, together with Estelle, during their stay. Estelle elects not to accompany them, making a show of needing to settle Karel into his new home.

Willem's relief at seeing his brother in such a good state of health is evident.

He claps him on the back, "Pieter, it is so good to see you looking so well. It is a great relief to me."

The two men set off together to outspan Pieter's oxen. Feile, Kleinbooi and Klein Frantz are then tasked with herding Pieter's livestock towards the natural reservoir that flows a few miles away from the house. Here they will graze with Willem's animals.

The four girls come back outside, giggling and laughing, and everyone helps to unpack the wagon, which has been drawn around the side of the house. There is no space for Pieter's wagon in Willem's barn.

Before long, all items that Pieter's family brought with them have been carried into the house. With so many people staying for an extended period, Sannie is pleased to have the extra blankets, pillows for the beds and additional pots and cooking utensils to supplement her own.

Later that afternoon, Pieter shows Estelle the hen house, and they walk a short way around the farm. The heat of the day has gone, and the evening is cold. It is drier and dustier here, and they can see nothing but stones, thorn-trees, and termite mounds, huge reddish structures that rear up towards the sky.

"What are those tall trees over there?" Estelle points at a group of trees in the distance.

"Those are blue gum trees," Pieter smiles at Estelle's evident joy as she gazes at the vast loneliness of the land.

I hope she'll be happy here.

July 1900

At the end of July, Pieter and Willem leave to return to the struggle. Willem's two weeks' leave had ended weeks before, but the news of the fall of Pretoria on the 5th of June and the subsequent occupations by the Khakis of the nearby towns of Ventersdorp, Potchefstroom and Klerksdorp resulted in his delaying his return to his commando.

"Our capital is now in the hands of the enemy," Willem declared bitterly on the day he should have returned. "Our flag, which has flown over this city for so many years, has been torn down and trampled by the British, who have been trying to destroy our people for a hundred years. I don't know what to do now. Is the war over?"

Pieter gently counselled him.

"All is not lost, Willem. Let's wait and see how our officers decide to deal with these new developments and then we can make our own plans."

"But they have already failed," Willem stormed. "Our president fled Pretoria and the city surrendered with no resistance. The subsequent attempt by General Botha and his Burghers to stop the Khakis from entering the Transvaal Highveld has also failed. You heard the news. They were forced to retreat at Donkerhoek due to the overwhelming numbers of Khakis. Four thousand Burghers with twenty-three guns is no match for an opposing force of over fourteen thousand Khakis with seventy guns."

"We'll go into town next week and hear the latest news, Willem. We can then make a decision about what to do, okay?"

"I'm thinking of accepting Lord Robert's offer and taking an oath of neutrality. At least then I can stay here on the farm in peace and not risk my livestock being confiscated. I'm tired of this war, Pieter."

"We'll talk again next week, Willem. Once we have more information and can make a proper assessment of the situation."

The following week, Pieter and Willem visit the general store in the local town. They return with exciting news.

"Our officers held a war council meeting at Balmoral recently. They've adopted an entirely new military tactic. We'll no longer be employing defensive or passive tactics but will be employing a new strategy of attacking the Khakis as frequently as possible and attempting to obstruct their communication routes."

"How will that work practically?" asks Marta.

"The Burghers will be divided into small groups which will all act independently of each other. The aim is that the Khakis will have to divide their own forces and this will make them more vulnerable to our attacks," Willem waves his arms around in excitement.

"In addition to the Burghers under General Botha, another four commandos are being re-organised including our Lichtenberg Commando," Pieter informs the women.

Later that evening, Pieter engages with his brother about their proposed return to the fight.

In a low, calm voice he says, "You have a hard choice to make, Willem. You can accept Lord Roberts' offer and surrender your weapons. His words could be sincere, and you might get to keep your farm and your livestock. The alternative is that you go to the Potchefstroom District and join up with the Burghers there. This option is risky as if the new military strategy fails, you'll be branded by the Khakis as a rebel and punished accordingly."

"What are you going to do, Pieter?" Willem asks plaintively. "You're faced with the same choice."

"Not really, Willem. My farm is already lost to me because I deserted it. My livestock is here, but I've no land and no home," Pieter is shocked by the bitterness in his own voice.

"I can't believe we are having his conversation, Willem." Sannie's voice cracks like a whip and her words drip with disgust. "The strength of our army in the field must be preserved," she continues. "If you two aren't prepared to return to your commando, then Marta and I'll have to take your places. Someone must fight for the *Volk.*[1] We won't stand by and let you two cowards undermine our hopes for a free Afrikaner nation."

Sannie's frank and disrespectful comments about him and his brother surprise Pieter. He knows that Marta is also keen for him to return to the war, and that is the correct way for her to feel, but she isn't as unpleasant and rude about it as Sannie.

"You are shirking your duty towards your country, Willem, and I'm ashamed of you," Sannie continues coldly.

Willem glowers at Sannie. "It is not your place to comment, Sannie. Of course, Pieter and I plan to return to the fight. We needed to know what was happening first, that's all. We didn't even know where to join our commando before today."

"I'm glad to hear this ridiculous discussion is finished then," Sannie is not suppressed by Willem's admonishment of her. This topic is too close to her heart. "Would anyone like some more coffee?"

On the morning Pieter leaves, Marta and his daughters accompany him to the barn to say goodbye. Marta is grim and terse, and Renette and Suné stare at him glumly. Only Estelle seems controlled and expressionless. He says goodbye to each of them and then turns to look at Estelle.

"Help your mother and look after your sisters." Looking into her green eyes with his bright blue ones, he wordlessly communicates his hope that her relationship with Marta will be better now that she has her *Tannie* Sannie and her cousins to keep her company.

Estelle wraps her arms around him and whispers, "Maybe Mama will be nicer to me now, Papa. I really hope so."

MICHELLE

TOM TAKES A FALL

July 2019

Alice and Michelle sit on the couch in her lounge drinking warming cups

---

[1] A nation of people, in particular, the Afrikaner people.

of coffee. Michelle has a log fire going in the grate and the room is warm and snug. This is the first opportunity they've had to meet up for over a month and Michelle is starting to relax in Alice's easy company.

Alice updates Michelle about the terrific time she had in Cape Town, sharing stories about all the nightclubs she visited and interesting men she met. When she's exhausted all her news, she asks Michelle, "How have things been with you? Did you convince Tom to see Dr Stephenson?"

Alice listens intently to Michelle's update about the night terrors both she and Tom experienced while Alice was away and the visit to Dr Stephenson.

"I wasn't entirely honest about the situation with the ghosts when we last met. I hadn't seen them since the smudging, but I had heard them. The voices of Pieter and Robert were diminished, but they were always there, whispering together. A bit like white noise in an office.

"There was also this awful laughter. I know it belongs to the poltergeist although I never saw her. It was loud, obnoxious and pervasive. The smudging didn't seem to keep her at bay at all, if anything, it seemed to have made her darker and more antagonistic. The visions didn't stop either; I've had some terrible ones. I'm convinced these visions are somehow related to the poltergeist."

Michelle stops speaking, her lips quivering.

Reaching over, Alice takes Michelle's shaking hand. "I'm so sorry, Shelles. What is it like now? Has it remained the same or has the situation deteriorated?"

"I suppose it's deteriorated. Over the past few weeks I've seen the shadows of Pieter and Robert in the corners of different rooms. They've not spoken directly to me or manifested in a more substantial way like they did when I first saw them. I don't know if this changed behaviour is because of the smudging or because the poltergeist is somehow suppressing them."

Michelle takes a gulp of coffee, giving herself a moment to think. Setting her cup back down on the table, she continues. "I believe the poltergeist dominates the two male ghosts, but I could be wrong. She has threatened both Tom and I physically and is aggressive and angry. The behaviour of the two male ghosts is different, less threatening, but that could change. I just don't know what to think about it all."

Estelle, the poltergeist's name is Estelle. I don't want to give her a name because it makes her too real.

Alice considers Michelle's words for a moment before sharing her opinion.

"It could also be that the smudging and St John's wart are working and restricting the behaviour of the two male spirits. These preventative measures don't seem to have impacted the poltergeist as much, although she hasn't threatened you physically recently, has she?"

Alice looks at Michelle expectantly.

"No, I haven't seen her. I've only heard the laughter and experienced the nightmares I told you about. I find it disturbing that she can infiltrate my dreams, Alice."

Alice nods.

"I agree with you. Even if the preventative measures are stopping the poltergeist from manifesting and harming you physically, she must be very strong and determined to be able to infiltrate your subconscious while you are sleeping."

"From what I've seen of her, she is certainly those things and more. She bears a terrible hatred towards Tom and I don't know why."

Michelle thinks of the girl in the room, the one the unseen man had called Tracey and shudders.

Maybe I do suspect why, but I'm not ready to speak to Alice about those suspicions yet.

Forcibly pushing this thought from her mind, Michelle brings her coffee cup slowly to her lips, watching it fixedly in order to avoid meeting Alice's eyes.

"And Tom, how has he been?" Alice looks at her with searching eyes.

"Tom's behaviour has not improved since Dr Stephenson confirmed that he doesn't have a brain tumour or any other kind of malady of the brain. His moods change so rapidly, I find it difficult to judge how he'll react to anything I say, even the simplest things like dinner is ready.

"He's taken six weeks' leave from work. He had long leave due and he decided to take it now. He told me he wants to relax and focus on overcoming his recent insomnia and anxiety. To all intents and purposes, he appears to be taking every possible step to get better and follow Dr Stephenson's advice."

"Really," Alice is interested. "What steps has he taken?"

"He's seeing a physiotherapist once a week to treat the tension in his neck and upper back. He's suffered from chronic pain for a few years but he's never been willing to see a physiotherapist before. He's always preferred to treat his symptoms with pain killers and muscle relaxants. He told me the treatments involve acupuncture and they've helped to release his knots of tension."

Michelle is gabbling in her relief that Alice has not picked up on her odd behaviour and pursued a line of questioning about Estelle's reasons for hating Tom. Her deception has caused the colour to rise in her cheeks.

Withholding information is the same as lying. But I'm not lying, Tom hasn't done anything wrong. I'm sure he isn't a rapist.

"He's resting a lot during the day as his nights are still disturbed. He appears to sleep soundly during these daytime sleeps, but when I've checked on him, I've noticed that his forehead is often puckered up into little wrinkles of agitation and disquiet, as if alien thoughts are intruding on his rest. He is pale and haggard and looks ten years older than he did three months ago."

Michelle pauses again, gathering her thoughts.

"The sleeping pills seem to have made matters worse and he has started walking in his sleep. Fortunately, he doesn't go far, just around the rooms on the second floor, but it is worrying."

"What about sex? Have you made love lately?"

Alice's intense look and question make Michelle squirm uncomfortably.

"No, not recently. He is behaving weirdly about any sort of affectionate gestures and pushes me away if I so much as stroke his hair or touch his arm. It's awful, he's making me feel like … like a leper."

"Have you tried asking him about his behaviour and why he is reacting so strangely?"

A deep sigh escapes Michelle.

"Yes, I have asked, but he won't answer. He puts his fingers in his ears and screws his eyes tightly shut, just like a small boy. I don't know what to do as he won't even consider seeing a psychiatrist or a psychologist. I'm starting to wonder if I should leave him. I can't go on like this."

Alice nods sympathetically.

"I understand how you feel, Michelle. Is there someone else who's close to him who you could discuss this with? Not necessarily your thoughts about the poltergeist, but someone who could convince him to see a psychiatrist. There must be some reason why the poltergeist has zoned in on him the way she has. There must be something in his past that she believes requires vindication, perhaps on behalf of someone else. Do you have any ideas at all?"

Again, the unwanted thoughts flood her mind.

Tracey, who's Tracey and why did I see her in my vision? Who's the unseen man who assaulted her? Could it be Tom? No, that's a ridiculous idea. I'm not going down that road, even in my own head. I'm sure Tom had nothing to do with the death of that woman.

"I suppose I could try speaking to Carl about it," Michelle floats the idea. "He's called a few times to see how Tom's doing. They've known each other since university and they worked their way up at the firm together. They started the corporate finance practice at Kellerman, James & Thompson together ten years ago."

"I think that's a good idea. He may be able to tell you a bit about Tom's past and talk him into seeing a psychiatrist."

"I don't know if he'll tell me anything, assuming there is something to tell. He's loyal to Tom. If I can convince him that it's in Tom's best interests to see a psychiatrist, he might help to convince him. I know he's worried. He asked if Tom was having a mental breakdown."

"Mmm, you may be right. Carl's misguided loyalty to Tom might make him a poor subject for this exercise. What about Trevor? He might be able to tell you a bit about Tom's past. They also go back a long time, don't they?"

Michelle pulls a face.

"Yes, they do, and he might. If I buy him a few drinks he might confide in me. I'll go and see him although I don't like the man."

* * *

In the early hours of the morning, Michelle lies awake in the spare bedroom. She's slept here for the past month as Tom's restless thrashing and moaning all night keep her awake. The sleeping pills force him into a drug-induced sleep but do not seem to stop the nightmares.

The room is pretty with pale lemon curtains and bed linen and a vintage dressing table. It is white and very delicate looking, in a style called French Louis XIV.

I was so happy when I selected this dressing table for this room. Could it really have only been three months ago?

She's been awake since Tom staggered in during one of his sleep walking episodes. She'd gently led him back to his bed and told him to go back to sleep, in accordance with some advice she'd read on the Internet. Tom refused to discuss his sleep walking with his general practitioner or consider seeing a psychiatrist.

I'm not sure he even believes me when I tell him he has been walking in his sleep. He claims he doesn't remember anything about it.

Her conversation with Alice replays in her mind. Her guilt is uncomfortable. There are a lot of things she'd deliberately omitted to tell her friend.

I never told her the details of my vision, or was it a nightmare, involving the woman called Tracey. What I saw was date rape, I'm sure of it. I also never mentioned the newspaper article I found about the suicide of Tracey Atkinson. Tom's quoted in that article. Why him? Kellerman, James & Thompson employs six hundred people in its Pretoria office. He must have known her well to be quoted in that article, and yet he's never mentioned her and neither have any of his colleagues or friends.

She also hadn't mentioned Tom's escalating drinking problem to Alice. The frequent nights out with Trevor when he came home barely able to walk. The only benefit was that the nightmares seemed less intense when he was drunk.

That's probably why he's doing it, to escape the nightmares. How did this happen? How did our lives descend into this complete mess of alcoholism? I suggested that we sell the house and move somewhere else, but he won't hear of it. He refuses to acknowledge any paranormal presences in this place, evil or otherwise.

Alice is right, I must find out if there is something in Tom's past that is causing these issues for us. Everything is pointing in that direction. The strange happenings in this house, Tom's disturbed nights and weird behaviour, the visions I've been experiencing, and even the tarot card reading. There's something I don't know about in his past and it's the route of our current problems. I'm going to speak to Trevor and see if he'll tell me anything. If I meet him in a bar, the booze may loosen his tongue and he might tell me more than if I speak to him sober. Not that I'm likely to ever catch him sober anyway.

Michelle falls into a thin and fitful sleep, waking up at 7 a.m. with the cold winter sun forcing its way through the light material of the yellow curtains.

* * *

Entering the restaurant, Michelle sees Trevor sitting at the bar, a neat whiskey in front of him.

Of course, he drinks them straight and without ice. He wouldn't want to dilute the effect of the alcohol.

Behind the bar counter stand rows of bottles, twinkling in the soft light. As she draws closer, she's sure she can see the shape of a bayonet reflected in the glass of an oversized whiskey bottle. She gives her head a little shake and plasters a smile on her face.

"Hello, Trevor, it's nice to see you."

Trevor rises from his tall bar stool and gives her a hug, in the typical manner of the directors of the firm on meeting one of the wives.

"Hi Michelle, it's lovely to see you. I haven't seen you since your housewarming party."

The lines in his forehead deepen momentarily and Michelle wonders what he remembers about that night and whether he doesn't think it was all a drink induced hallucination on his part.

"Shall we sit in one of the booths?" asks Michelle. "They're more private."

"Sure, let's order a round and we can sit in that booth in the corner."

Trevor drains the last of his whiskey and turns to the young bartender. "Another double, no ice. And for you?" Trevor looks at Michelle.

"I'll have a diet coke, please," Michelle can't drink at this time of day.

The bartender, a young man with a lovely smile, pours their drinks. He gives Michelle diet coke from one of the vats and she regrets not asking for a can. The drinks from the vat always taste different and not in a good way.

Carrying their drinks, they walk over to the booth Trevor selected and sit down.

Michelle wonders how to start, but Trevor beats her to it. "What is it you want to ask me about? Go ahead, I'm all ears." The words were slightly condescending, but Michelle thinks this is just his way of getting the discussion started.

He must know I don't like him. That I think he's a lush.

These thoughts shock her into speaking. "I want to know about Tom's past and, in particular, his relationship with a woman named Tracey Atkinson."

There, it's out in the open. He can either answer me or skirt around it. I hope he answers. If he doesn't, I'll have to find another source of information.

Trevor looks vaguely surprised, but he starts to speak. "Tracey Atkinson. That's a name I haven't heard for over ten years. Tracey was a girl Tom dated many years ago, before you joined the firm, I think."

He looks at her and she nods her affirmative.

"Tom dated Tracy for a few months in her final year of articles. As you know the firm doesn't encourage directors to become romantically involved with articled clerks, but it happens. Tom was quite a playboy at the time and had enjoyed a string of flings and short-term romances before he became involved with Tracey. His previous affair had ended on a sour note when he was caught screwing the girl on the desk in his office. Excuse my French," Trevor pauses looking uncomfortable.

"It's okay," Michelle encourages him, "I've heard that term before."

"Well, the executive board didn't take such carryings on in the office lightly and he was given a warning. At the time, he was also drinking heavily, but it was controlled and didn't impact on his working day.

There had also been a couple of incidents at social events which had come to the ears of the executive committee. He was told to get his act together and behave himself."

Trevor stops at the sight of the slight frown that wrinkles Michelle's brow.

"Go on," she says, "it's a bit strange to learn these unexpected things about Tom. He's always been such a gentleman towards me."

Except for recently. Maybe the old saying that a leopard never changes its spots is true, after all.

Trevor sighs heavily, his eyes sinking even more deeply into his eye sockets. "Tracey was assigned to one of his audits, this was before he branched into corporate finance. She was an excellent worker and received top notch ratings for her performance. That's always great for a partner, you know. Saves us some effort and work if the clerk in charge of the audit is reliable and does a good job. Anyhow, she was well rated among the partners, but she was a bit odd. Never socialised and was a quiet and withdrawn little thing. There were some rumours that she had been sexually abused by a relative in her past, but I never knew about that for sure. She was a strange choice for a man like Tom."

A slightly perplexed look crosses Trevor's face. "He befriended her, and they started going out together. He kept a lid on his drinking and wild behaviour and wined and dined her in a most respectable manner. Everything was going splendidly until the firm's year-end function in November 2010. Tom and Tracey attended together, and he reverted to his old ways and got very drunk. It was after 2 a.m. when they left together. Going upstairs to a room Tom had booked for the night. Booking a room wasn't an uncommon practice. Lots of people did it, knowing they would be too drunk to drive home after the party. It's one of the reasons the function was always held at a hotel. That, and the fact that few venues could cater for such a large group."

Michelle struggles to maintain her smile. The parallels between Tom's behaviour during his courtship with Tracey and his courtship with her are unmistakable.

But what went wrong with Tracey? Why did their relationship end?

Trevor stops again and gulps down the remaining half of his drink. He signs to the bartender to bring him another.

When the golden drink has been placed in front of him and he has taken a sustaining sip, he carries on. "The following Monday, Tracey didn't arrive at work. She called in sick which was most unusual. Tom's behaviour was odd too, he was quiet and introspective, and had a bit of a haunted look. She came back to work, more introverted than ever. The relationship between Tom and her ended abruptly and she just put her head down and worked even harder. She'd completed her training contract and was offered a permanent contract which she accepted, with the proviso that she wanted to transfer to the Johannesburg office. This term was agreed to. The audit partners wanted to retain her as she was a good worker."

He takes another large gulp and gazes into the amber depths of his whiskey. Inhaling deeply, he continues. "Tom's relationship with her ended and we didn't hear anything much about her for several weeks until we got the news that she had committed suicide. It was a terrible shock and it took Tom months to get over it. He stopped drinking and became a shadow of his former self. He didn't date again until he met you and that was a good few years later."

"February 2014," Michelle recalls the date immediately.

"Yes, February 2014. After he met you, he became more like his old self although he never drank heavily again until recently."

He looks at Michelle questioningly.

"He's been suffering from stress lately," Michelle evades his unspoken question. "A few references to Tracey Atkinson have come up and I thought it might have something to do with the source of his recent anxiety. He doesn't want to see a psychiatrist or psychologist to discuss his problems so I thought I would do a bit of an investigation myself."

"Tom's a good guy. I hope he comes right with whatever problems he's currently struggling with."

"So do I, Trevor, so do I."

* * *

Tom's behaviour takes a sudden and strange turn on Sunday evening. He staggers home, drunk, at 7 p.m., after spending the greater part of the day bar hopping with Trevor. Michelle has cooked dinner and the food is ready.

She dishes up while the food is still warm and they sit down to eat their meal at the dining room table. No wine is served as the thought of it sours Michelle's stomach and Tom prefers to stay with whiskey. Michelle makes inane conversation, unable to bear the loudness of her own distressed thoughts.

She's in the kitchen clearing up when a series of yells from the television room cause her to drop the plate she has rinsed. It falls to the floor and smashes.

Rushing into the adjacent room, she witnesses Tom in the grip of what seems to be some sort of religious fervour. He's throwing his arms around and babbling on about his past sins and salvation.

The television is showing an evangelistic programme. The pastor on the screen catches Michelle's eye. He's a tall and graceful man with greying brown hair and eyes that blaze out of his thin face as he imparts his message about God's love.

"God loves you," the television booms. "He loves each and every one of you. Those of you who've lived exemplary lives and those of you who've sinned. He loves you so much he sacrificed his only son for you."

"Hallelujah," the exulted shout issues from Tom's straining throat.

Sweat rolls down his face and his eyes glow with religious zeal.

Michelle is stunned. Tom has always adamantly declared himself an atheist. It's never worried her as she prescribes to her own brand of religion which does not extend to worshipping with others in a manmade structure.

Sitting down in a chair, she furtively watches her husband. She hopes she is observing him in a way that is not obvious as she doesn't want a confrontation with him. She's been observing him subtly for thirty minutes or more and he is getting more and more excited and caught up in the sermon on the screen, when all at once a transformation takes place. His vigour becomes quiet resignation and his bright and intense eyes become lack-lustre and dull.

Turning her attention back to the television, she watches the pastor who's embroiled in a healing process. A queue of disabled people have lined up, but this is not what's caused the change in Tom. He's looking at the woman on the stage who is in the process of being healed.

She's pretty, with long blonde hair and clear skin. Her lustrous eyes shine in her youthful face. She totters across the stage on medium sized heels and drops to her knees in front of the pastor. He reaches out towards her.

"What is your ailment, my child? How can I help you?" he intones.

Under the camera's watchful eye, the woman looks up at him.

"My name is Tracey Atkinson. I'm dead and I want to live."

The pastor is shocked. He opens his mouth and speaks forcefully. "I can't raise the dead. I'm a healer and God works through me, but I cannot give life."

The woman on the stage starts to fade, her presence becoming fainter and less recognisable until she can no longer be seen. The pastor and audience stare at the empty space where she'd been standing.

In the audience, a shrieking laugh destroys the heavy silence. The camera pans towards the sound and picks out a young girl. Her attire is unusual. She's wearing an old-fashioned bonnet which obscures her face, and a long dress with buttons all the way up the front. She looks like she's stepped out of an old photograph taken in the 1900s.

Laughter spews from her like vomit. "No, you can't raise the dead, Pastor John," she says between eruptions. "Only the responsible party can correct the evils of the past. Doesn't the Bible say, *an eye for an eye*, Pastor?"

Michelle glances at Tom, still seated in his chair. His face has taken on an ashy look. On the television, the pastor recovers quickly and moves on to the next person in the line. An elderly woman in a wheelchair is already rolling across the stage. The cameras re-focus on the pastor as he launches into his healing litany, this time with a more viable subject.

Tom gets up, moving quickly towards the drink's cabinet. He pours himself a strong neat whiskey and sits back in his chair.

"Do you want to come and talk to me while I finish in the kitchen?" Michelle asks hopefully.

"No, I'm enjoying this programme," his attention returns to the television screen.

Michelle finishes tidying up the kitchen and calls good night to Tom from the doorway. He barely acknowledges her comment. Turning away from him, hurt, she heads upstairs to her book and bed.

***

Every afternoon for the next two weeks, Tom disappears and comes home just before dinner at 7 p.m., stumbling through the door and disinterestedly rushing his way through the meal Michelle has painstakingly prepared.

Afterwards, he sits in front of the television, drink in hand, and watches evangelistic programmes about repenting your sins until well after midnight.

From 10 p.m. every evening, Michelle lies awake in the spare bedroom, listening to the soft drone of the television in the lounge and considering the steadily worsening situation with her marriage. His long leave is at an end and he needs to go back to work.

What should I do? Should I tell him I want a divorce?

She thinks about it, considers it, probes it, wondering how her marriage has gone so wrong in such a short space of time.

Eventually, Tom lumbers upstairs, takes a sleeping pill, and falls into bed. He tosses and turns in the vice-like grip of his on-going nightmares, until he finally falls into an alcohol and drug-induced sleep.

Disturbed by her thoughts, Tom's restlessness, and her own relentless dreams, Michelle's sleep is light and unfulfilling.

During the mornings, while Tom continues to sleep his drugged and disturbed sleep, Michelle does her client work and continues to do research on her book.

It's an uphill journey as she is tired and troubled, both of which inhibit her concentration. Eventually Tom leaves the house. She relaxes, her eyes refusing to stay open and her cotton wool mind losing focus, until she's forced to take a short nap in the lounge, lying on the carpet in front of the fire.

The Sunday night before Tom is due to return to work, Michelle lies awake even longer than usual, finally drifting off after 2 a.m. Exhaustion catapults her into a deep and dreamless sleep.

Thump! Thump!

Michelle jerks awake.

"Help me! Help me!"

Leaping out of bed she rushes out of her room and onto the landing. A crumpled and groaning heap lies at the bottom of the stairs.

"Tom," her scream is loud and piercing in the semi-darkness of the early morning. "Oh my God. Tom!"

Running down the stairs she falls to her knees, bending over his broken form. A tear splashes onto his exposed cheek.

He opens his eyes and whispers hoarsely, "Call the doctor. I think I've broken my spine."

His eyes flutter closed as he succumbs to the pain.

Michelle stands and tries to think what to do. A headache thumps painfully in her temples, making thinking hard. She closes her eyes and massages her forehead.

"Michelle," the voice has a strong British accent.

She looks up into the amber eyes of the British soldier. His voice is warm and soothing. "You need to call for an ambulance. Don't call the local emergency services, they'll take too long. Call your Community Active Policing organisation. They'll arrange an ambulance."

He's right. I'll call CAP, they'll get an ambulance here quickly. Where's my phone?

Her cell phone is lying on the coffee table in the television room, charging. She dials the emergency number of CAP and, after a single ring, a voice answers, "You have reached CAP, what is your emergency?"

"My name is Michelle Cleveland and I live at number 17, Irene Community Estate. My husband has fallen down the stairs and I need an ambulance."

"I can arrange that for you. What are his symptoms?"

"He's passed out now, but he said he thought he'd broken his back."

Tears run unchecked down her face and her voice fights its way free of her narrowed throat.

"Is he bleeding profusely?"

"No, I didn't see any blood."

"Okay, I'll call hospital and arrange for an ambulance. It'll take about twenty minutes. Don't try and move your husband and if he wakes up, try to keep him as still as possible."

"I'll do that. Thank you."

Michelle hangs up. Tom is lying immobile on the floor.

The ghost speaks again. "The medical staff will ask you what happened. He reeks of alcohol and they'll know he was drinking heavily before he fell. They may question you about his recent behaviour. Whatever he says when he comes around, don't mention anything about ghosts or visions to anyone. Most importantly, don't say that Estelle pushed Tom down the stairs. The authorities are better off believing that Tom's fall was an accident."

"Estelle? The poltergeist? She's Pieter's daughter, isn't she?"

"Yes, she is Pieter's daughter."

Oh my God, this gets more and more complicated.

Michelle looks at Robert, this strange unearthly presence through which she can see the wall of the entrance hall.

"Why is it better if people believe Tom's fall was an accident? It wasn't! Why shouldn't I tell them what really happening?"

"Because they won't believe your story. Only you've seen Pieter, Estelle and I. Pieter and I have never appeared to Tom and he's only seen Estelle once or twice. He's mainly heard her voice and felt her dark presence. If you start making wild accusations about a ghost pushing your husband down the stairs, the authorities may think you tried to kill Tom and guilt has made you mentally unstable. You'll make yourself a suspect in this crime."

Eyes wide with shock at this unexpected possibility, Michelle asks, "But what if Tom says he was pushed down the stairs by a ghost. Won't that implicate me anyway? People don't believe in ghosts and I'm the only other person in the house."

"If Tom says anything about ghosts, and it's unlikely that he will, don't corroborate his story. He has been drinking heavily and his word is unreliable. It won't be difficult for you to get witnesses, if necessary, to his recent excessive drinking as he's been doing it in public."

"Okay, I understand, and I'll do as you say. I didn't plan to say anything about ghosts anyway. Who would believe me? Do you know why Estelle did this? Why? Why does she hate Tom so much?" Michelle's voice is shrill and hysterical to her own ears.

"Estelle has a vendetta against Tom for her own personal reasons. Her evil is strong, and she has been preventing Pieter and me from visiting you. The St John's Wart and smudging have also made it difficult for us. They didn't affect Estelle as she is too powerful to be stopped by such things. Her anger and hatred have made her resilient and resourceful."

Lifting her hands to her temples and rubbing them, Michelle mutters, "What more can I do to protect Tom? I just don't know what to do."

"Michelle, Tom's back is broken, and he is paralysed from the waist down. He'll be in hospital for a long time. He is safer there than here as it'll be more difficult for Estelle to gain free access to him while he's in intensive care and under constant surveillance. While he's recovering, you need to help Pieter and me expel Estelle and her wickedness from all of our lives."

"Pieter and you? But you two hate each other. I've seen you attacking each other."

"We did hate each other, Michelle. The intervention of Estelle in all our lives has enabled us to speak to each other and set aside our own personal issues. Fortunately, neither of us became so entrenched in our bitterness towards the other that we followed Estelle down the path of no spiritual return. We have agreed to put our differences aside to overcome the threat posed by Estelle and hope that eventually, our individual stories will become known to prevent others from following similar paths of spiritual destruction."

The sound of an ambulance siren in the distance interrupts their conversation.

"I must go," Robert immediately disappears.

* * *

Just after 4 a.m., Michelle staggers back through her front door.

At least I remembered to lock it before I left last night.

After the paramedics had loaded the stretcher holding Tom into the ambulance, she had elected to follow it to the hospital in her own car.

It had taken hours to admit him, filling in form after form and answering numerous questions from the nurses and the doctor.

Climbing the steep, steep stairs takes the last of her energy. She changes into her nightie and pulls back the quilt on the bed, deciding that sleep takes precedence over other ablutions. The edge of the quilt catches on a book and it falls to the floor with a crash.

What the hell is that?

Stumbling back three steps, she sits down hard on the floor. The book has fallen open and she can see yellowing pages covered in spidery writing. The date reads as the 19th of November 1899.

ROBERT

ROBERT'S DIARY

19 November 1899

General Cronjé's laager to the south-west of Mafeking, broke up and trekked south today. My squadron was posted to the Heights and had an excellent view of the whole process. It was a curious feeling watching the long line of canvas covered ox-wagons, together with herds of cattle, moving away from the town.

"What does it mean?" asked Richard. "Will the siege soon be over?"

"I can't be sure," I told him, "but I don't think the siege will end yet, they have left plenty of men behind to continue to engage us. The fact that they have sent such a large contingent of their force to the south is interesting though. Their compatriots in the Orange Free State obviously need their support."

As the dust obscured the vehicles of the departing forces, Creaky's bombardment of the town and the sniping from the trenches, continued.

2 December 1899

Today, like every other day, started with Creaky discharging shells into the town and on-going sniping by the enemy's guns, which have been strategically placed to rake the town, Stadt and defences on the Heights.

As the day grew progressively hotter, the shelling slackened, and everyone, Boers and defenders, rested through the sultry noonday hours. In the late afternoon, the Boers roused themselves and the shelling recommenced, carrying on until about thirty minutes before sundown. The fighting has fallen into a daily routine which is quite predictable and I've learned to appreciate this peaceful half hour, before the inky blackness of night descends on the land.

The occupants of the town enjoy this short reprieve too and emerge from their bomb shelters to sit on the steps or sandbags and discuss the day's activity and the resulting damage. The shepherds drive herds of mules through the dusty streets to be watered and the goats and cattle are brought into the town for the night, after spending the day grazing in the veld as close as possible to the town for safety purposes. The Boers are notorious for stealing livestock.

Tonight, the supper tables in the mess hall buzzed with the news that Lieutenant-Colonel Wilson had received a letter from his wife, Lady Wilson, saying that she's being held captive at the Boer laager. Apparently, General Snyman will only release her in exchange for a horse thief named Mr Petrus Viljoen.

Lady Wilson is highly regarded by the men and the citizens of the town so much irritation and distress was expressed towards the Boers and their dastardly ways. We had all understood that she was safe at Setlagoli, approximately fifty miles away. It was a shock to find out that she'd been captured by the Boers and was now being used as a bargaining tool.

While I've been writing tonight, the Boers have been shelling the town. Every night they shell us for approximately an hour and as soon as Creaky utters its final booming "good night" at 9 p.m., everyone not on duty goes to bed, often fully dressed.

I will close by saying that I have made peace with the fact that I am a prisoner in this town until the siege ends. The days pass slowly but I try to make the most of them, after all, a day survived, is a day worth celebrating.

6 December 1899

I could have died yesterday. Twice!

The general store had barely opened its doors for the day, when I popped in to buy some tobacco. I was paying at the till when a shell tore through it and exploded in the next store, knocking over a civilian who was taken to the hospital for treatment.

The noise caused my ears to ring for a few hours afterwards, but thankfully, it passed before I went on duty at 12 p.m. The overdose of adrenaline made me slightly nauseous and everything I looked at for the rest of the day was overly bright and magnified in detail. It was a close shave and I am grateful to God for sparing me.

At 3 p.m. a thunderstorm blew up. My squadron was manning the defence of the riverbed when we saw the storm approaching. The sky grew dark as night, lit up at close intervals by brilliant streaks of lightening and accompanied by ferocious peals of thunder.

I gave orders for the men to gather our equipment, but the rain was upon us before we were half done and we were forced to evacuate when the river turned into a raging flood.

We dashed for shelter, water streaming from our hair and clothes as we ran through rain, so heavy, it was like a waterfall.

By the time we reached the town, the market square had turned into a lake, the streets had become rivers, and the bomb shelters and trenches were brimming with water. There was no risk of the Boers taking advantage of the chaos as their situation was even worse. They were in their trenches when the storm hit and had nowhere to shelter from the cloudburst.

Richard found me sheltering in the mess hall a while later. I was entertaining a few mates with some stories about my day. I cannot write a lie, so I'll admit right up front that I exaggerated a bit.

"God spared my life this morning and I played it forward by saving Captain Fitzclarence's life," I told them.

"Go on, Mate, tell us how God saved your life."

"I was in the general store this morning, when a shell came right through it. The force threw me into the air, and I missed being blown to pieces by inches."

I illustrated the small distance, using my thumb and pointing finger.

"It was terrifying, my hair is standing on end again as I tell you the story. I've been thanking God all day for guiding that shell right past me.

"The shell exploded in the next store and a civilian was knocked over. I heard he's fine though, he only suffered a few scrapes and lacerations."

I noticed Richard just then standing on the edge of the crowd and pulled him into our conversation.

"Hi Richard, how are you? This weather is crazy, the rain is still pouring down."

"Hi Robert, I'm glad I found you here. This weather is normal for this part of the world. The rain will stop soon, these storms always pass after a few hours."

"Come on, Robert," yelled one of the men. "Tell us the rest of your story. How did you save our good Captain's life today?"

I couldn't disappoint them, so I continued with my tale.

"When the storm broke, I was manning the riverbed with Captain Fitzgerald and some other men. We prepared to evacuate, but a mass of water came rushing down the river course before we had finished salvaging our equipment. Captain Fitzgerald was just behind Al and me when the flood arrived. It knocked the captain right off his feet and was sweeping him away when Al and I jumped back in and grabbed hold of him. We managed to drag him to the riverbank, and it all turned out well. He would have drowned, otherwise, and that's a fact."

"Three cheers for Al and Robert for saving the captain," shouted the men.

I must confess that their appreciation of our actions was gratifying.

Richard's prediction proved to be correct and at 5 p.m. the rain stopped as suddenly as it started. Everyone was soaked to the skin and shivering with cold.

B.P.'s staff at headquarters quickly rose to this new challenge, and by 7 p.m. dry clothing had been handed out to all the people who had no changes and brandy and quinine served to the men defending the trenches. The women and children were fetched by wagon from the laager and provided with blankets as needed.

I heard today that the men on Cannon Kopje suffered the most as all their possessions were swept away and their shelters flooded. They spent a wet and miserable night, but consoled themselves that the enemy were even worse off, with no way of drying their wet clothing or replacing it.

I know this is true because I watched some of our men open fire on the Boers as they attempted to emerge from their flooded trenches. This resulted in a lively retaliation which lasted a good thirty minutes.

I personally think the men enjoyed having a go at the Boers in retaliation for General Snyman's refusal to exchange Lady Wilson for Mrs Delpoort, a Dutch lady who had expressed a wish to leave Mafeking. The Boer general will only exchange Lady Wilson for Petrus Viljoen, a man who was convicted of horse theft before the war and falls under the jurisdiction of the civil authorities in the town and not the military. They don't want to take responsibility for giving up a convicted criminal and this has left B.P. in a difficult position.

7 December 1899

Lady Wilson returned to Mafeking today.

I arrived at breakfast to find all the men in a state of great excitement. B.P. had consented to exchanging Lady Wilson for the criminal.

Apparently, Lord Edward Cecil, the son of the British Prime Minister and B.P.'s Chief Staff Officer, came forward and said it was unseemly for an Englishwoman to be left in the hands of the Boers and transported by coach to Pretoria under who knew what sort of conditions. He insisted that the exchange be made on General Snyman's terms and undertook full responsibility for the decision.

The expectant excitement grew even greater when a short truce was declared between the Boers and us to allow the exchange to take place.

My squadron and Richard watched the exchange with great interest from our look out station on the Heights. The mule cart carrying Lady Wilson and her escort of Boers set off from the laager and met the British party, carrying a white flag and escorting Mr Viljoen, about two thousand yards outside Mafeking.

Through a pair of field glasses, I watched the Boer being handed over into the care of his friends. I'd heard from the chaps manning the prison that he didn't want to leave its relative safety and return to his "friends" at the laager.

At the same time, the mule cart carrying Lady Wilson was urged forward by the driver, charging onto the main street of Mafeking at a gallop.

The distant figures of B.P. and Lord Cecil rushed out to greet her and the men in the trenches gave three rousing cheers which we could hear all the way over at the Heights. We all joined in with gusto and were astonished at how, despite the boredom and the hardship of the siege, our English patriotism and pride is still strong among us.

Lady Wilson was quickly whipped away to safety, barely reaching the house where she was to shelter before Creaky fired a parting shell at the town.

Lady Wilson's ordeal came up again during supper.

"Do you think the Boers treated her badly?" asked Richard, his eyes wide with anxiety.

"Not at all. I heard she was treated with great deference by everyone, from General Snyman and *Kommandant* Botha to the least important of the Burghers. Apparently, they were all exceedingly civil towards her," one of the men who worked at B.P.'s headquarters confirmed.

That was a relief to both Richard and I. I must admit I've been quite surprised by these farmers. Many of them can speak good English and they are always well mannered, although their demeanour is often grave and almost dour.

For some reason today, the Boer whose life I spared in the trench on the night of the bayonets has been on my mind. He spoke excellent English. I wonder if he's still here in Mafeking, or if he was among the Boers who left with General Cronjé a few weeks ago. That's assuming he's still alive, of course, but I believe he is.

24 December 1899

Christmas Eve fell on a Sunday this year. B.P. decided to celebrate Christmas a day early as he wasn't sure if the Boers would extend their ceasefire to the 25th of December. Apparently they celebrate Christmas Day on the 1st of January.

I attended the Christmas service at the church and then headed for the gymkhana B.P. had organised from 11 a.m. to 2 p.m. There was a good line up of events including climbing the greasy pole for a pig, although there was no pig to win there was another prize, tent pegging, two pony races, and a polo match. It was a happy and relaxed gathering as everyone, residents and soldiers, let their hair down after a trying two months.

Richard's family attended the gathering and I enjoyed spending some time with them in between my participation in the sporting events. I spoke to Richard's father, Mr Johnson, for the first time since my arrival in Mafeking.

He is a gentleman and our paths rarely cross, other than a fleeting "hello, how are you?", as we go about our various occupations and duties in the town. If it wasn't for the comradery created by the siege and Richard's role as a cadet to my platoon, I doubt we would have ever interacted.

Samuel Johnson is a tall man, with light brown hair and a neat moustache. His responsibilities at the bank clearly lie heavily on his shoulders as a great deal of his conversation revolved around his work, even though it was a holiday. He asked me how long I thought the siege would last and sighed heavily when I said I thought we still had a few months to go, lamenting the huge impact of the war and siege on the economy and development of Mafeking.

He has a high forehead denoting his great intelligence and I got the impression he is a man who spends more time reading newspapers and books than conversing with his family and other people. He is every inch a gentleman and, despite his patriarchal attitude towards his family, it is obvious that he loves his children and adores his wife.

He told me that he is the fourth generation of his family in South Africa, his great-grandparents having been among the first English speaking settlers to be sent to Algoa Bay in the Eastern Cape in 1820. His family have maintained their ties with England and are opposed to the growth of Afrikaner nationalism in South Africa.

While I was talking to Mr Johnson, Richard's sister, Emily, came running over to show me her new summer dress. The skirt flared out as she spun around, giggling with delight. Eliza also had a new dress which she sauntered over to show off in a quiet and refined manner, which she clearly considered better suited her older age of nearly thirteen.

Mr Johnson positively beamed at his two girls, taking great pride in their fair prettiness, inherited from their mother. Richard also clearly inherited his blond hair from his mother, but he has a lot of his father's looks about his physique and eyes.

"I was so pleased that Dall's Store got in a supply of summer dress materials, laces and ribbons before Christmas," Mrs Johnson confided to me. "I made the girls these new dresses and they're so pleased with them. It's also lovely that they have the children's Christmas tea party this afternoon to wear them too."

Richard and I exchanged small gifts. Knowing he likes to write notes about everything, I bought Richard a diary for 1900, which I procured from a store in the market square. He gave me a pound of Von Erkom's prize medal Transvaal tobacco which I greatly appreciate.

Richard also showed me an extract from Friday's edition of *The Mafeking Mail Special Siege Slip No. 36* and we had a good laugh over an article entitled "Christmas Holidays", which illustrates the extraordinarily good sense of humour that prevails in the town, in spite of the siege:

Christmas Holidays[1]
Going away by train at holiday time being likely to "Boer"
us no
SPECIAL TRAINS
Will be run to
Lobatsi, Francistown, and other places of interest during
Christmas week.
Dutch inhabitants of Trenches, Earthworks and other sub-
urban localities wishing to visiting Mafeking need not take
RETURN TICKETS

---

[1] Historical Paper, The Library, University of the Witwatersrand Location: Johannesburg. Collection number A2706

but will be invited to remain here boarded and lodged
FREE
Upon production of a Mauser.

The band was delightful and played some lively tunes, and I enjoyed seeing Emily and Eliza's excitement and pleasure at the various events, especially when Richard came second in the lads' handicap race. It made a pleasant change to see all the children having fun and their pinched and frightened looks gone for a while.

Lady Wilson and Mr Weil, a local wholesaler and importer of goods, had organized a Christmas tree and tea for the two hundred and fifty children of the town, many of whom were living in the Women's Laager. The afternoon rang with the sound of their joyous laughter as they ran about, cheering shrilly as they waved their small Union Jacks.

"It's good to see the children enjoying themselves," said Mrs Johnson. "The conditions in the Women's Laager are awful. The women and children are living in wagons and tents, which are overcrowded and very hot at this time of year. Frankly, it isn't safer there because it is regularly shelled by the Boers, which is why I decided to continue living in town with Richard and the girls.

"During the periods when the town is being shelled, the women and children shelter in a dark and cramped trench. At the hospital we are seeing continuous cases of children suffering from inflammation of their eyes and fever as it is impossible to maintain proper hygiene and sanitation under those conditions."

"I think you're safer in your house than in the laager," said Robert. "Your bomb shelter is well built, and the conditions are much better and cleaner there. I wonder how much longer this siege will last?"

25 December 1899

All the troops were on duty on Christmas Day, but it passed quietly.

We quickly established that the Boers did treat Christmas Day in the same manner as they would a Sunday which translated into another day's reprieve from the shelling and sniping.

I attended the Church of England service in the morning. It gave me a lot of pleasure to hear the words of the Christmas service and join in the singing of the traditional carols, knowing that back home in England my friends and relatives would be doing the same thing.

At 11 a.m., my squadron relieved the look-outs on the Heights, who dashed off to attend the mid-day church service before partaking of a decent Christmas lunch in the mess hall.

It was a lovely, clear day and from our elevated positions we were able to see the countryside for miles around. The smoke from the Boers fires rose in lazy columns as they cooked their Christmas meal, but other than that, nothing stirred on the endless vista of yellowish-brown veld.

We passed the hot, stifling afternoon discussing the latest news of the fighting to the south. A lone messenger had managed to wend his way through the Boer forces the evening before, bringing news that the fighting was going badly for Britain.

"Three major defeats in six days is ridiculous," Jack Simmons declared. "Britain hasn't suffered a run of defeats like this since the Napoleonic wars, and those were nearly one hundred years ago. I'm embarrassed on behalf of our leadership."

His round face was bright red with emotion as he spoke with the fervour of youth.

Jack hails from Suffolk, same as me, and he's good sort. We've become good mates, but his hot headed and evocative comments can irritate me sometimes. Given half a chance, he's sure to ignore his orders and end up getting himself killed.

"The worst part of it, is that our troops are being annihilated by a bunch of … of ignorant farmers," Jack spluttered.

His remark reminded me again of the Boer in the trench, the one called Pieter whose life I spared. During our brief encounter, he came across as being well educated and informed. I couldn't mindlessly kill a man like him.

I think our military leaders have completely underestimated these Boers, who are intelligent and cunning, as well as being fanatical about their Fatherland and their *Volk*. They are completely different to the Sudanese many of military brass fought against in North Africa. The Boers have a strategy and it doesn't include getting themselves killed by facing our troops in frontal attacks.

"You mustn't underestimate these Boers," I told Jack, "they aren't ignorant. Most of them are good marksman, with the ability to judge distance accurately. We've witnessed their skill with their Mausers right here in Mafeking. You also know they avoid engaging in open battle. When they attack, they are always widely scattered, which makes them difficult targets. They also always use flanking tactics to try and achieve an advantageous position over our troops. Our generals tried simple frontal assaults which were doomed to failure. They didn't develop their military strategies based on a knowledge of the enemy."

Jack's expression was one of shock at these words, but I could almost see the cogs turning in his brain as he chewed over what I'd said. After weeks spent living like a mole and defending the town, Jack recognised the truth in my words. It didn't sit well with him though, to be forced to acknowledge the early errors made by our military leadership in this war.

I tried to cheer him up.

"The good news is that the government has sent more troops to South Africa. The dispatch said that twelve battalions of militia and twenty thousand yeomen are on their way. Lord Roberts has also been appointed to take command in South Africa, with Lord Kitchener as his chief of staff."

It was amazing how his gloomy countenance brightened at the mention of Lord Roberts. Lord Roberts, affectionately known as "Bobs" by the wider British public and his troops, is a well-known military figure. His military achievements in Abyssinia, Afghanistan and India have made him famous and, to top it all, he was the Governor of Natal and the Governor and Commander-in-Chief of the Transvaal Province and High Commissioner for South Eastern Africa for a short time in 1881 before being appointed to a position in India.

"That's excellent news," Jack exclaimed. "These Dutchmen aren't going to know what's hit them now that Bobs is taking over. He's also lived here in South Africa, even if it was only for a short period, so he has some familiarity with the countryside and the people."

Richard, whose face had been creased into lines of anxiety as he listened to this discussion, brightened and his face relaxed slightly at these last comments. I jumped in quickly, compounding the positive statements and reassuring him. There's no point in worrying the lad.

"Absolutely, Jack. Things are going to change for the better for Britain now that we have Lord Roberts here to lead us. Maybe this siege will end sooner than we think."

It was gratifying to see the boy's wide grin at these words.

A silence fell, and my thoughts returned to the Boer from the trench. For some strange reason I think of him often. The man seemed no different from many of my counterparts here in Mafeking. In fact, he's undoubtedly better educated than most of them, although I wouldn't say that to Jack.

During my recent trip home to England, I noticed a lot of propaganda demonising the Boers who went from being "Brother Boer" to "Dirty Boer" almost overnight due to the imminent prospect of war.

I remember, particularly, the last words of a poem written by Algernon

Charles Swinburne and published in *The London Times* just before I left to return to South Africa:

> To scourge these dogs, agape with jaws afoam,
> Down out of life. Strike, England, and strike home.[1]

I realised that his derogatory reference to dogs was to the Boers and it made me reflect on the government's campaign to dehumanise the Boers in the eyes of the public. I know for a fact that a lot of what's published is blatant lies. The Boers aren't dogs. They're European men, just like us. These false messages aim to invoke a hatred and will to kill the men who are conscripted to fight in the war. Men like Jack, who believe it all, and are ready and willing to die to defend Britain against them.

* * *

It's 11 p.m. and I've just received new orders from Lord Cecil. B.P. is planning to attack Game Tree Fort, a Boer stronghold to the north of Mafeking, tomorrow and my squadron will be part of the attacking force.

While the timing is unexpected, I am not surprised that B.P. is going ahead with this attack as we have a lot to gain if we are successful. Firstly, we'll capture Creaky and stop it wreaking further devastation on the town and, secondly, taking Game Tree Fort will open the line to the north allowing us to join forces with the British troops who are coming to our assistance from Gaborone in Bechuanaland. I am sure B.P. also hopes to gain some additional grazing ground for our cattle as the existing ground has been devastated by a plague of locusts.

More tomorrow as I need to try and get some sleep before my squadron's 3 a.m. rendezvous at Dummie Fort to learn the details of the plan.

28 December 1899

An awful lot has happened since Christmas Day and I am writing this from my bed in the convalescent home where I've been recovering from my injuries for the last two days. I am grateful to God for sparing me the loss of a limb, or my life, during the attack on Game Tree Fort and I am going to try to write a comprehensive record of my experiences over the past forty-eight hours.

In the early hours of the morning on Boxing Day, my D Squadron met up with the men from C Squadron and A Squadron at Dummy Fort. The

---

[1] From the poem entitled *The Transvaal*, written by Algernon Charles Swinburne.

atmosphere was charged with anticipation at this change from the defensive position B.P. had followed to date. We were all exhilarated at the thought of fighting upright and out in the open. I was tired of firing surreptitiously from a trench like a rat protecting its hole, showing vicious yellow teeth but never getting close enough to bite my tormentor, and my fingers literally tingled with adrenaline.

"C Squadron will lead the attack from their position near the railway line to the west of Game Tree Fort, with D Squadron supporting them," B.P. outlined the details of the offensive attack. "The armoured train will provide additional support with its Hotchkiss and a Maxim. The Bechuanaland Rifles under Captain Cowan will protect the right flank of C Squadron during the attack. One troop of A Squadron men, with three 7-pounder guns and one cavalry Maxim, will attack from the left, supported by two other troops from their squadron.

"Any comments?" B.P. looked around at the gathered men.

No one had anything to add.

"Right then, good luck men, I'll see you all again later today."

B.P. smiled, full of confidence at the expected success of his plan.

The stench of sweat and tension hung in the air as the camp waited silently and watchfully in the cold. My taut nerves made me certain that vengeful eyes were watching us from the cover of the surrounding vegetation. I twisted my head this way and that, looking for any signs of movement in the heavy darkness. I saw nothing. The only sounds were the heavy breathing of my comrades and the crunch of hard ground as they shuffled their feet.

At 4.30 a.m. the bark of the first gun rent the cold early morning air. It was still dark, and the flash shone brightly, momentarily dazzling us. Shells from the 7-pounders followed, soaring through the air and exploding around the target in brilliant flaming balls.

"The railway line's been pulled up about half a mile from here."

The news travelled along the lines of men, just as C Squadron prepared to charge forward.

"The armoured train isn't coming."

I watched C Squadron surge forward as a mass, each man focusing on his own steps, knowing that if he fell, he would be trampled by those coming afterwards.

This is it, I thought as my men readied themselves to follow. *There is no flight option left. Now we must fight to win or be slaughtered like pigs.*

I ran, legs pumping and bayonet held at the ready, to the discordant notes of the supporting artillery guns and the Maxim which intensified the din and swirled around me like an insane orchestra. I was conscious of the men of my squadron around me, as well as those of C Squadron about three hundred yards ahead of me.

A great surge of comradery surged through me as these men, my brotherhood, charged forward through the smoke, directly into a hail of bullets from the Boer musketry. Death seemed certain, but, at this precise moment, this did not matter to me; a cloud of red anger and lust for blood having descended over my mind.

The anger prevented fear and grew in its intensity as the occasional figure, including that of Captain Fitzclarence, dropped around me in small explosions of red.

C Squadron reached the fort, which was hidden by bushes, and the guns roared; the sound of the discordant orchestra growing and swelling. My men and I slowed our forward momentum as we watched more ghostly forms falling, to lie in ghastly bleeding piles on the ground.

The few men still standing started to fall back, shouting at my squadron to follow suit.

"The walls are too high … Impossible to mount without scaling ladders."

Their shouts filled the air, mingling with the gunfire and moans, groans and cries of the wounded.

One of my men, William, and I picked up Captain Fitzclarence as we slowly and deliberately retraced our steps. The blood lust had faded from the men's eyes and their moods had turned sullen. Expressions of dejection had settled on some faces.

The Boers stopped their fire as soon as the retreat commenced, and the resultant silence felt heavy on me, like a shroud. This behaviour by the Boers reinforced my belief that they are decent men. They could have picked a lot more of us off during this retreat if they'd kept shooting.

Moving backwards, lugging the heavy body, was immeasurably hard. My overtaxed leg and back muscles trembled, and my sweat slicked hands slipped and slid under the captain's arms. I expelled a huge sigh of relief when William and I were finally able to lay our burden down at a designated spot near to the stranded armoured train. My legs refused to hold me up any longer and I sank to my knees.

That was when I noticed the blood. A bullet had grazed my chest and I hadn't even noticed. Blood had stained my shirt and was running down into my trousers. It was strange how the moment I saw the blood immense pain seared the right hand side of my chest. It was like being slammed with a club.

I was helped into the armoured train, and waited there, while the stretchers were sent out for the rest of the dead and wounded.

Captains Vernon and Sandford, as well as Lieutenant Paton, were all dead, their bodies stretched out as if they were sleeping, except for their terrible head wounds. They'd been shot at the muzzles of their opponents' rifles while attempting to fire their revolvers through the loopholes in the eight-foot-high walls of the fort.

It was a gruesome sight and I averted my gaze, taking small comfort in the fact their deaths would have been instantaneous.

My colleague, Colin, who'd been shot through the leg, was carried onto the train on a stretcher. He told me about the exceedingly kind behaviour of the Boers following the retreat.

"They helped pick up our dead and wounded and expressed great sadness at our losses. There were a few young ruffians, who attempted to rob the dead and wounded, but their leaders did their best to restrain them.

"The ambulance officer who brought me in said the Boers were astonished by the gallantry of our men in staging this attack."

Conversation petered out as the pain from my injured ribs wracked my body, making breathing difficult. Beads of sweat had broken out along my upper lip and brow.

Colin's waxy face told the story of his own excruciating pain and we both fell into a restless semi-doze.

The train eventually arrived at the station in the town at 10 a.m. and the wounded soldiers, including me, were taken to the hospital for treatment.

Lying on my back on a stretcher, I gazed up at the bright blue sky through half closed eye lids and wondered at its unchanged beauty. It looked the same as it had yesterday before this morning's orgy of death and injury.

* * *

The hospital was in chaos. Colin and I lay side-by-side on our stretchers among many others; all waiting to be seen by one of the three professional nurses. Mrs Johnson brought us bottles of water and said that our wounds would be attended to as soon as possible.

"We're treating the worst cases first."

My entire side was burning with a dull fire and my teeth were tightly clenched to prevent deep groans from wrenching through my body and out of my mouth. They would achieve nothing and potentially add to my pain.

Colin's face had the clammy pallor of a man fighting his own pain battle within his battered body.

It was hot and airless in the packed room where the injured men all lay waiting. Snores, laboured and wheezy breathing, moans and groans and the sounds of retching and vomiting filled the room, creating a low background hum of sounds. I ignored it all, drifting in an out of a semi-conscious doze while the hours passed slowly and quietly, with no shelling from the Boers.

I came fully awake in the early evening when Mrs Johnson returned with one of the nurses to take care of my injury. The entire right-hand side of my chest was a mass of redness with a thick and bloody gouge running through it where the bullet had passed.

The pain was terrible as the nurse set about cleaning and dressing the wound and I fainted.

Later I was awoken and told that I was being moved to a convalescent home which had been established in the railway servants' institute, near the station.

"Two of your ribs are fractured and they'll take a few months to heal," said Mrs Johnson. "You'll rest at the home until the nurse declares you fit to leave."

A sudden feeling of enthusiasm spread through me as my muddled brain gradually absorbed the idea that I was being moved somewhere. I was being moved to a place for the soldiers who were less badly injured. Somewhere away from the stench of blood, urine and death overlaid with antiseptic. Somewhere far from the babble of the delirious, wretched cries and wails of those driven nearly insane by pain, and at whose heel's death nipped, and the sobs of the bereaved.

My spirits rose and I managed to smile at Mrs Johnson.

The journey to the new convalescence home in a hospital wagon jarred my wound, but I managed to stay conscious throughout the journey. As the wagons containing the sixteen patients drew up outside the main door, Creechy fired one of its projectiles, ending the Boers' self-imposed cease fire. They had presumably imposed it out of consideration for the town's sad circumstances.

The shell whizzed over our vehicles and burst with a deafening sound about one hundred yards from where the wagons had stopped.

The men in the wagon, including me, were too exhausted to react and remained calm and collected. We knew there were worse things in the world than shells that missed their mark. There was death at close range from a big Boer bullet, crushed and shattered chests, legs, and arms resulting in death or amputation and being blown to pieces by a shell.

When I closed my eyes, I could see the smashed and disfigured heads of my colleagues and friends. I shed silent tears as I thought of Captain Vernon, now dead, who had been so full of life and vigour the previous day.

All the patients were quickly settled into their wards.

I was interested to learn that Lady Wilson had undertaken the management of the facility, together with four other ladies and a partly professional nurse. A good woman, that one.

Later that evening, the bugle call of the *Last Post* sounded and all of us patients knew that the funeral for the men killed in action that day was in progress.

In the darkness of the night, I lay awake pondering this enigma called the Boers. They are decent men, of European decent just like me. I know they are decent by their actions. They could have annihilated us during the retreat, but they chose not to. Some of them would have known our officers and I heard it said that they were distressed by the whole incident and that afterwards, they appeared to be almost depressed by the whole sad event.

It is not easy to shoot someone you have met and spoken to at close range, especially when you admire their bravery.

I finally fell into a fitful sleep and Black Boxing Day, as it has become known, came to an end for me.

29 December 1899

Richard came to visit me today. He shared with me all the distressing details of the losses to our regiment.

"Captain Vernon, Captain Sandford and Lieutenant Paton were all killed."

I nodded; the memory of their disfigured bodies was still fresh in my mind.

"Twenty-one rank and file also died. Captain Fitzclarence was wounded along with twenty-two rank and file and four men were taken prisoner. The men are bitter about not being able to get into the fort."

"Are they?" I asked. "I suppose they would be. It's natural. Are the survivors feeling intimidated?"

"Not all of them," said Richard. "Some of them want to go back and have another go at the Boers."

"I assume those are men who weren't injured or close to the action?"

"Yes, it's the men who weren't injured. They've been saying that although it is a terrible thing that so many lives were lost during the attack, it was a necessary action as the Boers are a bad lot and need to be defeated."

I picked up my glass from the table next to my bed and drank deeply.

"Do you think the Boers are a bad lot?" asked Richard suddenly, a perplexed look on his young face.

My water went down the wrong way and I had a coughing fit which caused my broken ribs to grind against each other.

"Well," I said at last, when I could breathe again and the pain had subsided, "no, I don't think they're a bad lot. The few I've met have seemed decent people and one, in particular, was well-educated. They behaved kindly towards us during our retreat and, from what I heard, they were considerate and courteous to our men afterwards and helped with picking up our dead and injured and loading them onto stretchers."

Richard learned forward, listening attentively and with great interest.

"So no," I continued, "I don't think they're bad people. I think they're fiercely independent and that they brought this war down on their own heads, but that doesn't make them a bad lot. The Boers I've had an opportunity to speak to all say the same thing. They believe that God is on their side and will ensure they prevail in the end. They do not trust the British and believe our government has lied to them and is after their goldfields."

Richard nodded, "I've lived here in Mafeking all my life and the Boer men and women I've met have always been kind and hospitable. Some of the women and girls are pretty and most of them are excellent cooks."

Richard looks perplexed. "Do you think this war is all about the goldfields and that if there was no gold in South Africa there would be no war?"

Looking at Richard, I considered his question. I had never formalised my scattered thoughts about the reasons for this war.

"I only know what I've read and heard," I said at last, "but I've come to understand a bit about human nature and greed over my life. I believe that what the Boers say is right. This war is about increasing the wealth and power of the British Empire."

Nodding sagely, Richard sat quietly for a few minutes while he reflected on my answer.

"Is there any other news of the war?" I asked.

"Nothing from outside Mafeking. B.P. believes the Boers were forewarned about our attack from Dutch spies in the town. He said that the defenders worked through the night to turn the fort into a blockhouse with three tiers of loopholes for defence. On the morning of our attack, their garrison had also been doubled and the railway line had been ripped up between the town and the fort. Both General Snyman and *Kommandant* Botha arrived with reinforcements almost immediately after our initial attack, which he said was telling as the Boer headquarters was three miles away."

"That makes sense and we know there are a lot of Dutch spies in the town."

"Oh, and our regiment has been reorganised from four squadrons into three. It's because so many men have been killed," said Richard.

He hung his head suddenly and stopped talking as the sudden realisation of the horror of so many deaths in the four months since war had been declared hit him.

After this, I steered the conversation towards everyday events.

"How is your mother, Richard? Is she still volunteering at the hospital?"

"Yes, she has been run ragged over the past few days since the attack on Boxing Day. We've hardly seen her. Father worries about her travelling to and from the hospital with all the shelling. So far, she's been fine though."

Fifteen minutes later, Richard rose to leave.

"I'll come again as soon as I can," he said, flashing me a happy smile. "I'll keep you updated on the latest developments."

8 January 1900

Richard has visited me every day this week. He entertained me with the latest war stories and happenings in the town.

"There are no coffins available," he announced during one visit. "The bodies of the dead are being sewn up in shrouds and the Sisters of Mercy from the convent, take turns praying for them. Mother thinks it is most uncivilised and is upset about it. Father hasn't said anything, so I don't think he cares much."

I studied his face as he told this story. The paleness of his skin and the bruised looking dark flesh surrounding his eyes belied his claim that he is happy and well. The lad has seen too much of the worst of life and is not sleeping well.

"As long as the dead are treated with the respect and deference they deserve for their great personal sacrifice to our town and country, I don't think it matters whether they are buried in a coffin or not."

I hope my words give him the clarity he is seeking on this matter. Mr Johnson is a good man, but he doesn't seem to see his son's anxiety or understand his internal conflict as he tries to make sense of the death and destruction that surrounds him daily.

13 January 1900

Today, Richard arrived in a state of great excitement.

"The Boer besiegers of Ladysmith launched an attack on the British defenders last week and it was decisively repulsed."

This was an encouraging piece of news.

Ladysmith is a large town in Natal. The last news I'd heard about it related to the disastrous Battle of Ladysmith on the 30th of October last year.

A large British force had gathered in the town under Lieutenant General Sir George White, an elderly officer who had served mainly in India. He ordered a sortie of his entire force to capture the Boer forces who were stealthily surrounding the town.

This approach resulted in complete defeat for the British. His troops were driven back into the town after having suffered losses of one thousand two hundred men, killed, wounded or captured.

News of a defeat of the Boer besiegers was encouraging, especially in the context of Mafeking's own besieged status.

"The men are all celebrating the news," continued Richard, his eyes sparkling with pleasure. "The dispatch said that sixty-five Boers were killed during the attack and another one hundred and twenty wounded.

"It also said that on Christmas Day, the Boers fired a carrier shell into the town without a fuse. It contained a Christmas pudding, two Union Jacks and a message saying, 'compliments of the season.' Isn't that hilarious? The Boers do have a sense of humour, don't they?"

I grinned back at him, his enthusiasm was contagious.

"That is funny. I told you many of the Boers are intelligent and witty."

"There is also a poem that was written by one of the people in the town at the beginning of the siege. It is aimed at the Boer military leader, *Kommandant*-General Piet Joubert."

Richard stopped speaking to pull a crumpled piece of newspaper from his short-pants pocket. A collection of other items came out with it, including a bit of string and a nail.

He's still such a boy. He should be going to school every day and playing sport with his mates, not fighting in a war.

Opening the paper out, he smoothed it with his hands and started reading.

> To General Slim Piet[1]
> Hail mighty Oom: Jew Boer
> Proud leader of a dirty crew
> Who shell at night instead of fight
> as savage Bourbon Tartars do.
>
> Your deeds of valour at the sound
> the nations well may quake
> The sick and wounded down you strike
> The Church and Town Hall break.
>
> The nature folk you blandly strip
> of cattle clothes and money
> and thus you prove you're closely bred
> To sow and wolf or monkey.
>
> Oh slippery one at last you've hit
> The biggest marks in town
> Days twenty four you've done your best
> To shell the Red Cross down.
>
> But still it waves and up its back
> Stands honour, brave and true
> Our warrior lads but wait the word
> to meet and share and square with you.

"What does *slim* mean?" he asked when he'd finished.

"In South African English it means someone who has outwitted you. It is not an insult."

His forehead wrinkled with effort as he attempted to understand the poem's satire.

"The use of the word *slim* in this context is satire. The poet is ridiculing the general by saying his is clever and then clearly informing him that the shells he is firing into Ladysmith are only hitting soft targets like the churches, hospitals and civilians instead of the military. The poet is essentially criticising him for his stupidity while praising him for being clever."

"I understand now. Thanks for explaining."

---

[1] From "The War Report, The Anglo-Boer War Through the Eyes of the Burghers" by J.E.H. Grobler

The corners of his mouth turned up in a broad smile as he silently re-read the poem with greater understanding.

Seeing this boy learn and develop is rewarding and I'll miss him when the siege eventually ends, and I move on from Mafeking. Assuming it ever does end; it is relentless and endless right now.

27 January 1900

I haven't written for a while as nothing much has happened other than my slow healing. On the 15th of January, a lovely warm day three weeks after my admittance, I was finally released from the convalescence home.

I've recovered well and although I have a raised and unsightly welt of a scar, I'm alive and feeling strong and refreshed. My ribs still ache periodically, and I was warned by the nurse not to do anything that made them awaken and sing loudly of their recent abuse.

Frankly, it is unlikely this will happen as I've been put on light duties for three weeks until my fractured ribs are deemed to be completely healed. It's excruciatingly boring!

Nothing much changed in the town over the period of my convalescence. The continuous rattle of the guns from the trenches and the booms of the shells as they strike various buildings have become so familiar, they are barely acknowledged by anyone, other than to deal with casualties.

The men, starved as they are of news, excitement and exercise, are short tempered and irritable. They spent time, gathered, complaining about the viciousness and cowardliness of the Boers. The conversation I overheard today was particularly bitter.

"They shelled the women's laager deliberately, which is completely barbaric. We know it was planned as the Dutch women took shelter in advance of the attack," a great hulking soldier, called John Mason, bellowed.

"B.P. is hopping mad about it and has now issued an order that any person, including women, found guilty of treasonably corresponding with the Boers, will be shot. He has also undertaken to confine the Dutch prisoners in a gaol constructed in the laager. Ha! The future consequences for the Boers of shelling the women's laager is they'll kill their own people." His smaller friend grinned gleefully.

"B.P. is a smart man. That is bound to deter them from firing on the laager. They also keep shelling the hospital despite numerous requests by B.P. for restraint to be exercised," John Mason twisted his hands together as if he had the neck of a Boer between them.

"Did you hear what happened to Lord and Lady Wilson?" he went on.

I pricked up my ears at this reference as I am most admiring of Lady Wilson. I had witnessed her efficiency in supervising the housekeeping and procurement of food at the convalescence home. I'd seen her every day during my three week recovery period, endlessly rushing about overseeing the smooth functioning of the facility.

"No, what happened to them?" The small chap asked.

"They were having their supper at the convent where they are both convalescing from illnesses, when it was shelled. A shell burst about four feet above their heads and they were practically buried in rubble.

"It's a miracle they survived. I heard that Major Gould Adams was visiting them at the time and he also survived. The convent is right in front of the hospital and is under the protection of the Red Cross flag. The blatant disregard of both the Red Cross flag and the abuse of the white flag by these Dutchmen is totally unacceptable, they are cowards."

I didn't comment, or become involved in this conversation. It reminded me of my discussion with Richard about whether this war would have taken place at all were it not for the goldfields the Boers controlled.

I recently read a poem by Rudyard Kipling which was written before the war about this very question. I have recorded the most telling lines here:

> Sloven, sullen, savage, secret uncontrolled,
> Lying on a new lad evil of the old –
>
> He shall take a tribute, toll of all our ware,
> He shall change our gold for arms – arms we may not bear.[1]

Kipling's description of the Boers as "sloven", "savage" and "evil" is insulting and most definitely part of our government's pre-war campaign to dehumanise the enemy in the eyes of the public.

My reading of the second set of lines is that they are arrogant and demonstrate Kipling's belief that Britain has a legitimate claim to the gold of the Transvaal.

My thoughts led me to wondering if I'd fight this war if I were one of the Boers. I've concluded that I would.

Of course, some of the behaviour by the Boers is ungentlemanly and despicable, like firing on the hospital and the Women's Laager and ignoring the white flag, but their cause seems just. What a strange and contrary lot they are.

---

[1] From the poem entitled "The Old Issue", written on 9 October 1899 by Rudyard Kipling and included in his *The Five Nations* collection of poems.

I've been declared completely recovered and it is a pleasure to return to active duty despite the attitude changes that the heavy loss of life on Black Boxing Day have brought about in the men of my new squadron. They've all lost weight and their faces have a haggard and yellowish look about them.

I'm pleased that my good mate, Jack Simmons, is still part of my squadron, as is Colin, who has recovered from his leg injury and also returned to active duty. Richard will continue to support my squadron, by carrying messages to head office and other forts and positions.

The conversations on the Heights have changed and there is an undertone of dreary acceptance of our situation which, following the loss of life during the Boxing Day attack, the men have deemed unchangeable through any active interventions on the part of our leadership here in town.

We're all desperately hoping that relief will soon arrive from the outside world.

"Well, Robert," asked the lively Jack, "what do you think the chances are that support will come?"

I considered for a moment, "I think it'll come, Jack. Kimberley and Ladysmith have both been relieved and I believe we're next on the list."

"Do you really? I've been thinking that we may be sacrificed to the greater cause of Britain's ultimate triumph over these Dutchmen."

Richard's mouth dropped open in surprise. "No," he declared, "we haven't been abandoned."

Jack suddenly realised what he had said and the impact of his careless words on Richard's young ears and tried to backtrack.

"Yes, of course, you are right Richard. Help will come."

"Of course, it will," I confirmed. "We just have to sit tight and wait it out."

Grinning mischievously, I added, "after all, horse soup isn't that bad, is it?"

The conversation then reverted to food, or the lack thereof. There are a lot of mouths to feed in the town and, after five months of siege, supplies are sadly depleted.

The provisions that the Cape government sent to the town before the war were only enough to feed four hundred men for approximately two weeks. This pathetic attempt at support for the expected siege would never have enabled B.P. to continue his defensive position of the town. It was the foresight of the firm of Weil and Company, which had sent vast stores to the depot in the town in advance of the declaration of war, that enabled B.P. to make any sort of resistance at all.

Among the other stores in the depot of Weil and Company, were two tons of gunpowder and other ammunition, one hundred and thirty-two rifles, insulated fuses and electric dynamos for discharging mines and other miscellaneous articles. All of these were put to excellent use by B.P. in defending the town.

Jack laughed, "I personally don't think that horse meat's that bad, although I know the natives won't eat it. Their refusal leaves more for us though, doesn't it?"

"They think eating horse meat will give them the same sickness that the horses of Africa suffer from and make their heads swell," said Richard, who had interacted with the Baralong most of his young life.

"Lady Wilson told me, while I was in the convalescence hospital, that it was the natives' refusal to eat the horse soup that resulted in the introduction of sowens porridge."

"That makes sense," observed Jack, "What's it made from, anyhow?"

"It's made from the meal which remains in the oat-husks after they have been ground for bread. She said its immensely popular with the natives."

Richard pulled a face, "It tastes a bit sour to me," he said, "but I still eat it," he added hastily.

Richard's a good lad and never wants to appear obstructive or fussy in front of me or my men.

"Yeah, it is sour," I said, "but I'd rather have the porridge than my ration of six ounces of bread a day. The bread tastes funny and it's full of strange substances that I can't chew."

The warm day continued into a fine night and my squadron elected to sleep out on the Heights. It's great relief to be outside breathing the fresh air, rather than being confined in a bomb shelter which smells of damp earth and sour sweat.

I'm writing these words by the light of the moon, while sitting in my sleeping bag. The largeness of the dark African sky, and the freedom of the thousands of bright stars which light it up like small candles, have led me to reflect on how different my current life is from what I expected when I heard I'd been assigned to Mafeking.

I never thought I'd be eating horse sausages, sour porridge and dessert made from hairdressers' powder. I also never expected to be fighting using an old cannon constructed in 1770. I must admit that regardless of its age, finding that cannon half buried in the Stadt was incredibly lucky for us.

The construction of the Wolf is also an amazing feat by our engineers. Who would've thought they could construct a cannon which can fire an 18-pound shell 4,000 yards?

31 March 1900

My men were assigned to the Heights again today. It was a peaceful morning, and the monotony and warmth of the day caused my eyelids to droop heavily. The threat of falling asleep on duty was real and I started counting the butterflies to keep myself occupied and awake.

The unexpected rattle of gunfire from the north shocked us out of our lethargy and we watched in surprise as the Boer's eastern laager erupted into confused chaos. The Boers quickly formed themselves into a mounted force of over four hundred men and galloped away. The distant clatter of many hooves and the shouts and cries of the men mingled with the distant gunfire carried to us on the gentle breeze, as we sat speculating about what could have happened.

Next, the Mafeking trenches came alive. Guns blazed, throwing up puffs of grey smoke.

A mounted squadron simultaneously took off towards Game Tree Fort to the north to engage the Boers there.

"What's happening?" asked Richard.

He sat down next to me with his legs sticking out straight in front of him. I noticed how his knees formed knobbly lumps on his long legs which have thinned down considerably due to the new horse meat and sowens porridge diet. His eyes burned with excitement in his gaunt face. What a difference the last three weeks of semi starvation have made to us all.

"I don't know. The Boers have been slowly evacuating the trenches closest to Mafeking for the past week or so, starting with the brick fields trenches and progressing to their eastern trenches. I assumed their withdrawal was to do with the defeat of General Cronjé in February and the subsequent fall of Bloemfontein, but who really knows with these Boers."

"Maybe it's the beginning of the end for the Boers," said Richard.

"Maybe," I agreed. "How are your sisters?" I haven't seen Richard's family for some time and have been wondering how they're managing on the limited rations.

Richard laughed, "Emily's fine. She's adapted to life underground and is a real trooper."

"And Eliza?"

"She's getting very thin. She won't eat the locust curry and she makes a big fuss about eating horse and mule meat too. Girls!"

The last word exploded from Richard's lips, seeming to carry all his bemusement and confusion at Eliza's behaviour which, through his youthful boyish eyes, went against the principles of survival and was immeasurably strange.

"That isn't good, she needs to keep her strength up. Hopefully, this blasted siege will end soon, and we can all get something decent to eat."

2 April 1900

At daybreak yesterday, the Boers declared a truce in order for us to retrieve the bodies of our troops who'd fallen during the skirmish the previous day. B.P. asked for volunteers to accompany the wagons and I leapt at the opportunity of escaping the town, albeit for a short time and for such a miserable purpose. I desperately wanted a change of scenery.

To my surprise, the glorious early morning sky with its fluffy white clouds tinged with varying shades of pink didn't bring me the happiness I sought or expected.

Instead, the journey seemed endless. Trepidation at what I must find at the end of it grew with each jolting rotation of the wooden wheels over the rutted ground. My chin dipped gradually until it rested on my chest while I grappled with my desolate thoughts and ignored the fresh beauty of the unspoiled countryside around me.

I was vaguely surprised when a small contingent of Boers met our wagons at the site of the altercation and proceeded to help our small party of men seek out the bodies of our fallen comrades.

Once again, the enigma that is the Boers struck me. Their faces were sorrowful and their eyes downcast when they came across the body of a dead soldier, smashed by a bullet, and crumpled into a grotesque and twisted shape on the hard ground. Their expressions and words gave no hint of elation or pride at their triumph during the previous day's warfare.

My mind has subsequently grappled with the unpleasantness of having the faces of these Boers, my opponents, imprinted on my thoughts. These mental pictures have replaced my previous faceless and unformed images of a devilish enemy, upon whom I could fire without remorse, a scowl of rage upon my face and my heart wrapped in a protective blanket of

British righteousness.

The skirmish turned out to have involved a patrol of Colonel Plumer's men from the Rhodesian Regiment,[a] which had lost six men as well as two officers. I hadn't met any of them before, but it was still incredibly poignant.

It brought home to me that Colonel Plumer's Regiment is closer than we realised. The fight between his men and the Boers took place just over six miles from Mafeking. Even though the Boers drove his soldiers all the way back to Ramatlabama, about eighteen miles away, I am much heartened by their proximity.

15 April 1900

What a terrible day this has been. I sit here writing and wondering why God sees fit to litter the paths of the faithful with so much pain and suffering. Why, God? Why?

I was at the hospital visiting Jack, who'd managed to get himself shot in the arm a few days before. He was sufficiently recovered to sit on the edge of the *stoep* with me, his arm in a sling, and his legs dangling to the ground, drinking a cup of tea and enjoying the peaceful expanse of veld in front of us. The long grass bobbed and waved in a gentle breeze, the autumn having coloured it a rich golden brown. It soothed the eye and the soul.

By gazing straight ahead, it was possible to momentarily forget about the on-going war and the frantic activities of the doctors, nurses and volunteers in the building behind us, as they desperately tried to save lives and put back together shattered bodies. I could almost believe that everything was peaceful and as it should be in this rural setting.

I shifted my head slightly and a burned and blackened homestead came into view like an unsightly scar upon the landscape.

My eyes continued to travel and the white canvas coverings of the wagons comprising the Boer laager filled my sight. It was followed by their horses and, lastly, their livestock, much of which had been raided from the surrounding countryside.

A sudden flash of brightness caught my eye and I whipped my head in its direction. It was the glint of sunlight on the burnished metal of Creaky as the Boers brought its cannon up, ready to fire.

Boom! The sound echoed across the rolling veld and a thick cloud of smoke rose up above the huge gun.

From the centre of town came the noises of the explosion as the shell burst among the buildings. Shouts and cries indicated that the projectile had caused damage. The few lady volunteers who had been resting on the *stoep*, hurried away to prepare for any casualties who might be sent to the hospital.

The Boers set about firing heavily on the town. I helped carry some of the wounded soldiers who'd been lying on the *stoep* back to their wards. Those who could, limped away on crutches.

A short while later, a party carrying a stretcher appeared. It descended into the trench which led to the hospital and emerged at the other end. As it commenced crossing the recreation ground in front of the hospital, the large white flag waved by one of the stretcher bearers attracted the attention of the Boers, who started firing on the group.

My stomach constricted in anger and frustration at this immoral behaviour by the Boers. I can't understand why they have no respect for the white flag.

I opened the door as they approached, and the stretcher bearers burst into the hallway where a waiting nurse ushered them in the direction of the operating room. As the stretcher passed me, I caught a brief glimpse of the face of the victim.

Mr Johnson's eyes stared unseeing from within bruised and dark circles of flesh in his grey and bloodless face.

Overcome by shock and swaying on my legs, I sat down heavily.

"Oh my God, Richard's father has been hit by a shell."

Like a man in a dream, I tottered over to the door of the operating theatre and peered inside.

The table was already laid with carbolic lotion, lint and bandages, dressing dishes, sponges and an array of instruments. The stretcher was placed beside the table and the blankets that enshrouded the patient were removed.

The sight of the thick mass of congealed blood covering the prostrate form caused me to gasp. A nurse caught sight of me, standing horror struck in the doorway. Gliding over, she shut it firmly in my face.

I collapsed into a chair near the operating theatre and started my vigil.

Sixty minutes later, the doctor emerged, wearing his jacket. He walked towards the exit.

Rising, a sharp cry issuing from my dry throat, I staggered towards the doctor and laid a quivering hand on his arm.

"Mr Johnson? How is Mr Johnson?" I asked.

The doctor's brown eyes were compassionate.

"We couldn't save him. He's now at peace."

Reaching out, he and placed a comforting hand on my shoulder.

"I'm sorry."

MICHELLE

JUSTICE

August 2019

Tom's been in the hospital for nearly a month, a thick white back brace surrounding his body and an IV feeding liquid medications into his left hand.

He's a discontented patient and refuses to have the curtains in his private room opened. He says that the bright sunlight hurts his eyes. His skin is sallow, and anger and frustration have chiselled deep lines into his forehead and down the sides of his mouth from his nose to his chin.

He looks much older than his mid-forties and it shocks and dismays Michelle, who hates visiting him in this state of degraded self-pity but feels obligated to do so.

Initially, he'd slept most of the time but now, throughout her brief visits, he either rants about the poor quality of the nurses who have to do everything for him, including washing him and bringing him a bed pan, or gazes up at the television on the ceiling, mesmerized by the never-ending line up of evangelistic programmes he watches.

The only small patch of brightness is that the expensive medical aid is covering his lengthy hospital treatment in full. A diagnosis of medium to long term paralysis has been sent to his life insurer which will be making monthly payments in terms of his disability cover. At least she doesn't have to worry about money during this time of crisis and, for that, she is immeasurably grateful.

On Tuesday afternoon Michelle arrives at the hospital at 3 p.m. Tom is lying on his back in bed, a light sheet covering him and an expression of anticipation on his pale face. In the dim light of the enclosed room, he looks like a snake with his white shining skin and heavy eyelids, half closed over deep-set eyes. She shudders involuntarily as she leans forwards to give him a perfunctory kiss.

He has no idea what I suspect ... no ... what I know about him.

Out of the corner of her eye, she catches a rapid movement of his arm as he pulls it free of its light covering. Jerking her head in the direction of the movement, she feels his right hand close around her wrist.

Despite the tremendous pain it must have caused, he manages to pull himself towards her. His lips compress into a thin grey line as he determinedly prevents any expressions of his pain from escaping his body.

"You've got to help me, Michelle," he whispers hoarsely. "I need to walk. I'm a sitting duck for her now with my legs useless to me."

His hand is squeezing her wrist so tightly, its fragile bones grind together.

A grunt of pain burst from her clenched lips.

"Stop hurting me," she whispers, "Tell me what you want, and I'll try to help you."

"I want you to find Pastor John and get him to visit me here at the hospital. He knows about her. He's seen her. He can heal me and then, together, we can destroy her."

His strength depleted, Tom lets go of her wrist and sinks back into his pillows. He stares at her out of sharp burning eyes sunk into pouches of darkly bruised flesh.

"Okay, Tom, I'll try to find him for you."

In the face of his desperation, what else can she say.

I have no options.

"You'll find his contact details in my contacts on my computer," Tom closes his eyes with a gasp.

Within moments his breathing becomes soft and regular and Michelle knows he is asleep.

I know he's keeping things from me about his past and the ghost of Estelle. Maybe Pastor John's presence will get him to confess, or at least to reveal more information.

* * *

That Friday night, Alice sleeps over at Michelle's house. They'd become closer again during this time of tribulation for Michelle, and Alice is spending a lot of her free time visiting and supporting her. Michelle is pleased to have the company. It stops her from dwelling on the mess that is marriage.

The weather is already much warmer and Michelle has switched off the heating.

"I can't bear being too hot," she tells Alice.

"You're preaching to the converted. I don't like heated environments as they are breeding grounds for germs. I'm quite happy sitting here on the floor in my pyjamas and slippers."

With her crop of auburn curls and smooth freckled skin, Alice looks like a teenager at a sleep over instead of a grown woman. That night, she's again indulging in her favourite pink gin cocktails. Michelle joins her, craving a release from her responsibilities.

The doorbell rings.

"That'll be our food," Michelle jumps up and rushes to the front door.

Five minutes later she returns with their takeaways from a local Indian restaurant.

Unpacking the food onto the coffee table, Michelle revels in the evening's lack of formality. Her heart gives a twinge as she thinks about how much importance Tom places on their sitting down at a perfectly set table whenever they are able to enjoy their evening meals together. She hasn't bothered with this evening routine since he'd fallen down the stairs and been hospitalised.

It feels like a waste of time to set the table just for me. Tom would be disappointed at my laziness.

A small repressed cry squeezes through her tightly clenched lips.

"I'll get the plates and cutlery," Michelle swirls away from Alice to hide her tear-filled eyes.

They both heap their plates with fragrant rice, butter chicken and nan bread before Alice asks Michelle the inevitable question.

"What's been happening around here with your ghosts?"

Michelle chews her mouthful of food slowly, giving herself an opportunity to coral her thoughts into something coherent.

It's all been so strange.

"I haven't sensed Estelle's presence since Tom's accident and I haven't had any strange dreams either. I've seen both Pieter and Robert though. They've made regular contact with me since I removed the St John's Wort. That seemed to work, by the way," Michelle smiles at her friend.

Alice nods, "It does work, but clearly not for a powerfully malevolent spirit like Estelle."

"Yes, that is what Robert told me. Did I tell you that Estelle is Pieter's daughter?"

Michelle relates her interaction with the spirit of the British soldier on the evening Tom fell down the stairs.

Alice listens attentively and does not interrupt while Michelle is speaking.

She's such a good listener.

"I haven't interacted with Robert that intimately again, Alice. He makes his presence known though. I've caught sight of him silhouetted against the bathroom door at night. You know I sleep with the light on, don't you?"

"Yes, I remember that. Are you sleeping in the master bedroom again?"

"Yes, it is more convenient for my dressing table there and the en-suite bathroom. I'll think about what to do when Tom gets better and comes home."

Alice opens her mouth, as if to speak, but then closes it again.

I wonder if she was going to say, "if he comes home"? She doesn't need to say that; I already know he may not recover sufficiently to return home for a long time.

"I've been working on my book about the Second Anglo Boer War whenever I get a moment. I found a piece of paper in my office listing research references about Britain's participation in the war. It's proved to be a most useful resource for me and, judging from the old fashioned and spidery handwriting, it must have been left by Robert. When I finally went to bed on the morning after Tom fell, I found an old journal lying on my pillow."

Michelle stops and gazes into space, thinking about the journal.

"It contains an account of the life of its owner in Mafeking during the siege."

"That is amazing, Michelle. Do you think the journal belongs to Robert?"

"Oh yes, it definitely does. His name, Robert Kirkpatrick, is written in the front in the same handwriting as the note. The leather cover is cracked with age and the pages inside are yellow.

"The journal is a fascinating and heart wrenching read. It reveals a lot of detail about life in Mafeking during the siege and how it impacted on the attitudes of the British troops defending the town. It also shares a lot on the lives of the civilian residents. Robert developed a friendship with a local family named Johnson and became close to the teenage son, Richard. He was obviously a kind and caring man."

Michelle looks at Alice, it is difficult to put into words the huge impact reading this journal has had on her.

"I feel like I've been given a window into Robert's heart and soul, Alice. The journal reveals so many of his personal thoughts and ideas. He discloses information about Britain's anti-Boer propaganda campaign that ran before and during the war and he even included transcripts of poems that were written at the time, degrading the Boers and their way of life. These poems and the propaganda in general weighted heavily on his mind and caused him a lot of internal confusion and conflict. He obviously didn't experience the Boers in a negative way or see them as being ignorant and vastly inferior to himself. He definitely liked the Afrikaners and admired their determination and courage."

Again, Michelle stops. "Most importantly, Alice, Robert knew Pieter. He mentions him by name in the journal. Robert wrote in an admiring tone about Pieter's superior education. He also wrote that he spared Pieter's life during a British assault on the Boer trenches one evening."

"Wow, Shelles, so that is how they are linked. They had an encounter during the war. That does make sense. I wonder what happened to sour their relationship so badly?"

"I don't know, Alice. I haven't finished reading the journal yet. It's slow reading as I have to decipher the handwriting which is small and quite feint and blurry in places."

"What an amazing find and story. Have you had any further encounters with Pieter? Has he revealed anything about his life story?"

A worried look flitters across Michelle's face at the mention of Pieter.

He might be a ghost, but I sense that he is conflicted and there are strong feelings of anger, resentment and maybe even guilt, underlying his actions.

"I have spoken to Pieter. Not directly, but through the Ouija board," Michelle responds to Alice's unspoken question.

"Really, I wonder why he doesn't speak to you directly?"

"I can't answer that, but I'll tell you what happened."

* * *

The previous Sunday, Michelle had worked on the first chapter of her new book the entire afternoon. With Tom in the hospital and Alice away, there was nobody to distract her from her writing. She had visited Tom during the morning and had no plans to visit again that day.

By 6 p.m., she'd drafted an additional four thousand words and was pleased with her progress.

Hunger forced her to stop and think about dinner. Standing up, she stretched her aching neck and back and swung her arms in wide arcs to loosen her stiff shoulders. Her outstretched hand knocked the Ouija board from its resting place on the end of her desk. The box, with the planchette on top of it, tumbled to the floor and the board fell out, face up.

"Shit! Shit! Shit!"

She'd avoided touching the cursed Ouija board since its reappearance in her office. It sat in the same place for weeks, a horrible reminder of the poltergeist and her malevolent power.

Hands trembling, Michelle bent down to retrieve the items from the floor. Her hands touched the planchette and the temperature in the room plunged. The planchette throbbed, heart-like, beneath her fingers, and an uncontrollable urge to play the game seized her. Going through the motions of mechanically sinking to her knees, placing the planchette on the board and laying her fingers lightly on it, the actions of her body no longer seemed under the control of her mind.

The planchette took on a life of its own and moved smoothly from letter to letter without any assistance, or even force, from her.

T-H-A-N-K—Y-O-U—F-O-R—H-E-L-P-I-N-G—M-E.—I—W-A-N-T—M-Y—S-T-O-R-Y—T-O-L-D.—P-E-O-P-L-E—N-E-E-D—T-O—R-E-M-E-M-B-E-R.—I—W-A-N-T—R-E-S-O-L-U-T-I-O-N—O-F—T-H-I-S—C-O-N-F-L-I-C-T—A-N-D—R-E-D-E-M-P-T-I-O-N.

The planchette stopped as suddenly as it started. The board snapped itself closed almost trapping her fingers.

She rocked back on her knees, not feeling as disturbed by the strange message as she would have expected, given the circumstances. It feels right. A message from the past; from the ghost of the poor, unhappy Pieter.

* * *

"That's some story," says Alice. During their conversation, the two women finished their dinners and their drinks, and Alice suggests a refill.

"Good idea," Michelle pulls herself to her feet. "You make the refills and I'll pack the dishwasher and throw away the empty cartoons."

Thirty minutes later, they're back in their places on the floor, fresh drinks in front of them. Michelle is feeling the impact of her third drink of the evening. She rarely drinks more than one cocktail in a single evening.

Letting your hair down occasionally is a good thing.

"I've seen other indications of Pieter's presence around the house," Michelle picks up the thread of their earlier conversation. "I found a pamphlet requesting donations to the heritage foundation that maintains the two concentration camp cemeteries at Mahikeng. You know that Mahikeng was previously called Mafeking, don't you?"

Alice nods.

"I did some research and there are eight hundred and twenty-five marked graves in the large cemetery. Two of the graves particularly interested me, they belong to Marta van Zyl and Sannie van Zyl, both of whom died in the Mafeking concentration camp during the Second Anglo Boer War. Marta van Zyl was Pieter's wife so his family must have been interned in the camp.

"I think he wanted me to discover the connection between his family and the Mafeking concentration camp and that's why he left the pamphlet there for me to find."

"That makes, sense. Why do you think Pieter only communicates with you through the Ouija board and other non-verbal ways like the pamphlet you mentioned? Why doesn't he speak to you directly like Robert and Estelle have?"

"I've thought about that Alice. I think that Pieter is trying to protect me. There's bad blood between him and Estelle and maybe he thinks the less direct contact he has with me, the less I'll draw Estelle's attention and rage. It's the only reason I can think of for his behaviour."

Alice is nodding, "That does make a certain amount of sense. This whole thing is so weird."

"Alice," Michelle looks at her carefully, "I thought maybe now would be a good time to revisit the Tarot cards. What do you think?"

Alice nods slowly, "Okay, the timing does seem right. I'll get the box out of my car and let's do it."

Jumping up enthusiastically, she heads for the front door.

Ten minutes later the three drawn cards lay on the coffee table.

"The Justice card represents your past," Alice looks at Michelle keenly.

"What does it mean?" Michelle's tone sounds petulant to her own ears.

"It means that you have already made an important choice or decision in your life which is having long-term repercussions on you now. Justice does not indicate whether you made a good or bad choice at the time, it only indicates that you made a decision that changed your life's path at the time."

Startled, Michelle's eyes widen. "I wonder if this card relates to my decision to marry Tom?"

"Quite possibly," Alice takes a delicate sip of her drink, "your decision to marry a wealthy older man certainly changed your life. It enabled you to leave your full-time job and start your own business, which is something you wanted to do. You were also able to free up sufficient time to pursue your writing passion as a result of your new circumstances."

Michelle sits quietly for a moment, digesting Alice's comments. "Do you think I was so keen to change my career path and follow my writing dream that I overlooked ominous signs about Tom?"

"I can't answer that. You need to search your soul and seek out the truth in that regard. It may be murky and distorted. Our motivations and desires are not always clear-cut. Who knows, something may occur that brings illumination and spiritual enlightenment to you."

Michelle nods, "What's the next card?"

"It's the High Priestess and it's in your present position. This card signifies that you are best advised to carefully assess any information which is presented to you as the truth, but which you have a strong feeling is biased and ill-founded. Do you have any idea what information this could relate too?"

Michelle gulps a mouthful of her drink in a bid for time before finally answering Alice's question.

"No, I really don't know what it could mean."

Alice mixes them both another drink. This is a fourth for Michelle and she is feeling quite fuzzy headed.

"What's the last card?"

"It's a powerful one," Alice's pretty face settles into solemn lines. "The Hierophant in the future position reveals a strong pull towards an individual who will explain the meaning of life to you, as well as your role in it."

"I can't understand the meaning of that one either, Alice. This wonderful individual who is going to explain everything that is happening doesn't seem to have appeared yet and I feel totally lost and alone."

A robe of melancholy wraps itself around Michelle and tears well up in her eyes for the second time that night, threatening to burst the dam of her self-control.

Alice grins at her naughtily, "Let's go for a swim."

"A swim ... but it's August. The water will be freezing."

"Nah, it won't be cold. It'll be fun. Come on, Michelle."

In her drunken state Alice's arguments are convincing. The two women run upstairs like children and change into bathing suites.

Alice looks amazing in a mottled pink full piece costume and Michelle starts to giggle.

"I hope no one sees us. They'll think we're quite mad."

* * *

The two women run lightly across Michelle's small garden and through the back gate. Jogging along the brick path, they soon arrive at the large communal pool. The water glistens in the electric light of the ornate lamps that illuminate the tastefully landscaped area.

Michelle slips off her bathrobe and stands on the edge of the pool. Dipping her right foot into the cold water, she shivers violently, and jerks it out again.

"It's really cold, Alice."

Alice rushes up to the edge and leaps in, hitting the water with a huge splash and sinking below the surface. Her face breaks through the roughened surface and she squeals with laughter, just like a small child.

"Come on, Michelle," she calls.

A dark shadow hurtles across the surface of the water like a torpedo from an old war movie. Michelle's mouth gapes open as it whistles past her. A ripple of displaced air causes her to jerk her head around just in time to see the shadow perform a tight U-turn and head back towards her. It thuds into her like a cannon ball and she flies forward and drops into the water like a sack of potatoes. Her head surfaces and she gulps air.

"You whore!"

The words float on the air as the shape darts around the pool. They seem to bounce off the mosaiced edging.

"Your husband is a rapist and a murderer, but you refuse to acknowledge it."

Cold hands press down on Michelle's face. The water is too deep for her to stand in this part of the pool and she can't muster the force necessary to push back against the downward force. Her head slips into the icy water which fills her eyes, nose and ears. Adrenalin fuelled strength floods her body and she fights ferociously against the determined spirit pining her down. Her lungs are ready to burst when the pressure suddenly releases and her head bursts out of the water, like a cork from a champagne bottle.

"I'm going to kill you, whore," the voice snarls at her.

From this close, the shadow has features. Large piercing green eyes glow in a pale face, so fair the fine scattering of freckles on her nose stand out like dark marks. Recognition stirs as she gazes into the eyes of the young girl who had revealed her presence, firstly on her computer screen, and then on the television.

The spirit's thin face is surrounded by a thick mass of straight blonde hair that falls well below her shoulders.

The same blonde hair I saw in the shower drain.

Despite her youth, the ghost looks about fifteen or sixteen years old, evil pulses from her like a deviant heartbeat and a wicked red light burns within the depths of her brilliant eyes.

"Why? Why must you kill me? What have I done?" screeches Michelle, her eyes dilated with fear.

"Why?" the girl throws back her head and laughs. "Because you knew that he was guilty of rape and murder but did nothing to bring him to justice."

"But I didn't know," Michelle cries.

"Yes, you did know. There were signs all around you. You chose to ignore them just like my father chose to ignore my mother's abuse of me," the ghost's voice drops to a low tone, but it still reverberates through the air. "She neglected and ignored me and, when the worst thing that could happen to me did, she rejected me and said I was unclean and defiled. I hated her almost as much as I hated him. My father, Pieter van Zyl."

Her hands reach out again and deliberately push Michelle down beneath the dark water. Numb with cold and shock, Michelle struggles against the downward pressure.

Tom must be guilty of raping that woman, Tracey Atkinson, and that's why she committed suicide. That awful scene I saw during my dream must have been some sort of vision of what happened.

The last bit of oxygen in her lungs exhausted, Michelle sinks down into unconsciousness.

* * *

Michelle awakens in her bed with Alice lying asleep next to her. Alice sits up when Michelle starts to move.

"Are you okay, Michelle?"

"I feel okay, just completely exhausted."

"I'm not surprised. That ghost-girl tried to drown you."

Michelle's memories of the events of the previous evening return suddenly and she inhales air sharply.

"Oh my God! I remember now. That phantom tried to murder me. What happened? How did I survive?"

"Pieter saved you," Alice says simply. "He came surging across the pool like an avenging angel and knocked into the girl with such force, she simply vanished into thin air. He yanked you out of the water and carried you over to the pool side where he administered resuscitation procedures. I know it was Pieter because he looked exactly as you have described him and wore the same large hat."

Tears run down her cheeks as she explains how she was unable to move while the poltergeist abused Michelle.

"My muscles were frozen, and I couldn't move. I couldn't scream. I could just stand and watch as she pushed you under the water."

The ghost's words return to Michelle. *You knew he was a rapist and murderer. There were signs all around you, but you chose to ignore them.*

"Let's go downstairs and make some coffee. I need to tell you something."

* * *

Michelle regards the hot coffee in front of her. A curl of steam winds its way upwards and disappears. Without looking at Alice, she starts to talk.

"Estelle's vendetta against Tom and I is somehow rooted in a traumatic event from her past. She said so last night, in between trying to drown me."

Michelle gives Alice a weak smile.

"She has somehow linked this event, which I suspect involves some sort of physical abuse, with Tom and sees him as an evil abuser."

Michelle stops speaking and studies her hands for a few minutes. Alice waits patiently for her to continue.

"I recently discovered some information about Tom and a previous relationship he had with a girl called Tracey Atkinson. I think he date raped her, and she committed suicide as a result."

She stops talking and looks at Alice, trying to gauge her reaction to this statement.

"Why do you think that, Michelle. What information are you basing it on?"

Michelle tells Alice everything she's learned, including the details of her strange dreams, the newspaper articles and her discussion with Trevor. At the end of it all, Alice looks at her questioningly.

"But you can't know for sure he raped her and that's what triggered her suicide. Even if he did, why is Estelle holding you accountable for his actions? You didn't know, did you?"

"I don't know for sure that he raped her, Alice. I could only be one hundred percent certain if he confessed to it, but it is the obvious reason for the sudden breakdown of their relationship and her ultimate suicide. As for my involvement ..."

Michelle stops speaking again and looks at Alice with huge, tear filled eyes. She visibly fights for control of her emotions while Alice waits.

Finally, she speaks again, her throat gulping with the effort of suppressing her extreme emotions, "Estelle said there were signs of Tom's character and guilt, Alice. She said I chose to ignore them. Maybe she was right.

Looking back, I recall some odd conversations about Tom around the office before we got married. I never took them seriously though as I thought the other women were jealous of my new relationship. Maybe I have ignored characteristics and traits in Tom over the years that may have indicated something odd in his past. I'm just not sure."

PIETER

THE *BITTEREINDERS*

August 1900

Sliding off his horse, Pieter sighs with relief. After three days of intensive riding, he is glad to be standing on his own two feet instead of sitting in a saddle. He looks around at the fertile hills of the Gatsrand, appreciating this sheltered and well-watered spot.

"Whoever selected this area for our headquarters made a good choice, Willem. The local farmers will be able to supply the commando with food and other goods."

Enthusiastic comrades greet the brothers as they approach the five hundred-strong camp, eager to regale them with stories about their military successes of the past few weeks.

"Based on what we've just heard, General de la Rey made a good decision when he appointed Combat-General Petrus Liebenberg to reactivate the commando." Pieter watches Willem as he pickets their horses in a choice grassy spot.

"I agree, Pieter. Isn't it great to hear so much positive news?"

Leaving Mhlopi and Sipho to attend to the horses and look after their gear, the two men stroll over to join a group gathered around a fireplace roasting meat.

The food is plentiful, and Pieter serves three generous helpings of meat and mielie pap onto plates. He splashes generous servings of *sous*, a warm sauce made from tomatoes, onions and spices, over the food, and takes two of the plates over to Mhlopi and Sipho.

Returning to the gathering, he sits down to enjoy his own meal and catch up on the latest news.

"Tell us about the battle at Silkaatsnek."[1] Stoffel de Bruyn is an old

---

[1] Kommandonek and Silkaatsnek were the only two passes through the

comrade of Pieter's from Polfontein. "I heard it went well."

Stoffel's sunburned face lit up with a grin, showing teeth yellowed by years of smoking a pipe.

"That was such a great victory for us," he declares. "General de la Rey made mincemeat out of those Khakis despite the fact that the garrison was at double strength on the evening his Burghers attacked."

"Is that so. How did the commando achieve such a great success against such big odds?"

"On the night of the attack, the Royal Scots Greys, which had been defending the pass, was due to leave the following day and their replacement regiment, the Lincolnshire Regiment had arrived. The departing Greys were assigned to guard the Kommandonek pass that night and the replacement Lincolnshire Regiment was assigned to defend Silkaatsnek. The leader of the Lincolnshire Regiment made the mistake of not posting guards on the summit of the two high cliffs that overlook the pass. You know which ones I mean?"

Pieter nods, he knows the Magaliesburg mountains area which separates Pretoria and Johannesburg from the bushveld to the northwest of the Transvaal. Kommandonek and Silkaatsnek, the only two passes through the mountains, are strategically important to both the British and the Boers.

"Anyway, the entire Lincolnshire Regiment was positioned at the southern entrance to the pass. In the morning, when our men attacked from the summit of the pass, the Khakis were totally unprepared. The positioning of their guns within their emplacements of rock and barbed wire, made it impossible for them to elevate their guns sufficiently to fire on us when we attacked. Assistance from the Greys only arrived from Kommandonek later that morning after it received a message via a runner. The Greys only stayed to shell us for about an hour before they departed to ride to Pretoria as scheduled. By the evening, the Lincolnshire Regiment had run out of ammunition and surrendered, with seventy-two of its men killed or wounded."

"A fantastic victory," chimes in Willem, his excitement palpable.

"Yes, and one we must all thank God for. De la Rey's Burghers also acquired a huge booty of two guns, numerous horses and mules and a large quantity of rifles, ammunitions and even shells for the guns. The rifles and ammunition are especially welcome as many of us have run out of Mauser ammunition and are relying on British Lee-Metford rifles

---

Magaliesberg mountain range which separated Rustenburg and Pretoria.

taken from their dead and wounded."

"How long have you been here, Stoffel?" asks Willem.

"Long enough to assist General Liebenberg with the reoccupation of both Ventersdorp and Klerksdorp several days ago."

"You see, Pieter," cries Willem, "the war is not lost to us. We did the right thing rejoining our commando here."

Pieter doesn't answer. The way he remembers their conversations, it was Willem who had doubted the Boers' ability to win this war and who'd wanted to surrender.

The guerrilla tactics, and its successes to date, give Pieter hope.

Maybe if we Boers irritate the Khakis enough; they'll decide it is not worth the effort and leave. Wouldn't that be fantastic.

Pieter knows he is an ordinary man, a farmer, but he recalls the fable about the fox and the mosquitoes from *Aesop Fables*, his favourite book. In the fable, the fox realises that if the first wave of mosquitoes is driven off, a new wave will arrive with fresh appetites and that this will continue until they eventually bleed him to death.

We Boers are nothing in the context of the British Empire, but sometimes an ordinary man must fight for his convictions in the hope of improving his circumstances.

Thoughts of his daughters come into his mind. His duty is to them. He must fight for their future freedom.

* * *

The following morning, Willem and Pieter remain at the camp, enjoying the novelty of being in a robust gathering of Burghers who are, once again, optimistic about the war. They had slept under the stars the previous evening and it was bitterly cold at this time of year.

The cold had prevented Pieter from sleeping as his previously injured ribs ached. He had risen and sought the warmth of the fire around which several other men sat, drinking coffee and smoking their pipes. He'd exchanged ghost stories with them until exhaustion had chased him back to his sleeping bag.

That morning, the brothers put up their tent which would offer some protection from the night frosts. Mhlopi and Sipho fetch their horses from the grazing-ground and they ride out together to visit neighbouring camps. As they ride, Pieter watches a stream of new recruits riding in from the adjacent countryside.

At one of the other camps, Pieter meets up with Jannie Snyman, a comrade from Polfontein. Jannie's been injured and sports unsightly scars along his right arm. His news is less optimistic than Stoffel's.

"The Khakis are attacking our women and children on the farms in a most cowardly manner. Several Boer families in the far south eastern Transvaal have had their homes destroyed with dynamite and set alight."

Jannie's eyes tell of a great weariness of the soul and his previously solid light brown beard is now streaked with grey.

"The burning of farms has increased since General Roberts issued a proclamation that any of the men from the Krugersdorp district who are serving on commando and who do not surrender by the 20th of July will have their property confiscated."

"That is bad news," anger makes Pieter's voice loud and strident. "How can Lord Roberts justify using women and children as pawns in this war in such an unscrupulous way? Doesn't he know that his government signed the Geneva Convention?"

"It gets worse," Jannie is morose and defeatist. "The Pretoria families of the Burghers who are on commando, have been removed from the city and sent by train to Van der Merwe Station on the eastern railway line. There are over four hundred of them and they have literally been dumped in the veld in the middle of winter with no food."

"That is completely inhumane," gasps Pieter. "How have they justified such dishonourable behaviour?"

"Apparently, Lord Roberts blamed it on the lack of supplies in Pretoria."

"What has happened to these homeless people?"

"They were transported by wagon to Middleburg. I understand that from there, parties of families trekked with their livestock to the bushveld in the north. They should be safe there. The worst part is that the Khakis chose to resume their offensive while the people were travelling and a limited number of Burghers had to defend the rear of the convoy against this cowardly British advance."

A tidal wave of rage washes over Pieter. He is shocked and appalled by the ferocity of his emotions.

How could the British, who held themselves up to the world as role models of superiority and civilisation, behave in such an underhanded and cowardly way.

October 1900

Pieter is exhausted. His small commando has been on the march continuously for over two days and nights and the men and horses have an urgent need for food and rest. Pieter fights to keep his eyes open; he does not want to doze off and risk falling from his horse.

The group is leaderless, their *Kommandant* having been killed during an altercation with the Khakis at Fredrikstad, a railway halt about nineteen miles from Potchefstroom, from which they'd fled. The loss of their leader doesn't matter as the leadership style of the commandos is informal with each man making his own decisions.

Considering General Liebenberg's recent catastrophic decisions, Pieter is pleased to take charge of his own life again.

The wounded among them is far more of a weight on the fleeing survivors than the loss of their leader. Willem is wounded in the arm and has a bloodied rag wrapped around it. Fortunately, it isn't serious, and Pieter is cleaning it with brine as often as their wild flight across the country allows.

Other men have similar types of superficial wounds, the more seriously injured in the fight, including Sipho who was hit in the chest by a stray bullet, having been left behind to be treated by the British. In the circumstances, there was no other option for the fleeing Boers.

Pieter had witnessed Mhlopi die six weeks earlier when he had been hit in the head by a Khaki bullet when a British patrol had unexpectedly come across their encampment one evening. Pieter had seen him jerk suddenly backwards as if he had been hit by a bludgeon. He'd fallen and become motionless, except for his twitching fingers. Pieter had run on, head ducked low, seeking his horse and escape before a bullet could find him. Mhlopi was dead and there was nothing he could do for him.

Willem, Sipho, and he had all escaped without injury.

The loss of Mhlopi and Sipho weighs heavily on the brothers' hearts. The loss of these two devoted servants is more devastating than the deaths of some of their comrades. Life will never be the same again.

When the haven of a friendly farmhouse finally comes into view two hours later, the men virtually collapse off their horses and, after picketing their animals and eating a hasty meal prepared by the women of the house, fall asleep in the barn and lie motionless until the following morning.

While they are resting at the farmhouse, Willem and Pieter have an altercation over the disastrous result of the battle at Fredrikstad.

"General Liebenberg acted foolishly when he decided to attack Major General Barton's camp at Fredrikstad," says Pieter.

"Why do you think that?" Willem turns to look at him quickly, a frown of vague irritation on his normally placid face. "He couldn't know what would happen and he had the backup of General De Wet and his commando."

"Yes, he did have backup, but it was still stupid of him to plan an offensive attack on such a well-prepared British position. The outcome was almost assured to be defeat for us. Now, De Wet has run back to the Free State and our commando suffered severe losses and retreated. That is why we are reduced to hiding in this farmhouse instead of continuing to successfully disrupt the Khakis' movements and communications in the Gatsrand."

Willem's voice suddenly rises sharply, "That is very unfair of you, Pieter. General Liebenberg did the best he could in that battle."

"Potchefstroom will now be re-occupied by the Khakis who'll secure the railway line between the town and their supply base at Krugersdorp. They can also proceed with the burning of our people's farms and the theft of their animals and crops unhindered. This defeat is a disaster for us."

Pieter shakes with suppressed rage.

One of the other Burghers comes towards them, making pacifying motions with his arms.

"Don't shout, friends," he says. "You could give away our position to a Khaki patrol.

Willem turns towards the intruder, red-faced with anger.

"Don't come over here and try to pacify me when my own brother has turned against our *Kommandant*."

"I'm just pointing out that you are putting all of us in danger with your shouting."

"He's right, Willem. Let's set this argument aside for another day."

Willem turns and walks away. A short while later the disagreement is behind them and he and Pieter prepare for bed in an amicable manner.

The following day, replenished with limited supplies, the men move on not wanting to jeopardise the pro-Republican family who own the farm. The burning of farms and plundering of their livestock, crops, and even vehicles has become more common and widespread over the past few months as the British retaliate against the new guerrilla tactics implemented by the Boers.

During their evacuation of the Gatsrand area after the devastating defeat at Fredrickstad, Pieter had been horrified by the devastation that surrounded them in the farming district. Burned out shells of homes lay smouldering against the blue of the sky while piles of ash were all that was left of grain that had been piled up and destroyed by the Khakis. Most of the animals had been seized, together with wagonloads of fodder.

Our successes with blowing up the railway lines and bridges have come at a high price. It doesn't seem worth it. Who would have expected the British to have resorted to such lowly tactics?

That evening, the little group gathers around a small fire in a sunken basin in the veld. They enjoy a mug of their home-made mielie coffee with their meal, while fresh meat obtained from a bush-lancer[1] roasts in the coals. The smell is appetising, and Pieter is almost drooling.

Their resting spot has been carefully chosen and their fire laid with dry grass and sticks, to ensure the fire smoke cannot be easily seen.

Pieter knows that the bush-lancers chose their resting places with equal care, usually seeking out the thickest bushes for sanctuary from the Khakis and the commandos.

It had been a stroke of luck when they came across this Boer and his cattle late that afternoon. He was one of the bush-lancers who loved his cattle so much he would rather have lost his own life than have his cattle taken from him. The men on commando held bush-lancers like him in greater regard than those who had run away with their cattle to escape commando duty or those who hoped that by retaining their cattle they would make a large profit after the war.

"This mielie coffee isn't bad," Willem smacks his lips appreciatively, "but I prefer it with milk."

"It's a sore trial for a Boer to live without coffee," the Burgher stretches out his long legs and exposes the sheep skin patches that adorn his trousers.

Pieter leans forward and turns the meat over using a long stick. The men have discovered that, without salt, meat is most palatable when cooked directly on the white-hot coals as the meat acquires a charred, smoky and slightly ashy crust.

The Burgher chuckles and continues his story, "That bush-lancer was not pleased to see me. He said we'd already taken his best cattle and the Khaki and Australian military units had taken some too. He wouldn't sell me any as he could not do without the few he had left. Of course, I didn't let such an answer stand in the way of my finding food for us."

The conversation turns to plan making.

"What are we going to do now?" asks Willem. "The Khakis have

---

[1] Boers who chose to roam around the veld with their cattle, in order to evade the seizure of their livestock by the British soldiers, were called bush-lancers.

control of Potchefstroom now and the entire Gatsrand and Mooi River area."

"I think we should make our way back towards Gatsrand and try to meet up with what remains of our commando," Pieter looks around at his fellow Burghers to assess their reactions.

No one had a better idea, so it was decided that the group would head back towards the north-west.

April 1901

Darkness has fallen and Pieter sits near the fire, drinking mielie coffee and thinking about his wife and children. Its flaming warmth is welcome as the nights are already cold despite the fierce heat of the autumn daytime sun.

Pieter had seen his family yesterday for the first time in weeks. Marta was despondent, but Renette and Suné had rushed into his arms with tears of joy.

Estelle had been withdrawn and ill-looking. Her thin white hands lay lifeless on her lap as she sat in the chair in the *voorkamer*, listening to Willem and his stories. She was thinner and her back, neck and shoulders were set in lines of fear as if she expected someone to attack her at any moment.

The relationship between Marta and his oldest daughter had deteriorated and the two barely said a word to each other during his short visit. It concerned him greatly, but he hadn't been able to resolve the situation with either Marta or Estelle.

When he had mentioned his concerns about Estelle's withdrawn and frightened behaviour to Marta, she had been unhelpful and almost belligerent.

"Estelle is a disobedient and difficult girl and she brings trouble onto herself," Marta had said. "I can't be expected to understand or comfort someone who is so stubbornly anti-social and uncommunicative."

Estelle had been equally non-responsive to his gentle probing about her anxiety and state of mind.

"There is nothing wrong, Papa," she said, averting her eyes in a furtive way that Pieter noted with concern. "I'm just tired of the war and I miss you," her eyes filled with tears which she successfully fought back.

I'm sure her anxiety has something to do with Marta's rejection of her. She believes she's responsible somehow for Marta's attitude and behaviour. That's not true and maybe it's time for me to tell her the truth about her mother. I'll do it if the opportunity presents itself. I don't want to make a big thing out of it and possibly worsen the situation.

Not knowing what else to do, Pieter had taken her cold and limp hand and led her to his room. Extracting the old suitcase that held his grandmother's belongings from beneath the bed, he opened the old latches. He took out the leather-bound Bible which had belonged to her.

"I want you to have this Bible, Estelle. I know you'll treasure it as I have done. I particularly want you to consider John 8 verses 3 to 12."

He opened the beautiful Bible and started reading:

> And the scribes and Pharisees brought unto him a woman taken in adultery; and when they had set her in the midst, They say unto him, Master, this woman was taken in adultery, in the very act. Now Moses in the law commanded us, that such should be stoned: but what sayest thou?
>
> This they said, tempting him, that they might have to accuse him. But Jesus stooped down, and with his finger wrote on the ground, as though he heard them not. So when they continued asking him, he lifted up himself, and said unto them, He that is without sin among you, let him first cast a stone at her. And again he stooped down, and wrote on the ground.
>
> And they which heard it, being convicted by their own conscience, went out one by one, beginning at the eldest, even unto the last: and Jesus was left alone, and the woman standing in the midst. When Jesus had lifted up himself, and saw none but the woman, he said unto her, Woman, where are those thine accusers? Hath no man condemned thee? She said, No man, Lord. And Jesus said unto her, Neither do I condemn thee: go, and sin no more.
>
> Then spake Jesus again unto them, saying, I am the light of the world: he that followeth me shall not walk in darkness, but shall have the light of life.

He closed the Bible and handed it to her. "Keep it safe and read it often."

Taking it gingerly, she clutched it to her thin chest. "I will Papa."

He walked over to his saddlebags and opened one of the flaps. Pulling out his tobacco pouch, he removed two gold coins. He also removed his sheathed hunting knife. Taking the book back from her, he re-opened it and made a thin slit in the inside leather cover. He slipped the coins into the slit and shook them downwards. They made two small round rises under the leather. He closed the book and gave it back to her.

"Keep these coins hidden and use them if you ever need them. I don't know what the future holds for you and your sisters. Use this gold to keep them and yourself safe and for any emergencies where money can help."

Estelle didn't say anything. Her huge and forlorn eyes broke his heart.

Guilt washes over Pieter as he plays these scenes over in his mind. He knows something is wrong with Estelle and the relationship between her and Marta is worse than ever.

I had no idea, when I married Marta, that she would never accept Estelle as her own child. I expected her to grow to love her and treat her as her own, but that's never happened. She is resentful of Estelle's bloodline and the fact that her mother was an English gentlewoman.

The opportunity hadn't presented itself for Pieter to tell Estelle that Marta was her stepmother and that her birth mother had died during childbirth.

Maybe I didn't want to talk about it and answer the numerous questions she was bound to ask. My memories of Catherine are precious, and her death still pains me after all these years. I should have told Estelle the truth, but I didn't want to deal with my own loss and heartache. I let her down and I let Catherine down too.

He hadn't been able to talk to Marta about Estelle's evident misery as the scorched earth policy employed by the Khakis since the end of January had dominated the thoughts and conversation of the four adults.

Maybe I should have spoken to Sannie. She may know why the relationship between Marta and Estelle has deteriorated so badly lately. It's too late now and I'll just have to pray for them both and ask the Lord to guide them.

Estelle's poor health had been even more evident when he and Willem had left that morning. Her skin was wrapped tightly around her skull, making her green eyes look huge. The similarity between her and a lost Boer child he had found wandering starving in the veld some time ago, was overwhelming.

"Look after yourself, Estelle," he had said to her when he bade her goodbye. "I don't like seeing you looking so thin and frail."

"Yes, Papa," she responded, her voice devoid of all emotion.

Fingers splayed to make the most of the heat of the flames, his anxiety heightens as his mind, like a dog with a bone, worries at the idea of Marta, Sannie, and the children's unprotected position on the farm.

Their isolation amid the vastness of the Transvaal veld, populated by wild animals, poisonous snakes, and a variety of insects, has always worried him during his absences. More recently, the threat of an attack on the farm by either *bywoners* or natives, who have fled their jobs and now roam the veld, has been his main concern.

Recently, the Khakis "burned earth" policy has been added to his list of anxieties. He comforts himself as best he can with the knowledge that they have Karel, who has proved himself to be an excellent watchdog, and Mosiko, who is devoted to his wife and children.

Pieter has been traumatised by his recent experiences in the Gatsrand and Mooi River Valley area with this new burned earth policy.

In January, the Khakis had amassed a force of over twenty thousand men to sweep through the Transvaal, burning and destroying everything in their path. They no longer exercised any discretion and all farms were burned and their livestock and crops either expropriated or destroyed. Even more worrying was the knowledge that the Boer women and children were being picked up by the Khakis and incarcerated in concentration camps.

After the battle of Fredrickstad the same tactics had been implemented in the Gatsrand in an unrestrained way and the farms of everyone – Boers, British sympathisers, republicans, and foreign nationals – had all been targeted. The destruction bruises Pieter's heart and soul.

Unlike some of the Burghers, who feel a sense of freedom from the responsibility of caring for their families as a result of the concentration camp policy, Pieter is horrified at the thought of his family being swept off the veld and interned in some English refugee camp. Like the rest of the men in his commando, the burning of the farms and harsh treatment of their families has hardened his resolve to continue to fight the injustices heaped upon them by the British.

Low conversation hums around him as the men of the camp discuss the events of the day. The commando had utilised a successful hit and run style of fighting to attack and capture a British supply train and its guards.

The commando had taken as much clothing, equipment and munitions as they could carry, as well as some foodstuffs, to replenish their own supplies, which were running rather low. The men are high on the success of the operation.

Anger and worry make it impossible for Pieter to join in the excited talk or even to laugh at the stupidity of the Khakis who do not realise that the Boers are now far more reliant on British supply trains and their wasteful behaviour to replenish their supplies than on their own, or the native families, living in the veld.

Two weeks ago, Willem and he had trailed a column of British soldiers and collected a good supply of Lee-Metford cartridges which had been carelessly dropped and left lying in the dirt.

Can't they see that attacking our farms and incarcerating our families will not cut off our supplies? Unlike at the beginning of the war, our women are no longer our main suppliers.

The beginning of the war had been a shamble with the government, in its enthusiasm, failing to make any proper arrangements for supplying the Burghers with food while on their journeys to the front and afterwards. Many of the Burghers only had provisions for two weeks and expected the government, in accordance with an agreement with its citizens, to provide them with food thereafter.

This oversight caused great suffering, but fortunately, it was quickly remedied by the Boer women who turned every farmhouse and every city residence into a bakery. For the first two months of the war, all the bread consumed by the Burgher army was prepared by their women, who organised an effective division of labour whereby certain women baked the bread, prepared sandwiches and boiled coffee while others procured the needed supplies and still others distributed the food at the various railway stations through which the commando trains passed, or even took it directly to the laagers.

Pieter understands that this was a mass gesture of support for the war effort by their women, who had also taken over many of the laborious tasks on the farms including tending to the flocks and herds, working in the fields, and transporting produce along the roads using the long ox-wagons.

His heart constricts at the knowledge that cutting off supplies to the Boers on commando is unlikely to be the main aim of the Khakis with this new policy of destruction. Destroying their morale is their goal.

The Khakis do not understand our women. Putting them in concentration camps and destroying the farms will increase their hatred of the British and harden their resolve to keep fighting for the freedom of our nation.

Pieter and Willem eat their meal quietly and lie down to sleep, their heads resting against their stiff saddlebags. Sleep is slow in coming. The ground is hard, and they are bothered by numerous insects which are still prolific at this time of year.

MICHELLE

TOM'S CONFESSION

September 2019

Thank goodness they'd come. Pastor John and his assistant, Ruth, are her last remaining hope to stop the downward spiral of Tom's mind into madness.

The move from the hospital to a private room in a subacute rehabilitation facility in Irene has not done Tom any good.

During the day, he lies on his hospital bed, his face a doughy ball of flesh from which his eyes stare listlessly at a world in which he obviously has no further interest. His disinterest extends to Michelle and she feels invisible when she visits him, unable to draw a single word or sign of recognition from his immobile visage, which remains completely expressionless when she greets him.

It's as if he's lost his memory instead of the use of his legs. Only his eyes remained active, darting around furtively as if expecting someone or something to attack him at any moment.

"He raves, thrashes and moans all night, as if in the clutches of some terrible dream," one nurse confides. "He cries out and shouts, but none of us nurses can make out any specific words or names."

The unspoken words make Michelle cringe.

They all think that Tom has lost his mental faculties.

Knowing about the dreams, the reasons for his terror are apparent to Michelle. He's haunted by the relentless poltergeist who wants revenge for her interpretation of his crime. His nights and days are fraught with exhaustion and fear.

The deterioration in his condition over the past week since he had begged her to find Pastor John and ask for his help is startling.

Pastor John is standing in the corridor outside Tom's room when Michelle arrives at 10 a.m. She greets him with trepidation. She's not convinced that his colleague can help Tom, but she hopes for the best outcome possible.

She's already spent many hours on the phone with this man, explaining the circumstances of Tom's mental illness and accident in preparation for today's treatment session. She'd been completely transparent during these discussions and had explained all her anxieties and suspicions.

Pastor John had listened carefully and been supportive of everything she'd said.

"Your timing is fortunate, Michelle," he said at the end of their second lengthy telephone conversation. I have a colleague from the USA currently visiting me here in South Africa. He is a pastor, but he is also a genetic scientist who decided his talents would be better spent doing God's work than making pharmaceutical companies rich. He's developed a new treatment for paralysis involving gene therapy for spinal cord regeneration. I discussed Tom's case with Pastor Luke, and he's prepared to try to help Tom before he returns home in a few days' time."

"This is unexpected. How does it work?"

"I don't know the details, but it involves an injection into his spinal cord. The injection is followed by a series of physiotherapy treatments using transcutaneous electrical nerve stimulation, or TENS, to control the pain as the damaged nerves start to regenerate. I understand TENS works by delivering small electrical impulses through electrodes that are attached to the patient's skin. These electrical impulses flood the nervous system, reducing its ability to transmit pain signals to the spinal cord and brain."

"Can't we get this treatment for Tom though his current doctor? Surely there are genetic scientists here in South Africa who could perform this treatment for him?"

"Gene delivery strategies are a new area of medicine, Michelle. Pastor Luke is an extraordinarily intelligent man and I believe that his being here now, just when Tom needs him, is an intervention by God on Tom's behalf."

"I don't know what to say. It sounds like a wonderful opportunity and I'm sure Tom will jump at it if you recommend it. The alternative is a long period of paralysis with a chance of recovery many years from now."

"He many never run and jump again," Pastor John said, "but Pastor Luke believes he'll be able to get about with the aid of a walking stick."

A few days later, Tom gave Pastor John his go ahead for the treatment and the die was cast.

An intense and strong personality, Pastor John had determinedly pushed aside any further worries she'd expressed during subsequent conversations; even her concern about how he would get the staff in the rehabilitation facility to co-operate with this unorthodox brand of treatment.

"When are you going to start?" Michelle asks.

"Very soon. Your husband dozes through his days, but the nurses withheld his pain and sleeping medications last night at my request, so he'll be more mentally active today."

Pastor John looks at Michelle carefully. "You don't have to stay. Pastor Luke has me and my assistant, Ruth, to help him."

Oh no, the next hour is going to be an ordeal but I'm sticking around. There is no way I'm allowing this man to affect a sham cure and charge me a fortune for it.

"Thank you, but I'll stay."

"As you like," he smiles reassuringly, "I'm comfortable with that."

Through the open door, Michelle sees a woman bustling around the room, setting up equipment under the watchful eye of a tall, thin man. She lifts a small machine out of its box and places it on a trolley.

I wonder how Pastor John convinced the nurses to co-operate with him for this session and to withhold Tom's medications last night. I would have thought it was unusual for them to do so and dangerous too. I'm sure Pastor John must have bribed them to stay away.

"I'm ready when you are, John," the tall man calls from inside Tom's room.

Pastor John sweeps into the room, almost bouncing with excitement. Michelle tentatively follows.

"Pastor Luke, Ruth, meet Michelle, Tom's wife," Pastor John introduces his two colleagues, in turn. "Michelle, meet Pastor Luke and my assistant, Ruth."

"Nice to meet you both," Michelle smiles at them.

"Good morning, Tom," Pastor John's attention shifts to the injured man.

The prone figure on the bed opens his eyes and peers up at the pastor. His lips draw back over his teeth in an attempt at a smile.

"Hello, Tom," Michelle greets her husband.

He looks at her briefly with disinterested eyes that show no recognition and then shifts his gaze back to the pastor.

"This is my colleague, Pastor Luke, and my assistant, Ruth. We're going make you better, Tom," Pastor John's eyes are warm and compassionate. "Before we begin, is there anything you wish to say to me?"

"Yes, Pastor," Tom's uncertain whisper strengthens as he continues, "there is something I need to tell you. I'm a rapist and guilty of manslaughter."

Michelle stands and listens as Tom recounts the story of the date rape she's already witnessed in her nightmares. His voice is hoarse, as if the words are being dragged over sandpaper.

The circumstances leading up to the death of Tracey Atkinson, as revealed by Tom, are exactly those she'd already heard from Trevor.

"It was such a stupid thing to do," Tom's hands, lying on top of the bedclothes, tremble. "I've lived with the guilt of it for years. I stopped drinking heavily after that night. Meeting Michelle gave me the strength to stay off the booze and rebuild my life. I was lucky no one guessed the truth and I kept my job and position."

Yes, you were lucky, thought Michelle bitterly.

Suspecting something and knowing it for certain is not the same thing, she realises.

You used me to put it all behind you, but what about that poor girl. She lies dead in the cemetery, her life destroyed by your callous actions.

"Thank you for sharing this with me, Tom," Pastor John takes his hand gently. "In order for my treatment to work you need to have confessed your sins and allowed Jesus to remove your burden of guilt and hopelessness. Remember Matthew verses 11:28 to 11:30, Come to me, all you who are weary and burdened, and I will give you rest. Take my yoke upon you and learn from me, for I am gentle and humble in heart, and you will find rest for your souls. For my yoke is easy and my burden is light."

Tom is crying, the tears course down his cheeks and wet his pillow.

"I was a fool, a selfish and stupid fool. My guilt has always remained with me, even though I moved on with my life as best I could. I even bought an Ouija board. I saw it in the window of a shop I was passing one day and felt compelled to go in and buy it. I had a vague idea of using it to contact Tracey and ask her to forgive me."

"Did you use it, Tom? Did you try and contact her?" Pastor John studies Tom's face carefully.

"No, I lost my nerve. I've never believed in the occult, but what if I did succeed in contacting her and she wouldn't forgive me? What if she decided to haunt me?" His dry lips parted in a bitter grin. "I didn't know that she wasn't the threat to me."

Pastor John squeezes Tom's hand encouragingly.

"Let us pray. Turning to the Lord for strength in times of need is the best thing any of us can do."

The beautiful words of the prayer sooth Michelle and she pushes her anger at Tom's confession, and her devastation at his betrayal of her trust aside to deal with later. Now, she needs to focus on this miracle cure that the two pastors are proposing.

Pastor John's words calm Tom and his jaw and clenched fists relax.

"Let's get started," Pastor Luke removes a large syringe from its protective wrapper. "It won't take long, and Tom won't feel any pain."

The two men gently roll Tom over onto his stomach and remove the back brace.

Ruth pushes the trolley holding the small machine towards the bed. The control dials on the machine's face catch Michelle's attention, as do several electrodes linked to it which hang loose until Ruth attaches them to Tom's back.

"Hold his shoulders down, Ruth," Pastor Luke fills the syringe with a clear concoction from a small bottle. "This injection is directly into his spinal cord and feels icy cold as it travels up the spinal column. The unpleasant sensation could make him jump." He inserts the needle into the base of Tom's spine and presses the plunger down, slowly, and firmly. Once the plunger is empty, he removes it deftly and throws it into a bin marked "sharps".

The LED down lights embedded in the ceiling explode, showering bits of plastic down on the people and bed. The temperature drops.

Exhaling sharply, Michelle's breath makes a puffy cloud in the sudden chill.

The machine on the trolley creaks as its sides bow outwards. Crack! It splits in two. A crackle of blue electricity runs along the cords and the patient on the bed jumps. Ruth, who is still holding his shoulders, flies backwards and crashes into the wall.

Tom's legs and arms shoot out stiffly, relax, and then shoot out stiffly again.

"Oh my God, Pastor Luke shouts. "Oh, my dear God, what is happening?"

The man on the bed is dancing an electric jig, his eyes are open, but there are no eyes, only a bulging whiteness.

"Gaaaaah." A series of choking sounds escape his mouth and spittle rolls down his jaw.

"STOP IT!" shrieks Michelle, "It's killing him."

Snap! Snap! Snap! The electrodes pop off his straining back and fly across the room, hitting the walls and making small craters in the plaster.

There are smoking black rings on Tom's flesh where the electrodes had been attached.

Tom's body convulses into one last dramatic spasm and slumps into a boneless pile of flesh. A subtle smell of burning taints the air that Michelle draws into her shocked lungs.

"I WIN! YOU CAN'T UNDO MY WORK. CAN'T MAKE HIM WALK AGAIN!" The words echo around the room, bouncing off the stark white walls. "HE'S DEAD!"

An indistinct shadow, like a whirlwind, swirls around the room and plunges out of the closed window.

The room's temperature returns to normal.

* * *

Pastor John leaps across the room and starts administering CPR to the deathly white figure on the bed.

A groan refocuses Michelle and she swings towards the spot where Ruth hit the wall.

The assistant has pulled herself into a kneeling position and is cradling her head in her hands.

Thank God she's alive. Two deaths would be a complete catastrophe. How are we going to explain what happened to the staff and police?

Michelle makes a jerky move towards Ruth but freezes at Tom's loud command. "Stop, Pastor John, I'm okay." His eyes are open; they are his normal blue eyes and look attentive and alert.

"What happened?" he wriggles his toes. "My feet are tingling, ooooooh, it's driving me mad. I can't move. Someone rub them for me. Please!"

* * *

"The inflammation of the membrane in his spine has gone down," Doctor Haasbrook looks up from the scans he has been examining. "We hoped this might happen over time and Tom would eventually walk again, but the speed with which it has happened is unprecedented. To be honest, I've never heard of anything quite like this. Tom can move his legs and should be able to walk normally within the next few days. No doctor would have predicted this outcome, but it's happened."

"It's amazing," Michelle whispers.

"Once he's strong enough to be discharged from hospital, he'll require extensive physiotherapy at home," Doctor Haasbrook looks at Michelle. "My nurse will give you the contact details of a physiotherapist in Irene so that you can make the necessary appointments. I assume you'll be the one taking him to those sessions?"

"Yes, of course," Michelle's feeling dazed.

Who would have expected this outcome? Not the poltergeist, that's for sure. What will she do now that her plan to kill Tom has failed? Does she know he's not dead?

* * *

Pastor John, Ruth, Alice and Michelle sit in her lounge drinking cups of tea.

Michelle had left Tom sleeping. Dr Haasbrook said he would sleep for hours following his ordeal.

"Go home and get some rest, Michelle. The nurse will call you when he wakes up," he'd directed.

Michelle rests quietly, listening to Alice and Pastor John talking and making plans.

"Something must be done to deal with the spirits that are haunting this house and Tom," declares Alice. "I've personally experienced the power of this poltergeist, Estelle, and she isn't going to just pack up and leave now that her plan has been thwarted. She's going to try again."

"You said the other two ghosts, the ones called Pieter and Robert, are not dangerous. Is that correct, Michelle?" Pastor John looks at Michelle.

"Yes, I understand they want my help to change their existing situations as ghosts. They both want their stories revealed to the world. They're helping me do that through the book I'm writing. Robert confirmed that the two of them had a history together and he passed from this life carrying a burden of resentment and hatred towards Pieter. I don't know the details of what precipitated Robert's early death. My interactions with Pieter indicate he is seeking some sort of redemption for a past transgression. As I said, I don't know what he did or why it affected him so badly that his spirit became trapped here on earth."

"How do you feel about Tom?" Alice is sitting next to Michelle and pats her hand gently. "You suspected that he raped Tracey Atkinson and that it broke her mentally and resulted in her suicide. How do you feel about his confession and knowing that he did rape her and ultimately cause her death?"

Michelle stares at Alice. "I … I don't know," she whispers. "I lay awake all of last night thinking about what I should do. Trying to come to a decision. I knew, in my heart, that what I suspected was true."

The small group look at her expectantly. "What did you decide?" Alice probes gently.

"I'd decided that a divorce was necessary … that I couldn't live with a man who had committed such an evil act and then deceived me about it for the whole of our married life."

"Do you still feel the same, Michelle?"

"After the events of today and Tom's confession I feel so confused again. What Tom did was terrible and wrong, but he didn't intend for Tracey to die. Should he be forgiven? Does he deserve forgiveness? Is the poltergeist right in thinking he should die for his sins? An eye for an eye like it says in the Old Testament. I'm so confused."

"Do you remember the Tarot card you drew just before Tom's accident, Michelle? The High Priestess? You didn't know what that card signified then. Maybe its message was about this situation. Estelle clearly bore a huge grudge against rapists and men in general when she died. I agree that people should pay for their crimes, but Estelle's behaviour overlooks the New Testament's doctrine of forgiveness."

Alice's earnestness and Biblical reference surprise Michelle.

Pastor John nods his head.

"I agree with Alice, Michelle. You need to consider your relationship with Tom carefully and decide if you can find it in your heart to forgive him. He's suffered a lot lately. The Bible says:

> people should bear with each other and forgive one another.
> You must forgive the sins of others as the Lord has forgiven
> yours.

"You love Tom, Michelle. You had a good life together. Think about it carefully and then make your decision," Alice says firmly.

"I'll think about it," her voice trembles. "I want to see how he behaves when he comes home. I can't live with a drunk."

"I understand," Pastor John smiles at Michelle reassuringly, "I'm sure you'll make the right decision when the time comes. Meanwhile, we need to plan how we are going to deal with the situation of the three ghosts. We need to try to help them achieve the peace they are seeking, and by doing so, we'll also help Tom and you."

"What can we do? I've only been able to contact Pieter through the Ouija board and it's not an effective medium of communication. Robert's been more forthcoming, and I've spoken directly to him a few times. He did say that he and Pieter would work together to help us resolve the problem with Estelle." Michelle looks around entreatingly.

"I think," Pastor John considers Michelle and Alice in turn, ensuring he has their complete attention, "that we should try innovation and see if the spirit of Pieter will manifest itself so that we can speak to him. At the same time, we can try to get Robert to interact with us and Pieter. They'll be able to share their individual stories and reasons for remaining earth-bound after their deaths. They may also be able to shed some light on what happened to Estelle to make her so malevolent and embittered."

The two ladies nod their heads in unison.

* * *

The rosy flush of health colours Tom's cheeks. Michelle looks at him stunned, as he sits up in bed eating his dinner. It is three days since Estelle's failed attempt to kill him and the change in Tom is unbelievable. He's not only recovered the use of his legs, but his mind seems to have healed too. His confession has opened the festering wound in his soul and allowed the terrible infection that had accumulated over the years to drain away.

Pastor John's daily mindfulness sessions with him have also helped squeeze out the last of the poison and facilitate this amazing healing. The Tom lying in front of her in his hospital bed is the old Tom. The man she'd loved and married.

How do I feel now? I just don't know.

Dr Haasbrook's nurse had called her that morning. Tom had slept for twenty-four hours following his ordeal three days previously and, today, he had asked for her. Initially, it hurt her to know that Tom had asked to see Pastor John before her. She knows Pastor John has seen Tom twice already.

Tom explained the purpose of his meetings with Pastor John.

"I wanted to thrash out my emotions and thoughts before seeing you. Pastor John's helped me work through my guilt and remorse and I needed to do that before I could face you."

Seeing Tom so improved melted away any remaining irritation and resentment Michelle held.

She quietly watches him enjoying his chicken curry and then half of his chocolate fudge brownie before laying his fork down.

"I'm full, it's all delicious but I can't eat another thing."

"You need to give yourself some time, Tom. Your recovery is miracu-lous, but you must remember you were ill for weeks before the gene therapy."

"Pastor John told me what happened. It seems that the poltergeist inadvertently healed me instead of killing me as she intended."

"Yes, that is also what I think. Pastor Luke said the enormous electrical charge that passed through your body greatly accelerated the effect of the gene therapy he administered. As a result, you skipped the entire regeneration period and were healed immediately. Despite her negative motivations, she ended up helping you."

"I'm surprised Dr Haasbrooke has not investigated this further, Michelle. Why do you think that is?"

A gusty sigh passes through Michelle's lips and she shakes her head. "I don't know, Tom. That's puzzled me too. Pastor John said that the TENS machine shorted and, as a result, the current that passed into your body was much stronger than he intended. I think Dr Haasbrooke is so overwhelmed by your complete recovery in such a short period that he hasn't delved into the circumstances too deeply yet. I don't know, but Pastor John seems to be managing him and his questions."

"I want to come home, Michelle," Tom says, looking at her steadily. His eyes are clear and engaging. "I know I misled you and you have a lot to forgive me for, but I would like you to think about putting this behind us and trying to get our lives back on track."

Reaching out and taking his hand, Michelle looks into his eyes and shares what's in her heart. "I want you to come home, Tom, I want it very much, but I can't live with you if you are drinking like you were. If you want to come home, you must promise to go to the Alcoholics Anonymous meetings Dr Haasbrooke recommended and put the drinking behind you."

"I'm ready to do that Michelle. I'm worried that the poltergeist will try to come after me again once she realises that her attempt to kill me failed. I am also scared she will try to get at me by harming you, but I won't be resorting to alcohol again. I've come to terms with the reality of the situation and I realise that this poltergeist is not just a figment of my guilt and imagination. I thought I was going crazy and the booze helped me to cope with my feelings of inadequacy. I'm hoping that Pastor John will help us find a way to deal with Estelle and ensure that we can both live in safety going forward."

"Okay, Tom. Dr Haasbrooke said it would be at least four or five more days before he can discharge you. In the meantime, Alice is staying with me at our house and Pastor John and Ruth are just down the road so I'm as safe as is reasonably possible."

Michelle doesn't tell him about Pastor John's planned innovation to try and get the spirits of both Pieter and Robert to manifest themselves.

He'll want us to wait until he returns home before holding the innovation ceremony and I think it's better to do it when he's not there. Estelle may choose to appear and Tom's presence will make any negotiations with her impossible.

"What are you thinking about so deeply?"

Michelle smiles at Tom. "I'm just thinking how nice it'll be when you come home."

I'm sure Pastor John would have mentioned the innovation ceremony if he thought Tom should attend.

ESTELLE

FARM LIFE

August 1900

As soon as Papa and *Oom* Willem's mounted figures disappear into the distance, Marta starts harassing Estelle about doing more to help with the household tasks and farm work.

"You need to help more, Estelle, and stop all this running around in the veld gathering flowers or sitting reading your father's books. You know we have a shortage of labour on the farm and August and Solomon are having to do farm work and can't help us in the house."

Estelle eyes her mother with derision at this statement.

Of course I know about the labour shortage. I'm not stupid. I've noticed that some of the labourers have disappeared from the farm since our arrival here. I also know they are either supporting the Khakis or have returned to their tribal homes. How could I not know, you've complained enough about it.

Estelle keeps her thoughts to herself although she realises that Mama must sense her silent insubordination.

"Yes, Mama," she looks down, avoiding Marta's eyes.

"Well, don't just stand there. Go and collect the eggs from the hen-house. You're already late with that."

Estelle sets off briskly towards the distant henhouse, her back rigid and her head held high.

I miss Papa so much. How much longer can this awful war go on?

She thinks about August, *Tannie* Sannie's elderly houseman. She doesn't know him well, but he has always been there, working in the house, whenever her family made their visits to *Oom* Willem's farm in the past. His ready grin and the network of smile induced wrinkles around his twinkling brown eyes had always made Estelle feel welcome. Now the older man is having to help Mosiko and the other farm workers with the task of keeping the farm running.

I really miss having him inside the house. I've lost a friend.

Solomon is a middle-aged man who helped with the cooking and preparation of the meals. Kind and patient, he always had a broad toothy smile for Estelle although he never said much. He is also currently helping Mosiko with the livestock and the care of the crops. There is no home help anymore.

Mama and *Tannie* Sannie both employ houseboys rather than house-maids in accordance with the common *Boerevrou*[1] practice. Through overheard bits of conversation and observation, Estelle knows that *Boerevrouen*[2] prefer to hire male servants. Although it is rarely mentioned, Estelle also knows that this practice is due to a general fear by *Boerevrouen* that their husbands will become sexually involved with female workers. Estelle doesn't understand exactly what this means, but she knows it is linked to a woman's ability to have babies.

Whatever it is, she thinks, *it is a bad thing and I don't understand why the women don't just say no to the men.*

Without any domestic help in the house, *Tannie* Sannie and Mama assign certain tasks to their children, like making the beds, washing dishes and doing the laundry.

Lena and Hannekie take the clothes and linen and put them in the wash tub. Renette and Suné tread the washing up and down until it is clean enough for their older cousins to finish washing it. The two little girls regard this task as great fun and squeals of joy and giggles of delight fill the air as they splash about in the large tub.

Estelle hangs the washing outside on the wash line and brings it inside once it is dry. Hanging the washing outside is a horrible task and none of the women or children like doing it. The washing is ready to be hung outside at about 11 a.m. and the sun is high in the sky. Even though it's only August, it beats down on her bonnet covered head and body. Sweat runs down her body within the confines of her long sleeved dress and trickles down her cheeks and neck. Only her bare feet feel comfortable and free of hot and heavy constraints.

Mama gives me this job because she doesn't like me. It's a punishment.

One Sunday, after *Tannie* Sannie and Mama have cooked the dinner and Estelle and Lena have washed and dried a seemingly endless pile of pots and dishes, Mama broaches the idea of employing a native woman

---

[1] An Afrikaner woman, usually a farmer's wife of conservative outlook.

[2] Plural of *Boerevrou.*

to help them in the house.

"I'm dead tired tonight, Sannie. It is hard to manage the farm without Willem and Pieter and also do all the cleaning, cooking and washing on our own."

Tannie Sannie looks at Mama, a wary expression on her face, the tension is palpable. Estelle can sense it, but she doesn't understand it.

"Willem and Pieter are away for an unknown and indefinite period, Sannie. We need some help in the house while they are away fighting, and we are alone on the farm."

Tannie Sannie nods in acknowledgement of Mama's comment but doesn't say anything.

"Mosiko has seen how we are suffering, and he suggested that his wife and daughter come and help us in the house until our menfolk return. Mosiko has worked for Pieter's family all his life and we know his wife and children well. They are good people."

Tannie Sannie sighs deeply, "We could certainly use the help. I'm exhausted by the end of the day. The girls are wonderful, and they really try to help, but another set of hands would not go amiss. I agree to giving Mosiko's wife a trial period in the house, but why do we need his daughter, she is only a girl."

"I think Mosiko wants her to get some experience working in the house. It would give her an opportunity to get a job in a city later in her life."

"I think he has aspirations above his station in life, but I won't stop the girl coming and helping her mother."

Mama smiles, "I'll speak to Mosiko about it tomorrow."

I must warn you, Marta, that if it doesn't work out, I'll ask them to leave."

"I understand, Sannie."

"And when Willem and Pieter are here, they must stay away. The jobs will end when they men return home permanently."

"I'll explain it to Mosiko and make sure he understands."

On Tuesday morning, Mosiko's wife and daughter arrive early to start work in the house. Ardrina and Dorthea are quiet and unobtrusive as they go about their daily tasks and the entire family's burdens reduce considerably as they no longer have to gather and carry the wood for the fires, clean the house, and do all the washing and ironing.

Estelle and Dorthea are childhood friends. Estelle remembers slipping away from the house and going down to the labourers' kraal as a young girl. Ardrina welcomed her and allowed her to help with some of her household tasks.

Life in the kraal is so interesting. It was fun to cook outside over the communal fire and listen to Ardrina's stories about the Ancestors.[1]

"Tell me about the Ancestors, Ardrina," she would cry.

Ardrina would reply, "The Ancestors live in the spirit world of *Unkulukulu* and are regarded as intermediaries between the living and the spirit world. The ancestral spirits are known as *amadlozi* and *abaphansi* and make themselves known through dreams, sickness and snakes.

"We make offerings of home-brewed beer and animal sacrifices to the Ancestors to keep them happy and to ask them for blessings, good luck, fortune, guidance, and assistance.

"If bad luck occurs in the kraal, the *Sangoma*[2] is consulted to determine whether the occurrence is a result of witchcraft or due to the Ancestors feeling neglected or becoming angry. Once a decision as to the cause has been made, either a witch hunt takes place, or a sacrifice is made to appease the Ancestors."

Papa has always encouraged Estelle to visit Mosiko's family at the kraal. He understands her pleasure in their simple way of life and entertaining stories. Mama does not understand or like it. Now that Papa is away, she has forbidden Estelle from visiting the kraal.

"Why? Why can't I visit Ardrina and Dorthea at the kraal? Papa never minded."

"Your Papa is ignorant of the ways of society, especially for women. He's not here now to condone your unladylike behaviour and I'm not allowing it. It is time for you to start behaving appropriately, Estelle. I'll not have you bring shame on me and my children."

Estelle has no option but to stay away from the kraal, but at least the extra help in the house frees her a bit from the yoke of her mother's demands and expectations. She returns to her previous habit of taking long daily walks around the farm.

September 1900

Estelle's life on the farm has settled into a routine and the early spring days pass quickly and uneventfully. One afternoon in mid-September, a

---

[1] Indigenous religions believe that their ancestors can offer advice and bestow good fortune and honour on their living dependents. They also make demands and insist that their shrines be properly maintained and their spirits appeased.

[2] The spiritual healer of the Zulu-speaking people of Southern Africa.

thick cloud of dust appears on the horizon. Mosiko comes running with a warning that a great crowd of horsemen and ox-wagons is approaching. It is a Boer Commando, but not one from this district.

The disorganised gathering sweeps into the yard with a great deal of noise and commotion and sets about making a camp. The *Kommandant* comes to the door and knocks.

"Good evening, ladies," he says, "we'll be resting here overnight. I would be obliged if you could give us coffee and some milk."

His clothes are cared for, and he looks neat and respectable, despite his dishevelled appearance from riding hard all day.

The tension in Mama and *Tannie* Sannie's shoulders and necks is obvious and Estelle realises they are worried about this situation. Despite her misgivings, *Tannie* Sannie agrees to provide them with coffee and milk as is the custom and expectation.

"We can't provide you with any other assistance. Our supplies of flour, mielie meal and other foodstuffs are limited and we don't have to spare," she tells the *Kommandant*.

"Coffee and milk will be fine, *Mevrou*.[1] Thank you for your kind assistance."

"I'll fetch the milk, Marta, and Lena and Hannekie can start making the coffee." The straight set of *Tannie* Sannie's back and thin line of her mouth tells of her displeasure at this turn of events.

The making and serving of coffee for the men continues all afternoon and in between there are a few other knocks at the door.

A burly man with small, piggy eyes asks for kindling and wood. He is dirty and disreputable looking, his skin burned brown by the harsh Transvaal sun and his hair hanging in greasy clumps.

"We don't have any wood to spare." Mama points at the distant cluster of trees where the girls gather kindling for use in the house. "You can collect your own wood from the copse over there."

Mosiko cuts logs for their use but smaller kindling is necessary to start their fires or the large logs won't burn. Estelle knows their kindling pile is low and she was planning to gather more sticks and twigs when she went out walking that afternoon.

I wonder if Mama and Tannie Sannie will let me go now that all these men have arrived. I think they'll be more inclined to let me go if I take Lena and Hannekie with me.

The dirty man is clearly not pleased by their lack of assistance and

---

[1] Afrikaans word for madam or Mrs.

argues that they should be more helpful and give him the wood he needs.

Fortunately, the *Kommandant* hears the commotion and strides back over. "The ladies do not have any wood to spare, Koos," he says. "Do as they suggest and look for your own in the wooded area over there," he points in the general direction of the trees.

The man called Koos glowers at Mama but obeys the *Kommandant*. Slinking away towards the copse.

The *Kommandant* tips his hat at them. "I apologise for his behaviour. We appreciate the coffee and milk you have given us. Good afternoon."

He turns and strolls back to the laager.

A short while later, another man knocks on their door. His blond beard is scraggly and thin, and his greasy skin is spotty. He is still just a boy. His clothing is dirty and stained and he looks uncared for and neglected. He asks them for mielie meal.

This time *Tannie* Sannie is the one who turns him away empty handed.

"I don't like the look of some of these men. They're not keeping themselves or their clothing clean and have a wild look about them. That *Kommandant* is stupid," she continues as she closes and bolts the door, "a lonely farmhouse inhabited by two women and four female children is no place for him to make a camp with so many over-friendly men."

The younger children are anxious about all the strangers in the yard. They group themselves around Karel, clutching him wildly and hanging on to his thick neck.

At 4.30 p.m. Mama and *Tannie* Sannie realise that they do not have enough kindling for the morning fire. Even if they bank the fire carefully, it will not last the night and will have gone out long before the morning.

"What should we do?" *Tannie* Sannie asks Mama. "I'm not keen on sending the girls out to look for kindling with all these strange men around the place."

"If we don't send them to get some sticks and wood, we won't be able to start the fire in the morning and serve coffee to the men. They may give us trouble if we don't do what is expected. If the girls go now as a group, it won't take them long to get enough for tomorrow morning."

"Okay, you're right. Lena, Hannekie and Estelle can go, and I'll tell them to stay together."

* * *

Lena, Hannekie and Estelle set off towards the small wooded area, each carrying a basket. It is in the opposite direction from the temporary camp the Boers have set up in a nearby shallow dip in the land. The girls can smell the smoke from their campfires and hear the hum of distant conversation and laughter.

Estelle misses Karel who is not with them. Mama had told the girls to leave him behind.

"He might attack one of the men if we allow him to roam free. He's been growling at our unwanted visitors ever since they arrived. It will cause a lot of trouble if he bites someone."

Lena and Hannekie are deep in conversation about an upcoming event at the church in the local village and wondering if their mother will allow them to go. They don't notice that Estelle is falling behind as she dithers while collecting a bouquet of wildflowers.

At the start of the trees, Estelle is distracted by a cloud of white butterflies. She stops walking and watches them flying haphazardly in all directions. She has never seen so many butterflies altogether before and she stands for a while, watching them dancing across the veld and imagining they are fairies.

By the time she starts walking again, Lena and Hannekie have disappeared among the trees and she doesn't know which path they've taken.

"Bother," she mutters under her breath, as she chooses a path and rushes along it, stopping intermittently to pick up sticks and hoping to catch up with the two older girls, who are unlikely to have even noticed she's not with them.

An unkempt Boer looms up unexpectedly in front of her. Estelle's sticks tumble to the ground as surprise loosens her grip on the bundle of firewood she's been clutching to her chest.

Taking a careful step backwards, Estelle wraps her arms protectively around herself.

He leers at her, his thin lips drawing back over brown-stained yellow teeth, and reaches out, grabbing hold of her frail wrist in an iron grip.

Opening her mouth to scream, he roughly slaps his free hand across the bottom half of her face, effectively stifling the sound before it can erupt from her mouth. His rough, calloused hand abrades her skin, bruising her lips and cheeks, and his pungent stink makes her gag.

Drawing back his clenched fist, he rams it into her soft stomach. The pain is incredible, and she seems to choke on the trapped scream that reflects off his restricting hand and forces itself back down her throat.

The man's eyes glow with a heinous lechery as she wrenches her body backwards, trying to break free of his grasp. He lets go of her and she tumbles to the ground, thumping down hard on her back. A soft whimpering sound reaches her ears, like a distressed animal, and she realizes with horror it's coming from her.

Agony explodes in her right side as the man kicks her, his unyielding boot connecting with her ribs, just to the side of her budding breasts. Self-preservation causes her to try and roll away, despite the debilitating pain. He roars laughter. "Trying to get away from me, are you?"

She watches him unbuckle his belt and let his trousers drop. Dropping gracelessly to his knees beside her, he plunges his hands under her dress, yanking it up and ripping her underclothes down. Her gorge rises again at the ripe smell of his unwashed body as he forces her thighs apart and wedges his knee between them.

Gazing up into his ugly face she can see each course strand of his long brown beard and even the blackheads in his large nose. His breath is hot and moist on her skin. He brings his head down and rubs his face all over hers.

A terrible pain rips through her as he forces some stiff and unyielding part of his body into her delicate flesh. He thrusts savagely into her, hips pumping, and grunting like an animal, before stiffening and collapsing on top of her. A few minutes later he rolls away, crushing her injured side and forcing a deep groan from her.

She lies for few moments, unable to move, as he pulls up his trousers and buckles his belt. Glancing down at her, he grins, and then strides away, disappearing among the trees.

The sound of her rushing blood and gasping breaths roars in her ears as she lies in a sticky puddle. Her eyes flutter and her mind spirals down into blackness.

* * *

Two hours later, Mosiko finds her. She forces her eyes open at the sound of his familiar voice and looks up into his shocked brown eyes. Dimly she is aware that her dress is tangled around her waist and her thighs are sticky. Her stomach is on fire, but modesty forces her to try and roll over while her hands seek to pull her skirt down, hiding her nakedness.

She feels his tears drip onto the side of her face, running down her cheek and onto the hard ground beneath her.

Mosiko bends down and lifts her up. She writhes in pain from her damaged ribs. Holding her firmly, he sets off towards the farmhouse.

* * *

Estelle is aware of Mama opening the door to admit Mosiko.

"What is wrong Mosiko? What has happened?" she hears Mama ask him. The words swirl sickeningly around her aching head.

She sees the tears slipping from the older man's eyes. They create shiny paths as they run down his cheeks. His skin has a dull, greyish look as if he is terribly ill.

"One of the men attacked Estelle," he manages to say, lips quivering with suppressed anguish.

"Oh no, Mosiko. What did he do to her? Is she hurt?" *Tannie* Sannie comes up behind Mama and draws her out of the doorway. "Let him inside, Marta."

Turning to Mosiko, she says: "Take her straight to her bedroom and put her on the bed."

Mosiko lays her gently on the bed and leaves the room. It's not his place to stay and tend to her. He'll wait in the kitchen for Marta to bring him news of Estelle's injuries.

Mama removes Estelle's clothing and inspects her body.

"She has lacerations and terrible bruising. Her ribs are painful and there is swelling, but they are not broken," she says. "She has been defiled, Sannie. How could she bring disgrace upon our family like this?"

"It's not her fault, Marta," *Tannie* Sannie says softly. "She's a victim. You mustn't say such things."

"It is her fault, Sannie," Mama's harsh tone plunges into Estelle's fragile heart like a knife. "She put herself in harm's way. She didn't listen to my instructions about staying with her cousins. She never listens and now the worst has happened. Her father will be so ashamed."

A soft whimper of misery escapes Estelle's swollen throat.

"Let's not talk about this now," says *Tannie* Sannie soothingly. "I'll get some warm water and help you wash her and put on her clean clothes. Why don't you make a brine solution to clean her wounds?"

* * *

Estelle hears the door of her room open and someone enter. As she gradually awakens to a world of pain, her soul separates from her body and floats above it. The stillness of the small figure in the bed makes her wonder fleetingly if she is dead and her soul has departed her body.

Her physical body lies as motionless as stone, arms lying limply on top of the blankets, until *Tannie* Sannie gently touches her cheek. She sees herself react with great fear, jerking her body backwards and hitting her head against the wall behind her. She can see abrasions and marks on her lower face and around her wrist. They stand out cruelly against her pale skin.

Her soul re-enters her battered body and her eyes flutter open. She looks at *Tannie* Sannie. She's incapable of speech and makes no sound but watches warily as *Tannie* Sannie sets about caring for her wounds and bruises.

Why is Tannie *Sannie caring for me and not Mama?*

Tannie Sannie dips the rags she has brought with her into a bowl containing a brine solution. The open cuts and lacerations on Estelle's ribcage and body sting as her aunt applies the disinfecting mixture. *Tannie* Sannie's tears drip onto Estelle's exposed skin, warm drops of love and compassion that burn into her heart.

Estelle can't see the damage well from her lying position but knows from *Tannie* Sannie's reaction it must look terrible.

A soft knock sounds and Ardrina comes into the room. "Here is the poultice you asked me to make," she says quietly. "I made it from bread and wine like you said and then boiled the mixture over the open fire outside. It is cool now."

"Thank you, Ardrina," says *Tannie* Sannie.

Estelle feels her aunt's cool hands on her damaged flesh as she applies the poultice. "This will help with your bruising," she says.

Tannie Sannie dips a little bread in some warmed milk and offers it to her. Estelle eats a tiny amount and then turns her head away, staring with indifferent blankness at the wall.

"Let's leave her to sleep, Ardrina. I'll come back after supper to clean her wounds with the brine solution again. Please could you make another bread poultice this evening and I'll apply it. I'm also going to make her some beef tea as that will be easier for her to drink with her throat injuries."

Tannie Sannie and Ardrina leave and Estelle is left alone.

November 1900

Two months have passed since the attack that claimed Estelle's innocence and dealt the final blow to her relationship with her mother. Mama views her with disgust and visibly shrinks from touching her as if she has a contagious disease.

Estelle's care, during her period of convalescence, has been handed over entirely to *Tannie* Sannie and Ardrina.

A few days after the attack, *Tannie* Sannie had tried to explain to her what had happened. She told her about the sex act and its purpose within the sanctity of marriage for women to have children.

"Having sex with a man outside of marriage is a sin in the eyes of the church," she says. "Your mother is struggling to adjust to what has happened to you, Estelle, and you'll have to give her time. It's a terrible shock for her."

Estelle had turned away from her aunt, her body still so sore that moving was agony, and wept into her pillow. Tears slipped sideways from her eyes and trickled down into her hair, as she lay there wishing for death. Her mother had always hated her. No matter how hard she had tried to make her mother love her, she hadn't. Now her mother considered her to be defiled.

What will Papa think when he finds out? Will he reject me too?

Dawn arrived relentlessly every day, each one as joyless as the one before. Estelle never smiled and often sat on the *stoep* all day, gazing dully at the veld until it disappeared into darkness. She knew that *Tannie* Sannie was worried about her.

"She's too thin, Adrina, and so lifeless."

Estelle never heard her say anything to Mama though. Mama had withdrawn completely from her oldest daughter and barely acknowledged her existence.

She tried to pull herself together for Papa's sake, but she just didn't seem to have the energy needed to do it.

I'm just so tired and so terribly unhappy.

April 1901

Estelle is sitting on the *stoep* quietly reading when her mother comes sweeping through the front door, skirts rustling, carrying a basket of washing. Catching sight of Estelle, she sets the basket down and stares at her angrily, the corners of her mouth turning down. "Estelle, what are you doing? I've been looking for you to hang out this washing."

Estelle looks up guiltily. She was reading her great-grandmother's Bible and trying to find some comfort within the aged book covers. She knows Mama resents her ability to read and dislikes Papa's English family, especially now that the Khakis are burning the farms and land.

The confusion and horror of the events of just over six months ago still dominate her waking hours and overwhelm her sleep with nightmares and cold sweats. No comfort or understanding had been forthcoming from Mama, whose uncompromising condemnation are hard to bear.

Hope that the Bible might hold some answers to her despairing and depressed frame of mind had compelled her to sit outside, on this warm autumn late morning, and consider, yet again, the passage her father had referenced. She had read it repeatedly. Her mind probed it and considered what Papa had meant when he referred her to it.

Does he think that I'm a sinner? That I have fallen from grace like the adulterous woman in the Bible? Did he mean that he doesn't judge me? Or that Jesus would not judge me? I wish he had explained more so that I could understand what he meant.

Her mother's sharp eyes alight on the book in her lap. "What's that you've got, Estelle? Show me!"

Estelle is reluctant to part with her Bible and hugs it tightly to her chest.

"It's Great-grandmother Anne's Bible. Papa gave it to me when he visited us last week."

Mama looms over her, eyes narrowed to slits and cheeks bright spots of colour. "Give it to me now," she reaches down and wrenches the book from under Estelle's crossed arms.

Her hot breath on Estelle's face is pungent and overlaid with coffee as she roughly turns the fragile pages with her work-worn hands.

Abruptly she shuts the book and shoves it back towards Estelle. "Take it. Pray to the God of the English and see what good it does. No one in this community will want you, not now. You're no better than a prostitute."

The inference that she had asked to be attacked through her behaviour and deserved what had happened to her was not lost on Estelle, whose face drained of all its colour. "I hate you, you are the evilest woman alive. I wish you would die."

"I'm not going to die. You're not going to kill me the way you killed your own mother."

She stopped and clapped her hand over her mouth as if she could stop the words that had already been said. Turning abruptly, she walked back into the house, slamming the door behind her.

Estelle sat stunned for a few minutes, a strange and empty look in her eyes. Struggling to her feet, she walked over and picked up the basket of washing Mama ... Marta ... had left behind. Lifting the heavy load, she shuffled down the steps, like an old man, and headed towards the wash line.

Marta is not my mother. No wonder my life is so different from that of my sisters. Papa was determined that I should speak and read English, but he never insisted that they learned. He has never shown either of them Great-grandmother

Anne's things or let them read from her old books. Now I know why I never felt loved and why I look so different from Marta and my siblings. Why didn't Papa tell me?

INTERNMENT

May 1901

The family is seated at the table eating their midday meal when Mosiko bursts through the front door.

"The Khakis are coming. Lots of them on horses."

His dark brown eyes roll wildly in this head and sweat runs in rivulets down his face.

Cold sweat beads Estelle's forehead and she feels momentarily faint. *Oh, Lord, please protect me from these strange English men.*

Marta's face has the colour and texture of uncooked dough, as she pushes her chair back and rushes into the pantry where she starts shoving meat, bread, and butter into a waiting basket. Other parcels of food and kitchen implements are already packed and stacked against the pantry wall in anticipation of this dreadful day.

"Get the blankets off the beds, Ardrina," says *Tannie* Sannie as she heads for the front door, her ramrod straight back and stiff shoulders betraying her fear. The house servant and her daughter rush from the room to gather as many blankets as possible.

The soldiers clatter into the yard, their horses sending up clouds of choking dust. Through the kitchen window, Estelle watches two soldiers dismount and cautiously approach the farmhouse.

Karel, who has been lying under the table hoping for some scraps, crawls out and stands up. He growls a fierce, deep growl.

Tannie Sannie's voice, loud and strident, warns them of approaching trouble a few seconds before the soldiers enter the kitchen, rifles at the ready.

Karel continues to growl. The hair on his neck is standing on end and his eyes glare at the aggressive strangers.

"You are all required to come with us," shouts a red-faced Khaki with a peeling nose. "You have ten minutes to get what you need and come outside before we set fire to this house."

Karel suddenly stops growling and howls, his lips are pulled back and all the hair on his back bristles. He launches himself at one of the soldiers.

"Bang!"

The shot rings out and Karel stops in mid-lunge, falling to the earthen floor with a sickening thud.

The terrified youngsters stand up from their seats at the table and walk out of the kitchen. They go directly to their rooms and collect their pre-packed sacks containing their spare nightdresses, clothes, bonnets, and other essentials. *Tannie* Sannie and Marta had prepared well.

Estelle has packed great-grandmother's Bible into her sack as well as a lace handkerchief from Papa's suitcase.

He's going to be heartbroken at losing his suitcase, but I can't possibly bring it. It's too big and Marta won't let me.

The girls carrying their sacks, their eyes blank and shiny with shock, together with Mosiko and the two women clutching their precious parcels and the basket, exit the house. The walk across the dusty yard to the tree where the soldiers indicate they must gather seems eternal to Estelle, who believes she'll be attacked or shot at any moment.

Not wanting to show fear in front of the Khakis and shame herself and her family, she wills her fingers and legs to stop trembling. Focusing on the riot of yellow, red, and brown leaves that hang from the tree, as it parades in autumn splendour, calms her. The tree's indifference to her family's plight as they gather beneath its branches, feet crunching on fallen leaves, is astonishing to Estelle.

We'll be gone and our home will be gone, but this tree will remain, its branches reaching into the brilliant blue sky.

Several Khakis are dosing their home with fuel, ready to burn it to the ground. The two soldiers who had evicted the family from their house suddenly appear carrying burning logs on shovels. Within moments, the house is alight and the fire is spreading quickly.

Estelle opens her mouth to scream, Adrina and Dorthea are still inside, but just then they rush out of the open door, their arms laden with cushions and blankets.

The soldiers systematically round up the other farm workers and chase their families out of their huts in the kraal. They are herded into a group under another nearby tree where they watch in dismayed horror as their homes are also doused with fuel and set alight.

Renette's large, blue eyes overflow with tears as Mosiko leaves their family and walks over to join his fellow farm workers, their wives, and children, under the large tree. Ardrina and Dorthea stay with them.

Estelle puts her arms around Renette in an attempt at comfort, feeling her sister's stout body shaking as she desperately tries to restrain her emotions. Renette knows it is shameful to cry but she can't stop herself.

Estelle's own heart is broken at the unnecessary death of poor Karel. He had tried to protect them so faithfully and now he is dead, and Mosiko, the last link to her old, safe life on their own farm, has left them too.

They all watch silently as the soldiers systematically set about the destruction of their lives. The farmhouse, barns, and kraal burn to the ground. The crops are burned and trampled by the soldiers' horses, and the cattle, including those belonging to the farm workers, are shot dead where they stand in the veld. Even Ansi, the gentle milk cow is ruthlessly killed by the soldiers. Not all the Khakis are good marksmen and Estelle's gorge rises at the screams of pain from badly placed bullets.

I didn't know injured animals scream like human babies. Papa has never missed when he's needed to put an animal down.

The metallic stench of blood mixes with the oily scent of induced burning, as the thick black smoke blots out the sky and everything succumbs to the flames. The watchers cough and splutter, as the smoke and ash blow in their direction, and the roar of the flames fills the hot air.

Their eyes smart and run with tears from a mixture of emotion and smoke. Suné, who's been standing quietly, eyes wide and tear filled, suddenly opens her mouth, and vomits. Marta turns angry and astonished eyes on her youngest daughter but makes no move to assist her. Estelle pulls her handkerchief from her skirt pocket and helps Suné wipe her mouth. She kicks dirt over the stinking mess.

The guns crash repeatedly and eventually the screams and bellows of the injured cattle stop. The vultures have started to gather, circling and making raspy drawn-out hissing sounds as they prepare to fight over the carcasses. The winners would gorge themselves, making disgusting grunting noises reminiscent of hungry pigs or barking dogs.

A short while later a wagon arrives to transport them.

"You are going to a refugee camp," a young-looking soldier tells them, through an Afrikaans interpreter.

Tannie Sannie glowers at the interpreter and hisses "hands-upper" under her breath.

Contempt for the middle-aged interpreter fills Estelle's heart. She's familiar with this term used for Boers who have not only surrendered but are actively assisting the British army against their own people.

The children sit on the dusty ground, their faces white and pinched, as the two mothers, Ardrina, and Dorthea load the parcels, cushions and blankets, a field table, a bath, a pot, and a kettle into the transport wagon.

Estelle sits next to Suné, holding her little hand. The smell of vomit rises from her and Estelle thinks about what Papa had told her about the theory of miasma.

"The miasma theory is a medical theory that diseases are caused by a miasma or a noxious form of 'bad air' or night air," he'd said. "A lot of people still believe in this theory, including your mother, so please don't go against her on that point. I don't believe it. I agree with the doctors that cleanliness helps avoid diseases. Remember that, Estelle, and try to keep things as clean as possible."

A soldier gestures to the children to get into the wagon while Marta hands a bucket and two chairs up to them. The hands-upper pushes them off the wagon.

"Get in," he growls, "you can't bring anything more."

Marta refuses. A red flush of suppressed fury suffusing her face and neck.

"Please get in," says the young soldier.

Knowing Marta doesn't understand his words, Estelle watches her, wondering if she can tell from his actions that he doesn't want to hurt or humiliate her.

Marta looks at the interpreter. "What about our house servants?" she asks.

"You can take them with you," the hands-upper says.

Marta points to Ardrina and Dorthea. "Those two," she says.

Sadness descends on Estelle at these words. Mosiko won't be coming with them.

Oh Mosiko, I'm going to miss you so much. You've always looked out for me. You helped me when I needed it the most and offered me uncondemning support through your visible and solid presence.

The man nods and Ardrina and Dorthea walk over to the wagon and climb in.

"You'll have to look after them in the camp," the soldier warns, through the interpreter. "They get minimal rations."

Marta nods briefly and takes her place in the wagon.

There is no wagon for the farm workers. They must walk to the railway line regardless of their age or state of health.

Estelle doesn't know if the soldiers will leave them there to fend for themselves and grow their own crops or take them to one of the black concentration camps where they'll be forced to work, either growing crops for the British troops or digging trenches and driving wagons. She's aware of what lies ahead for the farm labourers and their families from her chats with Ardrina and Mosiko.

She also has a good idea of what lies in store for her own family at the concentration camp from overheard conversations when Papa and *Oom* Willem last visited the farm.

Suné joins Renette in her quiet crying as the wagon moves off, but Estelle does not cry. Her heart has turned to stone. They are travelling with little personal property, food and water and no hope for the future, but these Khakis will not break what little spirit remains to her.

At least they haven't harmed any of us.

She watches bitterly as the farm workers, including dear Mosiko, set off on their journey, shoulders slumping, and eyes fixed on the ground. Two of the women stumble along with their babies strapped tightly to their backs.

At least I have the gold that Papa gave me safe inside my Bible. I wonder if he gave any to Marta?

The families' trek from *Oom* Willem and *Tannie* Sannie's farm to the concentration camp starts on the 27th of May. Two days later, the convoy reaches another farm, where it stops to inflict its destructive objectives on the inhabitants.

The ten-year-old "man" of the house attempts to defend his home from attack, a bullet from his old rifle coming so close to one of the soldiers, Estelle sees the Khakis visibly jump.

It gives her a momentary feeling of satisfaction.

The Khakis responds to this pathetic defence by bombarding the house with gunfire. The noise is huge and makes the ears of the spectators sitting in the wagons ring.

The youngster suddenly staggers back from the window and disappears.

The Khakis approach the house cautiously, but there are no further gun shots.

A woman, whom Estelle later discovers is called Mrs Smit, opens the door, and the Khakis rush inside. Two of them soon emerge carrying the limp bodies of children; the boy she saw shooting from the window, and a small girl of about three years old.

The boy's head lolls backwards, and one side of his shirt and his left arm are soaked in blood. It trickles fast from his wounds and splatters onto the ground, making dark, sticky patches. The little girl's hair is clotted with blood from a head wound.

From a distance their faces look pale and lifeless, as if they are already dead.

The hands-upper speaks to the woman. "Get ready to be taken away within ten minutes."

She nods in acknowledgement of his command and goes back into the house, leaving the door open.

A short while later she re-emerges carrying a small trunk. Her other children follow her; six of them carrying blankets and clothing, and a girl of about thirteen years old carrying a crying baby. The hands-upper tells them to get into the waiting wagon.

One of the soldiers tears strips of cloth from a sheet and binds the two injured children's wounds. They are then lifted onto a wagon with their mother and siblings, ready to be transported.

A groan of pain escapes the boy and Estelle watches Mrs Smit's lips move in silent prayer; her eyes glazed over with dull shock. The baby's cries go on and on, as irritating a sound as the harsh cries of the hadeda birds first thing in the morning.

The Khakis round up the farm workers and leave them standing in a miserable group near the wagons as they set about destroying everything on the farm. Silent tears slide down their cheeks as the soldiers systematically break out the doors and frames of the farmhouse, chopping down the trees and slaughtering the animals. They then loot the kitchen before setting fire to everything, including the farm workers' huts.

Marta heaves a great sigh of despair as the wagons set off again, trundling steadily towards their incarceration at the concentration camp. Estelle is emotionless having wrapped her anger and hatred around herself like a cloak.

Once again, the native workers are herded in a different direction. The British administration has burned everything they possess but will not take any accountability for their welfare. They'll not even be sheltered in a concentration camp with a share of the meagre food rations.

The travellers are woken early the next morning and herded back into the wagons. Mrs Smit's oldest daughter, Isebel, holds the baby while her mother sits, her small daughter's head in her lap, and prays, rocking her upper body gently to and fro.

Her injured son, Sarel, half lies, half sits, against the side of the wagon, his breathing is laboured, and his lips have a blue tinge.

The intense poignancy of the scene pierces the protective layer of anger around Estelle's heart and it squeezes into a wedge of pain.

"No, no!" the scream jerks Estelle awake and her eyes fly open.

She'd dozed off, lulled by the endless motion of the wagon. One look at the ivory face pillowed in Mrs Smit's lap tells her that the little girl is dead. She looks like a beautiful doll except for the blood-soaked bandage wrapped around her golden hair.

Two hours later, Sarel breathes out a long, rattling breath. His chest does not rise again as he goes to join his young sister in her eternal sleep.

"I'm sorry," she whispers to Isebel.

"It's better," Isebel says, her eyes expressionless, "Henrietta was a frail child and would never have survived the camp. Sarel might have been sent away from us to a prisoner of war camp."

Mrs Smit says nothing. She just sits cradling the head of her dead daughter in her arms.

When the convoy stops that evening, the two children are buried in a single grave, each wrapped in a blanket. Estelle sees the blue still lips of the girl before the blanket enfolds her lifeless form.

The hands-upper says a prayer over the grave while Mrs Smit, whose name is Annette, stands dry-eyed but deathly white, clutching her wailing baby to her chest.

Estelle's chest burns with anger at the hands-upper's audacity.

How dare he pray over the graves of those innocent children who he has betrayed?

She sheds no tears; crying is for the weak. Her throat closes with hatred and she struggles to breath for several seconds.

I hope he goes to hell and Satan himself feasts on his rotten soul! That applies to all traitors and abusers of women and children. I'll survive and I'll make my presence known. Men like him will rue the day they crossed my path. This I swear in God's own name.

June 1901

Despite Estelle's trepidation about the camp, it is a relief when the wagons finally pass through its gates and they are off-loaded into a heap of sand. Annette Smit's baby girl has sickened during the journey and won't feed. There is nothing she can give to her and the child is sinking fast.

"Maybe we can get a few drops of brandy at the camp," says *Tannie* Sannie. "That might save her."

"Go and give your names to the camp superintendent, Mr McCowat." The hands-upper points towards a large tent in the distance. "He'll tell you what to do next."

Leaving the children to stand guard over their scanty possessions, Marta, *Tannie* Sannie, and Mrs Smit set off to report to Mr McCowat.

Estelle stands, holding her skirt up out of the dirt, observing the sea of white, bell-shaped tents pitched in straight lines at equal intervals all over the large and dusty field. It had once been veld but the grass has been hacked away leaving barren, exposed earth between the tents and in the cooking area. There is not a single tree in sight to provide welcome relief from the sun which shines down harshly, even though it's winter.

There are so many tents!

From her position near the gate, she sees a small number of defeated looking men and large numbers of thin and raggedy women and children. They are all sitting or lying listlessly in the dirt among the tents. A few black house servants and farm workers are scatted among them. None of them seem to have any sort of useful occupation or any energy to do anything.

Estelle is shocked at the filthy state of the people.

Do they not have soap and water to keep themselves clean?

When the women return, Isebel, who is holding the baby, looks at *Tannie* Sannie expectantly.

Tannie Sannie slowly shakes her head, "I asked the camp supervisor if he could give us a few drops of brandy for your sick sister, but he said no, he didn't have any."

Tannie Sannie's shoulders are slumped dejectedly and she suddenly looks shrivelled and old.

Tears slip from Isebel's eyes and make white streaks down her face which is still blackened with ash and soot from the destruction of her home.

How can anyone be so unfeeling towards a baby? Estelle thinks, *He must really hate us.*

Her soul fills with determination and her hatred burns brightly, fuelled by this new act of contempt and repugnance towards her people. She straightens her back, pushing her shoulders back, the will to survive reinforcing her soul like a steel girdle.

You're not going to defeat me. I'm going to survive this camp, no matter what, and one day, I'll get my revenge on men like you.

Carrying their parcels and other belongings, the new arrivals head for the tents. As they draw closer, a middle-aged woman dressed in a patched brown cotton dress and a bonnet rouses herself and comes over to them. "Hello, I'm Mrs de Wet. Come this way."

She leads them towards one of the tents. As they walk, Estelle notices several tree stumps, like keloid scars on the earth.

"Where have all the trees gone?" asks *Tannie* Sannie.

She has also noticed the stark landscape, devoid of trees and other vegetation.

"They have been cut down and their wood used for fires to cook food and boil water. There are none left now."

Mrs de Wet stops outside one of the tents. "There's space for you in this tent. Mrs Odendaal and her son are currently the only people living here."

She looks at Ardrina and Dorthea.

"I see you have brought your servants with you. No extra rations or blankets are provided for servants," she said. "Did the Khakis tell you that?" Marta nods.

The front flap of the tent is tightly closed. Mrs de Wet opens it and gestures for them to enter. Estelle's first impression is one of neatness despite the dim lighting and stuffiness inside the tent. A smell of sickness and impending death hangs in the oppressive air.

A woman in her thirties kneels on the floor next to a makeshift mattress. Her small son lies on the mattress, weak and frail. His face is flushed with fever and he has a hacking cough.

"I'm trying to keep him warm," the woman explains her reasons for keeping the flap closed. "He is shivering with cold."

"What is wrong with him?" asks Marta.

Estelle inhales sharply, preparing herself for the answer she expects.

"He has influenza. There are a couple of hundred cases of illness in the camp right now, a mixture of influenza, bronchitis, and enteric catarrh. There have been some dust storms lately which the camp doctor thinks are causing more respiratory illnesses."

Mrs Odendaal's chin quivers and she swallows hard. "My name is Hester Odendaal and this is my son, Hennie. I'm glad to have some company."

Estelle catches the look of fear that passes from Marta to *Tannie* Sannie. She watches Marta take a deep breath and introduce *Tannie* Sannie, the children, and their servants to Hester.

A few moments later, Annette Smit enters the tent with her children, who've been waiting patiently for her outside the tent. She lies the dead body of her baby down on a blanket. Dropping into a seated position on the hard ground, she sits, rocking herself to and fro, and keening softly.

Her worn and seemingly bloodless body is that of an old woman and the large eyes in her white face are wild and haunted. The death of her infant on top of the recent losses of her oldest son and toddler seem to have broken something deep within her mind. It is frightening to watch.

Hatred for the camp supervisor who denied the baby a few drops of brandy constricts Estelle's throat. The baby is dead. She'll never take her first steps, laugh and play with her older brothers and sisters or go to school. The camp supervisor did nothing to try and save her. In Estelle's mind, he is a murderer. Taking deep breaths, Estelle attempts to unwind the knot of anger in her stomach.

Marta looks at Annette, her eyes are sympathetic. "It's better that the baby died," she says. "She's now at peace with our Father."

Tannie Sannie's eyes flash anger. "The camp supervisor could have tried to help! Surely he could have found a few drops of brandy for Annette's baby somewhere."

"That is true, Sannie, but God expects you to forgive him. He'll not forgive our individual sins if we bear grudges against someone else. Worse yet, such feelings, if not repented, could cause Him to turn away from our people and our cause."

Marta quotes her favourite Bible verse about forgiveness.

"The good Lord says, 'If my people, which are called by my name, shall humble themselves, and pray, and seek my face, and turn from their wicked ways; then will I hear from heaven, and will forgive their sin, and will heal their land.' We must do as He commands."

Marta's words make Estelle feel ill.

She is so sanctimonious with all her praying and quoting the Bible at every turn. But where is her understanding and compassion? She has rejected me because she believes I'm defiled. Where is her ability to love unconditionally? I hate her!

"I'm going for a walk around the camp," *Tannie* Sannie ducks through the tent flap and walks away.

Needing to escape the cloying confines of the tent and the overwhelming anguish of the mother of the dead baby and the mother of the seriously ill boy, Estelle goes with *Tannie* Sannie.

She quietly observes when *Tannie* Sannie stops to speak to the other women, and notices how she averts her face in disgust from the few able-bodied men who have clearly deserted their commandos. Sannie detests deserters and has no time for weak spirited and cowardly men. She is proud of the fact that her husband is a *bittereinder*. Willem will fight to the end.

So will Papa, Estelle thinks, *he has put this war before his family and especially before me.*

One of the women seems less lethargic than the rest. She introduces herself as Mrs Carina Groenewald. "I arrived last week with my two sons." She points towards two small children who are sitting in the dirt drawing pictures with their grubby fingers. "You need to know that clean water is in short supply. The river water has been contaminated by the rotting remains of all the farm animals slaughtered in this area. The animals that have been preserved to feed the camp and other local people drink from the river and the banks are slimy with their waste which also washes into the water."

"Really," exclaims *Tannie* Sannie, "but those women are washing in the river."

"There are no other options," says Corina. "There is nowhere else to wash clothes or yourself."

"What about boiling the water for drinking?"

"There is no fuel," says another woman, joining in the conversation. "I'm Mariska Fourie and I've been here for five weeks."

"All the trees have already been cut down so there's no firewood left. Very few of us have pots in which to boil water, even if there was fuel for a fire."

Tannie Sannie says nothing about the pots she and Marta brought with them.

"Which tent are you in?" asks Mariska.

"We have been assigned to Mrs Odendaal's tent. Her son is very ill."

"Yes," says Corina, "the dust storms and lime-dust from Mafeking have caused outbreaks of influenza, bronchitis, and enteric catarrah in the camp, especially among the children and elderly." She looks over at her two little boys, their heads bent over their work. "So far, God has spared my boys and me."

Tannie Sannie looks at Mariska, "Do you have children?"

"Yes, I have a daughter of five years old. She is with my mother in our tent as she has contracted conjunctivitis. I came out for a bit of fresh air but will return soon to relieve my mother."

"Oh dear, how are you cleaning her eyes if there is no boiled water?"

"I'm using the river water. There is nothing else."

"There are also a significant number of children who have contracted laryngitis and some cases of malaria."

"Malaria! Really! But this is not a malaria area."

"No, but many of the camp inmates arrive with it. People are being sent here from other areas where there is malaria."

An elderly woman with snow white hair joins the gathering. "I'm Mrs van Tonder," she says, "but you can call me *Ouma*.[1] A delivery of British military blankets arrived this morning. Corina and Mariska have already claimed some for their families. If you come with me now, I'll help you

---

[1] *Ouma* is the Afrikaans word for Grandmother.

get a few before they are all gone."

"Oh, thank you, that is very kind of you."

Ouma van Tonder leads the way to the storeroom, a bleak grey structure that dominates the patch of dirt within which it lies. There is a queue of raggedy and weary-looking women waiting outside. While *Tannie* Sannie and Estelle stand in the line, *Ouma* van Tonder regales them with her story.

"My husband, Danie, and I are both seventy-five years old and were living in a women's laager up until a month ago when it was attacked by a convoy of Khakis who came across it unexpectedly. My husband was one of twenty men living in the laager. They were all too old to go on commando and had been appointed to help protect us."

"We were travelling with thirty wagons and carts and two hundred cattle and had been living on the veld for seven months prior to that attack. Various Boer commandos had been providing us with weapons, tents, food, and clothing.

"The Khakis overwhelmed us easily and proceeded to burn all our wagons, food and tents. They forced us to watch."

A distant look comes into the older woman's eyes as she remembers that day. "The soldiers set fire to the wagons first."

She describes how the yellow and orange flames had spread out delicately, tasting the dry tinder of the wagon frames, and how the bright sparks had flown high into the sky, fanned by puffs of the bitter wind, and settled on the canvas wagon covers which instantly burst into flames. As the wagons and tents burned, black smoke had billowed upwards, reaching a tremendous height where it was whipped to shreds by the wind.

"What happened next?" asks *Tannie* Sannie, forcing the elderly woman to return her wandering mind to the present.

"When they considered the destruction to be sufficiently complete, they marched our elderly guards, and the few boys of twelve years and older, away as prisoners of war. The women and the rest of the children were brought here."

"Were you scared?" Estelle asks.

"No," *Ouma* van Tonder's lips form a thin, straight line and she pushes back her shoulders as if in defiance. "The Lord has always preserved me until now and He will continue to do so."

Tannie Sannie and Estelle eventually reach the front of the queue and their lengthily wait is rewarded by their receiving three old and thin blankets.

"We'll still have to share the blankets," says *Tannie* Sannie, "but obtaining these feels like a small victory."

Speaking to the three women and obtaining the blankets puts a bit of a spring into *Tannie* Sannie's step. "The Lord has provided us with these blankets. The nights are already cold, and these will help," she announces happily to the occupants of their tent.

"What about food?"

The new arrivals have not eaten since early that morning and their stomachs are growling loudly.

Tannie Sannie has obtained the answer to that question from the other women. "It seems that the rations are more generous here than in some of the other camps."

Tannie Sannie details the rations they'll receive: a half a pound of meat, two ounces of coffee, three-quarters of a pound of wholemeal, one twelfth of a tin of condensed milk, two ounces of sugar and a half an ounce of salt per person per day.

"Unlike the other camps," she says, "we'll also be given some rice, jam and marmalade. Corina Groenewald said that the weight of the meat excludes the bone, so we are fortunate. My children will get half rations as they are under twelve years old, and Ardrina and Dorthea will only be given a small ration of meilie meal and salt."

"That isn't very much to sustain four healthy adults, two teenagers and two children. What about milk and fresh produce?"

"Corina said that milk, fresh fruit and vegetables, soap, candles, and toiletries are hard to obtain and have to be prescribed by a camp doctor as a medical comfort."

"How are we going to survive on these rations?" Marta bursts out. "The British are planning to starve us."

"We have no option but to survive on these rations, Marta. We are fortunate to be receiving meat rations. In most of the camps, the families of men who are on commando do not receive any meat rations at all. We have some candles and soap in our parcels. We must use these sparingly and make them last."

"You are right, Sannie. We must make the most of our situation and trust in God to help and protect us."

* * *

Three days later, the two families attend their first funeral in the camp. The doctor had finally come the day before to write out the death certificate for Annette's baby.

228

Two of her other children, Marieke and Ruan, caught colds during the trek to the camp due to sleeping outside in the cold night air. They are lying sick on their makeshift beds on the floor next to Hennie Odendaal, who is slowly recovering, but is not yet well enough to get out of bed.

Dr Kaufmann, who is Viennese and speaks no Afrikaans, attempts to look at the sick children. Hennie Odendaal and Marieke Smit have yellowish shiny complexions while young Ruan Smit's face is pallid except for a hectic flush on his cheeks which accentuates the dark circles under his fatigued looking eyes. All three sick children have clogged up chests and phlegmy, rattling coughs.

Marta leads their tent's inhabitants in a daily prayer that God will show mercy and not take another of Annette's children. Estelle joins in, but she has no faith in prayer. God has shown no inclination to assist any of the camp's other inmates, so why would he favour Mrs Smit's children?

The doctor cannot communicate with Annette and has no medical supplies.

He points to the hospital, an ominous looking wood and iron building, and indicates through actions that he wants to admit the children.

"No," refuses Annette Smit, "children who go to the hospital never come out."

"Hennie's not going either," says Mrs Odendaal, folding her arms across her body aggressively.

Dr Kaufmann can't understand them, but their rejection of his proposal is obvious. He snorts in disgust and takes his leave of them.

"What a rude and unhelpful man," complains Mrs Odendaal, "I'll never place my son in his exclusive care."

"I agree," says Marta, "we'll continue to treat the children using our methods."

Marta has managed to purchase a piece of goat's lard, a small bottle of wine and another of brandy, as well as a few other medicinal items which she keeps hidden in their tent for future medical emergencies. Estelle suspects Papa must have given her a few of his gold coins during his last visit to the farm.

Now I know about her coins, but she doesn't know about mine.

Each day, Estelle carefully watches Marta and Annette melt the piece of goat's lard and mix it in a small cup with a spoonful of turmeric. Using a warm knife, Marta spreads a small amount of the goat's lard mixture onto three chest protectors, one for each child. Lena and Hannekie had made the chest protectors by cutting squares of flannel cloth from an old nightgown and sewing two pieces of tape to each of them so that the protectors could be tied around the children's necks.

The sick children lie all day on their backs in their makeshift beds with the protectors applied to their chests and a piece of wadding, smeared with a little castor oil, between their shoulders.

"This poultice helps relieve oppressed chests in children," says Annette, noticing Estelle's interest.

Estelle smiles shyly at her. *I must learn as much as I can about healing practices. They'll help me with my goal of survival.*

Marta's cold attitude towards her has continued at the camp, but it no longer bothers Estelle, who has cut her stepmother from her heart and life.

She hasn't even noticed that I no longer care or react. One day she may need my help and when that day comes, I won't be there for her. Oh no! I'll watch her die.

In the early afternoon on the day of the funeral, a horse-drawn hearse halts outside the tent. The four women go out first, moving slowly as if with great age, and stand alongside it, followed by Estelle, Hannekie, and the younger children who are well enough to attend. Lena stays behind to attend to the sick children.

Seeing the activity, a motley collection of people, including *Ouma* van Tonder, Mrs Groenewald, Mrs Fourie and many other women and older children, as well as a sprinkling of elderly men, quickly gather. The *hensoppers* do not come, they know they are unwelcome.

"I'm sorry for your loss."

Mrs Odendaal nods in acknowledgement of Mrs Groenewald's sympathy.

"Why have these people come?" *Tannie* Sannie asks *Ouma* van Tonder. "They did not know this baby and have no reason to weep at her funeral. They didn't even know her mother."

"There is nothing for people to do in the camp. There are no occupations to keep them occupied or distract their minds from their unhappy circumstances. In this grim place of chronic boredom, a funeral is a source of entertainment. That's why they have come."

Estelle is disgusted by these words and moves away from the crowd, standing alone on the outskirts with her hands clasped in front of her and her eyes downcast.

A man with an unkempt grey beard and a back bent with age, assumes the role of minister and reads from his Bible, the cover of which is cracked and worn. His face is set in heavy lines of stern graveness.

Come to me, all you who are weary and burdened, and I will give you rest. Take my yoke upon you and learn from me, for I am gentle and humble in heart, and you will find rest for your souls. For my yoke is easy and my burden is light.

He then requests that a Psalm be sung and announces the numbers of the verses. Two ladies from the group start the singing, their voices cracking and rough at first, and then clearing as they get into their stride.

The rest of the gathering follow their lead, lifting their voices in song, and when the last notes have died away the old man says a prayer for the mother who has lost her child and says that she should be consoled to know that her baby has gone to walk with Him.

That ends the service which is limited to ten minutes by the camp authorities. Despite its short duration, the funeral is most touching and Hester, *Tannie* Sannie, and their children cry, their tears watering the hard ground.

Estelle does not cry. To her, tears are for lessor things like the loss of Papa's suitcase or moving from their farm and then again from *Tannie* Sannie's farm. It's not for something as permanent as death or the loss of innocence. These things remained incarcerated within your heart and soul forever. A relentless burden you can never free yourself from.

Annette is restless and uneasy all the way through the short service, behaving as if she does not quite understand what is happening. The women and older children who share her tent know that she is suffering sleepless nights and that the burning of her farm, deaths of three of her children, and the desperate circumstances of the camp are telling on her.

The man and some of the women place the rough wooden coffin containing the pathetically small body into the hearse and the crowd disperses, with most of them drifting towards the communal area. Annette and a few other women and children follow the hearse to continue mourning at the graveside.

Estelle stays behind to help Lena look after the sick children.

July 1901

Three long weeks after their arrival, *Tannie* Sannie, Marta and their families and servants have settled reluctantly into camp life.

Every morning, when the family passes the tents belonging to a group of *bywoners* on their way to the latrines, which are nearly half a mile from the main body of the camp, Estelle is obliged to listen to Marta loudly expressing her disgust at having to live in a camp with such dirty people.

"Look at the ground around their tents," she complains. "It's soiled with slops and rubbish because they are too lazy to dig a hole near the fence and bury it. They don't even use the latrines; they just do their business wherever they want to; it is completely unhygienic, and they are putting us all at risk of typhoid and other illnesses."

In some ways, Estelle doesn't blame them for not using the latrines which comprise a mixture of trenches, similar to those used by the army, and a bucket system which was easier for the small children. As she draws near, her gorge rises from the overpowering stench.

Ardrina carries the makeshift chamber pot that the occupants of their tent use during the night and empties it into the latrines. It's the largest cooking pot that Marta had managed to pack, and keep, on the day the Khakis attacked the farm. The pot is always overflowing by the morning and Estelle finds it revolting, but she is grateful she doesn't have to try and make her way to the latrines during the night or, even worse, find somewhere to squat away from the tents in the open.

Estelle can hear *Tannie* Sannie talking to Marta about Dorthea.

"Dorthea is not thriving and Ardrina is worried about her. She complains of being perpetually tired and lies sleeping on her blanket all day. She finds no joy or happiness in anything at all," says *Tannie* Sannie.

"I know what you mean," says Marta. "She is fading away."

"I don't know what more we can do for her. We already share our limited food with both her and Ardrina. There just isn't enough food to go around and we have no way of getting any more."

Estelle has also noticed the change with Dorthea. She's noticed it with several other children and heard *Ouma* van Tonder refer to them as fading flowers.

Now that she's decided to live, Estelle's determination to survive this camp and escape her oppressive life with Marta and her gutless father burn brightly within her, giving her strength to overcome the difficulties of her present life.

The greatest challenge is the lack of food. The relentless hunger wears everyone down. It surges upwards from their empty stomachs and burns new pathways into their brains. The pathways are called hate.

Marta, *Tannie* Sannie and the other women in the camp have learned to hate the Khakis. Their hatred is fed by the injustice of their confinement and the neglect and maltreatment they are subjected too.

Estelle doesn't care about the Khakis. They are determined to claim the Witwatersrand gold mines as their own and won't let anyone stand in their way. They are the oppressors and their behaviour is predictable. Estelle's anger is directed at the Boer men, who continue to resist the Khakis regardless of the consequences for their families. She is also disdainful and disinterested in her father who has lied to her and let her down so badly.

The second challenge is the relentless boredom. When her family first arrived at the camp, there had been a school of sorts that she had hoped to attend with her sisters. It had closed quickly when first the headmaster, and then two of the teachers, resigned. They were Uitlanders who had not been able to leave when war was declared. Despite their difficult circumstances and poverty, they were not prepared to work at the school for the low wages offered. Mr McCowat justified the low pay as none of them held certificates in teaching.

Following the closure of the school, Estelle attempts to teach her sisters to read and write using small twigs she's managed to procure to write words in the dust and draw letters. She also shows them how to do basic addition and subtraction using small stones collected from around the camp. It passes the time and Estelle is pleased with their progress.

The bitterly cold nights and freezing July winds are the third great challenge.

The last week of July is the worst weather of all. The temperatures drop drastically at night-time and a piercing wind whistles through the canvas walls of the tents. The days are often warm, with the mid-day temperature reaching up to twenty degrees Celsius, but after 4 p.m. the temperatures plummet and sometimes a biting wind gets up.

"Goodnight, girls," Estelle says.

"I'm so cold," says Suné.

Her teeth are chattering and her body shivers relentlessly. Estelle wraps her arms around her and holds her tightly. Behind her, Renette has cuddled up to her back in a similar manner. They are lying on two thin blankets, spread one on top of the other on the dirt floor, and are wearing all their clothes to stay warm.

Despite these layers, the icy cold seeps through the thin bedding that separates their bodies from the ground, making it so cold it is almost impossible to sleep. Estelle lies awake, her joints aching with inflammation from the chilly dampness.

When the morning finally arrives and the family ventures out to go to the latrines, Estelle hobbles along, the itching, red chilblains on her hands and feet making her life even more uncomfortable. All the children try not to smile as their dry lips crack open and bleed. She doesn't complain like her siblings do.

It makes no difference if I complain, and Marta will just say unkind things to me if I do.

The number of cases of influenza, bronchitis, and enteric catarrh in the camp climb daily due to the cold and continuous dust storms that blow up and billow around the tents, seeping into the makeshift beds, collecting in the folds of dresses, bonnets and underclothes and settling on food and cooking implements and utensils. The misery compounds among the inhabitants of the camp, but Estelle never murmurs a word of complaint. She crushes the discomfit and discontent when they rear their heads in her mind and focuses on waiting out this trial with determination and fortitude.

One day, Dorthea wakes up sweating and feverish. Her condition rapidly deteriorates, and she starts vomiting and suffering from bouts of diarrhoea. The overpowering and fetid smell of vomit mixed with diarrhoea seems to settle on Estelle's skin, like dust. She takes her sisters outside and keeps them out for most of the day.

Later the evening, when the girls are forced to go inside because of the bitterly cold wind that has sprung up, Dorthea looks so thin and diminished as she lies on her blanket with the blankets kicked off due to her fever, that Estelle feels real fear for the first time. It has never occurred to her that Dorthea might die, but she has lost so much weight she looks ethereal. Her skin is a dusky grey and her large brown eyes are lustreless and dull, as if they are covered by a layer of the infernal dust.

Estelle wakes in the morning to the wails and lamentations of Ardrina. "My baby," she cries, "my baby is dead."

She lies on Dorthea's blanket with her daughter's wasted body in her arms, keening and wailing.

The passing of Dorthea is not eventful in the eyes of the inhabitants of the camp who are too involved in their own efforts at survival to care about the death of the daughter of a servant. The doctor doesn't come and issue the death certificate for three days as he is overwhelmed by the numbers of sick and dying people in the hospital.

Tannie Sannie and Marta wrap the scrawny body of Dorthea in a blanket and lay it outside, alongside the tent. Despite the cooler weather, the smell of her rotting body is overpowering, making Estelle feel sick and dirty. Her heart is heavy with grief as she sits outside with her sisters, avoiding Ardrina's awful pain-wracked eyes which chill her soul.

Dorthea is finally buried in an unmarked grave in the cemetery. After the death of her daughter, Ardrina changes. Her broad, pleasant face loses its mild and perpetually contented look and her grip on reality slips. She wanders about aimlessly humming a traditional lullaby under her breath:

> Keep quiet my child
> Keep quiet my baby
> Be quiet, daddy will be home by dawn
> There's a star that will lead him home
> The star will brighten his way home
> The hills and stones are still the same my love
> My life has changed, yes my life has changed
> The children grow but you don't know my love
> The children grew but you don't see them grow.[1]

***

"It hurts, Mama," Hennie Odendaal complains, wrapping his stick-like arms around his chest.

His mother turns haunted and anxious eyes on him. He's complained relentlessly of pain ever since his bout of influenza in early June.

"Please Lord," she prays, "don't take my only child from me."

The instances of influenza and bronchitis in the camp have crept up to five hundred people, with another eight hundred suffering from enteric catarrh. Everyone is afraid of the rampant sickness and resultant deaths.

Annette Smit's face is also set in deep lines of anxiety and hardship. Her son, Ruan, had not recovered from his bout of influenza and now lies in the graveyard next to his baby sister. "Dear Lord, you have taken four of my children to be with you. Please spare my remaining six and let them stay here on earth with me for a bit longer."

Estelle knows that *Tannie* Sannie is also worried about Marta's mental health. A couple of days previously, Marta's night had been disturbed to such an extent that she kept all the adults and older children awake with her thrashing about and incoherent comments and moans. The following day she was unusually quiet, and her eyes held a tormented look.

The afternoon following Marta's nightmare, Estelle overhears *Tannie* Sannie asking her what is bothering her.

"Pieter is dead, Sannie."

"Why do you think that? You can't possibly know that he is dead."

---

[1] English translation of *Thula baba, thula sana* – a traditional South African lullaby.

235

"I do know. His spirit visited me in a dream last night. What made it so strange," Marta says, "was that we had an ordinary conversation. He told me all about how uncomfortable it is for the men on commando at night, sleeping on the hard ground in this bitter July cold, and with no decent coffee to drink when they wake up in the morning. I told him that camp life was also miserable and that I was afraid of all the illnesses that were spreading among the inmates. We were sitting in the *voorkamer* of our farmhouse and the paraffin light gave everything in the room a soft, golden glow.

"I didn't know I was talking to a ghost until I realised I could see the back of the *riempies* chair he was sitting on right through his body. He must have known from the look in my eyes that I knew he was dead because he gave me a look full of tender sadness and made me promise that I would look after myself and the girls as best I possibly could. 'You must fight to stay alive and return to our farm someday soon,' he said, '*Oom* Paul has provided for us so that we can rebuild after the war. He's also provided for our neighbours.' He stayed with me until the first light of dawn and then he dissolved into the brightness."

Tannie Sannie gives Marta a hug and together they pray for Pieter's soul.

A wave of dizziness overwhelms Estelle, standing in the shade of a nearby tent. Her knees buckle and she slides to the dusty ground, curling herself up into a tight ball. *Papa dead! He can't be dead.*

The ground is hard, and the dust is tickling her nose, but she can't stand. Her legs won't work.

Papa dead! Shock abates and anger replaces it. *Why did his spirit make contact with Marta? Why not with me? He doesn't care about me at all.*

The nightmare marks the beginning of Marta's withdrawal from life and the point at which she starts to lose all sense of time.

Estelle watches her surreptitiously, as she goes about her daily tasks, struggling to eek an existence out of the harsh camp life. It's as if time has been cancelled and she's just existing until the next phase of her life begins.

She frequently lapses into gazing vacantly into space, her mind retreating from her current environment to a safe place where she and Pieter are together on their farm. Seeing to the needs of her two daughters, Renette and Suné, seems to be the only thing that's keeping her going.

If she didn't have her two daughters, she would give up entirely on living. She certainly doesn't care about me. I might as well not exist at all.

PIETER

HELPLESS

August 1901

Over the past few weeks, Pieter has discovered how strong-minded Estelle is. He has tried repeatedly to make some sort of contact with her but every time she has rebuffed him.

Being a member of the spirit world is not at all what he expected. He's frustrated and angry at his ability to witness the lives of his loved ones unfurling before him without being able to intervene in any way.

Standing next to Estelle and Sannie, he watches with them as the new arrivals file through the gate of the camp. Their numbers are significant, at least five hundred men, women, and children, and possibly more.

"Don't they look awful?" Estelle whispers.

They are a particularly unhealthy-looking group. Their overly large dark eyes stare out of gaunt faces, ashy grey from malnutrition and sickness instead of a healthy shiny black.

Sannie looks at Estelle briefly, her face reflecting her unspoken and murky fears. "Yes, they look very ill."

The rations for the new inmates, who have been transferred to the Mafeking camp from the Taung black concentration camp, have been limited to mielie meal and salt for months and it reflects in their apathetic behaviour and emaciated limbs. Estelle knows this will not change for them going forward as the Mafeking Camp Commandant maintains the same ration policy for natives.

This latest development worries Pieter who decides to haunt the camp for a while and see how it develops. His spirit is tied to his farm in Irene but, for as long as his family is alive, he can manifest near any of them.

"Where's Ardrina?" Sannie asks later that afternoon. "She hasn't come for her dinner."

"I haven't seen her since this morning," says Lena.

"I saw her when we were watching the arrival of the new inmates," says Estelle. "She was standing with some women on the other side of the road."

An hour later, Ardrina has still not appeared.

"Lena, go and look for her. It's nearly bedtime and I don't want her disturbing everyone by coming in late," says Sannie.

Lena goes out and returns alone. "I couldn't find Ardrina anywhere."

Her bed is empty when the family goes to sleep, and she is still missing in the morning.

Estelle goes outside to start teaching Renette and Suné after their scanty breakfast of mielie *pap*.[1] There is no sugar or milk so the meal is tasteless and unappetising.

Pieter is shocked at the meagre rations. He'd heard talk about the poor treatment of the inmates in the camps before he died but witnessing it first-hand is entirely different.

Pride fills his heart as he watches his children sitting just outside the tent practising writing in the sand.

A short while later, Mrs Smit comes rushing past the little group and bursts into the tent where Marta and Sannie are doing their best to tidy up and sweep the floor.

"The new arrivals have brought measles into the camp," her thin face is flushed with anxiety and she flaps her hands around like two agitated doves.

"Measles! Are you sure?" Marta asks.

"Yes, definitely measles. One of the women who arrived yesterday asked *Ouma* van Tonder if there is a hospital in the camp. Her son is burning up with fever and has a red rash covering his body. He also has a hacking cough. I'm so worried. Hennie is still so weak after his influenza attack and I can only get a little condensed milk for him as a medical comfort. There is no fresh meat, milk or vegetables available to help build his strength."

"We must try to stay isolated from the new arrivals," says Marta. "It's the only thing we can do. Unfortunately, the lack of cleanliness by many of the camp inmates will aid the spread of the disease."

"There are so few medical staff and hardly any medical supplies available. There is no disinfectant, carbolic or Izal available and a limited quantity of chloride of lime; we are in the hands of God," Marta says to Sannie.

A few hours later, Ardrina comes staggering towards the tent. Tears make twin paths down her dusty skin and her hair looks greyer and patchier than before.

"Mosiko was among the new arrivals from Taung," she says, her voice

---

[1] A porridge made from mielie meal.

catching with sobs. "He died of measles during the night."

Sannie and Marta take her into the tent and get her to lie down on a blanket. She has not slept for over twenty-four hours and is on the verge of collapse.

Pieter listens as later, Sannie shares Mosiko's story. "After the destruction of our farm, the Khakis herded the labourers to the closest railway station and dumped them there. They joined an informal camp which had already developed. Every day, more workers arrived with nothing but the clothes they were wearing, and the numbers swelled. Life was terrible as it was winter, they had no food and nothing would grow. The people were starving."

Pieter trembles with rage as he listens. Lord Kitchener's "no work, no food" policy forces black refugees to grow food for the army departments in return for their own food. This heartless British policy dictates that black civilians are not officially rationed, nor provided with adequate medical support and building materials to build shelters. Its aim of reducing the financial cost of the war for Britain disgusts Pieter.

How could anyone be so inhuman? What's wrong with these Khakis?

"Masiko decided to strike out on his own and try to survive in the veld until the war ended and he could be reunited with Ardrina and Dorthea. He eventually drifted into the Northern Cape in search of food and work and was rounded up during one of the Khakis sweeps of the countryside. He was interned at Taung[b] where the only food the inmates received was mielie meal and a little salt. The squalid and filthy conditions, coupled with the poor diet, caused outbreaks of illness in the camp. The administration decided to move some of the inmates, including Mosiko, to the Mafeking camp."

Pieter's heart breaks as Estelle cries herself to sleep that night. She loved Mosiko.

* * *

Exactly twelve days later, Hennie Odendaal complains of not feeling well. "My body aches, Mama."

Pieter, who is hovering just outside the tent entrance where Estelle is teaching her sisters, can see Hennie lying on his blanket on the floor. His teeth chatter with cold despite the warmth of the mid-day sun.

"He's as hot as fire," Mrs Odendaal feels his forehead. "What should I do?"

Marta rummages through a pile of clothes and hands her a glass bottle.

"Give him a little brandy. It may help revive him."

Two days later the tell-tale measles rash appears on his thin, white body.

He is the first, but the other children succumb, one by one. First Suné, then Renette, become violently ill, and then Lena and Hannekie, both on the same day. Mrs Smit's remaining children all sicken and add to the confusion of prostrate people and blankets on the ground.

Estelle is the only one of the children who doesn't sicken with the virus. Pieter's pride in her grows as she helps to care for the other children who are lying on their rough beds, barely able to move their limbs or open their mouths to receive small sips of the foul water.

First, they are hot and throwing their covers off and then they are cold, their bodies shivering and their teeth chattering. The brandy is soon finished, and Marta is unable to obtain any more.

The four women make poultices for the children's rashes using some crumbs of stale bread mixed with a little of the medicinal wine. It makes no noticeable difference to their discomfort and suffering.

In other tents, similar battles are being fought by the weary camp dwellers as typhoid and whooping cough, as well as measles, swell the ranks of the sick and dying.

September 1901

Marta lies on her thin blanket. Her body trembles uncontrollably with fever, as if from the effort of merely breathing. Her hair splays out like straw around her gaunt face with its over-large and over-bright eyes. She is dying and she knows it.

Pieter realises that Estelle, who is the only one well enough to care for her, also knows it. She has witnessed both her beloved younger sisters being buried in the graveyard having succumbed to their illnesses.

Marta is the only member of her family still alive and Pieter wonders how Estelle feels, knowing Marta is dying. Her face is expressionless as she goes about her nursing tasks. He has not succeeded in contacting her, she has barricaded her mind against him.

Pieter's thoughts stray to the shallow and unmarked grave in the camp cemetery where his younger children have been buried in a mass grave, together with other children who had died on the same day. Not far away are the graves of Sannie and Mrs Odendaal. Their graves have rough markers.

Who would have thought I would experience so much emotional pain after death.

The death of her sisters has broken Estelle. She visits their graves every day. Pieter has seen that her eyes remain dry. It worries him that she cannot express her anguish through tears.

She's keeping it all inside and nursing a growing hatred for the British who have facilitated the deaths of everyone she cares about.

Estelle mops Marta's brow with a wet cloth. Tears trickle from Marta's eyes as the pain of loss overwhelms her, but Estelle's expression does not change. She shows no pity towards her stepmother and it alarms Pieter. He knows Marta has treated her badly, but he expects Estelle to feel some sorrow for her wretched circumstances.

Estelle is hugely resentful towards Marta and I don't understand why. There is more to the story of the bad blood between them than I know. I wish Estelle would allow me to contact her. Maybe I can help her accept and come to peace with the past.

Pieter hears Marta's soft mutterings as she utters her last words. "I'm coming to you girls. Mama, is coming. We'll all be together again with Papa."

I won't be there to welcome you Marta. I'm trapped here on earth until I can resolve my internal conflicts and guilt.

Marta's body relaxes, not in a rush, but slowly and inexorably. She exhales one last shuddering breath and she is gone.

* * *

Estelle sits in the dirt, her eyes vacant and dead-looking. Ardrina sits next to her, trailing her fingers through the dirt in a senseless pattern. They are the only two people left from their original group of two children, four teenagers, and three women who had entered the camp only three months ago.

Ardrina and Estelle had done their best to wash and tidy Marta's body before wrapping it in a piece of linen, ready for burial. There were no coffins available. Estelle had fashioned a headstone for Marta from a piece of slate. Now that these small duties were done and Marta is interned forever in the hard, cold earth, Estelle has nothing physical to focus on and passes her days staring into space.

Pieter's concern for her grows and he wonders what, if anything, she is thinking about.

MICHELLE

ROBERT'S REVELATIONS

September 2019

The room is clear of all furniture and clutter apart from four cushions in a circular formation, and two small wooden coffee tables, one on each side of the room. A white candle is burning cheerfully in the centre of each coffee table.

The door is closed, and Pastor John, Ruth, Alice and Michelle are all seated on a cushion facing each other. Pastor John gives Michelle instructions on how to encase herself in a protective bubble.

"Visualise a bubble of white light and step into it. Ruth and I envisage Christ's white light, but you are free to choose your own protector."

It has been agreed by Pastor John and Alice that a group meditation in advance of requesting Robert and Pieter to appear will fill the room with positive energy and make it easier for the two spirits to manifest physically.

Each person focuses on their own meditation while simultaneously concentrating on opening their third eye.

"Pieter," the pastor stretches out his arms as if embracing the room, "when you are ready, please join us for a discussion."

The pastor rests his hands palms up on the knees of his crossed legs. "We would like you to join us too, please Robert."

Time passes, how much Michelle cannot say. Her uncovered arms start to form goosebumps and she wraps them protectively around her body.

The temperature's dropped but it's nowhere near as cold as it gets before Estelle manifests.

"Hello," says a deep voice.

Opening her eyes, Michelle gazes into the melancholy countenance of Pieter.

Doffing his hat, he smiles and greets everyone. "My name is Pieter van Zyl and I died in July 1901 during the Second Anglo Boer War, or South African War, as I believe it's now called," his blue eyes twinkle.

"I'm Michelle and these are my friends, Pastor John, Ruth, and Alice. We are pleased to meet you, Pieter."

"It is time. Where is my English counterpart?"

"We're hoping Robert will also join us," Pastor John smiles broadly.

"I'm here, Pieter." The phantom in his Khaki uniform materialises near the doorway. "Don't worry, I'm not about to give you free reign to share your biased account of our story. I have my own details to add."

Pieter nods his head in acknowledgement. "We both have a story to share."

"Would you like to start, Robert?" asks Pastor John. "We would like to understand your life and how you came to be trapped in a ghostly form instead of moving on to heaven ... or hell."

"Okay, I'll share my story first. Are you all comfortable?"

"Yes, we're all fine," says Pastor John. "Go ahead with your story."

"I'd been stationed in Bulawayo, Rhodesia for a year when I received a telegram that my mother was seriously ill and that I should return home immediately. I arrived just in time to say goodbye to her. It was a sad time for my family who all adored our feisty and hardworking mother. She was a great cook too and prepared excellent meals. You never went without pudding in my mother's house." The phantom sighs deeply as he reflects briefly on those happy days.

"It must have been a difficult time for you, Robert," Michelle's eyes are sympathetic.

"I stayed home for a few weeks and spent some time with my younger brother, Charlie. One of his legs was a bit longer than the other and he had a severe limp. He couldn't run or play like the other boys, or work like them either, so life was difficult for him. He had a lovely nature though, always smiling, and happy and we were close.

"The pre-war propaganda aimed at dehumanizing or animalising the Boers was already in full swing during this time I spent at home. I was confused by it because I had met many Afrikaners during my time in Rhodesia and found them to be a decent lot. My experiences with the Boers didn't stack up with the portrait of them that was being painted by the local newspapers. I realised later that this was how the government prepared young men for war. They depicted the enemy in the worst possible light to fuel the soldiers' eagerness to kill without conscience or sympathy.

"It worked, that much I can tell you. I heard many of my peers and colleagues refer to the Boers as insolent, corrupt, and cowardly. Even I, who knew differently, got caught up in the demonisation of the Dutchmen, especially when we were under siege. Being bombed continuously will do that to a man."

These less pleasant memories solicit another heavy sigh from the ghost.

"Mind you, I don't believe that propaganda and brain washing can destroy a man's basic moral compass. In my heart I knew that this war was unjust and that it was the result of British imperialistic desires for greater economic power. Britain wanted the gold in the two Boer Republics and was determined to have it."

Michelle smiles encouragingly as Robert stops talking momentarily and collects his thoughts. The downwards turn of his lips and hunted look in his eyes betray his distress at reliving these memories.

"In early September, I received orders that I was to join my regiment in Mafeking as soon as I could. War was imminent and an attack on the town was considered inevitable. I booked passage to Cape Town aboard the *Dunnottar Castle*, a relatively new Royal Mail Ship that serviced the Castle Line between Britain and South Africa. My God, that ship was fast."

Robert's great excitement, remembering his journey on this incredible ship, was unmistakable.

"How long did the trip take?" Pieter asks, his eyes glowing with interest.

"I left Southampton on the 12th of September and arrived in Cape Town on the 3rd of October. It was such an exciting journey."

"That is fast," says Pieter. "What a great experience for you."

"After docking on Cape Town, I travelled to Mafeking by train. I was on one of the last trains to make it through before war was declared.

"I met Samuel and Richard Johnson on the day I arrived in Mafeking. Richard was a great lad, young and excited at having recently being recruited to the Mafeking cadet corps. His vision of war was glamorous, and he imagined it consisted of endless battles with short periods of eating, drinking, and sleeping in between. He had no concept at that time of the immeasurable boredom of being under siege, and having to shelter for hours at a time in a bomb shelter or trench."

Robert hesitates for a moment and Michelle uses the opportunity to take a sip from the glass of water on the floor in front of her.

"Richard was assigned to assist my platoon when we were on duty on the Heights. His job was to deliver any messages we needed relayed to head office or any of the other forts in the network. We became good friends and the two of us spent a lot of idle hours shooting the breeze and talking about everything. In many ways he reminded me of my brother, Charlie. He had the same lovely nature and interest in learning about everything. Richard took the place of Charlie in my life and represented what Charlie could have been if he hadn't been limited by his physical disabilities. You must understand that life was different back then and there wasn't the same support for disabled people as there is now."

Robert looks at each person in the group intensely for a moment. "You have no idea how people bond during a siege. Being shut up in a confined area with the same people for months on end is not for the feint hearted. Tempers start to fray, and altercations occur even within families. Richard was such an even-tempered young man. He never complained about anything and everyone liked him. He had a great sense of humour about the food shortages and we had a lot of laughs over some of the meals, especially towards the end when our menu became weird and comprised horse sausages, minced mule and curried locusts.

"He was also a great animal lover. I only saw him get really upset twice during the time I knew him. The first time was when one of the natives stole his cat for food. He was enraged because he really loved that animal, but when he realised that some of the natives who hailed from Johannesburg were starving, he found it in his heart to forgive the thief."

Pieter is leaning towards Robert, listening intently to his words.

"I had no idea it got that bad in Mafeking during the siege. Stealing someone's pet to eat is horrible," Pieter remarks.

"The food situation got really bad for the last two months of the siege. It wasn't only the troops and civilians in the town who were affected by the shortages, but also the natives living in the Stadt, especially those who weren't local. The local Baralong and Fingos had their own gardens which they used to supplement their food allowance, but they wouldn't share or sell any food to the five hundred natives who'd been driven into Mafeking by the Boers before the siege. They were totally indifferent to the plight of these poor unfortunates and left them to starve even though many of them had plenty of money. They were well paid by B.P. for digging the trenches for the defence of the town."

"That's awful. I can't believe the local natives were so hard and unfeeling towards those poor people," cries Alice.

"I was also surprised, but that's how it was. The natives were tribal and looked after their own."

Robert looks at Michelle who nods. "Carry on with your story."

"The second occasion when he became most upset was during an unexpected bombardment of the town. It was late in the afternoon and a couple of native shepherds were driving a small herd of mules down the main street when bullets and shells started flying. From our position on the Heights, Richard and I watched the shepherds take cover leaving the mules standing in the street. We heard the muffled whump of shrapnel as it hit the ground, digging up puffs of dirt, and then the screaming started.

It went on and on. It was one of the most terrible sounds I have ever heard. "It's the mules, oh my God, it's the poor bloody mules," one of my men shouted. "Shoot them, poor creatures. Someone shoot them!"

"The shelling stopped, and in the sudden silence, the screams were amplified. We all had our hands over our ears, but it made no difference, the shrill, high pitched sound rang inside our heads.

"A few moments later, a few soldiers rushed to the scene and shot the injured mules. Richard was horrified by this incident and the suffering enduring by those poor animals.

"When Richard's father, Samuel Johnson, was killed and I became his role model, he told me that he thought of this incident when he heard the news. He hoped his father didn't suffer the way the mules had.

"I became his role model before Samuel died, but I became even more important in his life afterwards. He was the only male in a home with his mother and two younger sisters and his responsibilities as the man of the house weighted heavily on him, especially when Lord Kitchener took the scorched earth policy to a higher level in January 1901. It was a scary time for everyone with food so short and the Boers riding around the countryside derailing trains and causing havoc."

Out of the corner of her eye, Michelle catches a flicker of annoyance cross Pieter's tired-looking face, but he remained silent.

"His mother, Mauve Johnson, a lovely woman, was concerned that he was becoming old before his time with all the home-cares he had taken on after his father's death. She also felt he was wasting his intellectual ability by not going to school. She arranged for him to start at an English-speaking school in Pretoria in June 1901. I was stationed in Pretoria at that time and she asked me if I could come to Mafeking and escort Richard to the school. I gladly agreed and prepared to make the journey, together with several of my men. Lord Kitchener had undertaken a new project of building blockhouses throughout the new colony of the Transvaal and I was given orders to check on the progress of the building in the areas surrounding Mafeking. We arrived on the 15th of June.

"I was killed a few days later. My men and I had spent the day inspecting the new blockhouses near Zeerust and were on our way back to Mafeking when we were attacked by a party of Boers. Unfortunately, Richard was with us."

Looking at Pieter, Michelle's sees a flicker of understanding dawning in his blue eyes. His grim mouth twists into a tight-lipped line of growing despair.

ROBERT

THE GREAT BURNING

May 1900

Robert stands in the cemetery saying his goodbye to his fallen comrades and some civilian friends.

It's so ugly here.

The regular lines of limestone mounds, each sporting a simple wooden cross, lie within a small square of brown stone wall. Even the vegetation is unsightly, comprising a few scruffy fir trees and scraggly bushes of geranium.

Maybe now the siege is finally over, the cemetery will be improved. Some green grass and a few shady trees would make such a difference.

Robert makes his way over to a civilian grave where a lone boy stands, his back towards Robert, gazing at the town's empty railway station, hospital, and other relics of the recent siege.

"Richard," he says quietly.

The boy turns and looks at Robert with aged eyes in a young and flawless face.

"How are you, Richard?"

"I'm tired, so utterly tired," he says, his expression is one of mingled sorrow and anger.

Robert nods acknowledgement. The civilians of the town who have struggled to work, cook, and clean during the seven long months of gradually reducing food supplies and continuous shelling are tired. The British soldiers who fought in the trenches and lived underground for months are tired. The doctors, nurses, and volunteers who worked in the hospital and convalescence facilities and who dealt with the bodies of the fallen are tired. The relief column which marched for miles on end across the rolling veld in the dusty heat of the late autumn days and the bitter cold of the nights, is also tired. Everyone is tired.

"How are your mother and sisters?" Robert asks, remembering Mrs Johnson's pinched and hopeless face on the day of Mr Johnson's funeral several weeks ago.

"They'll be alright," says Richard. "We'll all be alright now that the siege has ended. Normal life will resume, although it will be without my father."

"Yes, it'll be without your father. I'm so sorry, Richard."

Richard smiles at him. "A least I still have my mother and my sisters ... and you. You'll come and visit us often won't you, Robert?"

"Of course, Richard. I've decided not to return to England, but rather to join the garrison at the Eland River Post. Eland River isn't that far from here so I'll be able to visit you and your family from time to time. I'll come as often as I can. You are like a brother to me."

Richard did not attempt to conceal his delight at Robert's words; he beamed.

August 1900

Robert stands in the centre of the barricade admiring the men's handiwork. For the past few weeks, everybody has been busy building rough stone walls or breastworks called sconces.

As reports and indications of the growing army of the enemy around them increase, further defensive measures are taken. Robert and the other survivors of the Mafeking siege draw on their recent experience to aid their preparations for the anticipated battle.

A makeshift defensive perimeter has been established using ox wagons to create barricades. In addition, the sconces have been blinded with earth at the front and topped with biscuit boxes, bags of flour, and boxes of Australian mutton.

It's the best we can do in the timeframe, but our position is still weak, Robert thinks.

The main position of the Elands River garrison is at a farm located on a small ridge about 0.6 miles away from the river. There are two small positions located on hills to the south, a bit closer to the river, called Butters' Kopje and Zouch's Kopje, after the leaders of the defending troops.

The entire area of the camp does not cover more than five acres and is surrounded by hills from which it can be shelled. The men know they are not in a good position to defend themselves, especially as the main camp only has one 7-pounder mountain gun and one Maxim, with another Maxim being in the possession of Captain Butters who is defending the position on Butters' Kopje.

"It's amazing, isn't it?" says Jack, coming up behind Robert. "Who would have thought we would be preparing for another battle so soon after the fall of Pretoria and the British occupation of Rustenburg?"

"I did wonder if it was really over," says Robert, "or whether the Boers would formulate some new plan. They have an awful lot to lose, don't they?"

"I can't say I felt like that. It seemed as if everything was going right for our leaders after the relief of Mafeking. We had established garrisons throughout the Marico District, including the towns of Mafeking, Zeerust, Lichtenburg and Rustenburg, and our patrols were going around disarming those Boers who had not surrendered their weapons. Many of them had already surrendered."

"Sure, a lot of Boers did surrender, but the Aussies said at the time that not many Mausers were handed in. They anticipated further trouble from dissident bands of Boers, especially those under the command of Generals Koos de la Rey and Christiaan de Wet, who are still hanging on to the hope of victory for their respective republics. There are pockets of resistance all over this area and especially in the Magaliesberg."

"The Aussies say that the dissidents have been going around to all the farms for the past fortnight and coercing all the Burghers who had laid down arms to re-join their commandos. Apparently, they have used threats and even personal violence to force resisting Boers to take up their arms again. It's a bad situation."

A perplexed look crosses Jack's face, "Did the Aussies really anticipate further problems? I didn't know that. They've been bringing in stores and forage found at farms for a few weeks now."

"That is true, in some cases they have managed to get in before the dissidents and commandeer what we need from the farms. If the farmer is there, they are paid a fair price for what is taken, but if he is away without permission, his property is forfeited. In many cases, however, the dissidents have already been to a farm and have taken everything, including all the men."

"Aren't the dissidents more likely to attack Rustenburg than here? It seems to be the most vulnerable of our garrisons, being the most easterly and far-flung."

"Rustenburg is vulnerable and retaking it is also a matter of Boer pride, but Elands River Post is the logical target, isn't it? Think of all the supplies we have here. Last time I checked there were over fifteen hundred horses, mules and cattle, large quantities of ammunition, food, and other equipment, and over one hundred wagons. That's pretty tempting for bands of Boer guerrillas, don't you think?"

"Yes, I hear you, Robert, but I still think an attack is highly unlikely.

What do you think of the Aussie troops?"

"They're not bad blokes. Their loyalty to Britain is undeniable, but most of them don't like the idea of burning the farms of dissidents. I've heard them talking and they find it cowardly and distasteful. I also get the distinct impression they consider their combat skills to be superior to ours."

"Do they? I haven't really spoken to many of them. Why do they think their fighting skills are better than ours?" The bemused look is back on Jack's face.

"They look down on us Tommies because they have better bush survival skills than we do. They're a rum lot, really. They haven't got a good word to say for the Boers who they think are uncouth and lacking in hygiene, and yet they hold the native soldiers in high esteem.

"It's rather odd to me, because the Aussies and the Boers actually have a lot in common, but there you go. I guess they see themselves as British first and Australian second."

"It's interesting that they view the native soldiers with such favour. I was on patrol one afternoon, during our march here, and was looking for a place for us to outspan for the night, when I came across a small herd of buck. I took a few shots at them, but I missed, and they all disappeared like the wind. I carried on and soon came across a small pan of water which would be a great resting place. Next to the pan was a farmhouse and as I drew near enough to become visible, a woman opened the door and came out. She was trembling with fear because she'd heard the shooting and thought it was the Baralong come to loot her farm and stock. She said that Colonel Baden-Powell at Mafeking had given them guns and they were using them to intimidate the elderly men, women and children on the farms and steal from them. She intimated that there'd been instances of rape and murder in the area."

"My God, that is terrible. B.P. should have disarmed them after the relief of Mafeking. I heard he didn't want to offend the Baralong who had helped with the defence of their Stadt and the town. I thought it was a short-sighted view at the time, better to disarm them and risk offence than have them running wild causing trouble."

* * *

The gathering of men around the campfires throws strange and dark shadows in the glowing reddish yellow light as they lustily bellow out the final refrain of *Soldiers of the Queen*.

It's the Soldiers of the Queen, my lads,
Who've been my lads,
Who're seen my lads,
In the fight for England's glory, lads,
When we have to show them what we mean:
And when we sat we've always won,
And when they ask us how it's done,
We'll proudly point to ev'ry one
Of England's soldiers of the Queen!
It's the Queen!"[1]

When the sing song finishes, the men put their quartpot[2] on the campfire and stand about talking.

"There's nothing like some good news to bring out the best in soldiers," grinned Jack at Robert and their new Aussie mate, James Cawthorn.

"Yeah, it's a relief to know that General Carrington is on his way here with his relief column. Our position's not exactly strong, is it?" says James.

"The Boers will never attack Elands River," declares Jack, "Don't you agree, Robert?" Robert looks at Jack speculatively but doesn't answer.

Never say never, is what I think. I didn't expect the Boers to instigate some of the attacks they did in Mafeking. It is best never to underestimate these Boers.

Several of the other lads, however, agreed with Jack.

The evening ended with Colonel Hore calling for "Three cheers for the Australians" and the singing of *God Save the Queen*.

* * *

Robert stood to attention as the first dirt was thrown into the graves of the men who had died during the battle. The Queensland Citizen Bushmen fired volleys in acknowledgement of their dead officer and, in between, the buglers played the different bugle calls. Of the bodies interned in the ground, twelve were soldiers and four were native porters. There were also fifty-one people wounded during the battle that lasted only eleven days but felt like a thousand years.

Despite his grief at the loss of colleagues, who had become his friends, gladness filled Robert's heart when he saw the Union Jack still flying on

---

[1] *Soldiers of the Queen*, also sung as *Soldiers of the King*, was composed and written by Leslie Stuart in 1898.

[2] A portable boiling pot that held a quart of liquid and was placed over a campfire to heat food or boil water for tea.

the crest of a nearby hill.

Despite our small numbers, we held firm.

"Hi Robert, a sad occasion isn't it?" says Jack, his voice husky with emotion.

"Yes, yes, a terrible fight. I thought we were goners when firstly General Carrington's garrison was ambushed and withdrew and then B.P.'s relief garrison turned back. We really did well in the circumstances."

"I worried about the lack of water the most," says Jack. "Not having a water source within the camp and having to send patrols out at night to collect water from the river, was pretty scary."

"I must admit, old chap, that I was worried about water too. When the Dutchmen attached Butters' Kopje two nights in a row, I thought our water supply would be lost but good old Captain Butters and Lieutenant Zouch managed to repulse them both times, protecting their positions and keeping our water supply open. It was worse than Mafeking in that regard, wasn't it?"

"Yes, you can't live without water. We had a water supply in Mafeking, so that was never a concern."

"Do you remember on the second night of those attacks, when the Dutchmen tried to advance under cover of a flock of sheep and goats which they drove before them. Weren't they surprised when Captain Butters fired the Maxim at them?"

"The Dutchmen are an unethical lot," says Jack. "My mate, James, was lying injured in the Mafeking hospital when it was fired on by the Boers. It was clearly marked with a Red Cross flag at the time. One of the Boer artillery shells struck it and he was further wounded by shrapnel."

"They are a rum lot," Robert agreed. "Many of them are educated, tolerant and kindly but they abuse the white flag and the Red Cross flag too."

"Well, Lord Kitchener did eventually come to our rescue and it all turned out well for us, except for the loss of so many animals. I hear only two hundred survived the siege which is a terrible shame."

"I hope the people of Mafeking are safe," says Robert. "Now that this siege is over, I hope I can make a quick visit there to check on the Johnson family."

December 1900

Pretoria is an oasis in the burned desert created by Lord Robert's scorched earth policy.

Robert had arrived exhausted after the hasty retreat of his brigade, under Major General Clements, from Nooitgedacht near the Magalies-berg Mountains. The disastrous battle against Boer commandos, led by Generals Koos de la Rey and Christiaan Beyers, resulted in the death or wounding of sixty-four of his peers and the capture of fifty-four men and one hundred and eighteen wagons.

The brigade's flight through a barren and desolate countryside, populated only by numerous scavenger birds feasting on the rotting corpses of thousands of dead cattle, sheep and horses, was horrific and Robert had to avert his eyes and numb his mind to retain some vestige of belief in his own leadership.

The normalcy of the city of Pretoria is an antidote to some of Robert's bitterness. Lord Roberts' headquarters, known as the Residency, is situated in a charming suburb known as Sunnyside. The beautiful setting abounds with shady trees and burbling streams against a background of high hills. The distant and miniature forts which crown these hills are the only reminder of the on-going war and their seeming insignificance in this delightful setting diminishes their status as reminders of the on-going Boer resistance which has brought so much suffering down on the heads of the rural civilian population of the Transvaal.

As Robert walks the bustling streets of the business district the smooth-ness with which both civilian and military business is being undertaken acts as a salve to his bleeding soul, softening the mental and emotional scars that have developed during the past three months.

I don't think my soul will ever fully heal, but at least the pain will reduce, and the rough edges of my scabs will not rub so roughly against my beliefs.

The Transvaal National Bank and the Natal Bank are forcible remind-ers that President Kruger, the man affectionately known as *Oom* Paul by his people, deserted them during their hour of need, taking all the gold coins and bars they held with him to Delagoa Bay.

Gold is the route of all evil in this terrible war. My country wants it and could not tolerate the Boers potentially developing their two republics into wealthy and powerful economies. Britain deliberately set out to take the Boers' land and bring it under the Union Jack. It seems the gold turned the heads of the Boers themselves. I've heard stories of corruption and fraud among influential Boers and I've heard it said that their President ran off with all the wealth of his country packed into his departing train.

Robert knows he is disillusioned by the events of the past few months. The siege of Mafeking had ended on a high note with stories filtering through of the ecstatic joy and celebrating by the English, far away on their island across the ocean.

The circumstances of the siege had been unpleasant and often boring, but there had been a comradery and a sense of British pride in the ability of the troops to withstand the discomfort and continuous shelling of the town. He had read somewhere that thirty thousand shells had been discharged on the town.

He grins when he thinks about how the troops had clamoured for their gift of chocolate from Queen Victoria after the siege. Naturally, the tins of chocolate sent to the troops fighting in South Africa as a Christmas present from the Queen had not made it through to Mafeking during the siege.

The recall of B.P. after the battle of Elands River was immeasurably disappointing to Robert. B.P. had played a major role in his life for seven months during the siege and the troops had held him in high esteem. His recall felt like a slap in the face.

He's discussed this with Jack, who is stationed in Pretoria with him.

"B.P. was held accountable for the escape of the Dutchman guerrilla, Christiaan de Wet and his convoy, through the Magaliesberg Mountains,"[c] says Jack.

"I know, but it doesn't seem right that he was held entirely accountable. There were others who played a role in that fiasco. What about Lieutenant General Ian Hamilton? He didn't listen to direct orders?"

"I agree that there were others who played a role in the whole sorry story, but when you are in charge, you are the one who is held ultimately accountable."

"I know, I know," says Robert, "but it doesn't make me feel better about B.P.'s recall. I also don't like the path this war has taken. Having to implement Lord Roberts' scorched earth policy in the Magalies Valley for three months has turned my stomach. I'm glad to be stationed here in Pretoria now, away from all that burning and destruction."

"I get you, mate and I'm glad too. Thank God for the incident at Nooitgedacht[d] which got us out of that hell hole, even if it was bad for our side."

"Hmmm," says Robert. "The outcome of that battle also upsets me. I've heard through the grapevine that Lord Kitchener has blamed Major General Clements for our defeat at Nooitgedacht and I think that is unfair. It's being said that he made a poor strategic choice of position when he chose Nooitgedacht farm as a camping site and that he chose it for all the wrong reasons.

"We were both there and know that he followed the advice of the

English-speaking farmers in the area when he chose that camping site. We also know that he was let down by headquarters and received no relief from Major General Broadway and his men who were stationed nearby."

"It makes me mad that Kitchener is trying to pin this defeat on Clements. He, Broadway, and headquarters are all equally responsible. I suppose Lord Roberts didn't want to leave South Africa under a cloud of potential incompetence and poor decision making."

"You are right as always, Robert. Lord Roberts ensured that he departed South Africa a hero having conquered the Boers and added two colonies to Great Britain's repertoire of territories. Anyhow, he's gone now and there's nothing that we can do about any cover-ups so we may as well think about more cheerful things."

The haberdashery is directly ahead, and Robert's thoughts turn to Christmas and the purpose of his trip into town.

"What are you doing for Christmas this year, Robert? Are you planning to join us for lunch at the hotel?" Jack asks.

"Nope, I'm planning to travel to Mafeking tomorrow and spend a few days, including Christmas, with Richard and his family."

"That is great, you are fortunate to have a family to go too."

"I know," smiles Robert, "although this will be a difficult one as it's the first Christmas since Mr Johnson passed away. I'm glad to be getting away though. It'll be good to see everyone in Mafeking and I'm glad I can offer the Johnsons some support."

Entering the store, he waits patiently for the elderly storekeeper to attend to him. He knows exactly what he wants. Lengths of pink and yellow ribbon for Eliza and Emily and a package of fine lace for Mrs Johnson.

They won't have anything like this in Mafeking with so few of the supply trains making it through to the town.

* * *

That evening, lying in his bunk, Robert reflects on Major General Clements again and considers what he thinks of the man.

Following the battle at Elands River, Clements had taken his duties in implementing the new scorched earth policy seriously. The men under his command, including Robert and Jack, had been lined up and ordered to ride through the countryside, burning every farmhouse in their path. It no longer mattered whether the men of the house were home or what their allegiance was, all crops were destroyed, and all livestock killed. The ground was rank and defiled with blood and gore mixed with ash and blackened veld grass.

Robert abhors this new policy of Lord Roberts'. He despises himself for being instrumental in implementing it but feels he has no other option. His dreams are filled with Boer women, their faces stoically accepting, and children crying quietly in their distress, as they watch their homes burning. He is left sleep deprived and despondent.

Many Boer women have taken to the veld in their ox-wagons, abandoning their farms before the arrival of the troops, and endeavouring to survive on their own, or in groups, by adopting a nomadic lifestyle and living in their wagons. They take their cattle and sheep with them, thus ensuring the family's food supply, as well as their loyal workers to shepherd them.

Some of the displaced labourers have joined the British forces, while others have taken to the veld, wandering in aggressive bands, attacking, and pillaging the remaining farms and any women's laagers they happen to come across.

It's a disgrace to leave women and children homeless and at the mercy of marauding desperadoes. I imagine that's why Lord Roberts has established a refugee camp in Pretoria.

* * *

Robert is shocked to see the town rising out of the burned and black countryside instead of the vast expanse of the usual wide and shallow bowl of dried out, green yellow veld. Dust and ash move in lazy dark clouds and settle thickly on the dark muddy water of the occasional shallow pan or watering hole. He knows about the great burning, but it is still a shock to see this.

The town looks much as he remembers. Most of the houses still bear signs of assault and the marketplace has a dilapidated and desolate air despite the attempts at Christmas festivity.

He knocks on the door of the Johnson home and Richard rushes to the door to welcome him, followed closely by his mother and sisters. He's pleased to see that they all look well and are plumper and rosier than when he last saw them.

The delicious smell of home cooking makes Robert's stomach growl loudly. Mrs Johnson has made a splendid traditional supper of toad-in-the-hole using local sausages and her mother's recipe for the batter. There is an apple pie for dessert.

Robert welcomes the change in fare from the meals served at his barracks, especially the apple pie, which is served with clotted cream. Each bite fills his mouth with the delicious combination of slightly sour apples and plump cooked raisins, marinated in a spicy sauce and wrapped in Mrs Johnson's special sweet pie pastry. While they eat, the family share all the local news.

Mrs Johnson passes him the bowl, urging him to take a little more cream.

"What do you think of this scorched earth policy of Lord Roberts'? It is causing an influx of refugees into the town which is still struggling to recover from the siege."

Robert reflects on his answer before speaking. "I'm not in favour of burning the farms and destroying crops and livestock. I feel as if I'm behaving like a criminal when I'm forced to participate. It's one of the reasons I was glad about Jack and my relocation to Pretoria. I don't have to bear witness daily to the devastation of the civilian population."

He looks at Mauve Johnson and Richard to gauge their reaction to his words. They are both nodding in agreement.

"I don't like it at all," says Mrs Johnson. "The women's laager has been transformed into a refugee camp to accommodate all the destitute families that are flooding into Mafeking and the surrounding towns."

"There is a refugee camp near Pretoria too," Robert puts down his empty port glass. "I was speaking to one of the ladies in Pretoria who's been assisting at the new camp in Irene. She told me that Pretoria has been flooded with refugees ever since the war started. Some of these Boer families were being housed in a camp on the banks of the Apies River near Pretoria and she was part of a group of women who were assisting at that camp. These families have now been moved to the Irene camp and she's working as a volunteer nurse there. The conditions sound awful."

"What's happened to the women and children who were already living in the women's laager?"

A shiver runs down Robert's back as he remembers the squalid living conditions in the laager during the siege. "They're still there. They're impoverished and require on-going relief. Would you like a cup of tea? I'm going to make one for myself."

"A cup of tea would be lovely. Thank you."

Robert turns to Richard as his mother leaves the room. "How are you, Richard? I believe all the schools are still closed. What are you doing with yourself now?"

"I'm studying here at home with Emily and Eliza. Mother has given me some of my father's books, and I'm using these to continue my studies as best I can. He had an interest in economics, which I suppose is natural seeing as he was in banking. He also had an interest in the theory of evolution, and I've been reading about Charles Darwin and his works and ideas."

"He's getting on well too," says Mrs Johnson, smiling at him fondly as she re-enters the room carrying the tea tray. "Richard is quite academic and interested in continuing his education. I'd hoped the schools would be reopened after the end of the siege, but it doesn't look as if that's likely for a while to come. We are managing though. Emily and Eliza have been practising embroidery and applique. Girls, why don't you show your work to Robert?"

After Robert has admired and exclaimed over the girls' handcrafts, which are excellent, he takes his leave, heading for The Dixon's Hotel where he's spending the night.

* * *

Robert arrives at the Johnson home at 12 p.m. on Christmas Day, his arms filled with gifts for the family.

Mrs Johnson and the girls have prepared a marvellous traditional dinner which is followed by a real English plum pudding.

"What a wonderful surprise," Robert declares, savouring each delicious mouthful. "How did you manage to get this? I know very few supply trains are getting through with the Boers sabotaging the railway lines so effectively."

Mrs Johnson smiles gently. "I'll let Richard answer. He's the one who procured the Christmas pudding."

Richard grins hugely, "I did some work for Mr Weil helping him clear out the company's depot in town. He gave me this as part of my wages. He knew you were coming to spend Christmas with us and he wanted to help make it a memorable one."

"Well, he certainly succeeded," says Robert, patting his full stomach. "That was great."

In the early evening, Robert walks with the Johnsons to the Church Hall where the children are putting on a nativity play. Eliza plays Mary and looks perfectly sweet with her long golden hair and calm blue eyes. She has the pink ribbon Robert gifted her for Christmas tied in a pretty bow on top of her head. Emily is a sheep and does a lovely dance with the shepherds and the other sheep.

Tumultuous applause follows this performance as everyone gives vent to their pleasure at the normalcy of this Christmas and enjoys the relief from the everyday worries caused by the war.

Robert drops off to sleep that night thinking about his mother back home and his younger brother who died of scarlet fever two years before. His involvement with the Johnson family and Richard has helped to fill the hole in his heart that has never gone away. The memory of his brother will never leave him, but now he can remember the good times without being overwhelmed by the pain of his loss.

June 1900

Robert is on his way back to Mafeking. He hadn't planned to return in the middle of the year, but he'd received a letter from Mrs Johnson several weeks earlier asking him if he could escort Richard to the new school that has opened in Pretoria.

> Dear Robert
> I hope you are well and are finding your duties in Pretoria bearable.
>
> I received a letter from a friend of mine, Mrs Partridge, who lives in Pretoria, saying that Lord Milner has opened a secondary school for English-speaking pupils in Pretoria. The school opened on the 3rd of June with Mr Charles Hope as the headmaster.
>
> I have been fortunate enough to obtain a place in this school, called Pretoria High School, for Richard. I believe he will benefit greatly through continuing his education as he is a bright young man.
>
> I am reaching out to you as I am unable to leave the girls and accompany Richard to Pretoria. My brother-in-law, Richard's Uncle James, and his wife, will provide a home for Richard during his time at the school. James is in the Cape for business for several weeks and is unable to make the trip to Mafeking to collect Richard and take him to Pretoria.
>
> I know that you are close to Richard and thought you might be able to arrange some time off to escort him to the school on my behalf.
>
> I look forward to receiving your response.

Yours sincerely
Mauve Johnson

Robert immediately put in a request to travel to Mafeking and collect Richard. His superior had been willing to allow the trip but had asked him to take ten of his troops with him and perform an inspection of the blockhouses that were being built in the area.

He'd written back to Mrs Johnson informing her that he and his men would be arriving in Mafeking on the 15th of June and would bring Richard back with them on their return to Pretoria later that month.

* * *

Robert jerks awake, the memory of his dream so vivid it brings him out in a cold sweat. In the dream he, Richard, and his men had ridden into a Boer ambush while checking on the progress of the building of the blockhouses around Mafeking. The man whose life he'd spared in the trench in Mafeking, the Dutchman called Pieter, had risen from behind a clump of bushes and taken aim. His hate filled blue eyes blaze as he trains his rifle on Richard.

It's morning and the sun has splashed the sky with a rosy blush. It's time to get moving as he and his men need to get their inspection of the local blockhouses finished today. They are due to start the return trip to Pretoria the following day.

Mentally pushing the strangeness of his dream aside, Robert does his ablutions and goes downstairs for breakfast with his men.

The men have eaten and are enjoying a cup of tea when Richard comes into the breakfast room. He's dressed in his cadet uniform and has a backpack over his shoulder.

"Hi Robert," he says cheerfully, "Mother said I could come with you today to see the blockhouses under construction. She's packed me a lunch," he holds out the backpack.

His grin is so broad it seems to take over his entire face.

The dream briefly flashes into Robert's mind, but the idea of disappointing the boy is unendurable.

It was just a dream.

"That sounds like a splendid idea, Richard. I would love to have your company."

Thirty minutes later the men and Richard are mounted and trotting out of town.

260

The initial blockhouses had been built in March of the previous year on the orders of Lord Roberts to protect his army's main supply route, the railway line between Bloemfontein and the Cape. They had proved to be effective and not one bridge where these blockhouses were sited and manned was blown up by the Boers.

Lord Roberts was now implementing Lord Milner's suggestion that the blockhouses be extended away from the railway lines and across the veld.

It is a good idea. If there are enough blockhouses, the Boer dissidents will be literally fenced in. It'll also facilitate the establishment of supply depots away from the railway line and give our troops a greater range when they are pursuing the Boer commandos. The poor sods don't have much of a chance now.

Later that afternoon, Robert, Richard, and the troops pass a rocky outcrop scattered with intermittent clumps of thick bushes on their way back to town. It's been a long day and the tired men are looking forward to reaching the hotel and having a good evening meal.

"Bang! Bang! Bang!

Despite their training, the horses jump nervously in reaction to the sound. Robert swings around in his saddle and looks towards his men and Richard.

One of his men has slumped over in his saddle. The prancing movements of his horse cause him to slip sideways, falling in slow motion down the side of his anxious animal. The bloody mess that was once the top of his head comes into view. Death must have been instant.

Other shots ring out and other men fall.

"Noooooo!" the sound tears from Robert's throat like a siren.

I must protect Richard. His family has already suffered so much loss.

Grabbing his rifle, he fires an angry shot towards the rocks. Around him the churning hooves of horses kick up clouds of reddish dust as his remaining men attempt to escape the next round of fire. He desperately tries to move his horse so that Richard is shielded from the sniping.

A sole man rises from behind the nearest bush. He's hatless and his blue eyes blaze fiercely from his lined and weather-beaten face. It's the man from the trench in Mafeking whose life Robert spared all those months ago.

Robert bellows profanities, as he fires at Pieter.

For Robert, the attack ends quickly. He feels the bullet tear into his body, wrenching him from his horse. There is no pain, as he slips from this life, but hatred towards Pieter, the man who has done him such a grievous injustice, together with a desire for retribution, tether his soul to the physical world.

MICHELLE

PIETER'S CONFESSION

September 2019

Robert is somehow diminished; his spiritual form having faded as he ended his story.

Michelle offers him a short reprieve. "Why don't you take a short break now, Robert, and let's hear what Pieter has got to say."

Robert smiles at her gratefully and nods agreement.

"Pieter, please go ahead with your story."

"*Goeie middag,*"[1] says the ghost in his rumbling voice. "I'm pleased to meet you all, and I'm especially glad to finally get to speak to you properly, Michelle."

Michelle gazes at the spirit of the Boer. He's not ominous or frightening and has an eager expression on his translucent face.

He wants to tell us something important.

"Hello, Pieter, I'm also pleased to have this opportunity to learn more about you," she replies.

"Hello," murmur the other three occupants of the room.

Robert doesn't speak, merely stares expectantly at him.

Pieter smiles and reverts to English. "You have no idea, Michelle, how delighted I was when I first realised that you could see me. You are the first person I've been able to communicate with since my death in 1901. I've spent many years trying to make contact with my daughter, Estelle, but her heart and mind are closed to me. I haven't specifically tried to contact any other people; I didn't know it was possible, until I met you. I don't know why you are able to see and hear me, but I'm grateful, and now it seems that others can see and hear me too."

Michelle thinks about the Ouija board, packed away in the drawer of her desk. *It's interesting that I'm the only person who has seen Pieter's ghost in all these years. I hope ghost sightings won't become a regular event for me.*

She shudders slightly at the thought.

"I'm pleased to meet you too, Pieter. Your English is good."

"My grandmother was English and so was my first wife, Estelle's mother."

---

[1] Good afternoon in Afrikaans.

"That makes perfect sense," Robert interjects. "Your English is excellent, and I wondered if you had English relatives or connections."

His eyes twinkle with pleasure in recognition of their common heritage.

The lines of anxiety etched around Pieter's mouth relax slightly in response to Robert's friendly look.

"I'm glad you speak good English, Pieter. I'm sorry to say it but my spoken Afrikaans leaves a lot to be desired. You have mentioned a few times that you need my help. What is it you believe I can help you with?"

"I died a bitter man, Michelle. My own home and farm, and those belonging to my brother, Willem, were destroyed by the Khakis during the Second Anglo Boer War. My wife and daughters, as well as my sister-in-law and two nieces, were transported to the concentration camp at Mafeking. I knew they had little chance of surviving the harsh conditions and widespread diseases in the camp. I vented my anguish and rage on others before my death and my resultant guilt prevented my soul from crossing into the afterlife and finding eternal rest. I need to share and explain my actions during the last weeks of my life so that my soul can find peace and ascend to heaven.

"You have undertaken to write a book about my life and that of my family. I'm glad. I want my story told. People must remember the camps and the terrible hardships suffered by my people. I also want to tell you about my last days on this earth. You won't find that sort of personal and detailed information by doing research as it was never recorded. It will also help me cleanse my soul."

"I'm happy to help you in any way I can," says Michelle. "I would love to write your story and ensure the memory of the hardships your family suffered during the war is kept alive for future generations."

Pieter walks over to the large glass doors which open onto the outside patio. He points at the jacaranda tree in the garden.

"I planted that tree, you know, on the day my family and I fled our farm. It was a few days before the Khakis captured Pretoria."

"Did you really?" says Michelle. "It is a beautiful tree. I didn't know that a jacaranda tree could live that long."

"Yes, they can live for up to two hundred years if the conditions are right."

Pieter turns away from the window and seats himself, cross-legged, on the floor. His mouth is set in lines of determination. "I killed Robert," a strangled half sob escapes his throat. "I did not know that until he told his story, but it was me. I'm the one who killed him.

"The day he died, my brother and I, together with several other Burghers were lying behind a cluster of rocks near Mafeking, watching the road.

"We were making good use of our time by filing the tips of our Mauser cartridges and making them into dumdum bullets. Before the incarceration of my family, I scorned the use of dumdum bullets because they cause such severe injuries and large-scale bleeding, but the cruel behaviour of the Khakis towards our women and children had changed my attitude. I thought God would forgive my making dumdum bullets as it was the Khakis I planned to use them on and they deserved it. Of course, I was wrong."

Michelle gazes into his burning and tormented eyes.

"As we lay behind the outcrop of rocks, we saw a group of eleven horsemen approaching. We all remained perfectly still and let them approach to within five hundred paces. They were British soldiers. One of them was an officer; all their uniforms were smart and new. I remember noting that with anger. My own clothes were ragged, and my shoes had holes in the soles from wear. I wasn't very clean either. In the beginning, we had been able to wash our clothes when we camped, but as Lord Kitchener's noose tightened around us from January 1901, we needed to be perpetually ready for immediate flight so washing clothing fell by the wayside.

"One of the Burghers, a trigger-happy man, opened the firing. He shot and killed one of the Khakis; I can remember seeing his head dissolve in a spray of red blood. The rest of us followed suit, shooting wildly, and the bodies of four other men fell heavily from their horses, hitting the ground and raising clouds of red dust on the road."

Michelle notices Robert's keen attention to Pieter's words.

"In the few moments before I shot him, the officer tried to manoeuvre himself in front of one of the other horsemen. I raised my Mauser, took careful aim, and fired. The officer fell forward, as if in slow motion. His foot remained caught in the stirrup with his body in a horribly twisted position on the ground.

"Four of the horsemen took hasty flight, but one just sat there, staring in the direction of our rocks, completely dumbstruck. He slowly raised his hands. We could see that he was not a man but rather a boy of about fourteen years old. That was obviously why the officer tried to protect him. I thought it was his son.

"I raised my Mauser again and was just about to fire when Willem put his hand under the barrel and pushed up my rifle."

"Don't shoot, Pieter," he said. "That boy is defenceless and not a threat to us."

264

Michelle looks at Pieter, "What did you do?"

"I shot him. My rage was so enormous I could not stop myself. I'd lost everything of value in my life as a result of the war.

"The boy didn't die immediately. My shot was off and he lay on the ground, twisting and turning in that infernal red dust, until one of the other Burghers came out from behind the rock and put him out of his misery."

Pieter hides his face in his hands in a gesture of defeat. "I was so bitter against the English."

Robert glides over and sits down beside him. After a few moments of watching Pieter's internal struggle, Robert reaches out and places a comforting hand on his shoulder. "I understand how you felt, Pieter, and I forgive you."

The two ghostly men continue to sit like that for a few minutes. Pieter absorbing Robert's compassion and sorrow, and then he continues speaking. "About a month later, I died. My commando had an unexpected encounter with a larger party of Khakis. We were trying to scavenge some food supplies from a burned-out farm when the patrol suddenly appeared.

"I ran but I had to duck under a barbed wire fence on the farm. It caught the sleeve of my jacket and while I was freeing myself, a soldier shot me in the chest. I was left for dead.

"A short while later, Willem came galloping across the field. Stopping, he dropped to the ground, pulled me off the wire, and lifted me onto his horse. Somehow, he managed to support me across his saddle and lead me away to safety. I died later that evening."

Pieter stops speaking. For a long time, he sits quite motionless.

"I'm sorry, Robert. Sorry for allowing my anger and bitterness to overwhelm my better nature. Richard died a boy because of me, and, although you say you have forgiven me, I can never forgive myself."

"Did you know I spared your life? On the night of the bayonets, when Lord Baden-Powell ordered us to attack you in your trenches?" Robert looks at Pieter. There is no malice or bitterness in his expression. "I recognised you before you shot me, and I died with the knowledge that the man whose life I'd spared killed me and the boy I regarded as a son. It was hard to bear at the time."

Pieter's large frame sags and folds in on itself. Michelle would not have believed that a ghost could have such a severe reaction to shock.

"That was you?" he gasps the words as if recovering from a gut punch.

"Yes, that was me, Pieter."

Michelle studies Robert's face, assessing the physical changes that had taken place over the past hour. The stern mouth that had defined Robert's features in Michelle's mind, had softened into a less formidable and unyielding shape. The hard and determined look in his eyes had disbursed, replaced by a look of understanding.

"The fire of my hatred for you has burned for over one hundred years, Pieter." Robert's voice is soft and gentle like a summer breeze. "I fed it on anger, disappointment and an unfounded sense of what is just and right. I was disgusted by Lord Kitchener's burned earth policy and his cruel treatment of the Boer women and children. Somehow, despite my own strong feelings in this regard, I failed to have any real understanding of how this impacted the Boers and their attitudes and frame of mind. I can see now how wrong I was to blame you for my death and, more importantly, the death of Richard. I didn't appreciate how the war broke down everything in your life, your sense of community, farming lifestyle, self-expression, individuality, freedom and, finally, your family."

Robert reaches out towards Pieter again, "I'm sorry, Pieter. Please forgive me for my lack of understanding."

Pieter just nods, unable to say anything.

Robert smiles, acknowledging the unspoken sentiment. His ghostly form becomes more transparent. "Thank you, for helping me find peace and move on."

Michelle has a last glimpse of a faint wavering shape and then Robert is gone.

Pieter hauls himself to his feet and crosses back over to the window. He looks at the jacaranda tree for a few minutes and then looks back at Michelle. no one else in the room seems to matter to him, he focuses solely on her.

"I want to give you something. It's my legacy."

He points at the magnificent old tree. "If you dig beneath the roots of that tree, you'll find the Kruger coins I hid the day I left my farm. I would like you to donate half of the value to charity. The other half you must keep, Michelle. You can use some of it to finance our book. I want my story told. I want people to remember the horror of the past and ensure its circumstances are never repeated."

Michelle stands up and moves next to him at the window. She smiles into his sad eyes. "Of course, I'll do that. Are you sure you want me to take half of your money? Don't you have any living relatives?"

"No, my brother betrayed me by not looking after my only surviving child, Estelle. There is no one else and I want you to have it for helping set Robert's soul free from its perpetual torment."

"What about you, Pieter? How do we set your soul free?"

"How can I free my soul from the eternal guilt in which I've wallowed, like a pig in muck, for over one hundred years? How, please tell me how?"

Pieter is standing with his back to the large window. The green grass of the garden and the flower beds, filled with daisies, marigolds, pansies, and daylilies, in their bright spring colours, can be clearly seen through his transparent form, making a mockery of his anguish and self-depreciation.

"I failed my daughter, Estelle, when she needed me the most. I didn't sufficiently defend her against the jealousy of her stepmother, my wife, Marta. I never even told her that Marta was not her real mother. I knew that there was something wrong with her when I visited my family for the last time on the farm before they were taken away by the Khakis, but I never pushed her to tell me what had happened. I found out about Marta's mental abuse of Estelle after I died. I also learned that she was brutally raped and abused by one of the men from a commando which sought shelter and aid at Willem's farm. She was only thirteen! The man was an animal and he was never brought to justice for ruining my daughter's life. Estelle never recovered from that ordeal and Marta turned her back on her entirely. Treating her like an outcast."

"Oh no!" cries Michelle.

Her eyes fill and the tears overflow. They course down her cheeks unchecked.

Alice rises and comes over to her. She pulls her into an embrace and rests Michelle's head on her shoulder, patting it gently. Alice's eyes are also overflowing and the colour in her cheeks has flared up into a blotchy red rash.

"I've never been able to contact Estelle, not during the years before her death, nor since. She's kept me out of her life most successfully, turning away when I tried to reveal my presence to her, and ignoring any messages or signs I left. I wanted to confess to her, to tell her that I'm so sorry for my neglect and sins and beg her forgiveness. I've never had the chance though. She has never given me the chance."

He stops and breaks into a horrible laughter, as unnatural and hellish as the laugh of the Devil himself. "I cannot explain my transgressions to her and seek absolution from her. Until I can do that both of us will remain locked inside our personal prisons of guilt, resentment, and hatred."

Michelle reaches out towards Pieter, looking for a way to offer him comfort and support, but her hand passes through him.

She glances at Pastor John helplessly, hoping he'll give her an indication of what she should do. He catches her eye and opens his mouth to speak just as the closed door opens. Estelle stands on the threshold. She is bonnetless and her thick blonde hair frames her delicate face with its large green eyes. Her narrow feet are bare, and she is wearing an old-fashioned floor length dress from the beginning of the twentieth century.

"Estelle, my dear little Estelle, come to me?" Pieter holds out his arms towards her. The girl in the doorway does not come forward, but looks at him, her eyes hard and glittering chips in her white face.

"Estelle, please forgive me. I did what I thought would be best for you, for both of us, when I married Marta. I knew she was jealous of you and she saw your mother in your features and everything you did, but I thought she would get past that when she got to know you. I had no idea she would grow to resent you more and more as the years passed. Having her own children made her worse and not better as I expected. She accused me of favouring you, teaching you to speak English and reading with you but not doing the same for Renette and Suné. I only discovered how she felt after I was wounded and came home to convalesce and by then it was impossible to remedy the situation with the on-going war and my leaving to join the fight again so soon afterwards."

Estelle looks at him, different emotions and expressions working her face like colours on a canvas. Despair won. "It's too late," she cries.

Pastor John starts to rise to his feet. "It's never too late, my dear."

She casts a furious and tormented look in his direction, and he flies backwards, hitting the wall with a heavy and ungainly thud.

"What do you know?" she shrieks, "It's too late!"

"Why, Estelle?" pleads Pieter. "Why is it too late?"

"Because I've already killed him and my soul is condemned to eternal damnation. I waited for you, Papa. I waited and waited, but you didn't come. *Oom* Willem told me you gave up on living when you discovered we had been sent to the concentration camp. How could you do that? How could you give up and leave me all alone?"

"I'm so sorry, Estelle. I did not expect any of you to survive the camp. I didn't want to be left on my own and my own selfish despair dominated my actions."

"But you left me on my own, Papa. First on the farm where I became the victim of that terrible man and then when you visited us for the last time and left me behind with that awful woman you married. She blamed me for what happened with that rapist; she said I was tainted and not fit to live in her house and associate with her children. She nearly broke my spirit and when the soldiers came to the farm, it was a relief for me to escape her hatred and abuse.

"The camp was awful, but in many ways, it was better for me. Marta relented and allowed me to set up an informal school for my sisters and some of the other children in the camp. This helped to pass the time and gave them some structure to their days. My mind was occupied with thinking up new lessons every day, it helped me to forget my own pain.

"After the measles epidemic, I was left alone as the only survivor from our tent. *Ouma* van Tonder invited me to live with her and some other orphaned girls. I wasn't friends with any of them but they didn't know me and so they didn't judge me. I was just another orphan who needed emotional support and who pitched in with them to try and keep alive until the war ended. Conditions in the camp improved once spring arrived and there was less sickness and disease.

"When the war ended, Papa, I waited for you to come, but you didn't. *Oom* Willem came instead and asked me to go with him and help to rebuild his farm. I had no other option, so I went with him. and was happy until he remarried, but his new wife didn't like me either. No one ever liked me.

"Now you have come, but it is too late."

"Tom's not dead, Estelle," Michelle says quietly. "Your attempt to kill him by interfering with the gene therapy backfired. It actually helped to restore over ninety percent of the functionality in Tom's lower body that he lost when he fell down the stairs."

"Really, is that true?" she looks at each person in the room, an unfathomable look in her bright green eyes. They all nod, affirming the truth of Michelle's statement.

"I think ..." Estelle stops, thinks, and then speaks again, "I think I would like to meet him."

"Why? Why do you want to meet Tom? You said that you hated him and were even prepared to sacrifice me as an accomplice to his crimes. What has changed?" Michelle scrutinises the poltergeist's face. *I'm not sure I can trust this young woman.*

"I've spent many years resenting my father. I blamed him for my miserable childhood and took the view that he had betrayed me by marrying Marta and putting his desire for a wife and more children above my happiness and well-being.

"I never realised how difficult it was for him, a young man left on his own with a young child to bring up. The implications for him of my having an English-speaking mother and a father who had an English-speaking grandmother and was anglicised from the perspective of the Afrikaans-speaking community in which I grew up, never occurred to me."

Estelle pauses and Michelle considers her glib words. They have a slightly insincere ring.

Why do I feel that she trying to sell me a story?

Pieter's eyes sparkle with unshed tears and his voice trembles as he responds to his daughter's commentary. "It was difficult for me, Estelle. Your mother was never accepted by our neighbours or my acquaintances and it made life hard for her. She felt like an outcast. I thought that if I married Marta our community would accept you."

Estelle nods in acknowledgement. "I suppose they might have if Marta had ever accepted me, but she didn't. She was a strict Boer woman and had been raised with a deep suspicion of the English and a resentment towards them because of their continuous perceived infringements of the rights and freedoms of the Boer Republics.

"I believe your devotion to me and determination to conserve my English heritage infuriated Marta and was seen as blatant favouritism towards me."

"You may be right about that, Estelle. I never discussed these things with her. I assumed she would understand why I thought it necessary to preserve your heritage."

"Well, she definitely didn't understand. I also blamed you for the fact I was attacked, and my virtue was stolen from me. That was unjust of me, what could you have done? You were away on commando. Marta's ill treatment of me, coupled with the unfortunate circumstances on that day, conspired to bring about my destiny. I was fortunate to survive the beating I took at the hands of my attacker.

"Marta rejected me afterwards. She was a deeply religious woman with set ideas that had been ingrained in her from birth. She was not able to apply any perspective or common sense to the situation. I was lucky to have *Tannie* Sannie who did a lot to care for and comfort me. I was not grateful enough for the love she gave me."

"Sannie was an incredible woman, Estelle. She loved you and held no unfair prejudices against you because of your English blood. I am grateful to know she tried to care for you."

"Oh, yes, *Tannie* Sannie was always kind and considerate towards me."

Estelle shifts her gaze back to Michelle. "When you moved into this house, Michelle, I knew what Tom had done. I was able to rifle through his mind like a filing cabinet and I quickly found those thoughts, anxieties and the guilt that related to the death of Tracey Atkinson. I thought that I could relieve my own pain by tormenting him and making him suffer for his ill-treatment of Tracey. It didn't work and I didn't feel better so I kept upping my abuse of him in the hope I would eventually find some respite from my own on-going torment.

"I became more and more desperate and angry when I didn't achieve any sense of personal absolution, until I pushed him down the stairs that night. I followed up my initial actions by trying to kill him through infiltrating the TENS machinery and electrocuting him. Now that my father has revealed so much to me about our past, I feel a need to meet Tom and see whether I can forgive him. I don't want to be a ghost forever; I need to move on."

A faint unease comes over Michelle at Estelle's last words.

What if she can't forgive him. Will she try to kill him again?

"In order for you to meet Tom, Estelle, he would need to come home. I can't bring him here if you are going to jeopardise his safety. If you want to meet Tom, you need to promise me that you'll not harm him regardless of whether you can forgive him or not."

Michelle is aware of the complete silence. She looks around. Everyone is looking at Estelle expectantly.

"Of course, I understand that, Michelle, and you have my promise that I'll not harm Tom before or during the meeting."

"What about afterwards, Estelle?"

Estelle smiles but it doesn't reach her cold eyes which are like chips of green jade. "I promise I won't harm him after the meeting either."

Michelle hesitates.

Can I trust her? She has done some terrible things and tried to kill Tom. What other options do I have? Pieter and Estelle both need to find redemption and Tom and I need to be free of them both, especially the highly unstable Estelle.

"Okay, if Tom agrees, I'll arrange for you to meet him after he comes home. You must give him two weeks to recover and regain his strength before the meeting. Do you agree to those terms?"

"Yes, I agree."

The two ghosts fade away and the four participants gaze at each other.

"I did the right thing, didn't I?" Michelle's face is grey and her eyes agonised. "What else could I have done in the circumstances?"

Pastor Jim smiles encouragingly, "It'll be alright, Michelle. We'll prepare for the meeting."

PIETER

UNTIL DEATH DO US PART

July 1901

Pieter is lying on the ground with his head in Willem's lap. A makeshift bandage, made of a piece of ripped shirt, is bound tightly around his chest. It's done little to stop the flow of bright red blood from the bullet entry wound.

Pieter shivers violently in the bitter cold of the evening. The commando has made camp in the shelter of an outcrop of rocks, but it only offers a bit of protection from the cold wind and his attentive brother has no extra blankets to wrap around him.

The July weather is brutal. Every evening, the men go to sleep in their homemade sleeping bags wearing all their clothes including their rain jackets and heavy coats. When they awake in the morning, their sleeping bags are covered in a layer of frost and their bones seem to ache from the cold.

Thoughts of Willem's burned out farm fill Pieter's mind. He and Willem had visited it recently in the hope of replenishing their supplies and that's when he'd seen the devastation. The blackened and roofless structure had stood, lonely and partially destroyed, in the middle of the patch of dirt that had once been the yard. A variety of birds, predators and others, gathered on the roofless walls, like dark spectators at a funeral.

As they'd travelled through the veld in the vicinity of the farmhouse, the stench of rotting animals carried on the wind from the herds of sheep, goats, cattle and horses slaughtered by the Khakis had been overwhelming. The water in the dams was undrinkable as it was full of bloated carcasses.

When they rejoined their commando, a friend had remarked on his appearance. "What's happened, Pieter? Your hair and beard are streaked with grey and your skin looks like an old man's."

"Willem's farm has been burned by the Khakis and they've taken our families."

"Oh, that's bad. I'm so sorry. Do you have any idea where they've been taken?"

"The concentration camp at Mafeking would be the logical place to take them, but we've no way of knowing for sure. We don't even know if they're alive."

Over the past few months, terrible stories about the semi-starvation, poor conditions, and diseases at the camps have circulated among the various commandos as they travel around the countryside, evading capture by the Khakis and wreaking as much havoc as possible. Tales of the escalation of contagious diseases at Mafeking concentration camp torment Pieter, who is sure that's where the two families have been taken.

Pieter had discussed his concerns with Willem many times.

"I don't believe our families will survive the camp, Willem. The people have little food and no cleaning materials. I've heard there's no clean water. Our families are rural people who have never been exposed to diseases like measles, they have no immunity to these terrible illnesses."

"I'm also worried, Pieter, but we need to control our fear. We are fighting for our independence from these British oppressors. You must not forget that."

"I haven't forgotten, Willem. My head aches with my hatred for these cowardly and inhuman beasts."

"I understand how you feel, Pieter, but you must be more cautious. You have become completely reckless in your behaviour during our skirmishes with the Khakis. Getting yourself killed isn't going to help our people, our country or our families. Our wives want us to continue the fight and expect us to overcome the obstacles that the Khakis throw up in our path. You know this is true, Pieter."

Pieter does know this is true. Marta would want him to continue to fight. The last verses of a popular song about the so-called refugee camps, composed by one of the Burghers, comes into his mind:

> But thanks to our wives, for they do not care
> Whatever the hardships they have to bear,
> They willingly suffer their woeful plight
> If their husbands stand firm for God and the right.
>
> By her noble example the Burgher's wife
> Still gives him strength to continue the strife
> And she cheers him on with all her might
> To stand up firmly for God and the right.
>
> O Afrikander! Be staunch and true
> For that's what your wife is expecting from you

You will help her to make the burden light
By standing firm for God and the right.

Willem doesn't know about Pieter's guilt. He isn't aware that Pieter never loved Marta and that he married her out of convenience when his beautiful and gentle Catherine had died, leaving him to raise Estelle alone.

Catherine was his true love. Hers is the face that haunts his dreams and dominates his memories. He's tried to treat Marta well and with respect, but there's no love. Marta knows she's his second choice. Knows she'll never replace the beautiful English girl who played the piano and sang popular English songs in her lilting accent.

He loves all his daughters and dotes on Suné and Renette, but Estelle is his special girl, the child of his true love. Marta has sensed this unintended favouritism and takes it out on Estelle when he isn't there to defend her. It's his own fault for being transparent with his emotions and for not being true to himself when he made his decision to marry Marta, on the recommendation of his mother, ten years ago.

Willem's entreaties to take care of himself make no difference to Pieter, who cannot hear them through the tumultuous racket of his own guilt and confusion. Rage gives him focus and the courage to ride straight into each fray, completely impervious to his personal safety. He no longer cares if he lives or dies.

His behaviour towards the Khakis is aggressive and even heartless, but he's being dragged along by the turbulent current of self-destruction.

Today, during an unexpected altercation with a troop of Khakis, the inevitable had happened and a bullet from a Khaki's gun ripped into Pieter's chest, causing one of his lungs to collapse. Pieter had been left to die, but Willem had managed to return for him, lifting him on to his own horse and getting them both away to a safe place in the veld.

Pieter sees the pain in his brother's eyes. Willem knows he is dying and there is nothing he can do to save him.

"Willem," Pieter whispers thickly.

"Yes, I'm here."

"I killed three Khakis today, Willem."

"You did, Pieter. You are a hero."

"No, Willem, I'm not a hero, killing is a terrible thing. I'm ready to go now and finish my part in this war. I believe I'll be reunited with Catherine in heaven one day. It'll only happen once I've atoned for my recent sins. Good-bye, Willem."

The last words are barely a whisper.

"Good-bye, Pieter."

Pieter's chest rises slowly for the last time and he lets out a long shuddering breath. His spirit, tormented by guilt due to his recent actions, is not yet ready to leave this earth. It lingers as Willem digs a hole in the cold, hard soil for his discarded body.

MICHELLE

October 2019

"The nurses say he is doing well, and the nightmares have stopped."

Michelle looks at Dr Haasbrook, waiting for his questions. Hoping she can answer them without betraying Pastor John, who has been so good to Tom.

"He is eating well, sleeping well and can walk unaided. I think he is ready to be discharged."

Michelle blinks in surprise, as the doctor's comments sink into her brain. "That is great news, Doctor," she lets out a tremulous breath. "I thought he would be paralysed for life."

"With injuries like your husband's, the patient may eventually recover. It usually takes a long time though, especially for someone of your husband's age. Despite all our medical interventions, the only real cure is time and patience. The patient's attitude and determination to recover and walk again also play a role."

Michelle looks at him sharply.

"When Tom was admitted he had a drinking problem and was suffering from recurring nightmares and chronic insomnia. The prognosis for him wasn't positive and I thought we might need to admit him to a private psychiatric hospital for a period. I thought he might try to harm himself or attempt suicide."

"Yes, I had the same worry. His mental state was unpredictable and worrying. But that seems to have changed now. When I saw him yesterday, he was just like his old self again."

"The feedback I'm getting from the nurses and staff indicate that Tom is mentally in a much better place now, Michelle. The nightmares appear to have stopped and he is alert and interested during the day. When he was first admitted, he took no interest in anything. He spent his nights thrashing about frantically and often called out in his sleep.

"Since the therapy applied by Pastor Luke and Pastor John, not only is he walking, but he is also reading and watching television. I'm not going to ask you about that treatment, Michelle. It was unorthodox and illegal, and I could press charges against both of them, and Ruth too. I'm not going to because it worked. Somehow, whatever they did, it worked, and not only can Tom walk now, but his mental issues seem to have been resolved."

Michelle's shoulders relax and she realises how anxious she has been about Pastor Luke and his gene therapy. Her muscles burn in protest at the sudden change.

I'm going to pay for my anxiety.

A tension headache is already nibbling at her temples.

"I've emphasised to Pastor John the gravity of what he did by facilitating that gene therapy. Pastor Luke could have killed Tom and it is an act of God that he didn't. I hope you understand that, Michelle."

"Yes, of course I do."

Dr Haasbrooke shrugs lightly, as if shaking off his thoughts and concerns before moving on to other things.

"Tom has expressed a desire to go home. I got the impression that your marriage was under severe strain and I'm not sure if that's an option for him. He'll need constant supervision and his progress must be monitored. I don't know if there'll be any unexpected side effects from the treatment that was administered."

"What kind of side effects?"

"I'm not sure. Maybe numbness, stabbing pain or chronic prickling, tingling or burning sensations, that sort of thing. I just don't know what to expect so I'm hoping for the best while preparing for the worst. Anyhow, what I want to know is will he be moving back home and are you in a position to monitor his progress and call me if there are any symptoms that you feel unable to cope with alone?"

"He asked me if he could come home, Doctor Haasbrooke. I've thought about it and I've decided to give it a try. He can move back for two weeks and I'll see how that goes. If he reverts to heavy drinking and abusive behaviour, I'll have to relook at the situation."

If Estelle can't resolve her antagonism towards him and find closure for her past, both our lives will be at risk. Estelle needs to completely accept the terrible experiences of her past and embrace the transition towards her future and away from what is finished and unalterable. Can she do that? I just don't know.

"Okay, that sounds reasonable, Michelle, and I cannot press you for more. On that basis, let's go and speak to the nursing staff and Tom about his discharge into your care."

Two hours later, Michelle is driving Tom home. One of the nurses had pushed Tom in his wheelchair to the front entrance and Michelle had brought her car right to the door. The nurse had watched Tom walk over to the car, climb into the passenger seat, and fasten his seatbelt. Satisfied, she had waved at them and turned away, returning to her post in the orthopaedic ward.

During the drive home, Michelle explains to Tom everything that has transpired with the ghosts and, especially, with Estelle who wants to meet him. He listens carefully but does not comment other than to ask if Pastor John can attend the meeting.

"Yes, Pastor John and Alice will facilitate the meeting, Tom. You don't need to worry about being left alone with Estelle. Pieter, her father, will also be in attendance."

"Okay, I understand," Tom says and turns the conversation towards lighter topics.

He really does seem to be back to his old self.

* * *

Ten days pass. Michelle keeps a careful eye on her husband. He doesn't display any unusual symptoms and experiences no nightmares. His sleep is restful, and he wakes each day looking healthier and stronger. Michelle also sleeps soundly and has no terrible dreams.

They return to their daily routine of eating dinner together. The spring weather is lovely and warm, and they sit at their table on the patio enjoying her tasty homemade meals. No wine is served during these meals; the bottles stay on the shelf in the pantry. The levels of the hard liquor in the bottles in the liquor cabinet remain unchanged. He doesn't touch them.

Every third day, he goes to physiotherapy. Michelle offers to drive him, but he refuses.

"I'm well enough to drive myself and I enjoy driving."

When he comes home and kisses her in greeting there is no alcohol on his breath.

Michelle's love for Tom resurfaces. She's never stopped loving him, except perhaps for the short period following his fall when he deliberately rejected her. Her early thoughts about divorce remain unsaid and hope for their future burns brightly within her.

During the ten-day period, Tom has seen Pastor John daily. Michelle is not part of their sessions, but Tom emerges from them happier and more resolved to stay away from liquor and heal his life.

"I've decided to make a monthly donation to the women's shelter in Pretoria," he tells her following one of these sessions. "I can't change the past, but I can do something proactive to change the future."

He also starts talking about returning to work and has an early discussion with his colleagues about re-starting in the new year.

"Fortunately, we have lost a few of our partners to immigration so the firm needs me. I'll have a written warning about drinking during working hours on my file for three months. After that, if there are no further transgressions, it will be removed."

Michelle hopes they have traversed this dark period in their lives and better times lie ahead.

There is still the outstanding issue of Pieter and Estelle that needs to be dealt with. The meeting with them has been arranged for day fourteen of Tom's return home. Pastor John, Ruth and Alice have all agreed to be in attendance and plan for the session to follow the same pattern as the previous one.

In preparation, Michelle and Alice are teaching Tom about meditation. Michelle smiles inwardly as Alice gives instructions.

"Close your eyes, Tom, focus on your breathing, in and out, in and out. Try to focus solely on your breathing and not become lost in thought. When that happens, that is awareness, and you must return from your distracted thought to the breathing."

Tom meditates with dogged determination, trying his best to follow Alice's instructions. Michelle practises her own meditation. She's making progress and her ability to observe and let her thoughts and feelings go without becoming caught up in them is increasing with each session.

The day before the planned meeting with Pieter and Estelle, Michelle and Alice enjoy a cup of herbal tea in the kitchen. The sun is shining, and the large windows throw patches of brightness everywhere. It is a warm and happy place to sit and chat.

"Do you remember our Tarot card reading in April, Alice? The one when Tom was away on a business trip and the haunting was just beginning?"

"Yes, I remember it well, Michelle. You drew The Chariot, The Moon and the Ten of Swords. Why are you asking about that?"

"I've been thinking about the meaning of those cards. The message in The Moon card about your partner having hidden secrets seems so apt in retrospect. Tom did have a secret that he kept from me. Estelle seemed to think that I knew about the situation with Tracey or should have known about it based on Tom's behaviour and office gossip. I've thought long and hard about this and I honestly didn't know. I had no idea he had something so sinister hidden in his past until I started having the dreams instigated by Estelle."

Michelle seizes both of Alice's hands.

"What do you think, Alice. Do you think I deliberately turned a blind eye to indicators of Tom's offence? Was I selfish and blinkered for my own personal benefit?"

"No, Michelle, I don't think that. You couldn't have known unless someone told you. People don't look for fatal flaws in their partners and don't expect them to be deceitful. Estelle is wrong about that and it is probably natural for her age. She died young and has retained the mindset of a teenager.

"When you are young everything is black and white, there are no shades of grey. That is why university students are so determined in their protests and cannot easily be swayed from their mindsets. Their life experiences are too limited for them to make any allowances for human nature in their thought processes.

"As people age, they mellow and gain more understanding about what makes other people tick and make the decisions and choices they do. I'm hoping that Pieter's interaction with Estelle has empowered her with more understanding and empathy for others."

Michelle nods, "I hope you are right. You have made me feel better about my own role in all of this. I had thought that the Ten of Swords card meant that my marriage was finished, and that divorce was the only solution for me. I've come to believe that Tom and I will stay together and the period of his deception has come to an end, allowing us to overcome the obstacles that were placed in our path."

Alice smiles, "I'm delighted you have revisited that reading, Michelle, and discovered the deeper meaning indicated by the cards. In the circumstances, I agree with your thoughts and conclusions."

Alice reaches out and embraces Michelle.

ESTELLE

THE BITTER ENDING

June 1902

"The peace treaty has been signed and our men have laid down their arms," says *Ouma* van Tonder, bustling into the tent.

Her voice brings Estelle to her senses. She's been sitting with her elbows on her knees and her head propped up by her hands, daydreaming.

Maybe daydreaming, she thinks with a stab of fear. *It's more like my mind just stops working and my thoughts scatter in all directions like seed thrown to the chickens.*

It has been over nine months since Estelle's sisters and *Tannie* Sannie passed from this life and were buried in the camp graveyard. During this time, her mind has become prone to frequent wanderings. She would forget what she was doing mid task while her mind went off on some tangent, or she would simply sit, gazing into space, not thinking of anything at all.

Am I losing my mind? Am I on the path to madness?

Despite her outraged resentment towards the Khakis due to their cruel treatment of her people, the deaths of everyone she holds dear, and her resultant determination to live, she could have fallen into a pit of hopeless despair from which there was no return had it not been for the constant kindness and ministrations of *Ouma* van Tonder.

This astonishing old woman had withstood the ravages of the diseases which swept through the camp and subsequently took many of the surviving orphans, including Estelle, into her care, making them feel loved and infusing them with a will to live.

The new camp commandant, Mr Cook, had called the ladies together a short while previously to tell them the war was over. In her strangely apathetic state Estelle couldn't say how much time had lapsed since *Ouma* van Tonder had shared this news with the occupants of her tent.

"The women all cheered him," *Ouma* van Tonder confided to the rapt group of listeners. "He is a good man and, since his arrival in January, our situation here in the camp has improved greatly. We now have better medical treatment, proper schooling, and our own church. The food has been much better too, and we have been given fat meat and even fat tinned meat."

"Peace," murmurs Estelle.

Her mind circled the word, probing at it and questioning its significance for her. Her thoughts started to drift away again when understanding suddenly hits her.

Peace has come. That means the camp will no longer be required and we'll be sent home. Where will I go? Who'll want me? Maybe Papa's still alive.

A tiny flicker of hope lights in her soul.

I don't know that Papa is dead. Marta dreamed he died, but that doesn't mean it's a fact.

Estelle fights off her apathy and tries to focus on the swirling sounds around her. At *Ouma* van Tonder's words a few of the older girls have started to talk excitedly.

"Are we really at peace now? What are the terms? Have we given up our independence?"

"The peace negotiated have agreed that our forces will lay down their arms and will recognise King Edward VII as their lawful sovereign."

"Oh no, what sort of a future is that for us? We'll be slaves under British rule," cries one girl.

"My God, oh, my God, why have you deserted your people," says another.

Ouma van Tonder looks at the girls sternly. "The terms of the peace treaty are not perfect, but our Burghers have all been granted amnesty and the British government is making an amount of £3 million available to assist with resettling our people and supplying them with necessities such as food, seed, farm implements and livestock. You must thank God for your blessings."

"We have been sold out for £3 million," grumbles a voice.

"Yes, and Britain now controls all of our gold. This negotiation is all for their benefit and that's the truth."

Estelle gets up and goes outside. She needs to think over everything she's just heard.

Maybe Papa will come for me and everything will be all right.

* * *

Life in the camp changes over the next week as Burghers arrive and are reunited with what remains of their families. In some cases, there are no family members left to greet a Burgher, and he leaves alone.

Estelle overhears a lot of excited talking about the future.

"What are we going to do now?" is a common question.

Some of the Burghers are unsure, but others are immediately returning to their destroyed farms to get their lives restarted.

Days pass and no one comes for Estelle. Each morning she gets up, dresses, and waits for Papa, who never comes. Gradually, she slips back into her old habit of gazing, unseeing into space. Her mind becomes less and less focused as it alternates between rage, frustration, bitterness, and humiliation.

On the Saturday following the coming of peace, Estelle is standing at the fence of the camp, watching a line of ants marching to their anthill. *Ouma* van Tonder is leaving that day. Her only surviving son out of four children had arrived the day before and plans to take her to live with him on his farm. Estelle's mind skirts the question of what she'll do once *Ouma* van Tonder has left.

I'll really be alone once Ouma leaves.

She hears footsteps on the gravel path behind her and swings around quickly, ready to scream for help.

Several of the Burghers returning to the Mafeking, Zeerust, and Lichtenburg districts have taken refuge in the camp while they rebuild their farms. The sight of these burly men with their lined faces and bedraggled beards almost paralyses her with fear. Ever since they started arriving, memories of her ordeal nearly two years previously have filled her thoughts, and her sleep is broken by horrible nightmares of being throttled and abused by faceless men with large hairy hands and foul-smelling breath.

"Estelle, it's me … Willem."

Oom Willem stands in front of her, hands hanging limply at his sides. His expression stricken and dark circles of exhaustion surrounding his eyes.

"Willem … I'm so happy to see you." She looks behind him, expecting to see her father there. "Where is Papa?"

"Pieter is dead, Estelle. He was killed nearly a year ago. I'm so sorry."

She screams. The hope she had wrapped around herself like a protective cloak dissipates and the truth lies before her in all its stark barrenness.

Papa is dead. Marta was right when she said he had been killed.

Falling to her knees, she wraps her arms around her head and wails, giving herself over entirely to her loss and grief. Time passes, she has no idea how long, and then she starts coming back to herself.

She looks up at *Oom* Willem, who is still standing there patiently, waiting for her storm of weeping to pass. Stoic and emotionally control-led, he has no idea how to offer comfort to his niece, so he just waits for her self-control to reassert itself.

"What am I going to do now?" she asks. "There is no one left."

"I also have no one left, Estelle. It's just you and I now. If it makes any difference to you, I'm glad to see you."

Estelle's eyes are large and wounded. "I'm glad to see you too."

"I'm going back to my farm," says Willem. "I'd hoped my family had survived the camp, but that's not the case. At least I have you and we can re-build the farm together."

Estelle nods. There is nothing else she can do.

August 1903

Estelle has been at *Verward* Psychiatric Hospital,[1] in Pretoria, for nearly four weeks. She'd been admitted by *Oom* Willem at the insistence of his second wife.

Her inability to focus her mind and the memory lapses she'd experi-enced while in the Mafeking camp remained long after she'd left and started her new life on the farm with *Oom* Willem. Her condition escalat-ed after *Oom* Willem met and married a much younger woman called Madeleine.

Madeleine, a tall and well-built woman with powerful hands and arms from years of hard work, was deeply religious and fervently Afrikaans. Estelle's lapses into English, ability to read and write in English, and enthusiasm to read her Great-grandmother Anne's Bible deeply frustrat-ed Madeleine, who doesn't like Estelle and makes no bones about that fact.

The stress of trying to please Madeleine drives Estelle further away from reality as she seeks solace and oblivion within the sanctuary of her memories. Stopping her work in the middle of a task, Estelle often sits there staring at it, a dull and half-questioning look on her face, for up to an hour.

"That girl is completely odd," she'd overheard Madeleine complaining to Willem. "You can't explain anything to her without her mind drifting away to other things. She always looks confused and apathetic. I find it deeply distressing. I can't ask her to help with anything like cooking as she loses focus halfway through and is likely to burn the house down."

---

[1] *Verward* is an Afrikaans word meaning confused. This hospital is fiction-al.

After this conversion, *Oom* Willem had tried to speak to her about her lack of focus and attention. His attempted intervention had not helped. Estelle tried to stop her mind from wandering by attempting to pull it back, but it always drifted away again. No matter what she did or tried, indifference always crept back in, dissolving her thoughts like sugar in water.

Estelle's relationship with Madeleine deteriorated steadily, until one day, Madeleine's hand flashed out, unexpectedly, and struck her across her jaw. Estelle, with her slight frame, fell where she stood and lay stunned on the floor. She never cried or called out, but her bitterness overflowed and turned to hatred.

Over the months the beatings continued. Willem knew. His mouth turned down at the corners when he witnessed Estelle jumping in terror at Madeleine's threatening behaviour and cutting words. Estelle saw acknowledgement of the situation in her uncle's eyes, but he did nothing to intervene. She knew that Madeleine was pregnant with his child and he was hoping for a boy. His blindness to Madeleine's cruelty towards her fed Estelle's hate, making it grow and grow.

When her son, Charl, was born, Madeleine decided she didn't want Estelle living under her roof anymore.

"I don't want her around my baby, Willem," she declared. "I'm concerned she'll negatively influence our son with her peculiar ways and mental absences. She'll set a bad example for him."

Willem had agreed and quickly arranged for Estelle to be assessed at the mental asylum in Pretoria known as *Verward* Psychiatric Hospital. After her diagnosis of being mentally unbalanced and chronically depressed, she was hastily admitted due to the risk of her committing suicide or becoming dangerous to others.

Her initial impression of the hospital had been of a beautiful building, situated on large and pleasant grounds with a tranquil atmosphere. It was a deception.

The inside is entirely different, housing significant numbers of patients suffering from a variety of mental ailments including idiocy or feeble mindedness. All the windows are covered with metal bars, the toilets are filthy, and the whole hospital reeks of rancid food and human waste. Aggressive patients who are deemed to be a potential threat to other inmates or the staff, are kept separately in a fenced off ward, like animals.

Treatments for all patients are the same. Bromide is used as a sedative and an anti-convulsant and chloroform mixed with alcohol is used as an anti-spasmodic. Patients suffering from epilepsy and other seizure disorders are treated with digitalis to regulate their heartbeat.

Estelle does not display aggressive fits of temper or experience fitting or seizures, so her treatments are less severe than some of the other inmates. Her periods of mental vacantness are treated with blisters, intended to draw out the excess blood causing her insanity and distract her from her disordered thoughts.

The blistering process is painful and increases her hatred towards those responsible for her plight. The revolting features of her rapist are locked into her memory and his face has become representative to her of all abusive men. During her treatment sessions she focuses on him and all others like him. Her hatred commands her to seek retribution against everyone who has hurt her or other affected women.

Men who hurt women need to pay. Need to suffer like I have.

Her hatred and malevolent thoughts became her focus and enabled her to fight off her apathy.

Someone must stand up for abused women. Who'll do it? Why, I will, of course.

These thoughts are far more effective to her perceived mental recovery than the open bottle of ammonia the hospital staff wave under the noses of the inmates. The wandering, apathetic look disappears from her eyes and they became direct and sharp.

February 1904

The pair of eyes peer through the crack in the door. A cunning and malignant look lies within their dark and demented depths.

Estelle sits on her bed examining her few possessions. Great-grand-mother Anne's Bible lies open in front of her as she slides her gold coins back inside the cover.

The doctor says I'm doing much better now and may be able to leave the hospital soon. He says he'll help me find somewhere to live and get some sewing work. I also have this gold to help me get started with my new life.

"Give me that book." The voice, loud and grating, makes Estelle jump.

She looks up to see Adele Kruger standing next to the adjacent bed. Adele is prone to fits of aggressive temper and lives in the fenced off ward. She is pregnant and is occasionally allowed out, under strict supervision, to walk in the garden.

"What are you doing here, Adele? How did you get away from the nurse?"

A sly smile stretches her lips, "Mrs Ferreira? I gave that silly old woman the slip. It wasn't difficult, she is so fat and slow. Now, give me that book." She reaches out her hand for it.

"No, you can't have it. This is my book," Estelle clutches the Bible to her body and draws back from the huge deranged creature in front of her.

A terrible cry of rage escapes from the woman's gaping mouth as she lunges forward, clawing at Estelle's neck and face and tearing great red welts into her soft flesh. She is immensely strong, more like a wild animal than a human. Estelle kicks out at her and then draws in a great breath, tensing her body. Her breath rushes out of her as she uses all her strength to wrench herself away.

If I can roll off the bed, I can go under it and escape.

Adele holds on to her with incredible strength. Her hands reach up and tightened around Estelle's neck. The fingers tighten until Estelle's vision dissolves into blackness. She feels her mind going fuzzy and floating away.

* * *

Estelle looks down on her body lying on the bed. Her skin is bluish due to her death from suffocation.

She loves her new presence as a ghost.

At last, I'm free of my tainted body and the limitations of my earthly life. I'm free now to do as I please. All of those who have wronged me or any other innocent women, had better watch out.

PIETER

TRAPPED

March 1904

After Estelle's death, her spirit returns to her old family home in Irene. Pieter goes with her. He could have haunted his brother but wants nothing to do with him after Estelle's demise, the blame for which he lays firmly at Willem's feet.

His alternatives are to haunt one of the places he has inhabited during his lifetime and the Irene farm is the natural choice.

Acknowledgement of his spirit's presence is no more forthcoming from Estelle after her death than before it.

MICHELLE

FORGIVE AND YOU'LL BE FORGIVEN

October 2019

The candle flame dances and jumps, throwing flickering shadows on the white walls. The curtains are drawn against the beautiful bright day outside the large windows. The five people wait, seated cross legged on cushions on the floor with their hands relaxed in their laps. On a small table in the corner of the room, lies the Ouija board. It casts an unnaturally large and block shaped shadow on the ivory wall.

A surreptitious peep at the faces of Pastor John and Alice remind Michelle that this isn't an ordinary meditation session. Their eyes are unnaturally bright, darting about as quick and restless as a bird's.

Shifting her gaze towards her husband, his peaceful expression and calm eyes surprise her.

Next, she focuses on the ghostly shape of Pieter squatting on the floor. His body is twisted and shrunken within the rough, homespun shirt that encases it. His ragged trousers, patched with homemade leather, are loose around his diminished legs. Even his hat sags with age. The memory of how Robert looked at the end of their last meeting, just before his ascension from his holding position as a ghost to the next life, drifts unbidden into her mind.

Pieter's process of redemption is underway. I don't think he'll be here with us for much longer.

The door bursts open. Estelle explodes into the room, eyes blazing, and with some object held out in front of her.

Michelle strains to make out what the object is, it looks like a smart phone. As she watches a mass of phosphorescence bursts from the smart phone, twinkling in the dimness like stars.

A sharp sour smell fills the air. It is the smell of fear as adrenaline filled sweat leaches from the pores of the watching group.

The room comes alive with shadows. The shadows of women of all shapes, sizes and ethnic creeds. Women wearing the brightly coloured traditional colours and designs of Africa; Hindu women wearing saris; Muslim women wearing hijabs or burkas; European women wearing

Victorian clothing; American women wearing jeans and T-shirts. The women have one common feature, their baleful and glittering eyes.

The shadows multiply into thousands. They swarm everywhere. Some have scarred faces and twisted bodies, but most are beautiful with the glowing good looks of youth.

Estelle starts to chant, "Me too, me too," and the shadows catch the refrain. The words howl around the room like a strong wind.

A loud crack fills the air, and the group, who are all still seated, launch themselves instinctively backwards.

In front of their horrified eyes, the floor splits open from the door, right across the room to the window. The crevice widens and a noxious smell rises from its steaming depths. It is a horrendous smell, the smell of suffering, death, corruption, and blood overlaid with the odour of burning and charred bodies.

Estelle's eyes fix on Tom. "I've come for your soul, Tom. You and I will both pay for our crimes by burning eternally in the fires of hell."

The poltergeist moves forward, her claw like hands reaching for Tom's arms, ready to drag him with her into the crack from which burning lava heaves and surges. The shadows swirl eagerly; their faces greedy as they prepare for the kill.

The group on the floor are frozen, appalled. All except for Pieter, who rises to his feet and, as if prepared for such an emergency, holds out an ancient leather-bound Bible.

"Stop, Estelle," his voice booms out. The sound shocks the shadows into silence and the chanting cuts off, plunging the room into silence.

Estelle halts. Pale and breathless, she looks at her father, every muscle quivering with anxiety and expectation.

Pieter glides over to her, the Bible held up like a shield. "This is your Great-grandmother Anne's Bible, Estelle. She is waiting for you in heaven. She wants desperately to meet you and to love you."

Reaching out, he takes her white hand in his. "I love you Estelle. You are my little girl and I'm so sorry I went away without doing more to protect you from the jealousy of your stepmother. I'm also sorry that I never told you about your real mother, instead I let you believe that Marta was your blood mother knowing that she had rejected you. Will you forgive me my sin against you, Estelle?

"Your mother and Great-grandmother Anne are waiting for us, you and I, to join them. We'll be a family again. Please Estelle."

Estelle takes a slow and blundering step towards him.

"I came to kill Tom, Papa. I hoped retribution and my own resultant burning in the fires of hell would free my soul from its torment."

"Forgive me, Estelle. Forgive Tom. Let's move on together. Please Estelle. I love you. Your mother and grandmother love you."

"Oh, yes Papa." She falls forward onto her knees, her arms raised to him in supplication. "I love you too, Papa, and of course I forgive you."

"Let us pray together, Estelle, one last time."

> Our Father, who art in heaven,
> Hallowed by thy name.
> Thy kingdom come.
> Thy will be done,
> On earth as it is in heaven ...

As the words of the beautiful prayer fade away a strange sucking sound emerges from the crack. The shadows swirl, forming into a swiftly moving tunnel like a tornado. The crack gapes, draws in the tornado, and closes, sealing itself shut.

In the corner, the Ouija board implodes into a flaming ball. It reduces to ash within moments, not throwing up a single spark or piece of burning debris. One minute it was a board game and the next, a pile of smoking ashes.

Tom rises and takes a hesitant step towards Estelle. "Hello Estelle."

"Hello Tom, I'm glad to see you looking so well."

A glorious smile lights up her face as she speaks. The phantom looks so different from the malevolent and spite-filled creature from a few minutes earlier that Michelle barely recognised her. She can't believe that this young woman really is Estelle. The cold and glittering beauty, underpinned by heartless cruelty, and eyes filled with hellfire that had previously defined her face, are gone, relaxing into a sweet and pretty countenance dominated by pure and gentle green orbs.

Estelle looks at Tom, understanding further softening the lines of her face. "I know that you regret your past actions and that you have taken steps to redeem yourself. We cannot change the past, but we can change the future. The Bible says:

> If my people, who are called by my name, will humble themselves and pray and seek my face and turn from their wicked ways, then I will hear from heaven, and I will forgive their sin and will heal their land.

"If the Lord can forgive and not judge, then so must I. *For if you forgive other people when they sin against you, your heavenly Father will also forgive you.*

Good bye, Tom."

Tom smiles at her and then she is gone.

December 2019

The past few weeks have passed quietly for Michelle. Her life revolves around her client work and her writing.

The book is progressing slowly, the amount of research involved being greater than she had originally anticipated. The available information and records relating to the Second Anglo Boer War are incomplete and even conflicting, depending on whether it presents the British or the Boer point of view of events.

Neither Pieter van Zyl's nor the English boy's deaths seem to have been recorded so Michelle decides to write a fictionalised biography of the van Zyl family's story which allows her to fill in the blanks and missing pieces from her imagination. She need never tell anyone that her ideas originated from ghosts.

Tom is the same as the Tom of old in many ways, but there are differences. He has continued to volunteer his time at a local shelter for abused women and children. Together with other volunteers, they have painted the building and planted a vegetable garden. Toiling in the garden is having therapeutic effects on Tom and he is letting go of some of his perfectionist tendencies and connecting to others who live in a markedly different world to his.

After every gardening session, Tom tells her about his afternoon. After experiencing some initial setbacks, he has quickly come to except that no matter how carefully he plans and executes this garden, there are some factors that are out of his control like inclement weather and invasions by insects.

"I've realised, Michelle, that the pursuit of perfectionism is a waste of time," he laughs, "especially in gardening. I've spent my whole working life seeking perfectionism in everything I do. It led to my heavy drinking and partying when I was younger and frustration and strained relationships later in my life.

"My experiences of the past year have shown me that there are some things in life we just can't control, and I'm more at peace now that I've accepted this. This lesson is invaluable and is going to help me tremendously when I go back to work in January."

Michelle has also matured and become more of an individual, at peace with her abilities and life choices. She continues to meditate and embrace the mystic.

Together with Alice, she has re-visited the meaning of the second Tarot card reading during the period of the haunting. Her drawing of the Ten of Swords had caused her to question her motives in marrying Tom, but she has realised that her motives were pure.

"I love Tom, Alice, and I've always loved him. It is the strength of that love that enabled me to accept his past mistake and help us both move forward. The haunting did draw certain elements in our lives to a conclusion, but the doors that closed were the negative and hurtful ones and the changes that have come about are wholesome and positive.

"Estelle presented Tom as an evil man who raped an innocent girl and stood by while she self-destructed and that is not true. His actions were not pre-meditated and other factors were involved which led to the eventual outcome. He did a terrible thing and has paid a high price in guilt and self-abasement, even if I exclude the events of this past winter and Estelle's attempted revenge. He has channelled those emotions into positive outcomes with his involvement with the women's shelter and I've forgiven him. I believe that our experiences have helped us discover the true meaning and direction of our lives."

* * *

The gold, if it exists, still lies beneath the tree. Michelle has researched what would happen if she did discover any missing Kruger gold. She could not keep them, or even decide on how the proceeds should be used, they would have to be turned over to the state. She doesn't want the money for herself and she doesn't want to sacrifice the magnificent jacaranda tree to find the gold that would not be used for the purposes its owner intended.

The gold discovered in the Transvaal so many years ago has brought enough conflict and destruction to the people of her country. Some things are better left alone.

During October, she and the other residents of the housing complex will enjoy the tree, attired in its splendid royal robe of purple flowers. Some things are worth more than money.

NOTES

[a] Prior to the declaration of war, B.P. had gone to Rhodesia to raise two regiments for the purpose of protecting the borders of both Rhodesia, a British colony, and the Bechuanaland Protectorate, which remained under the British crown. In September 1899, B.P. had moved to Mafeking with the Bechuanaland Regiment under Colonel Hore.

Colonel Plumer and his regiment, together with some of the British South African Police, had been stationed at Fort Tuli in Rhodesia, for the purposes of watching the northern and north-western borders of the South African Republic and attempting to keep the railway between Bulawayo and Mafeking open when war broke out.

During the early days of the war, native runners had brought frequent news of the clashes between the men stationed at Tuli and a force of over seventeen hundred Boers. After the withdrawal of the Boers towards the south in November 1899, Plumer's Regiment commenced stealthily moving along the railway in the direction of Mafeking with the intension of helping B.P. Plumer had arrived at Gaborone in the Bechuanaland Protectorate in January 1900, and had since pushed on, reaching Lobatsi, only sixty miles from Mafeking, on the 6th of March.

[b] Limited information is available about the black concentration camps during the Second Anglo Boer War. Some limited research is available in a document entitled *Land, labour, war and displacement: A history of four black concentration camps in the South African War (1899-1902)* by Garth Conan Benneyworth.

The following extract from this work is telling about the lack of available information in this regard: *Fieldwork proved critical to gaining an insight into the experience at Taung. The sheer number of graves and possible size of the cemetery shows that, as with the camp at Dry Harts, some sort of calamity occurred there; one that is not recorded anywhere in the written archive. This means that establishing fatality numbers in the black camps and commenting on their experiences using only the written archive, as scholars do with this information, remains a flawed exercise. Fieldwork at Vryburg established the terrain, yet there is very little visible on the surface.*

[c] On the 10th of August 1900, General de Wet's commando, accompanied by a huge wagon laager, crossed the Gatsrand, pursued by a massive British force. De Wet's laager proceeded to Frederikstad where it joined up with General Piet Liebenberg's Potchefstroom Commando. From there, the com-

bined force proceeded northwards to the Modderfontein area where they were attacked on the 12th of August by a significant British force.

Realising that he had no chance of victory against the attacking British army, De Wet fled with his laager and on the 14th of August, he successfully crossed the Magaliesberg at Olifants Nek pass thereby escaping the encircling British army. This was a blow to the British military leadership, who had been determined to capture the famous guerrilla, and Lord Roberts sought to assign blame.

Lord Baden-Powell oversaw the Magaliesburg area. On the 6th of August, he withdrew his troops from their defensive positions at Olifants Nek and Magatos Nek passes through the Magaliesberg mountains and, together with his Rustenburg force, marched to the assistance of the besieged garrison at Eland's River in accordance with his orders. Halfway there he received a message from Lord Roberts that the Eland's River Garrison had surrendered and that he should return to Rustenburg, join up with Lieutenant General Ian Hamilton and his men, and then proceed to the Commando Nek pass. Lord Baden-Powell did not reinstate the defences at the Olifants Nek and Magatos Nek passes.

Shortly after dropping Lord Baden-Powell and his men off at the Commando Nek pass, Lieutenant General Ian Hamilton received a wire from Headquarters, giving him a direct order to march down the Hekpoort valley and occupy the Olifants Nek pass on the morning of the 13th of August. If he had done that timeously, with Lord Baden-Powell's men occupying the Commando Nek pass, there would have been no escape for De Wet.

Lieutenant General Ian Hamilton did not recognise the urgency of this correspondence and replied to Headquarters that he was not going to occupy Olifants Nek pass itself but would rather block it from a distance. There were two roads running westerly, either of which could have been chosen by de Wet. The Olifants Nek road was more difficult to travel as it is steep and shut in by two mountain ranges which allowed no view on either side, while the other road was easier to travel and provided an unbroken view of the open veld. On the night of the 12th of August, Hamilton had to make his own decision about which road to occupy, as the communication lines with Pretoria had been cut by the enemy. Hamilton also knew that Olifants Nek pass was already occupied by the Boers, although it seems that this was not known to de Wet's pursuer, Lord Methuen and his men, or even to de Wet himself. Regardless of his reasons, Hamilton elected to defend the easier road and that turned out to be the wrong choice and de Wet escaped. Lord Baden-Powell, as the officer in charge of the area was ultimately held accountable.

[d] The Battle of Nooitgedacht was fought in the Magaliesberg mountains on 13 December 1900 when Boer commandoes, led by Generals Koos de la Rey and Christiaan Beyers, combined to deal a defeat to a British brigade under the command of Major General Clements. Subsequent to this defeat, Major General Clements was accused of making a poor choice with his selection of a camping site and of failing to prepare adequate defences, distribute ammunition, gather intelligence, maintain alertness, and post effective sentries and patrols.

In his defence, Clements selected the site for the camp on the advice of the English-speaking farmers in the area, who had always been reliable sources of intelligence. At the time of the attack, many of his men had been called away for service elsewhere and the brigade was short of firepower and supplies. The instructions Clements received from Headquarters were also muddled.

Clements force was hugely outnumbered when the Boer commandoes attacked before dawn. It was three thousand Boers against twelve hundred defending British troops. Clement's forces didn't stand a chance, especially as the morning was to hazy for Clement to send a heliograph to the nearby Major-General Broadway and his men so they didn't come to his assistance.

SOURCES OF INFORMATION

The War Reporter – The Anglo-Boer War Through the Eyes of the Burghers

BCCD: British Concentration Camps of the South African War 1900-1902 (https://www2.lib.uct.ac.za/mss/bccd/Histories/Mafeking/)

Land, labour, war and displacement: A history of four black concentration camps in the South African War (1899–1902) by Garth Conan Benneyworth

Commando, A Boer Journal of the Boer War by Deneys Reitz

Australians in the war by Effie Karageorgos

A visual and textual re-storying of the diary of Susanna Catharine Smit (1799–1863) by Marlene de Beer

The Three British Occupations of Potchefstroom During the Anglo-Boer War 1899–1902 by Prof Gert van den Bergh

A woman's world at a time of war: An analysis of selected women's diaries during the Anglo-Boer War 1899–1902 by Helen M. Ross

The British Scorched Earth and Concentration Camp Policies in the Potchefstroom Region, 1899–1902 by Prof GN van den Bergh

The South African War: Implications and Convictions of Post-war Politics and Policy by Jaffar Shiek

Map – Military Survey of Pretoria and the country north and east

A tool for modernisation? the Boer concentration camps of the South African War, 1900–1902 by Elizabeth van Heyningen

Battle of Stormberg – Wikipedia

Battle of Elands River – Wikipedia

Blockhouses of the Boer War by Maurig Jones

The Treatment of "Everyday Life" in Memory and Narrative of the Concentration Camps of the South African War, 1899–1902 by Helen Dampier

Manliness and the English soldier in the Anglo-Boer War 1899-1902: the more things change, the more they stay the same by Sheila J. Bannerman

History of Mental Health Services South Africa Part 11. during the British Occupation by M. Minde

The Project Gutenberg eBook, Mafeking: A diary of a siege by F.D. Baillie

The Project Gutenberg eBook, The Relief of Mafeking, by Filson Young

The Project Gutenberg eBook, South African Memories Social, Warlike & Sporting from Diaries Written At The Time by Lady Sarah Wilson

Project Gutenberg's A Handbook of the Boer War, by Gale and Polden, Limited.

ABOUT THE AUTHOR

Hello, my name is Robbie, short for Roberta. I am an author with seven published children's picture books in the Sir Chocolate books series for children aged 2 to 9 years old (co-authored with my son, Michael Cheadle), one published middle grade book in the Silly Willy series and one published preteen/young adult fictionalised biography about my mother's life as a young girl growing up in an English town in Suffolk during World War II called *While the Bombs Fell* (co-authored with my mother, Elsie Hancy Eaton). All of my children's book are written under Robbie Cheadle and are published by TSL Publications.

I have recently branched into adult and young adult horror and supernatural writing and, in order to clearly differential my children's books from my adult writing, I plan to publish these books under Roberta Eaton Cheadle. My first supernatural book published in that name, *Through the Nethergate*, is now available.

I have participated in a number of anthologies:

- Two short stories in *Spirits of the West*, a paranormal anthology with a frontier and Western focus, edited by Kaye Lynne Booth;

- Two short stories in *Spellbound*, an anthologies of horror stories with a twisted fairy tales focus, edited by USA Today bestselling author, Dan Alatorre;

- Two short stories in *Whispers of the Past*, an anthology of paranormal stories, edited by Kaye Lynne Booth;

- Three short stories in #1 Amazon best selling anthology, *Nightmareland*, a collection of horror stories edited by USA Today bestselling author, Dan Alatorre;

- Three short stories in *Death Among Us*, an anthology of murder mystery stories, edited by Stephen Bentley; and

- Two short stories in #1 Amazon best selling anthology, *Dark Visions*, a collection of horror stories edited by USA Today bestselling author, Dan Alatorre.

- And have a book of poetry called *Open a new door*, with fellow South African poet, Kim Blades.